ALAN WARNER has w... ...r (which was filmed in ... Ladies), *The Stars In T...* ...ted for the Booker Prize), *The Dea...* ...n won the James Tait Black Prize), *Kitchenly 43...* ...historical fiction, *Nothing Left To Fear From Hell*, published in 2023. He is a senior lecturer in Creative Writing at the University of Aberdeen.

IRVINE WELSH is a writer who lives in Edinburgh, London and Miami Beach. His most recent novel was *The Long Knives*, and his forthcoming one is *Resolution*.

JOHN KING is the author of ten novels – *The Football Factory*, *Head-hunters*, *England Away*, *Human Punk*, *White Trash*, *The Prison House*, *Skinheads*, *The Liberal Politics Of Adolf Hitler*, *Slaughterhouse Prayer* and *London Country*. He has also written two novellas – *The Beasts Of Brussels* and *Grand Union* – and numerous short stories. John enjoys drinking beer in public houses and listening to loud music. He lives in London.

THE *Seal* CLUB

THE VIEW FROM POACHER'S HILL

ALAN
WARNER

IRVINE
WELSH

JOHN
KING

LONDON BOOKS BRITISH FICTION

LONDON BOOKS
39 Lavender Gardens
London SW11 1DJ
www.london-books.co.uk

This collection first published by London Books 2023

A catalogue record for this book
is available from the British Library

ISBN 978-1-7396983-1-7

Printed and bound in Great Britain by
CPI Group (UK) Ltd, Croydon, CR0 4YY

Typeset by Octavo Smith Publishing Services
www.octavosmith.com

CONTENTS

Migration *Alan Warner*   7

In Real Life *Irvine Welsh*   47

Grand Union *John King*   235

MIGRATION

ALAN WARNER

LILY HANSFORD

WHEN LILY HANSFORD was year ten at secondary school in Dorchester, she got friends with Angelita Sharma – who was half-Indian and that. Apparently, people in town and round the villages could be a little bit funny with Angelita, cause she was half-Indian and that. Lily couldn't ever, ever see how this mattered; Angelita was dead funny, beautiful: glistening black hair, long-stepping with gorgeous lively eyes. Her dad was Indian and that: junior doctor at hospital in town.

Once, when the osteopath consultant was called away, Lily Hansford had a brief examination from Dr Sharma himself, on one of her monthly trips to the hospital. Angelita's mum was the district nurse from Broadmayne as well. Angelita Sharma joked that some months Lily might see her parents more often than she did.

Of course, by then people were funny round Lily Hansford too, so it brought them together.

Even in year ten Angelita Sharma had wore real short, sequined skirts and polished boots to the three school dances – she looked blooming great.

'We like shit that shines,' Angelita told Lily and others as they downed vanilla vodka from plastic shooters in among the shadows of the ill-lit school car park.

'What? You mean cos your sort of Indian and that?'

'Hell yeah, of course.'

'That's brilliant,' said Lily Hansford.

Angelita Sharma snogged little Bill Dorren at Easter dance, up against the mural; touched his thing through baggy jeans. More than once, she claimed.

'Don't tell Dad. Or either of the bloody Coretta sisters,' Angelita Sharma told Lily Hansford. Down at the bus stops.

'How would I even word something like this to your dad? Even though he's a doctor?'

'Suppose. Don't tell Mum then.'

'Well, life was like a box of chocolates...'

Angelita completed the line in the accent, and they both screamed with laughter.

The Dorrens moved to Worthing soon after, and Angelita Sharma was not sorry.

Lily Hansford and Angelita Sharma spent a great deal of time in their bedrooms, trying on clothes, makeup, shoes. Lily loved putting Angelita's hair up in all different styles. They loved *Forrest Gump*. Yet what they really coveted and cultivated most, like a savage private cult, was Lily's mum's copy of the *Xanadu* soundtrack on an old cassette – until they each got their own personal copies on CD. Lily Hansford and Angelita Sharma were deliriously devoted to Olivia Newton-John and the dizzy trajectory of her career in all its forms.

The Hansford family were taking a holiday abroad that year – outside England! Usually, the three of them just went for ten nights to some country hotel, as long as it had an indoor swimming pool for Lily. Some days, Lily's dad, Tom Hansford, would drive all the way back from the hotel to his workshops to check on constructions and the office, leaving Lily and her mum, Carol, round the pool or having classic chicken club sandwiches from room service with the telly on.

Lily was furious that this foreign jaunt was gonna interfere with the ambitious plans she and Angelita had for summer – a day trip to London to see the Hippodrome and Buckingham Palace; so she squared it by asking if Angelita could come with them on their holidays too. It was negotiated – but very formally – with both sets of parents meeting one evening at Lily's parents' old farm. The girls went off together upstairs to listen to *Xanadu* after a very short appearance, while the parents worked out the holiday details over gin and tonics. Angelita even got a brand-new giant suitcase: all spangly. They were going to some resort on the Med in Spain and all that. A rented villa with a pool! These words were beyond exotic to them. They were often repeated at school in the jealous company of others.

*

On a floor mattress in Lily's bedroom at Maurwood, Angelita slept over the night before departure, and they both yapped with helpless excitement, so much so that Lily's dad came along the upstairs corridor in his bloody embarrassing stripey pyjamas, knocked, put his head in and told them both to wrap it up as he couldn't get a wink and he had a very long drive ahead.

The girls slurped down Coco Pops at 4.30 a.m. in the open-plan kitchen.

'Aren't you both a bit – overdressed?' enquired Lily's dad. 'Where's your tracksuit?'

'Packed, Dad.'

'We're just going to be at the motorway hotel in France tonight.'

'Oui, monsieur,' stated Angelita Sharma.

'There might be decent boys on the ferry, Dad.'

'Oh God.'

The four of them set off before light, under a full-lit coin of a harvest moon which travelled with them, flashing through the thin trees on the trunk road.

Tom wanted the radio on for traffic, but *Xanadu* totally dominated the Range Rover sound system.

'Is that bleedin Cliff Richards?' Tom Hansford asked.

Lily's mum, Carol, sniggered.

'Course, Dad. Get with it.'

'Cliff Richard,' Angelita corrected him.

Both girls fell asleep in the back of the Range Rover well before the ferry at Poole.

Lily's mum and dad were of the Hansfords and the Stricklands; their parents were the usual farmers who had lived for generations along those reaches of farmland between Whitcombe and Broadmayne village but had mostly quit the hassles of actual farming. Lily's mum, Carol Strickland, was an only child too, and Lily Hansford grew up in her mum's converted farmhouse with the dormer windows; big seventies extension built by Grandad Strickland back in his last days. Grandad Strickland had often shouted orders at the roof contactors from up on his tractor seat before driving onwards for the day. A flat-topped rectangular chimney was clamped onto its westerly end for the new living-room's grand brick fireplace – in times when we all assumed fireplaces would be with us forever.

The farmhouse was named Maurwood after the elms and three-hundred-year-old oaks over across the river bend, visible from the north windows.

'Knights In White Satin' riding through them, Lily's dad often imagined after he moved in – but not quite. Yet through those young trees in 1694 had ridden a troop of horsemen with a sealed message for Queen Mary II – who was soon to die of smallpox up in London. One of those riders had left an ink plan of their route, clearly marking '… *river woodes of Maude by Weetcombe*' as a cooking-fire stop on their eastwards itinerary. Headmaster Peter's local-history group had once given a lecture about it in the village hall, with coloured slides on an overhead projector.

Lily Hansford remembers so much of being little on the old farm, her mum saying, 'Our new chimley's for when Daddy gets into one of his tempers, all his steam goes straight up and shooed away towards town, back where it belongs.'

Yet Lily's dad, Tom 'Curly' Hansford, was a mellow man of good heart. Only became upset at the workshop when multiple aluminium-barn orders were on; he would drive home in some fury over one of his toolmen. Tom shouted first at Carol, then at the new spotlights in the kitchen ceiling; he would turn on the lunchtime ITV news and shout at that for about four minutes; sometimes he could even be seen outside, circling the rockery of the landscaped terrace, still waving a hand before the distant woods and at the skies before he slammed the door of the new Range Rover then drove back off towards town, forgetting he'd had no lunch. Just as well Lily chose school dinners four days a week back then to get all that year-eight and year-nine gossip. She was at the hospital other days.

Once, when she was nine, Lily was awoken in her bed, and her dad gently reached in and lifted her in both his arms. Accompanied by her mother, Lily's dad carried her carefully downstairs and out into that summer's night. The three of them there among the rockery shrubs with Lily still hoisted in her father's arms. A comet's greenish tail was stroked across the sky among the burbling stars. It had been on BBC Television's *The Sky At Night*. Her parents whispered as Lily looked up too. After a while she fell asleep in the cool air and woke happy in the morning, back in bed.

Tom suffered itchy backs then, said it was the stress and risk from the bank loan after buying over the second yard; he had one of those wooden-bead covers on his driver's seat. Carol changed the soap powder brand six times until the village pharmacy hit on the right ointment.

When she was little, Lily often found her dad at lunchtimes with his Barbour jacket folded over his forearm, rammed under one of the door lintels of the extension, his shirt and full weight pressing hard against the sharp edge of the doorway, slowly gyrating on his itchy shoulders, singing Baloo the bear's song from *The Jungle Book* film. Once, as he scratched and sang the song in front of Lily, there was a sudden sharp snap. All the varnished wood on the left-side door frame tore away from the wall, the plank of the lintel dropped smartly down from above as he, then the door frame, collapsed to an A shape in among a mighty scatter of dust and plaster lumps. No video cameras, no phones, or it could have been on Harry Hill's show.

In the green photo album there is a coloured Polaroid of Lily's mum before she married Tom, standing outdoors by the chimney in a halter neck; she must be about eighteen. Looks great; Carol always thought she had buck teeth, but they are just smiling teeth, which make her appear happier. Over her bare shoulder – which is bleached white in the sun's flare – is that completed chimney, but the roof isn't all the way on yet, and her grandfather's brickwork is still to be completed. Through the bright, ascending gaps of nine or ten absent bricks – like missing teeth – you see all the way south towards Chalky Road and the white horse; the coast and Channel beyond are accounted for by an inexplicable burnish to the sky. Today's rockery then is just a swirl of chalky, hard-overed vehicle tyre tracks.

Carol Strickland met Tom Hansford not at Pony Club get-togethers, nor the town pubs on a Saturday, nor a farmers' dance or at cricket on a Sunday with hungover village lads; not under the disco lights of the three annual school dances – though they were only a year apart there. Neither of them ever went to Riotz! nightclub in town either. Maybe they were just a touch country-snooty? They met when Tom came round to her dad's firm, Strickland Meadow Out-housing, when he was thinking of investing in it. Tom's own father had willed the farmland at Ketlent to him for development, but suddenly left Tom fatherless at twenty-one. Carol – tall, long earrings – was still on the typewriter in her dad's office in them days, dresses on those mornings her father was in, short skirts and heels when she knew he was away at the golf course or down seeing the accountants in Poole.

'How do you type with them fingernails?' was the first thing Tom Hansford ever said to Carol Strickland, nodding. It was a short-skirt day; he had wanted to catch the place without the boss breathing down his neck. He wasn't to know how soon he would become the boss's son-in-law.

'How do you think with all that daft hair on you?' Carol came back at Tom.

Cheeky versus cheeky, and he liked it.

He also liked – less than two weeks later – that he never could get the bloodstains completely out of his white M&S shirt, originally bought for school. Those very same, long manicured nails of Carol Strickland, up at night by the Hanging Tree. The rear of his Ford Escort Ghia. Tom claimed it was henceforth that his back started to itch, and she would scratch it for him regularly.

Tom and Carol got along like mates as well as lovers – a lot in common – no interest in colleges or universities; school and teachers were just a bit of a time-wasting laugh; they both left with a couple of A levels between them because their parents had businesses to be getting on with in the real world. Never read a page of *Under The Greenwood Tree* again, like they were forced to in the classroom. Both ate Sunday pub lunches quick, not talking but looking each other in the eye, often chuckling privately as if they were getting away with something mischievous. They both liked big dogs and they liked horses, though never owned any because of the Lily thing; even in their late teens they both loved James Herriot books, *All Creatures Great And Small*, and *Last Of The Summer Wine* on telly. First on the farm road to get a video player.

She stuck with Blondie, and he had a bad weakness for The Moody Blues – almost every album. They went to church together about five times a year, as well as for their parents' tragically early funerals, schoolmates' predictable weddings, midnight mass on Christmas Eve.

Tom made Carol mad one Easter when he turned up for church in football gear, back when the village still had a five-a-side team before the pitch was turned over to housing. She was so embarrassed. Tom borrowed someone's anorak from the hooks in the porch, wore it zipped up throughout the service, with his bare legs and his studded boots which shed muck on the flagstones as they clicked.

Every election they both unthinkingly voted for whoever the local Tory candidate was, though the Conservative always got in anyway – hey, who else would they vote for?

This slightly glamorous couple even once had a frisson of country scandal about them, by Broadmayne standards. Driving back from the Trueloe Hotel Harvest Ball, August before they were married, they gave a lift to Bart Jones, who they had been at school with – handsome, popular fellow who had been the star of the town's under-21s football team – cheekbones, quietly modest. He was with his French girlfriend, who he'd found in Weymouth where she was on a hotel-management exchange. She had a stunning name – Océane – and the looks to go with it.

All four shared a plastic bottle of cider in the car, so, over-the-limit drunk, Tom stopped by Swan Bridge. The Ford Escort Ghia got parked well up off the Dell Road in case the Police Land Rover came cruising round that way. All four lay talking and laughing across the bonnet and roof, gazing up at the curdled moon while they smoked the French girl's perfumed Gauloises cigarettes – or were they Gitanes? Carol was first to suddenly pull down her denim miniskirt, the Blondie *Rapture* T-shirt got hauled over her permed hair. Océane followed, completely naked – being French – and the two young women jumped in together, screaming, and burst apart the lunar medallion, which floated like a lifebelt in the middle of the black pool.

They say all the clothes came off the male participants also, who dived in to join them; Tom's curly hair went as flat as Carol's perm. It was ever spoken that Carol Stickland had laid her buck teeth to the French girl's lips and kissed her cider-and-French-cigarette mouth as studiously as a guy first kisses a girl, then all together, the couples were exchanged for long passionate clinches and caresses in the slow moon water. It was said Océane had a prominent scratch across her tanned back the next day. Blah blah blah. Who manufactured or spread such fine details we shall never know – could it really have been Océane herself in The Old Plough, with that beauty spot on her lovely face? Who cares? It was a scandal of such elation it might as well have been the blabbing fields, elms and dawdling moon river itself that spread the word.

But the world moves on, and scandal gets forgot round Broadmayne; it's between Tom and Bart whatever happened with the girls that night. Bart soon moved to London as a junior trader in a big bank. And Océane ? Who knows? Bart did send a big bunch of flowers to the hospital when Lily was born. By the way, Lily was born *well* over nine months after the swan-pool night – you know what silly rumours get like round those parts.

They made good time in France and took their first night in a motorway hotel close to Toulouse, where Lily and Angelita had a room to themselves and spent most of their time taking long showers and ferrying ice cubes from the corridor ice machine to their room to consume a big bottle of Coca-Cola with; so much ice was collected they eventually filled the sink with it just for amusement.

The four of them went to a café, which was accessed by crossing an enclosed walkway right over the motorway, and the girls paused there to marvel at the dashing, corner-lit roofs of the juggernauts streaking south below them from where they stood in the eerily bleached light of the air bridge. The girls firmly refused all foodstuffs except burgers and chips.

*

The next dawn, urged to haste by Tom, they drove onwards. Unfamiliar cypresses lined the roadsides and embankments, the trees' tall foliage made transparent by velocity. As the day before, the girls jeered while Tom sped down the fast lane overtaking truck after truck. Vehicles carried strange numberplates, Dutch containers ferried flowers south, Polish vehicles moved obscure loads, oil tankers of unusual brands serviced the petrol station forecourts. Continental families favoured campervans. The girls waved warmly if they overtook any vehicle with *GB* oval bumper stickers, carrying familiar numberplates. Several times, a high-performance sports car came up to the Range Rover's rear, and Tom indicated then moved into the slower lane for the pursuing vehicle to surge ahead, while the girls demanded he made pursuit – but he did not. 'Flash foreign git,' was all Tom muttered.

Late that afternoon they detoured off the motorway, tempted astray by some guidebook Carol had in her lap but which she could not consult in detail claiming car sickness. They parked in a gravel space and dined at a country restaurant with some sort of reputation. Though it was summer, they were seated in a salon by an open, circular wood fire, which flamed while glowing logs shifted. All four of them became flushed and removed outer clothing. Angelita and Lily were resolutely unimpressed – even appalled – by the menu. They guzzled Coca-Colas and insisted on chips, which had to be concocted *à la carte* off the menu. Tom kept repeating and explaining these three words as it was the only French he knew, apart from *sole meunière*.

Carol ordered an omelette, and Tom braved steak. When the food arrived the girls descended on their chips, but Tom and Carol surveyed their fare with distress. The omelette was a sort of blubber and the steak violently raw. They were sent back, Tom repeating the phrase, 'Well done, if you please. Well done, if you please.' The waiter returned the dishes to the table. Carol endured the omelette, but inside the browned exterior was a yolk froth. Tom sent the steak back yet again after the first cut of his knife. The steak returned. Tom protested to the waiter that it was still not done proper. This time the waiter just left the table without the steak.

'Bloody heck, he's just ignoring me now.'

Lily sniggered. 'Dad. Embarrassing.'

Clientele were staring.

'Just eat up your food now,' Lily mocked, shaking her head and sweeping her curls away from her lightly sweating forehead.

They fell silent as a man appeared next to their table in chef's whites.

'I am sorry, but it just isn't done,' Tom mumbled.

The chef held a blackened griddle pan, scooped the steak from Tom's plate and stood, holding the meat into the open public fire next to them. 'Enough?' he asked repeatedly, 'Enough?'

'A bit more, if you please.'

'Enough?'

'A bit more, if you please.'

Huffing, the chef blasted the meat fragment in the naked flames several minutes more. All the tables around them, populated by continentals, were watching this performance.

'Okay?'

'Okay.'

'That is not well done. That is destroyed,' the chef informed him in perfect English, as he slid this crisped and now shrunken fragment onto Tom's plate.

The others had completed dining, so Tom chewed alone.

They crossed the Spanish border, and the enormous sun had shifted its angle in the sky to a new configuration, which they all found uneasily alien. That night in the cactus and odd, aggressive-looking plants of the parking area – all of which were floodlit from below – bizarre insects drilled and thrummed, crickets chattered from the sides of the hot walls. Tom was annoyed they had arrived so early at this second booked motel; hidden over an embankment the motorway roared and whooshed. He maintained that if he could have motored onwards they would have almost made their destination of Puerto Bajo on the Costa Blanca, but he admitted they would have arrived too late to collect the keys to the rented villa from the agency office.

The girls insisted on wheeling both their large full suitcases into their motel room to consider their numbered and varied contents. They changed into shorts and T-shirts, and, despite the terminal hour of night, sunglasses were hoisted into their fringes. The girls soon complained to Tom and Carol no ice machine was present at this lodging, though they still lingered about the corridors hoping to meet other guests – doubtless with teenage boys in tow.

Late in the night Tom rose alone while Carol slept. Paranoid, he had gone out into the car park to check that the locked Range Rover was secure and to ensure the petrol cap was untampered with – though he knew this was slightly foolish. He stood there, marvelling at the dull heat of the night. An aircraft crossed the planetarium sky at cruising altitude, with its cherry collision lights visibly blinking. Tom felt a bit ashamed that, despite being a grown man, he was a little intimidated in a strange new world, and a little homesick already.

Tom thought of the empty rooms of Maurwood back across the English Channel; of he, Carol and Lily suddenly not inhabiting those spaces – he could sense the silence of the distant, familiar home and their own very particular vacancy in every room. The individual fibres of the synthetic carpets' weave would be springing fractionally upwards due the absence of their daily treading feet. He, Carol and Lily seemed as disappeared as those historical riders who had passed through the woods in... when was it... 1694? He also remembered a night when Lily was little, and he had carried her out to let her see a comet; he imagined himself holding Lily's frail body up to the ancient starlight, like an offered sacrifice, but that was an awful and false memory; he never did that. Carol was there.

He took a few deep breaths and shook his head. The driving. Wished he still smoked. Things seemed a bit easier when poor Lily was younger; he feared the end of innocence approached and what would the world do with her?

They motored south slowly, taking several long refreshment breaks, and arrived in Puerto Bajo at dusk to collect the villa keys. The town stood on the burning shore like a receiving cup being filled with the luminous light of the Mediterranean; in evidence was a shocking, clear light like none of them had ever witnessed before, even in the slow-moving summer evenings of Dorset. Here, twilight bats darted round the pine trees, like charcoal scraps thrown up by thermals; frantic insects formed undulating clouds under vertical streetlamp filaments, harsh fluorescent strip lighting signalled out frozen moments in passing, crowded cafés, liked embedded tableaux among those more softly illuminated streets.

The rental villa stood high on the hill, among the bougainvillea lanes of the residential range. To impress every new set of arrivals, the swimming pool and interior lights had been left fully illuminated beneath the fish-blue sky of stars; the villa's modern, box-like white walls, its sharp edges against the night, and its square windows made it a cradle of opalescence. The chlorinated azure glow of the large swimming pool threw ribs of trembling light upwards, stirred by the pumps, and printed them onto those first-floor ceilings in wave patterns – as if the occupiers were involved in monitoring mysterious but invisible phenomena, now adumbrated in symbolic form.

Angelita and Lily were so overwhelmed they ran to claim a first-floor front bedroom where both stared down at the pool glow and the wide moon emulsions of the sea, visible from these huge windows.

'This is the best place in the whole of the whole world,' Lily Hansford announced.

'Well it is pretty damn brilliant,' said Angelita Sharma.

'It's the kind of house I believe Olivia Newton-John lives in,' declared Lily.

'Shit yeah,' Angelita confirmed.

PUERTO BAJO:
CHAD'S POINT OF VIEW

SATURDAY NIGHT, ME, Jake Ingram and Lily Hansford are sat up from the beach on the terrace of The Jealousy Bar. Usual table, all three of us not talking, heads bent forward in the mood lighting, as if saying prayers back at primary school. The halogen-like up-glow of Lily's phone is showing the fat-free creamy cup of her swan neck.

Me, Jake and Lily are sending messages to each other on our private, three-person messaging group – blocked to all humanity but for us. Our thumbs are Xbox firing on the keyboards; sometimes Lily grimaces at autospell deviations.

The shallow cocktail bowl of a Ready-For-Lift-Off? with three straws has been placed on the table before us by that Munchkin waitress with the frilly shorts that they all wear to try and make their short-leg asses look more appealing during a ten-hour shift, leaning across tables retrieving plates and sodden coasters.

We are gossiping about Kate Goodenough, who is over by the bar with a Spanish local boy. I just posted:

She has gone Native, poor thing.
:-) what a loss for English decency.

Lily sends me an instant smiley face. Jake posts:

Maybe a taste for burro, cos we all
suspect Kate likes up the ASS too.

Lily answers with a smiley face. Then I do.

Yet striding over to our table comes bloody Kate Goodenough herself, pegged up on red heels with her lip stud. Her beau from the Spanish comprehensive school is pulled behind her by his arm. She's been with him all summer: Paco Martínez or Lafuente or Jiménez or whatever his *apellido materno* is – does it matter? Posh dopes in England have them double-barrelled names but *all* Spanish do. You can never remember so many names, and why should you? It's double the work; an imposition. Actually, Paco Whatever is okay. Semi-sussed, and his dad is quite rich for a local high-school kid. Estate agent, of course – what else? Paco knows he's Spanish and can't help it, chip on shoulder, wants to chomp on a superior species; a tiger with a sudden taste for English flesh.

'Chicos, amantes, coño, una noche más de Lift Off.'

Although she has never been there once in her seventeen years, Kate pronounces the name of the drink in perfect Thames Estuary English. Me, Jake and Lily each immediately click off our private messaging group to smirk up at her.

'Paco, tío,' Jake says, holds up an arm, and Paco, wearing a stupid Baloncesto vest with the number forty-two, does that gangsta-arm-grab-thing with him. I just nod. Lily mumbles, almost whispers through her lips, 'Kate, guapa.' As if she is forcing Kate's name up and into her memory. As if Kate's name is just something Lily forgot and remembered at the last moment. Kate bends to air-kiss Lily, who turns her face thoughtlessly left/right to receive.

'Cómo estás, Kate? Getting plenty exercise?' Jake grins.

I smile.

'Oh, wouldn't you like to know?'

'No,' Jake says bluntly, cutting, like a dead thump.

In English she says, 'Give us a suck on your straw then.' Kate bends down, touches the straw, pointing it towards her mouth with her acrylic nails, angles it into her lips. If it moves at all, I am at the wrong angle to potentially see Kate's dress move slightly up her tanned thighs, but Lily is at the correct angle to watch that toned rump pop outwards. But with feminine restraint and delicacy, Lily doesn't even glance at it at all. Disappoints me. Lily'll have seen it enough at PE – though she's mostly excused. I notice the Spanish mumps at the next table – young guys with fucking cloth wrist-bangles and rough beards, all taking a peek for use in their later hand-jiving; they'll be jealous of slim Paco getting a good ration of pure Albion.

'Don't swallow it all in one go, Kate,' I chip in.

'Fuck off,' warns Paco in English, but laughing. I am sure he blushes under that perma-tan. Moors and Christians, man. I am not so sure the Christians won; not before the Moors had spread their love about, that's for sure.

'Where have you been tonight then?' I ask without interest.

Kate has her cocksuck-lips round that straw-end, and, sure enough, I see the greenish tint of some Ready For Lift Off?, jump up the interior of the candy-stripe tubing, and she turns her eyes round all three of us: pure Newcastle cable porn.

Paco talks for her in English. 'Just the usual, man. Socco, a visit maybe at Kandala for some *chipitos*, then Strawberry Dancefloor.'

'Big excitement. Strawberry Dancefloor forever.' Jake shrugs and pretends to boogie in his seat; Paco shrugs, acknowledging the ultimate small-town boredom of what Puerto Bajo is for us. Swimming pools are not enough, it seems.

Kate Goodenough straightens. 'Ooo, that stuff will rot your teeth.'

'It puts hair on your chest, Kate.'

'Paco's all right there.' Jake smiles.

Paco laughs, beats his fists on his chest.

Kate turns to smile at Lily, as if Lily is jealous of ape hair on a young guy – she hates it! Kate's face looks good in makeup, though. You can see it's an hour's work and the mascara pulled back delicately behind each eye. She has a metallic gold band round her slim, tanned but over-toned right bicep. But it's more muscle than youthful slimness, like Lily. Kate's shoulders are just that bit too muscley from behind for me and Jake – what with all Kate's sea kayaking and water-volleyball shit.

I say, 'Hey, Kate, you're looking great. You look like a shining Nefertiti.'

She frowns, 'Titty who?'

'She's a dancer at Benidorm Palace,' Jake says.

I laugh, speaking English real quick, so I am not sure nor do I care if Paco follows, 'Nah, she was queen of Egypt in the times of the pyramids. The pharoah's wife. Akhenaten's Old Lady. You're like a delicious Egyptian queen by the Nile, Kate. Covered in gold with thirty cats following behind you.'

'Chad Lucas, you are so strange.'

Lily says quietly, enforcing the mockery, 'But you *do* look great.'

'Thanks, darling. Thank you, Chad, for the history lesson. Spot who is getting A in history again.'

I say coldly, 'Ancient Egypt isn't on the history syllabus Kate,' and she looks momentarily flummoxed but replies in English.

'Well, I hope I'll be sitting next to *you* on exam day, and you can show me your answers.'

'I'd show you anything you want, Kate. You know that.'

Jake laughs, and even Lily smiles. I don't know why we all don't just get a hotel room.

'Who's that mump bloke over there?' Jake frowns up at the bar, and we all turn to stare.

'That's Colin. He's a hairdresser at Aspirations in the port. Look at his hair.' It's a boyband quiff, and he gives every bloke the same haircut as him. 'Look at that plonker over there. Colin cut his hair. And him. Over there. You can fucking tell.'

'I could do better,' Lily says.

Me, Jake and Lily are English – okay? Nothing to be ashamed of in that. It's our culture. Okay? Accepted, I have only been to England once – London/Madame Tussauds/Windsor Castle – Jake's been loads of times and Lily's a blow-in; she actually lived in Dorset till she came over here with her mum and dad – or, as she coolly calls them, with a correct French accent, *les anciens*. That explains the Combine Harvester accent she had when she first arrived, though it's Essexed-out a good bit since.

Me, Jake, Lily, we all attend the fee-paying English-speaking Academy. The Caddy over at Puerto Feliz – final year. That makes us English. Right? Speak English at home. A-level curriculum, English history: no Barça or Real, no fucking Atlético for us, only Man U or Chelsea, Shakespeare and *David Copperfield* and Henry VIII's wives: Catherine, Anne, Jane, Anne number two, Catherine number two, Catherine number three. Unimaginative Christian-namers those fucking Tudors. I only need one wife: Lily.

Jake Ingram and me been like bros since Mrs Gillingham's old pre-school group up by the grotty public pool. Same as all the Caddy, we won't go to the public pool ever any more cause we all have our own great pools in our parents' homes, right across the villa range. I did once pull Carmel, a skank-chav English girl at the public. Fourteen – first snog. Hers too, she claimed. She had nice little ones but a sweat rash between them. She wasn't even comparable to Lily.

The public, though it is big (Olympic size), is all South Americans and now Russians (the poor ones, not like the Petrovs up the Caddy), and there's broke Polish/Eastern Euros from all those no-place countries – Estonia or wherever. You can't tell one father from another: a snaffling face, eyes everywhere, checking out clothes and mobiles. Gold crucifixes, parents' fashions jammed in 1987 – in winter, leather jackets on the men, like the guy from *Knight Rider*, big cardies on the plum-faced mums. Charity-shop fodder. In summer, speedos with masses of knob and bollock flash on the sun-loungers. Russkis have those potato heads that just move across from left to right like a boulder, little greedy eyes slammed in the middle. Money money money money NEEYET. The daughters can be hot, though. Good legs and arses with no cellulite, cause of a low history of toxins in the gene pool from loser communist times.

When you ask for a Coke at the public poolside 'bar' they don't have it in a glass bottle or even a tap dispenser – they hand you a World Cup can out of an underpowered fridge – one of the prehistoric ones with a flat, manual sliding top, not a six-foot silver frontloader like our parents have in all our kitchens – and then served in a fucking plastic cup. No ice and lemon or nothing. Not like the café-bars, bistros and restaurants down the front by the beach, which our parents take us to every Saturday or Sunday for lunches.

Even Arab kids have started appearing at the public with their shit plastic footballs from the *chinos*. I don't mean money Arabs, like Tarif up the Caddy. Morocs: white-van drivers, who pick up used washing machines, electrical goods and busted deckchairs from the roadside bins. Welcome to the EU, the cream of the North African educational system – not lawyers and doctors exactly. But they want a decent future for their kids, which is fair enough. These Moroccan dads in their crap, out-of-date, Serie A and English club strips. I like them, though. They're never pissed out their heads, bolting up rice-based dishes on a Saturday night, like all us expat Brits. Their women folk've fake Christian Dior scarves in a thirty-degree heat – the women sharing one pathetic can of

Coke warming in the plastic cups while the hubby gorges café solos and cheap fags, shouting into their crap old mobiles. Spotted on the back-road recycle park, a clapped-out Zanussi: go the A-Team!

The East-Euro kids piss in the pool showers, Jake says cause they've no bathrooms at home. They use shampoo in there, for fuck's sake. He says it should be called the *pubic* pool, what with all the foreign hairs in it. Says you can't tell head hair from pube among this lot.

Jake and me took Lily up to the public once just for her to see the circus. Not swimming, of course, just scoping it out. Jake told us, 'Check out the discontent – the men don't drink, the women don't sun-bathe. Wrong fucking country, mate.' But my thought was that Spain's just Morocco with Ray-Bans. Lily smiled at the very edge of her mouth, but there was that touch of tight hesitation, of pain in her lower lip, which I very much recognised. She's so sweet she never criticises a soul. Even the English chavs who go to the local Spanish high school.

Lily sometimes does mass and all that with her parents – Church of England service out of town, doesn't mean she's Spanish – fuck no. Look at her. She's English as it comes. Lily's skin is the whitest skin Jake and I have ever seen. Her hair is so jet black it makes her skin even whiter. Her bikinis are black too, which adds to it all; the top with the hanging-down jewel-chain between each tit, bottoms that immediately snap up between her arse-crack with the second stride when she walks over to dip her fingertips in a swimming pool. She stays long and white every summer for a great deal of time, no matter how many weeks we spend in and round our respective family pools. Her mum and dad, Tom and Carol – who are dead nice – have a huge infinity, with rotat-ing, rainbow-coloured lights under the water. The three of us circulate. The Drifters, Jake's old man calls us. We use the pool where the paren-tal units are currently out of the villa, quickly packing up and moving on when they come home from Spanish lessons, yoga, photography club or pissed from boring lunches in some new restaurant; we move over to the next pool on our mountain bikes with Lily doing a backie, or sometimes side-saddle on the cross bar with Jake or my cock in our Burberry swimming shorts touching against her kidneys – her bare back with its micro-bikini thread.

Then over two days in late July or early August – like forked cream that suddenly thickens – Lily Hansford goes latte-coloured, and she stays there. Yet no matter how brown Lily is by 15 September, no matter if she's been scuddy by the pool, living down on the beach, jet-skiing, on the quad bike or out on Logan Morgan's old man's fucking flash speedboat – it doesn't make a blind bit of difference come winter; Lily Hansford is flour-white again by each Christmas. It's funny really. When she first came to live in Spain, Lily told us she cried when she realised a suntan went and just peeled away in the shower every autumn. She had believed first time you got it, a suntan stayed on a person for ever and ever. Just like a scar on a tit job.

June-to-September holidays, Lily spends all her days by pool or rocky beach with Jake and me, starting at factor thirty and never going below fifteen, beneath a hire-parasol on the shore, UV leak tans her up grand, as Jake or I drape a towel across her shoulders by 3 p.m. Unless it's early morning and no one is about, not even me and Jake can spread factor thirty on her shoulders and lower back at the rocky beach, only by the family pools. People talk, and it would be bad for Lily while we're still at school if the truth were known. I mean everyone at the Caddy suspects I am totally in love with Lily Hansford, but they don't actually *believe* it – and that's the important distinction. We're so unnaturally tight there's even a rumour she's my second cousin anyway.

So white. Not much is pure white in Spain: the summer sky forever blue with the odd Lily-coloured cloud. All villas are painted white like a big elephants' graveyard scattered over those green moonlit pine hills; but when you look close at the walls of all our villas under the full moons of the seasons, and imagine them as Lily's naked body under starlight – nothing's as perfectly white as Lily Hansford's skin is.

Those mammoth skinny-dipping nights at the Sun Cliffs where she was like a glow-in-the-dark watch hand; you could see her lanky arms and legs waggling down in the black water. A white wall is all coated in dust, like the white cars and everything else white in Spain; it has peeling and blistered bubbles, festery blemishes. The red rains come up from Africa and stain the pure whiteness. There's no virgin snow. Nothing white stays white in this recent world: new T-shirts turn knicker-grey; white plastic bags and shoes go nicotine with oxidisation.

Only the big paper blocks of computer A4, the pack just freshly opened at school, compare to the whiteness of Lily's still and beautiful face, her long-spined back, her pert tits and punch-bag-tight arse.

Sometimes the three of us will be lying by one of our folks' three swimming pools. Lily will be tummy down, Wikipedia on her laptop. She's so white at the start of summer you need your brown polarised Ray-Ban sunnies on just to stare at her. The way she lifts her bum off the sun-lounger, the way she hoists it just an centimetre or two, as if in childbirth or in some business-like, private gynaecological manoeuvre. We know it's just sweat pooling on her ruby belly button piercing – which matches the red jewel hanging from the chain on her black bikini top. I, or sometimes even Jake, move over, put two palms on her lower back, or sometimes, if none of our parents is around, we risk our tanned hands on her and gently pull the white skin tauter. What we are trying to do is see if veins or blood vessels exist on down through that white skin, but there is fuck all. Though she has been getting electrolysis on her bikini-line, she doesn't have any black body hair either. It's weird. They are blonde. 'Give over,' she'll murmur. 'You'll actually *give* me thread veins.'

Look. Make your own psych evaluation, but Jake and me, we've spent most of our lives looking at women's and girls' near-nude bodies by swimming pools and on the beaches of Spain. Started with his mum, and even mine and my big sister, from even before our balls dropped and we started wanking off. We have seen the historical changes – from bush to Brazilian, from tangas to ankle bracelets, from natural to silicon – after the implants scare, we could spot redone silicons at seventy metres on the sand. From Botox to tramp-stamp-tats when we were eleven to what's now called Body Art. (A tat, any ink, would be wrong on Lil's double-whipped-cream skin.)

In come smartphones, so girls have more tan on their backs now than on their fronts, cause they're always lying on their tummies, Facebooking or texting; those young girls of the new summer, beneath vertical sunlight, heads hidden under towels and T-shirts the better to see their phone. We know girls' bodies and we know their skins, and nothing compares to the air-con-cool smooth snowfields of Lily Hansford.

Me, Jake and Lily can stand up above the Saturday beach on the paved walkway and look down onto the sand through our polarised sunnies. We see most of the Academy girls spread out down there in their latest Mean Girl groupings with a token hot boy – John Ingersoll usually, with his lemon-dyed fucking surf locks. Sometimes when a girl is lying face down you can't tell if the thin lace across her back is her bikini-top thread or if she's topless and it's actually a thin, delicate strand of dark sea kelp that adhered to her shoulders as she swam back in through the surf. We've seen and rated the bare tits of every fifth year of the Caddy, and you wouldn't get such opportunities in England, Jake assures me.

You can spy all the local or Caddy girls among the summer blow-in touristicos: Caddy gals have no beach brollies, no fold-away deckchairs, no airport thriller books; they just fry away down there with a small towel each, fake designer shoulder bag from the Sierra Leonean beach touters, smartphone in Union Jack, One Direction or Taylor Swift carcasses. Mind you, Spanish lads from the *pueblo* just have a towel each too, but baggy surfshorts in nineties style on their over-skinny legs; Barça tops, fucking stupid number-one buzzcut geometrics, Mohican hairdos that Dad told me Gazza Gascoigne wore back in ancient history: those losers have all been hit in the head by a bull at least once in their lives and have no smartphones either. Me, Jake and Lily, we stand there blinking down at the beach and the sea glare, our bleedin' destiny. Two mins flat and one of the Caddy girls bleeps me or Jake a text (never, never weird Lily):

> c u watching come down swim
> race ya to platform xxxxxx :-)

Fuck off. I have Lily. We just wave back – too cool to text.

Just to get the timeline correct for you here. I fell in love with Lily Hansford the day she arrived at the Caddy in nerd glasses when we were all sixteen. She got put in one year behind to catch up on her Castellano. Got to know her at breaks when she started wearing contacts. Jake and I agreed I was going to marry her round about then. One sunset, I started snogging Lily on the sofa in their huge upstairs front room as Jake choked at us. He surprised us and started seeing that slag Mary Townshend. Then he was going out with Mᵃ Carmen Cardona for a while – who was at least an improvement.

All last summer that black bikini has lasted, now this one too, and I begged her not to replace it, though it's so far up her arse crack she grumbles and finger hooks at it every five steps, which adds to her swaying gait. Lily Hansford's black bikini bottom rides up her arse crack for a specific reason. When Lily's with us, those Mean Girl bitches ask me and Jake to race them out to the swimming platform off the beach for a singular reason. Lily swims underwater like a fish – as we all do – but she ain't a fast swimmer, because Lily Hansford is deformed since birth. She has gammy legs. Okay? They are beautiful legs, but they are both beautifully gammy. That first day when she came to the Caddy, she hesitated at the classroom doorway then moved forward to the closest free desk between Kate Goodenough and John Ingersoll, ignoring the farthest and best one by the window. The whole fucking class held in a tension and glanced delightedly at each other as she limped and swung. The bunch of prejudiced ignorant cunts. Lily Hansford's left leg is about five centimetres shorter than her right, so she swings as she walks and throws her slim teenage body forward slightly, as if continually dodging infinite, machine-fired tennis balls which just skim her sides. Not just that. Her right leg, if you give it your undivided attention – as I do – is fractionally thinner than her left leg. You'd think it would be the other way round, wouldn't you? The shorter, weaker leg should be the thinner, but no, the supporting, stronger leg is just one centimetre slimmer if you really study it and compare it closely. If you hold the leg in both your hands. As I have done. Both legs are bloody crackers, very long, slim, shapely things, perfect knees and right down to those ankles that will never swell like my mum's did. Even when Lily's ancient and in her thirties, and pregnant with my babies, her ankles won't swell. She herself said it's like she has the legs of two different gals fitted on her, and they are there for me alone, to share – the two different girls' legs and the rest of Lil's body – like she said to me once: she's a Frankenstein made out of other girls' bodies, sure enough. If you think, it makes me and her a super-freaky-foursome in bed, her and two other girls' legs attached to her when I'm writhed up on her duvet in the afternoons with air con that pops her nipples the better for me to touch them with my teeth.

For years now Lily's seen a private physio here in Puerto Bajo: Mr Jamie – he used to be a physio at fucking Wimbledon, man, and those same hands that massage Lily's beautiful milk legs, those fingers that touch at her fatless tummy, have massaged Federer and brilliant Tsonga.

Jake and I slightly have the hump that Mr Jamie – who's sort of ancient – gets to feel her legs like only I do, to massage them, and he puts Lily on the running machine while holding her by the slender waist. We've been along to watch many a time. His fingers just touch each side of Lily's hoody top, and you think he's some kind of paedo, but no, he's measuring the degree of swing to the left as she jogs on the belt. He's watching her as she grows, wary that she gets misaligned; he senses and divines the pressures that are going on within her leg muscles, the strain her walk can put upon her growing spine. But since she is so tall and slim, he says she's actually getting better. Reckons she'll grow another four centimetres taller. Tells us skyscrapers are designed to sway in the wind, just like Lily Hansford is. I confess to Jake it turns me on, watching him go through the touchy paces with her, and Jake laughs, calls me a true sicko. Almost everything Lily Hansford does turns me on.

Of course, up the Caddy and behind her back, Lily is called by different school years: 'Limpin Lily', 'The Disco Champ', 'Ian Dury's Granddaughter', 'Lopsy Lu', 'Pissed Again', 'The Morning Drinker', 'Stryder', 'Reacher', 'Oscar Pistorius' – you fucking name it. Yet she's more of a beach babe than any of the straight-walking basic-pleasure-model skanks of the Caddy.

In summer Jake and I understand why my beloved spends every possible day on the rocky beach with us and why she prefers the stony coast of the Sun Cliffs far away from the sandy beach. She also has a preference for the pebbled shore by the string of beach bars. It's because *everyone* walks weirdly on a stony beach in bare feet. We all swing from left to right, we all tiptoe painfully and carefully forward; with no elegance we enter and stumble from the uneven edge of the surf or, drawing ourselves from the water, our arms are held out for balance. Even Kate Moss would look ungainly getting out of the sea on a stony beach.

Lily appears as normal as any of us do on an uneven stony beach, and she loves this. Everyone moves like she does. Nobody on that whole busy beach can tell she has gammy pins till, beyond the dunes and pampas-grass tufts, she reaches the sand-streaked pavement back up on the road and she begins that cute, slightly spazzy swing to the left. It reminds me of her energies and movements when she's riding the eagle on top. It's like Lily's always fucking, even when she just walks between us arm in arm if we're drunk.

But once you put Lily in water, where she sprawls and frolics for hours, she is free, and she knows it; she looks the same as everyone else, the instant our legs don't touch the sandy bottom an equality is at last established, the prejudice against her from other people vanishes and her black hair glistens from the sun above as if it has white paint splashed in it. She is like a queen walking incognito in normal clothes among her subjects.

Lily laughs more in the pool and seawater than anywhere else; she's not serious and even slightly sombre, as she is during sex. She swims till the narrow tips of her thin fingers prune, though Jake and I worry about jellyfish scarring that cherished skin, so we patrol either side of her for hours, ready to take the sting for her if we spot any spineless medusa puffing near her paleness. Jake kicked a jellyfish away from her once and got a good dose on top of his right foot, and it being the public beach there wasn't even the opportunity for me to piss on it, as I would by the Sun Cliffs. I have a filthy fantasy: I sort of hope Jake and me get stung by a brown stinger during the nightswimmings at the Sun Cliffs so Lily will stand above one or both of us and, slightly bent over, pee down on our burning skin, but we might as well leave this delicious prospect to fate, tide and currents. I told Jamie this. 'Ah, you sicko,' he said.

*

Lily has a huge collection of ra-ra skirts. Okay, I know ra-ras are a bit ancient and past it, but call it retro-chic or fuck right off. With her two wonky long pins, these skirts don't shorten her figure at all. She stands still a great deal, and this gives her a restive, meditative presence on the edge of any busy, loquacious group. The reason for this is because, when she stands still with her brown eyes following the current speaker, the disparity between her legs is briefly invisible, but for mine and Jake's trained and devoted eyes. And when she does walk, often in heels on Saturday nights, the swinging of the ra-ra skirt still only plays around her white or latte upper thighs, somewhat disguising the lively swaying motion of her natural stride and its lively cant – as if she's just hurrying. Notice how she always arrives with a sense of urgency, reaches out for her seat-back in a café or in The Jealousy, and then, with a quick arm, swiftly slides the seat out and tugs it back in beneath her descending arse and then she falls still and meditative – to her mind, invisible.

If she wore a straight, coloured skirt, the fabric would move up and down her thighs more, the way her dark, nasty school skirt still does, drawing attention to her uneven gait. She doesn't like that. All her straight skirts are white or slightly flesh-coloured or they match her latte tan, so the fabric riding on her thighs is not so noticeable. Great layered hair with gentle curls. She's gonna be a hairdresser, show that mump Colin from Aspirations how it's done.

God, she's beautiful.

SPOILED. I WOULD say she was spoiled – maybe we all were back then. I mean look, her parents always just did whatever Lily wanted, but you know cos of how she is, it was just a bad limp then (I wouldn't say 'bad' to her face, use that very word, but it actually was bad); didn't everyone and their dog make such a bloody fuss about Lily Hansford's famous limp, and me being brown-skinned and us going all around together? I won't say we were 'fixed at the hip' cos that's a bit close to the bone about Lily's, oh, I wouldn't say 'close to the bone' either – oh, anyway. Okay she was and is my best friend, it was a big limp, but her disablement, her – what's the proper bloody word these days; you can't use 'handicapped', can you? – her mobility issues, but even if she hadn't been how she is now – or then – mobility, her legs, she might have been spoiled by her folks anyway, maybe? I was. But I love her and always have and always will, and now I have been asked to, I will begin to tell her little story to you – though I have never told a story before. Wrote down I mean; obviously, I have told a story at Tokens Wine Bar to the sales girls and Human Resources colleagues and that. Not a Wrote Down Story, though. I don't drink alcohol much any more when I am there by the way – it's more cos of Dad being a doctor…

Lily Hansford went to secondary school with me, and we were absolute best mates always since forever having a laugh and that, then what happened to us is, her family moved abroad cos of her. From here to Spain. Though I didn't know why anyone would leave here other than for just going on holidays? In fact, I was with her the very first time she ever went down there into Spain with her mum and dad. A back and forth that was to be her life really. Funny what you remember. What a laugh that first fortnight was for us two. Lovely, but there were some awful bars and places there we went into, and

God it was hot. And the boys awful, real scrap snappers, trying to get us both to, well you know the usual daft-lad fantasies. Lots thought I was a Spanish girl cos of my skin colour and would speak straight to me in that language – Get out my face, mate, I am English, I said a few times. They don't like us English, think we are all slappers out for a legover, but look, for girls it's the weather is it not? – we have to go around half-naked in that shitty heat, so that brings in the wrong sort of blokes from all over the place. From all over the world, cos Spain is full of half-naked girls all summer long, what are you gonna get? You have to pour talc on your bits every night, or you might get a right awful rash. But I recall once Lily and I left this night bar place, it was truly awful, frightful I would say, we didn't even order a Coca-Cola, just went in and went straight back out of it again. It felt like Dorchester Prison or something, the canteen of it, with a pool-snooker-billiard-table thing that had a man sleeping on it with his T-shirt rolled up, beer belly, and 'wanker' written on his forehead in someone's lipstick. Written in English at least. So Lily and I turn round and walk back out and onto the street, as we look back behind us all giggles – guess who else was leaving that bar, through the door at the same time with us? A single bloody cockroach, Mister Cock-roach, flitting down from the step and scuttling off along the pavement behind us all on his own. That's how bad a dump it was, even the cockroaches were leaving. Oh we laughed and laughed, oh it was a scream. Always thought cockroaches looked like dates – you know the ones in the box you buy in supermarkets with the plastic fork? (cut this bit out of story) Anyway. Oh, just to add there was one lush nightclub there, though, but we were too young-looking/young to get inside so one night we got Carol – Lil's mum – to just drive us down and just stay sitting in the car in the car park outside just to watch and nose the people coming out, but honest this was already 3 a.m. and dunno if I had ever been up so late in my whole life back in them days, just there was no people coming out in one big rush, just like in England there would be at Riotz! in Dorchester – there was just no hour it seemed to just close. People just came out in dribs and drabs, at all times, through all nights and just bloody hell, there were even people just going *in* at all hours!

We started to nod off in the back of the car to be truthful, so Carol drove us back up home, but not before a bloke came over to the car, ignored us and knocked on the Range Rover's driver's window – tried to ask Mrs Hansford back into the club with him! Fancy! Lil's own mum, bloody heck, shit in the milk! Carol was so flustered she switched on her windscreen wipers and we drove off. Funny what you remember. Bloody hell, when we got back to the villa thing, Tom started shouting at Lil's mum about why on earth she had been driving the Range Rover about at all hours, and she explained that it would kill our curiosity about bloody night spots and... a right old set-to they had. We went straight to bed and fell asleep very nicely to their row. Funny what you remember.

So after we get back to Dorchester, Lily is all 'Spain this and Spain that, best place on earth', and this goes on for a bloody year or so, then all of a sudden I am all brokenhearted cos my best mate, doesn't she up and off to Spain, and I have to start hanging out with the bloody Coretta sisters? So Lil's brilliant mum and dad, Carol and Tom, just lock up their big long house at Maurwood, and get a caretaker to keep it up all okay and take Lil down to Spain there on a trial run, and they rent a posh villa thing there in what's it called? Puerto Bajo. Pool. Air conditioning. Street fiestas. Bars open till three in the morning. Next thing, the sweltering summer on the beach and the flirting is all over and Lily has snogged and a bit more, might I venture, six boys in a summer – the bloody sassy sasser – and they are putting Lily into a private school there, called the something Academy, where she has to repeat the whole fifth year, but she gets more A levels, oh shit in the milk, imagine having to relive one whole year of school again, even in Spain with the sun always shining! No thanks, you can return that to sender, mate!

We wrote each other texts and sent photos galore and sometimes we would phone each other on the good reception line, but Lily had to hide in the garden and whisper with louder chirping insects you could hear all about her, cause her dad saw the mobile phone bills. She wants to know all about my disastrous engagement to Hamilton Caldwell, against my dad's wishes. God, me and Hamilton went out for ages before we married. WHY?

So didn't she meet this guy too, at that school there? English bloke but left England dead young, almost when a baby, and lives out there and that, and first he seems okay. Chad Lucas. Met him when they came back on a visit, Lil all wanting me to like him loads and loads more than I really did, you know? Now I already know what happened to Lil and I, both our first times with bloody blokes, and she knows mine. She travelled to Southampton where handsome Paul Logue from a couple of years above us at school was at university doing electrical engineering, and she just turns up at his actual student union place somehow, and he was there drinking beers with his mates, and, like, Lily was in her amazing green top and that skirt I bought her and the long overcoat that made her look sophisticated and older – and cos it was so heavy it didn't move so much when she limped. She was like Hey Paul what a coincidence eh can we talk cause I really like you so that was that. She told me, just the two of them back in his flat in the afternoon it was like, a guys-only flat and truly frightful. Pigsty. Newspapers for curtains. No cups or mugs or glasses. They used actual CDs as coasters for cans of frothy beer and open CD cases as ashtrays, and a guy once peed out the first-floor window onto a car roof, and Lily said Paul told her this: there was no fridge. The freezer compartment had never been defrosted on the fridge and they were so hungry one day after smoking – how do you spell it? mary-wanna? – they noticed a pack of fish fingers entombed in there, in the ice at the back of the little freezer box, buried right into the ice, but they couldn't tug it free, and, being guys – imagine the total bloody horror of this – it being a guys' flat, they didn't have a single bloody hairdryer between them in the whole bloody house to defrost the ice box with. How blokeish is that? Men are just... unthinkable beings. A house with no hairdryer. So, they took a hammer to the freezer compartment to try to chip out the ice and get at the grub, but they broke the little pipes and all this blue coolant stuff burst out and soaked the fish fingers in their box and the fridge stopped working forever, even like the normal fridge-fridge bit. Funny what you remember. And after Lily and him had done it together on his single bed where there was a used sticking plaster trapped in the sheets at the bottom, he said, Look Lily, you are so beautiful. From the waist up. But you go all wonky towards the knees, you look great, till you walk about, but I still find you weirdly sexy. Imagine that, being called weirdly sexy? Lily lay on her tummy to use up the other condom cos we were distinctly curious to experience what it was going to feel like that way (as we had previously debated, and I experimented the same with Hamilton Caldwell WHY?) and he did it with her then said, Lily, I don't really want to be seen hanging about with you down at the union, the wonky way you walk, and people might think I'm doing the horizontal dance with you out of sympathy, as if I need that rep, as if I need to do it with anyone for mercy, but you are welcome to stay here tonight as you are so weirdly sexy and look, I am going back to the union for a couple more pints with the lads, and I'll get more condoms on the way, and I'll be back in a few hours, so make yourself very much at home here. The TV and games console doesn't work just now, but I think Dave has a radio in his room. That's all actual. What he said. Shit in the milk. Fucking blokes, eh?

After he had gone Lily was delighted to be able to get out of there still in the afternoon, and off home on the train, cos she was gonna have had to spin her parents a right old one if she had stayed the night, so. Hurt like shit on the train she told me.

So this guy she met in Spain was Chad, and he seemed dead nice in some ways, like a mega-intelligent-type guy, and I met him that once when he came over here, but in other ways he was a rude dude, abrupt, impulsive (?). A snob too, as he said he was surprised I didn't go to university cos my dad was an NHS doctor, and he said he was surprised I spoke – I can't remember the word, but he said he was surprised I spoke all-local-like, if you know what I mean? I noticed Lil's accent had got less local, more Essex. Bit of a pervert too, I heard from Lil, and I found him sort of racist judgy about people as well – I got the impression he didn't think I was English enough just cos I have brownish skin, that sort of dumb thing – and this coming from him-the-bugger, with the perma-tan who had hardly set foot on bloody English soil in his own whole bloody life and he's bloody starting to get bloody graces with me about what is being English and what bloody isn't. I was more English twenty times over than him, voted Tory, ate Sunday roast, paid years of taxes, and though I am Hindu a bit, I walk through the cold nights and buy the Christmas trees every year and watch the Queen's Speech. I told him straight that he was an expat, and I told him what my dad had once said to me: expat is a concept the English invented so's they are never immigrants or migrants no matter where they go to in the world – they are always bloody expats. No other nation was sly enough to have invented this idea but us. Chad blinked at that one, I can assure you, and you could see he didn't like hearing that, and Lily was trying to change the subject. If you really dibbed it up, I was English thru and thru, it was him, sloshing about in lots of swimming pools in Spain with his university-thinking ideas – go shit in a tall glass of milk, mate, you are some kind of half-baked beach bum in daft sunglasses, and you don't know where ya come from. I do. And a swivel head too, forgot we don't pose around wearing pricey sunglasses all the time in good old England, and his roving eyes followed each pretty waitress across the room behind your head while he was actually talking to you! I told Lil to watch for that, not to get engaged to him, but she didn't listen, and that was that. They got engaged then married, and she was Lily Lucas – which at least has a nice ring to it. Lasted about three and a half years, till he was found having an affair with some English skanker old schoolmate cheerleader-type bitch on that seafront there. So Lily run off too, back living with her folks, and had a romp with his best mate called Jake Ingram, who, from what I could work out, was always mad about her anyway – that put that cat among the pigeons. Do they have pigeons down in Spain? Maybe I mean Eurasian doves? Her physical condition was a bit worsened by then, that no one saw coming. She was meant to have been getting better, but it was her spine by then.

By that time Mr Hansford – Tom – had decided to take really early retirement, or at least let a manager run the barn-building stuff he did so well with, and that went okay for a good few years, but then that manager left, and the new one was a right clown, so Tom ended up coming into Gatwick and Bournemouth on EasyJet with his suntan almost weekly. Then Lily made her big decision. She had got mad about hair-dos and wanted to open a hairdresser's down there in Puerto Bajo in Spain, so guess what? Carol and Tom financed it all, every penny. Lil had done a health & beauty course over there in Spain. I was still engaged to cursed Hamilton Caldwell WHY? – lost half of the price of my first flat in the divorce after I married that idiot – you know how it is, you don't notice it even when it's in front of your nose when you're younger. He fancied my dad's house more than he fancied me, I think, cos I had put on this bit of weight, just piles on after your early twenties, doesn't it just? He thought Dad was loaded and would buy him a car – so we got married too, and it didn't last, but at least I met Lucien shortly after the divorce thing/separation, but by that time I was working quite high up at British Telecom – well, high up for Southampton division.

So Lily is running her own hairdressing salon called Lillian's in Spain. I went over to take my holiday after Hamilton Caldwell WHY? and it was great, and Carol was working there too. Then guess what? Tom and Carol decide to sell their place: Maurwood, all that beautiful riverland and house that's been in the family like forever back in all English history, as they are an old family of here, not like mine. They sell the barn-building biz, move lock, stock and barrel out there to Spain, they buy a big villa. With a pool that had a waterfall thing coming right through it. A year and a bit later, after she had split from Mad Chad, Lily comes back and stays with me in my new flat in Southampton for a holiday, and though we try to climb up Toot Hill together, Lil's mobility isn't as good, and she has a blue metal walking stick, but we go to stay at my dad's house (my mum and dad had divorced by then) in Dorchester, and I drive her out to look at her mum and dad's old farm, Maurwood like I said, and she starts to cry. It's sitting empty but was bought by a property developer who'll probably turn it into flats.

Lily and me we go on a night out to Riotz! And she leaves the walking stick at home, she can't dance any more, but a guy gives her his number after she snogged him. I didn't snog anyone, and I am feeling too old for that, and she texts him and meets him the next day. John Kitchener, and if you think about it you will remember him because his brother had the two ironmongery shops, one off High East Street, while he just went fishing all day I thought he was an idiot, but he was nice-looking. Were you in a car accident? was one of the very first romantic things he asked her in Riotz! She denies he said that, but it's funny what you remember, and she said, Yes I went under a tractor when I was a little one. Anything for a snog.

Suddenly she is cancelling the flight back to Spain, and Carol is going nutz cos of all the hair appointments Lily is blowing out with their regular clients down there, but Lily is gadding about with John Kitchener, day after day here, who has a nice flat in town where she immediately starts staying, and I have to go back to work in Southampton. John Kitchener works with rural affairs or something to do with... land registry? or... goodness knows what. Then she drops the bombshell to Tom and Carol. She is moving in with John Kitchener, and in fact she is moving back to Dorchester; she has missed England so much blah blah. Can you believe it? Well, they wait for the latest not to last – but it bloody well goes and does, to all our astonishment, let me tell you. Though Lil can't have kids, I get pregnant by Lucien and have Mareeta, who is all healthy, thank God.

So, Carol and Tom sell up in Spain after two years of waiting in vain for Lil and John Kitchener to fall apart, and they return to live here. They sell the Spanish villa and sell the lease on the hairdressers in Spain and back to England they come. They rent a nice bungalow on the edge of town, towards Winterborne Herringston past the Tesco's, and paying a big rent open a new hairdresser's in the middle of town, yup Lillian's (the second), for her to have as her own, though by this time Lil is not doing so well with her legs, there is another new misalignment, so she can't cut hair herself standing any more – she used to be so well angled for the task. Then suddenly she and John Kitchener have a bust-up because they find out he is seeing a lady who actually came to get her hair done at Lillian's before going on dates with him! The woman was getting a bloody discount too! Blokes, eh? So that was Lily back living in Dorchester.

Lily told me she once cut a weirdo's long blond hair all off as he now wanted a skinhead, so she scissored it away and shaved it down, and he had a tattoo of Jesus Christ spread out all across his head skin hidden in under all that hair, the crucified arms stretched straight out to each ear, the head and chest down towards the back of the rubbery folds on his neck fat. The guy was chuckling to her, 'Bet you didn't expect to be seeing him today, luv. Ever think about God?' Funny what you remember.

*

So for those of you who ask now, this is how Hansford's Garden Centres came about.

Tom and Carol had bought that nice bungalow just out of town, but Tom was restless to get another business up and going, so he makes a big investment in the garden centre out by Stinsford, mainly expanding the garden-shed and landscaping-firm side of it, which does really well during the boom years, and he buys out the whole centre in rivalry with Dobbies. Everyone spending money on posh gardens and upmarket sheds, and a lot of London folk with money are around buying holiday homes in Dorset they want all done up; outsiders and yuppies a lot of them, banging on about how great the community feel is down our way, with their bloody mushroom foraging and SUVs – though they aren't farmers. Ryce Rowles, who me and Lily were at school with, always was a weirdo, but he was charged by the police for threatening behaviour – he was shoving DVDs of that nasty weird film *Straw Dogs* thru the letterboxes of incomer cottages – had over a hundred copies back at his house, and though he is a weirdo, I found it quite hard not to admire him.

Now Lily had been doing okay, being single again, and we all started to breathe a sigh of relief. But Lily speaks good Spanish, and she had been attending a 'Spanish interests' group which has some local Spanish folks in it, and a gaggle of Spanish-holiday-home-owners. They all met once a month in a room they booked at the town hall and talked about Spanish food and culture stuff. One day a guy walks in whose name is Oscar Izquierda Martínez, who has taken a job at Boots the Chemist in town. Lily asks where he is from. He is from Puerto Feliz, a town about a mile and a half or less from Puerto Bajo. Lily tried to tell me, Tom and Carol one night that Oscar's name derives from the fact an ancestor was once left handed. We all knew it was only a matter of time and, sure enough, within a year Lily is heading south again with Oscar, and she moves back to Spain, to Puerto Bajo, linking up with old schoolmates.

Though this time Tom and Carol refused to get involved in financing the move, and they are furious at Lily for not even taking an interest in the hairdressing salon they set up for her here, which is run by Carol.

There was a big bust-up between parents and daughter for a while, with her down in Spain with this bloke Oscar, who it turns out is divorced with two kids in their early teens and an orbiting ex-wife. I soon sensed from Lily this was a larger cast than she had in mind – Oscar was just on a spree if you asked me, and Oscar was none too inspired when he learned that, especially in winter, Limping Lily starts to spend a few days a week having to use a wheelchair!

I would often drop in at the bungalow or at the salon and quietly report the latest I heard back to Tom and Carol from the stuff that reached me from Spain. I recall Carol once expressing amazement that Lily has so many boyfriends, and she said something: There are tastes for everything in this world. Funny what you remember. Gradually Tom and Carol started communicating with Lily again, but not much money got sent to her.

One day I was back from Southampton visiting Dad – Mum too, who was living then out towards Buckland Ripers with her new boy-friend nicknamed Poleman Rupert, who owned a tree-surgery business which his sons handled. Tom Hansford phoned me, asked me to meet him up at the south garden centre. He had bought two large garden centres by this time, and they were doing very well indeed. We had tea and cake in the café there, where it seemed some of the schoolgirls from our old school, working Saturdays in the café, didn't even know Tom owned the place, the way they banged his teapot down and his eyebrow shot up as he looked at me. He didn't seem to mind, though – in fact he seemed very happy.

With it being a nice day, Tom suddenly asked me to leave my car there and to get in his new car for a drive – we motored up out of town and round the ridge, down to the car park at Man O' War Cove, since it was lovely weather, we looked out towards France and towards Lily, I guess. Then we drove back townwards; he took a detour up and over, past Swan Bridge, the Dell and the Hanging Tree, round onto the farm road. When we pulled in outside with his new Range Rover – the one with the bigger engine – the chimney outlined against the sky, there was a Knight Frank 'For Sale' sign planted by the stone gates of Maurwood farm. 'Look! It's up for sale,' I said. 'Yeah.' He smiled. 'It has been through two different owners, but they never did nothing with it. It was meant to become flats, but the developers had trouble with permissions. I just bought it. Don't tell Carol. Or Lily. I don't have the keys or we could take a snoop around inside.'

For a single instant I didn't know why I was so very, very deeply moved by this moment, then I realised. Tom didn't have his own daughter with him here to come and show to her this huge gesture, so he'd taken me here instead, as I was all he had. I was so overwhelmed – what he had done seemed so… right… for Carol too, who I know missed her old family place. I burst out just crying, like Lily had that time I took *her* here, and, crying away, I leaned over and hugged him, and Mr Hansford hugged me back.

I was crying for our lost innocence and our youth too, and all the things that pass and life does to you, and we rarely get the chance to grab back at. Then Tom said he felt a change coming with crazy Lily's health, and I knew what he meant, I had sensed it too. He said Spain had been good for her health, that's why he tolerated it over all the years, and all the wasted money, and the stupid boys and men, because Carol and Lily were all the world to this man – but she could hardly swim safely any more and had been using a wheelchair more and more.

He said, 'Dry your tears now, love. It's so strange, Angelita. Maurwood has this huge downstairs doesn't it, with no stairs, no steps, all on one level, and it's like it was built for a wheelchair user long before ever Lily had even been thought of, or born into this world, and Carol's people lived here since, well since, since all that England has been. That's why I never felt at home down there in Spain, and, all told, there wasn't much but sun, dust and cheap liquor. The sun was good for my itchy back, though. And anyway, these days if you have the money, you can kit out an interior lift for the upstairs, but she can easily live downstairs to start with, and well, with the french windows she'll be able to get the chair straight out, and I can get slabs laid all over the garden so she can motor around to her heart's content. We'll get ourselves some horses and dogs at last, but gentle old ones from the horse and dog rescue, a bunch of them. Those horses will come trotting to her at the fence for hay when the land is white with a frost. Blimey, look at the state of that rockery. Need to get that fixed up by some of the lads at the centre.'

*

And that's how Lily Hansford came back to Maurwood last spring-time. Carol, Tom, me, Lucien and little Mareeta, we all went out in two cars to meet her at Bournemouth Airport. She was in an airport wheel-chair and got trundled into Arrivals by a worker in a high-viz jacket. She still had her passport in her hand. In the Range Rover, after Tom had physically lifted his daughter into the back seat, Lily told us Oscar Izqiuerda Martínez said 'hello', but he had also said, in the last days of their relationship, that he was sure her family could take better care of her than he ever could, because Mr Hansford was a very good man with considerable resources.

I was sitting beside Lily in the back seat, holding her hand like in the old times. There we sat with our torn, raw hearts.

Tom said in his gentle, older voice, his curly hair grey now, 'That does sound like a very left-handed comment to me.'

Oh. We all laughed.

My daughter and husband were following behind in our Renault, so we all journeyed together, on through the great ripening fields back up towards Maurwood above the river, as Carol switched on the Spotify thing. *Xanadu*, for a singalong – which was an old favourite of ours, funny as it sounds.

IN REAL LIFE

IRVINE WELSH

LITA (1)

An anaemic, wispy light filters insipidly through dark clouds that hang heavy over the sixties-built housing scheme. At a windswept bus stop stands Lita McCallum, sixteen, five-foot-four and just over fourteen stone. From close range this weight cedes most distinguishing feature to Lita's mesmerising jade-green eyes and the striking thick, dark brows topping them.

In her hand a bag of crisps. Lita has sadly come to the end of this snack; shards lacerate her busy mouth, allowing the healing, satisfying tang of salt into the wounds. She tips the last of the debris down her throat. The wastebin is fifty yards away and overflowing. Lita briefly looks at it before discharging the packet to the mercy of the whipping winds; watches it satisfyingly sweep skywards over the busy dual carriageway that diverts airport cargo to the docks.

There is nothing going on in any of the streets: no neighbourly banter, no children playing. Then a shrill scream of pain and despair batters in muffled reverb off the three- and five-storey blocks before fading into the roar of the lorry engines tearing down the main road. Lita barely registers this sound. She's focused on the bus stop's red advertisement, the reassuring and challenging golden arches. It suggests comfort, tells her everything is going to be fine. Then she touches her expanding, bulbous stomach. Feels the chord of her tracksuit bottoms cut into her waist. Shame and despair sweep over her as she loosens the tie to afford some relief.

Then a woman comes past, almost from nowhere. She pushes a double stroller containing loud, bubbly twins. Lita wonders how much this interloper has witnessed of her manoeuvrings. Looks at her in out-raged violation, which slides into a sneer as she ascertains the woman has still not registered her presence. One of the children jabs, from a chubby fist, an accusing finger at Lita.

The woman finally looks startled as she passes Lita, as if it takes *longer for this object to clear the sightline of her peripheral vision than it should. Lita's still-thin lower lip curls in surly judgement at the departing bony, shapeless mother.* **Fertility treatment,** *she thinks.* **Aw they fuckin twins.**

It is as if the children, given life by their mother, have literally sucked it from the host, destroying not only her breasts but leaving her entire body a desiccated shell. **Too fuckin auld for bairns: must be verneer fuckin forty, dirty fuckin hoor,** *Lita scoffs at the departing back. Even feels like* **saying something** *to the* **frumpy bitch,** *but lets it slide. The bus comes along, and she reluctantly pulls a tired, sweaty mask from her pocket, hooks it onto her ears and climbs aboard.*

Recently sacked by a local bakery for poor timekeeping, Lita has been sent by the Employment Office to be interviewed for a sales job at a boutique in town. She disembarks at the West End, the covid-and-lockdown-hit city springing to a tentative August life; its citizens striding with purpose, yet still chambered in their own worlds, looking relieved, yet hostile and cheated at the same time.

The shop is situated in a busy, narrow, cobbled street, down which Lita has never walked before, in a central part of town she scarcely knows. However, she is able to find it with the GPS on her smartphone. She is even slightly early. This is good. At the government place they had stressed punctuality was important, and it gives Lita time to have a cigarette. She looks up and down the street. A café selling all sorts of pastries, which make her mouth water but which are probably dear and shite compared to Greggs. A pub: but not one that sells Tennent's. In fact, three pubs on this short strip, yet the only one in her scheme shut down several years ago.

Lita finishes her fag and stamps it out on the pavement. As she warily enters the shop, a smartly dressed girl is coming out. As they almost collide, the girl bellows, – Soooo sorry, without breaking her stride. Lita first scrutinises her in departure, then whiplashes to the dresses on display and the racks of designer jeans. Panic rises in her; a series of knots in the pit of her stomach, she realises that there is not a single item of clothing in the shop that will fit her.

Then a slender and elegant woman, almost devastatingly handsome, is at her side, greeting Lita enthusiastically. She introduces herself as Lily Margelos, the shopowner. Born and bred in the city centre of

Edinburgh, Lily has just interviewed university student, Fionula Hoskins-Blythe, who passed Lita McCallum on the way in. It was a very good interview. Call-me-Fin had asserted, 'I'm attracted to this post as I love the customer interface of the retail industry, and I see it as a great opportunity to develop interpersonal and problem-solving skills which will stand me in good stead in my chosen career in public relations.'

Lily had overrun with Fionula, it was such an engaging chat. Yet she is happy to see Lita. The girl is massively overweight and her style leaves a lot to be desired, but Lily's motto is: don't judge, inspire. – Hello, I'm Lily. You must be Lita.

– Aye.

– Do come in, Lily escorts Lita into a back room with several chairs, a sink and microwave. – Coffee?

– Aye, says Lita. – Mulk n four shugur.

Lily prepares the coffee, and the two women sit down. – Well, Lita, what attracts you to the retail side of the clothing and fashion industry?

– Ah wis jist telt tae come here.

– I see... Lily Margolis feels her brows involuntarily arch.

After the ten-minute interview, Lily thanks Lita for her time, informs her that she still has other people to see before making a decision and that she will be in touch.

– Sound, Lita says, anxious to get out and spark up a Lambert and Butler. She heads to the newsagent's across the road to get more cigarettes and a Twix and Mars bar for the bus ride home. Jayden, her boyfriend, is due round later, and she has an empty house, with her parents up in the Highlands. It is shaping up to be a good day.

– JAYDUUUN!

Thir's slavers droolin oot the side ay his mooth, dribbling oan muh fuckin neck n ower muh bedspread. Ah shouts oan um try n git ehs cock up muh fanny but eh's no hard enough. Like loads ay laddies doon oor bit: been watchin too much porn oanline! Whin eh munches they Viagras or smokes that pipe eh jist wants tae stick it up yir erse n that shite's mingin n yi'll nivir git a bairn that wey! Ah'm fuckin sixteen n tons ay muh mates huv goat bairns n ah ken whit thir sayin behind muh back: 'how come Jayden's gied other lassies bairns but isnae able tae gie you yin?' N ah go: 'cause eh wisnae fuckin watchin aw that porn back then n eh could git it the fuck up a lassie's fanny!'

But no now. Naw. Jayden jist rolls oaf ays, gits up then lights up a fag, switches oan the laptop. Then eh's aw excited again, bit cause ay watchin a bunch ay boys fightin at the fitba, but no really at the fitba, jist in the street somewhaire. Jayden points tae the screen, 'that's me!' eh goes aw hyper but eh's no really fightin, jist waving ehs airms n bouncing oan the baws ay ehs feet. – Aye barry, ah goes. Ye cannae really tell it's Jayden cause thuv aw goat the same baseball cap n Stone Island jaikit oan.

Jayden kens ah'm no that bothered but then eh sais, – Ah'm no fussed aboot ridin ye right now.

– How no? Is it cause ah'll no dae that strangul stuff? Ah telt ye if ye git wide like that again, muh brars'll fuckin tan yir heid in!

– S'no that.

– How then?

– Look ay ye, eh sais, lightin up a fag, turnin ehs mooth down, that wey ah dinnae like, – yuv goat aw fat.

Ah just goes, – Ah've goat mare curvy, that's aw. You nivir heard ay Beyonce, ya daft cunt, n ah gits up oot ay bed n shakes ma booty at um.

Eh jist turns away fae ays n goes tae the windae! Ehs legs uv goat goose bumps. – Thir's a difference between bein curvy n bein fat.

– Fuckin beat it, Jayden.

– Naw ah'll no fuckin well beat it. *You* fuckin beat it.

Ah jist looks away cause it'll jist cause arguments n Jayden's goat a temper. Eh kens no tae batter ays but, or muh brars would cut ehs fuckin baws oaf. No that thir much guid tae um, fuckin ehsel up by watchin the fuckin porn like that.

Ah want a fuckin bairn. It's ma fuckin time.

JAYDEN (1)

The lounge in the flat is empty except for a burst green couch, from which foam stuffing erupts. There's also a battered table decorated by ringed mug marks and melted pools of candle wax. There are no carpets or lino, just the cracked black tiles common to all dwellings in this block, but in this case, uncovered.

The non-resident owner of the flat, Dessie McCallum, overweight, flabby gut hanging across his trouser belt, is possessed of large black eyes and tight thin lips, which work in harmony to spew contempt at the outside world. Dessie has a thin growth on his chin, complementing a slightly receding number-two haircut, and his expression of intense but tired hostility successfully conveys to his visitor, Jayden Templeton, that the host feels that just being in the same room as him is a massive concession. Dessie does not like having Jayden here, but his sidekick Mufty is in the jail, so a link has broken, compressing the supply chain. Dessie has no love for the Templeton family and loathes the idea of Jayden shagging his young sister. He's heard through the grapevine that this skinny seventeen-year-old jailbait shitbag feels that this romantic status gives him a certain clout with the McCallum family. One day, Dessie resolves, he will disabuse the young man of this delusion.

For the moment, though, such hands have their uses. But the business done, the handover silently undertaken, Dessie now just wants shot of Jayden. He pointedly holds open the front door of the second-floor flat he bought from the council, which he keeps for such transactions.

Jayden leaves with a surly nod and walks the two deserted streets to his home.

The antipathy that Dessie has for him is reciprocated. Jayden's fear of Dessie and brother Clinton, along with his need to keep on their right side for business purposes, makes him believe he is chained to their obese sister. What should have been a six-month summer-school romance has now gone on for two years. Worse, Dessie, unlike Clint, bears a strong resemblance to Lita. The large dark eyes, the thin lips, the eyebrows not only thick but also conjoined, though the spines sprouting above Dessie's nose are more substantial than the light downy hairs that connect Lita's brows. But they convey the same now-unarousing message: **McCallum.** *But most of all, while welcoming the pocket money, Jayden resents how much drug-dealing eats into his gaming practice time. To make it as a pro you had to put in the hours.*

Arriving home, Jayden heads to his bedroom and opens the bags, pouring the contents out on a small folding table. He chops out one line and smashes it. It's decent. Then he starts cutting the cocaine with Vim, talc and baby laxative. His share of the mark-up will pay for the small luxuries in life, like beer, cigarettes, digital TV and online gaming subscriptions.

As he works fastidiously, his brother, twelve-year-old Jarred, enters.
–What ur ye daein?

– Mind yir ain business! Git the fuck oot!

– It's ma room tae. Ah need tae dae muh homework.

– Fuck off doon tae the kitchen n dae it thair. Homework… waste ay fuckin time. Whae the fuck does homework?

– Ah like history, but, so ah dae it, Jarred says and departs.

Jayden doesn't look up, carries on mixing and bagging his merchandise. He hopes Lita doesn't call around again.

That fat cunt gits oan ma fuckin wick: gaun oan aboot bairns aw the time. Skelp her fuckin jaw if it wisnae fir they big fat paedo brars ay hers. Peshlay that Dessie: cunt's a fuckin Cadbury's feast, nae doubt aboot that! Clint's awright oan his ain, but eh ey backs Dessie up. Aye, she's pit oan the coral reef bigtime n ah've goat the evidence oan muh fuckin phone: us doon at Cramond two years ago whin she wis a ride. Back then ivray cunt tried tae bang her so it wis barry whin she sterted gaun oot wi me bit, ay.

Looked a bit like that wee bird oan Pornhub, hur in that *Barely Legal.* Cunt, couldnae believe she wis twenty-two! That's what ah'd like: a sophisticated aulder lassie. But ah widnae lit her dae porn. Aye, we'd dae scud, but jist oan the camera phone n jist fir us tae watch.

Aye, Lita wis barry at first. That pleated skirt, aw short so ye could see they wee knickers. Decent bit ay tit oan it. Didnae fuckin last, but ay. Piled it oan. Cannae pass a McDonald's. Ah like a Big Mac n a chocolate shake as much as any other cunt, bit no aw the time. Small doses, ay. But see whin ah git oan the Nintendo, ah kin dae something she cannae: ah kin sit for ooirs, even days, eatin fuck all. That's what keeps me aw trim, except fir a wee bit ay a gut fae the Stella n cider. Bit that's awright cause Stella n cider ur barry.

So ah'm best gittin the fuck away fi that Lita. We've been gaun oot fir fuckin ages now, nearly two fuckin years n that's mental. Scary. Way past time fir new fanny, tae git it up other lassies. Yins thit ur intae rough sex. Ye dinnae see Stanley Stonker oan Pornhub ridin the same burd for two fuckin years! Nae cunt wid watch that! If nae cunt wid even *watch* it, how should ye huv tae pit up wi it *in real life*?

Ah fancy that Andrea Raeburn, n no cause she's goat a snobby name, cause she's no posh, no here in the scheme, but she's no aw fat n ye'd be able to find her fanny withoot riggin some fuckin scaffoldin in front ay her tae hud up that Ned Kelly n they Eartha Kitts! Hi hi hi! Ah sais that tae muh mate Jordan the other day thair! Andrea's in oor group n she's guid oan *Fortnite*, n she wis at the school but ah dinnae mind ay her. It's funny how some burds thit wirnae rides at school sortay blossom whin they leave, n other yins like Lita...

... anyway, Joshy Boy Eight rode that Andrea, so ah'm gaunny git a hud ay hur. Seeken that cunt's pus. Hi hi hi! Huv tae watch Lita disnae find oot but!

People moan thit thir's nowt tae dae these days, but thir's plenty tae dae. Uh feel like sayin tae muh ma, whae jist sits thair, yuv goat aw they fuckin video games, things like that *Dispersal, Deterrence And Damage: Exterminate Them!*, which is the best game ivir. Better than *Call Ay Duty* or *Fortnite*, cause ye kin only git it oaffay the dark web. We play it in our group J-Firm oan encrypted software. What makes it that barry? It's no jist cause it's violent n ye git tae torture n rape n aw that, which makes it mare excitin; it's mainly cause as well as winnin by bein last man standin in the community situ, ye kin play it oan yir ain, or against sumday else fir a score. (T-Zone Rushmore fae California, highest ivir at 126,739.) Even whin yuv won, as ah maistly dae in J-Firm, either me or Joshy Boy Five, ye kin keep gaun n play against the game in order tae build that total. Ma highest is 83,674. Nae cunt in ooir community is even close tae that! JB7 goat 68,384, n JB5, what's that cunt's best? 61,947! Fuck All!

That score gied ays great publicity n took ays fae thirty-two subscribers up tae forty-seven. Jist three mare before ah start makin money. Then ah keep gaun n build up muh followers n subscribers, till ah'm a fuckin pro. N ah've goat the personality, like Limmy whin eh's oan *Dying Light*. It's aw aboot huvin a laugh n makin it as a pro. Aye, *Spersul, Deterrunce N Damitch: Sterminate Thum!*; muh ma could be takin an interest in aw that instead ay sittin aroond aw depressed n bored, gaun oan aboot the auld days. Nae cunt gies a fuck aboot that! Now ye go oanline n ye huv the time ay yir life. Ye git oan thair n yir ready tae smash any cunt! Then ye go oantae *Secret Love* encrypted porn site n watch some sexy wee hoor git monstered by Stanley Stonker, Adam Assbender (The Brutalizer) or Gasman!

Ah huv a look at the top twinty lassie gamers oan YouTube. Thir's quite a few ay thaim thit ah'd ride. Be barry tae huv a ride ay a lassie gamer fir a burd, hi hi hi. That SSSniperwolf lassie is mint. But they git subscripshins through bein sexy. If yir a laddie, be a barry laugh like Limmy n me, or if yir a lassie be a ride. PewDiePie n cunts like that wur only barry cause thuv goat tons ay staff. Wi could aw dae that.

Twitch is bettur thin YouTube, but ah dae baith, mind. Hud that argument wi Joshy Boy Six the other week oan Facebook: aye, it goat heated but whin we goat the githir naebody wis bothered. Mates kin dae that.

LITA (2)

Preparing to go out and meet her friend Siobhan, Lita McCallum watches mail cascade through her letterbox. Amongst the home-delivery leaflets and red bills, a letter with her mother's handwriting on the front. Home alone has been Lita's lot for three weeks. Her mother and father, Gertrude and Kenny, had gone 'up north for a few days', specifying nothing other than looking after her ailing grandmother in Fort William, then the more generic 'travelling in the Highlands'. They offered no indication as to when they would be back.

She opens the envelope to find fifty pounds inside, with instructions to feed Russell, the sleek black cat with the white whiskers and bib, which always seemed to announce serious dining intentions. Lita hadn't seen the grossly overweight feline in a while and suspected he owned multiple households. She scoops some food into the bowl any-way and heads out into a rainy August day.

Andrea Raeburn, collar-length brown hair wet from the short walk from the bus stop to her workplace, enters the Live and Let Dye hair-dressing salon. She is met with a frown, through a visor worn by camp Serbian Marko. He had taken over the business from a local woman who sold up and retired to the Algarve. Andrea pulls on a mask as Marko thrusts a white towel into her hands. – Get yourself dry, then clean up that floor, he pouts, going back to his covid-masked client, Amelia Sprake, who sits under the old-school dryer.

Andrea quickly heads to the back of the shop, towels then blow-dries her hair, putting on her visor, emerging with a broom. While sweeping up, she steals gazes at Amelia, one of the legacy clients Marko panders to, but nonetheless plans to displace through a slow remodelling of the salon. His strategy is to make gradual improvements, so as not to scare off the old guard. The fully fledged transformation will be held off until the new tramline comes through, and with it, a more affluent clientele.

Marko is showing Amelia a covid meme on his phone, and they are laughing. Catching Andrea looking, they invite her to join them. While not fully understanding the joke, she is delighted to put the broom down and share a giggle with them. Just then, two figures, one thin, pushing a stroller, the other chunky, walk past the shop window. The rectangular one looks in, dispensing a hateful glance that makes Andrea turn away.

– That cunt Andrea in her fuckin daft hairdressur shoap, wi hur stupit face covur, did ye see hur, ah sais tae Siobhan.

– Nuht, Shiv goes, lookin back, as her bairn, Beyonce, makes a funny noise in the stroller. Nae kid ay Jayden n mine's wid make daft noises like thon. – Ah ken that's hur shoap, but.

At least that fuckin rain's stoaped, n Shiv opens the zipped front ay Beyonce's strollur. – Gaunny batter her fuckin cunt right in, ah goes. – Ken how?

– How? Shiv goes.

– Saw Jayden lookin at her in the street the other day.

Shiv turns tae ays bit ye cannae see hur eyes the wey her hair's fawed ower her face. – Nowt wrong wi lookin, she tucks the flap ay wet, greasy hair behind hur ear. – Did eh say anythin?

– Nuht, ah goes, – bit she's a wee snobby hoor. She wis in Newland's class at school. Thinks she's fuckin bigtime cause she goat that hair-dressin apprenticeship.

– She ey sais she's gaunny open her ain salon one day.

– Aye, will she fuck; fill ay hersel that bitch.

– But Jayden nivir sais nowt aboot fancyin hur, Shiv goes.

– Nuht, but it's no jist cause ay that she's gittin battered.

– How's she gittin battered, Shiv goes, then Beyonce throws her rattle oan the groond. – Beyon-say-ay! Shiv picks it up n pits it back in the stroller.

– Saw her in Top Shoap up the toon the other week. Hud a funny pair ay troosers oan n a new sortay pair ay Congress All Star shoes. Ah sais tae her, pointin tae the troosers, like, did ye git thaim in here? She jist looks doon her nose at ays n turns away. Shi's wi this other fuckin snobby wee hoor, no fae oor bit, n thir laughin at ays, bit tryin tae cover thir mooths n make oot like thir no, ken?

– Aye, Shiv nods.

– Need tae fuckin well cover it eftir ah've fuckin well battered it n knocked aw the teeth oot ay it, ah goes.

Shiv goes aw nervous at that n starts chewin the ends ay her hair, like she ey does whin ah say some cunt's gittin fuckin leathered. – Then, ah tells Shiv, – that wis jist that time last week whin ay wis meetin you here, at McDonald's, ah sais jist as we go intae the resturint again n git settled.

Ah think Shiv worries sometimes thit ah might turn oan hur n batter her cunt in, but that widnae happen cause she's muh best pal. She kin git awfay nervous, like Jayden's ma, whae tried tae cull ehrsel n wis oan aw they puhls. Come tae think ay it, Shiv's ma's ey oan they sortay puhls n aw. If it gits handed doon ye feel sorry fir the bairn.

– Aw aye… that wis jist last week.

– Aye, ah goes as wi gits settled doon in they seats. Shiv hud Beyonce wi her in the stroller that time n aw. Ah looks at the bairn. – She's getting big.

– Aye, Shiv goes.

Ah tells her aboot that Andrea, walkin aroond thinkin thit her ain shite smells ay fuckin roses, but Shiv's jist starin intae space, eyes aw glazed like she's no right in the heid. – Ur you fuckin listenin, ah goes.

– Nuht, ah cannae concentrate oan fuck all, she sais, lookin aw feart, – it's they puhls the doaktir gied muh ma, that Doaktir Claire. Meant tae be fir her depression n anxiety.

Ah'm fuckin scoobied here so ah goes, – But see if she gied thum tae yir ma, how the fuck dis that affect you?

She turns roond n sais, – Ah dinnae feel right aboot things n ah git nervous around the hoose… n then shi looks at Beyonce, – … she starts moanin… so muh ma gied ays some puhls n ah feel awright whin ah take thum. Bit it's sometimes like ah'm no really thair, ken.

Ah nods, but ah looks at the bairn, thinkin: *see what you've goat in the post*. So ah goes up tae git a Big Mac n Diet Coke. Ah gits served by that boy Jordan, steys near Jayden's bit, well no the Crescent, but the Terrace, or mibbe the bit ay the Crescent thit's near the Terrace. But ah widnae classify that end ay the Crescent as Jayden's bit. But anywey, eh's pally wi Jayden. – How long ye been here, ah goes.

– Last week, eh sais. – What's yir mate's name, n eh looks ower at Shiv.

– Siobhan, ah tells um. – How did ye git the joab?

Jordan shrugs they thin shoodirs ay his. – Dinnae ken. Ah jist goat telt tae come here, eh goes.

– Guvirnmint?

– Aye. Ah goat a lettur.

– Through email?

– Nuht, through the post. Fishul lettur.

– Aw, ah goes.

Jordan's goat really bad spoats oan ehs face, n workin in the grease in McDonald's isnae gaunny help. Shame cause eh'd mibbe be a ride if eh didnae huv they spoats. Eh fancies Shiv, ah think. Ye kin tell cause Jayden said sumthin tae um once n perr Jordan pure goat a beamer!

Shiv shouts ower, – Git that Coke Zero cause it's better thin Diet Coke!

But ah goes, – Naw, it's too late, lookin at Jordan, cause eh awready poured us a fuckin Diet Coke.

– Aw, Shiv goes, – disnae matter then.

So ah git the food oan the rid tray n ah gies that nervous radge Jordan a wee smile n eh shrugs wi ehs coupon same kulur as the tray!

Ah takes it ower tae Shiv. She's nowt tae be depressed aboot, she's goat a bairn! Even if Beyonce is a bit spazzy, jist in the feet, like, bit ah widnae say nowt tae Shiv's face aboot that. It's the likesay me that should be depressed; nae bairn n fuckin Jayden no wantin tae git busy, n no able tae git it up, n whin eh does n then eh wants it aw anal like in the porn fulums whaire the boy goes, 'you love it up the erse, ya filthy bitch/slut/hoor', n the bird jist gasps like it's no fuckin borin n sair. A waste ay fuckin spunk.

Fuckin Jayden better ride ays in the fanny the night, cause ah'm pittin oan muh Victoria's Secrut! Ah'm gittin up the duff one wey or the other! A loat ay daft cunts huv bairns whin thir too auld. Fuck that. Despite aw Jayden's faults, ah think eh should still be Moderatur ay J-Firm instead ay Joshy Boy Five. Jayden's the best player so it's only fair, n JB5 should see that. That Jordan's in the group but he's no much ay a player. Usually eh's the first cunt tae git pit oot oan *Call Of Duty* or *Fortnite*. Spoats like that must take away yir confidence but.

– Ah think Jordun fancies you, ah goes tae Shiv.

She looks ower at him, aw spazzy, shakin n tremblun, n ah watches him turn away wi a fuckin beamer like they plukes'll explode n splatter custard aw ower the fuckin place!

JAYDEN (2)

The thin woman of thirty-nine years heaves in the heat, hauling air into nicotine-compromised lungs as she hung her washing out in her back green. Clipping the heavy, wet jeans of her eldest son to the line, she looks at the deep slash marks on her wrist, so red and angry against her white skin that almost reflects the blistering sun above.

Following her second suicide attempt, this time with the razor, Manda Templeton's medication had been altered. It was uncomfortable, but now essential, to wear long sleeves in this heat. How her wounds throbbed. What had she been thinking? All she could do was thank any superior power there may be in universe that it was Amy next door, rather than her sons, Jayden or Jarred, who found her.

Her washing all hung, Manda looks satisfyingly at her work before stepping back into the kitchen. The laundry will dry quickly in this heat, if it lasts. Sliding open a cabinet, she takes her pills from the three bottles. Fills a glass with water and washes them down.

Then she hears her eldest son, Jayden, coming downstairs, his feet thumping. He ambles into the kitchen and takes a carton of milk from the fridge. As he glugs it back, Manda wants to shout: put it in a glass, but by the time she finds words that are buried in medication and outrage, he has gone back upstairs. The fridge door hangs open, with the milk carton on the worktop.

*Upstairs, Jayden slumps back on the bed. Looks at his PC. Prefers it to PS4 or Xbox as an operating system. The phone was okay for keeping your hand in when you were out, but you needed to specialise to make it as a pro, in hardware and software. **Call Of Duty** and **Fortnite** were best for his career development, but the illegal **Dispersal, Deterrence And Damage: Exterminate Them!** is the most fun. He'll go onto Discord, set a challenge for **Call Of Duty: Warzone**, and get Joshy Boy Five fucked off. Then J-Firm will see who the Moderator of the Community should be. His mouth is dry and dopamine cravings surge* *through him. But his eyes water and his head pounds with too much screen time. He'll take a break; distract himself with thoughts of real life.*

Ah'm no wantin a bairn. How wid uh? What's the fuckin point whin the human race is fucked anywey? Nae bairn'll huv a great life: aw it'll aw be is tons ay fuckin worry. Even for posh yins thit send bairns away tae they schools, whaire they git fuckin nonced up so they then try tae fuck up ivray other cunt's life. Well they fuckin did it n aw, cause ivray cunt's fucked, even thir ain bairns whae'll huv tae live in a concrete bunker undergroond aw thir days. Whit kind ay a fuckin life is that? N doon here, it's even mare fuckin pointless.

N bein a bairn's fuckin shite. Ye find yirsel in this daft place wi they big cunts ye dinnae ken, n ye dinnae even like cause n they dae everything fir ye, then they tell ye what tae dae, n git aw stroppy if ye dinnae. Sometimes ye feel like tellin them tae git tae fuck. Fuck's the point, but ay? Later oan they say: ah did muh best fir you. Ye jist look at thum n think: *ye did fuck all fir me.* Anything you did, ye did for yirsel. Because ah wis aw aboot yir ain pride or ego, or it wid gie you something tae dae, because ye wir scoobied as tae whit else ye could dae wi your miserable fuckin life, or it wid *cement the love* between you n some other cunt, whae, let's face it, wis nivir gaunny stick aroond, n if they did they wid only drive ye fuckin mental. So aye, *do make it* aw aboot you, because it eywis fuckin well wis. You fucked it up cause ye gied yir hole tae a fuckin bam cause ye wanted something that wid gie ye love because nae other cunt aroond wis gaunny gie ye it. Ah even telt muh ma that once. She jist goes, aye, well thir's mare tae it thin that. But see tae me? Tae me that wis hur admittin the fuckin point. No thit she's any use, jist lies around greetin n watchin telly aw day.

And nae bairns wi a fat cunt; that's at least one thing me n muh ma kin agree oan!

UNCLE GLEN (1)

Glen Urquhart looks in the mirror, admiring the crest on his navy-blue short-sleeved Fred Perry shirt. Lifts it up at the front to reveal an almost flat stomach that is the envy of most of his contemporaries. Delighted, he runs his hands through his dark hair, a little greying at the short-cut temples but still abundant. Surveys the well-trimmed tache he's recently taken to sporting. Flashes a pearly smile, enjoying the reciporication of the image in the reflection. Then he puckers his lips and blows himself a kiss.

Who's a handsome laddie, then? Still got it!

He leaves his Albert Street flat in tidy order. The letting agency man had the spare keys. He hopes the renters, due in tomorrow, don't do too much damage. Even though the festival is greatly reduced due to covid, people still wanted to get away. The coronavirus and Brexit had made overseas travel prohibitive, so UK holiday flats were in demand. Outside, it's now cold for August, though yesterday felt like a heatwave. Of course, now that the festival was on this was perhaps inevitable.

Glen heads round to his yard and picks up the van. Drives to the scheme. The closer he gets he's increasingly swamped with memories, as the haar rolls in from the river and he feels as if he is driving into another world that will enclose him forever.

If ye believe in a material world like me, ye want tae look your best. Style is a socialist construct, an expression ay individuality and freedom. No like aw they daft wee drones oot there; told how tae think, dress, what to drink, eat, what tae say. Robbed ay a thinkin mind: brains frozen by lack ay use. Stuck in front ay screens aw day. Blocked like drains. Capitalism is jist like communism; geared tae human servitude. It takes it longer tae become a polis state but it does a mare thorough job.

Philly Matheson got that. I'll miss him, even though it was years since ah'd seen him. Ah'll miss *the prospect* ay seeing him. That has gone, wi the man himself.

But this is all a wee bitty despondent. We ken teenagers live a reductive life oanline, ma nephews Jayden n young Jarred being cases in point, and aye, it *is* depressing n scary tae witness that shite. Aye, and of course, there's the ongoing destruction ay the working class, nae *work* and melted doon into an uneducated scummy rump of demented idiots just waiting tae huv thir hate-clit tweaked by the snidey billionaire-owned media.

But ken what ah personally detest maist, even though ah've been nae angel masel with the drugs, fightin n chorin in my ain youth?

It's that they've nae fuckin manners now.

Even though we wir taught tae peeve, n no pass up any knock-off, we wir ey taught manners. *What dae ye say?* Aw the time. Yir ma. *What dae ye say?* Yir faither. *What dae ye say?*

Excuse me, please n thank you.

They nivir git taught that now. It's no thair fault; thir parents jist gied up. Like oor Manda. So what else can the daft wee cunts dae if naebody taught them otherwise? Aye, it's the nae manners thing thit gits me maist. It's fuckin hard tae like some cunt wi nae manners.

Philly Matheson got that.

Ah ken what thir thinkin, aw they lassies at the library where ah go tae get my books: *that Glen's an awfay handsome felly n eh's goat manners.* Ah once took the two nephews aside n telt them: *you'll never git your hole offay any decent lassie withoot manners.* But they never knew their faither, Gary Templeton, n trust me, they were better oaf withoot that bam. Mind you, eh wisnae a bad gadge back in the day. Before the drugs took hud, n then it wis endy story. Their ma? Well, dinnae get me wrong, ah love my sister Manda, but she's a bit ay a radge n aw. Picks the wrong man every time.

And here ah am, back in the scheme, parking the van. Made sure ah took aw the tools oot ay it back at the yerd. Gits up tae Manda's jist in time for my tea on Friday, fish from the van. She greets ays n offers ays a fag. First accepted, second rejected. Ah've broat some flooirs, roses, oot ay Tesco, n she pits them in a vase. – Wish other men were like you n oor dad, Glen. They stoaped making men like that. You were the last ay them.

Well, aye. And I would add Philly Matheson tae that list.

Muh sister Manda's a thin lassie wi a moon face and long broon hair in a centre parting. It's goat they grey roots, which eywis seem tae appear as soon as she leaves the hairdressers, but never grow longer than a couple ay centimetres. They locks dinnae half play cruel tricks oan her! Everybody sais thit Manda was a looker back in the day, and ah was mortified when she sooked the cock ay my best mate Davie Cunningham, a popular lad whae signed s-forms for Hibs. It made ays aw para that Davie only saw our friendship as a means ay getting oaf with my sister and things wir nivir quite the same wi us again. Of course, the likes ay Davie would never look at Manda now. Mind you, Davie's in worse shape, in fact eh's no longer wey us thanks tae a road traffic accident in South Africa. Daft cunt wis ey dodging aboot in fast motors.

First Davie; now Philly Matheson. Aye, the times they are a-changing.

Well, it's no that easy being one ay the few lads ay ma auld crowd that's looked after hissel, ah can tell ye. Only been back here a few weeks, but ah hear thum tryin tae rip the pish, usually when ah'm oot oan ma bike. Aw they waddling fat bastards, standing ootside the pubs, guts expanding in their cheapo knock-off trackies. What these cunts forget is that their wives and girlfriends, and sometimes their daughters, well, they aw want rode by Glen Urquhart. Right they do. And ah kin get it up withoot aw that Viagra and crack that the dafties are intae. And forget that Tinder pish: aw ah dae online is check that Facebook for fifteen minutes in the morning, then same in the evening. Make a rendezvous wi the lassies. Whae needs Tinder?

One thing ah willnae have is a smartphone. Yir fuckin owned by the capitalist state when ye start that nonsense. Naw, ma wee Nokia for texts n calls does me. Smartphones encourage bad manners, checkin thum aw the time. And ye dinnae need it. You just need to ken where tae go. Like the Hotel Viva! Been ma spot since ah did their plumbing.

Eftir the move tae Hemel Hempstead, the last place ah thought I'd find myself was back in Edinburgh, and now the fuckin scheme, ay aw places! But a temporary measure n only tae make sure Kid Sis is okay. Dinnae git ays wrong, ah had great times up here running wi the boys and rollin wi the punches. The battles ootside the chippy, rows up the toon, aye, those were the days. But ye need tae grow up.

So then Lucinda and me got together: a Barnton lass fae the other side ay the tracks. Her family was a bit stuck up, n they'd heard aw aboot the Urquharts, *and* it's fair tae say our reputation did precede us, but what could they dae in the face ay love? Ah mind ay taking ages at Terry's ower in Pilton getting that name tattooed across muh chist: LUCINDA. Forty bar and a boatil ay Grouse tae keep his hand steady.

Then Roxanne came along and we were happy. Got a nice house in Camo, oot towards the airport. Steep mortgage, but fuck it: me making plenty poppy, legit as well, through the plumbing business. Ye never go hungry if you're a good plumber, but it's fuckin hard graft. Dinnae let any cunt tell ye different.

Then came the move tae Hemel Hempstead: the Double H. My idea: too many bams up here, willnae let the past stey where it is, and ah wanted away fae them. As they say aboot the weight ay history: tragedy and farce. Thoat Hemel Hempstead wid be a better shot. The good part ay the Double H, mind; doon by the railway station. Funny, but railway stations are often in the shite part ay toon, but the Double H bucks that trend. We moved intae a nice big hoose on the main road. Doon the street, the Harvesters: a great, family-run local boozer. Great roasts on a Sunday. Lively discussions, cause ay a lot ay Tories doon there; well the English in the south really do think different fae us, but a few good lefties as well. Great laughs. Roxy settled in well at the local school. And me: making even mare money in the plumbing business than up in Edinburgh. The good life: local golf club membership, the lot.

Of course, she threw aw that away, that fuckin Lucinda. Still cannae understand her logic. It was when Roxanne got aulder n Lucinda had decided tae go tae university. Ah wis all for it; as a socialist ye have tae value learning. Ah was even a bit jealous: where was *ma* education? Aw ah did was graft and maybe the odd drink after work in the Harvesters wi ma mates Chris Proctor and Nige Blakeley. Then she comes in one day and looks around the hoose and goes in a snooty Barnton accent: is this all there is?

Ah kept quiet, but kent three things fae her tone. First, she was riding somebody else. And ah figured it was some cunt back in

Edinburgh. Lucinda was ey headin back, seemingly tae visit her ma whae was meant to be sick, but ah never saw many signs ay that. That wis numero duo. The third thing ah kent was that it had been going on for a while.

She left the house two weeks later. Went back up the road tae see Mister Fancy. Turns oot he wis this personal trainer, an ex-Raith Rovers player. Cunt was playing away fae hame. Lucinda said we'd sort out aw the stuff wi Roxanne later. Of course, Roxy wanted tae be wi her ma, no that Lucinda was fussed at huvin her aroond. At seventeen years auld ah swear that lassie had never gied us a moment's trouble. Goat oan great at that school: brilliant results in the GCSE exams. Of course, when she went back up tae Edinburgh that aw changed. She reacted badly to the split and went oaf the rails. Staying oot late. Fellys. Drugs. The auld usual.

Of course, Lucinda, the great independent woman, couldnae cope. She calls ays up n goes, you huv tae come up here n help out wi her.

Ah sais tae her, aw ma business is in Hemel Hempstead!

Aye, but yir daughter's here in Edinburgh!

So, well, a good plumber will never go hungry – and ah'm one ay the best in the business – so back hame it was. Ah headed tae the flat in Albert Street ah'd bought a while back n rented oot tae students. Up n doon oan the A1 in that van or oan the Kings Cross–Waverly choo-choo like a fuckin yo-yo ah wis, before Manda sterted the hari-kari drama, n then this lockdoon shite, so ah thoat ah'd better stick aroond.

Now Philly Matheson's checked oot. The murderer? Capitalism.

Of course, ye get aw the snide comments in some ay the boozers. *Aw so that Hemel Hempstead didnae work oot for ye?* Ye feel like tellin the cunts: *aye it did work oot, but ah came back for famelay. Understand that? Famelay? Sacrifice? Tae look eftir muh ain.* Then ah got intae that bother wi glessing Paul McFadden for makin a comment aboot Roxanne. Ah telt the copper that came by: any faither wid dae the same. Eh just nodded at me n telt me to git doon the road. McFadden jist hud a wee cut on the chin: only a few stiches. Deserved a lot mare. Fair play: cunt never grassed ays or sought any comeback. Admitted eh wis oot ay order n that it was a wind-up in drink that eh took too far. Fair enough.

N fair play tae Roxy, though, she took a telling and got herself the gither. Got intae university. Leicester. Economics. Got a nice felly now, fae a good family. Rarely comes back tae either Edinburgh or Hertfordshire. Can you blame her eftir Lucinda wrecking our hame in the Double H?

Aye, since Lucinda left ays for that Raith Rovers cunt, ah've been huvin the time ay ma fuckin life. Dinnae get ays wrong: at first it was very bad news. Ah struggled for a bit and resented having tae sell that beautiful Hemel Hempstead hoose. Ah'd built an extension and a conservatory at the back. Best part ay seventy grand, which, fair enough, increased the value ay the place, but a lot ay TLC went intae that construction. Ah was pretty annoyed, ah kin tell ye. Went on a bender in Ibiza wi Nige and Chris, staying at one Nige's Ibiza properties. Ah'd went oot n did the plumbing on it. Mental times. Nige was in process ay splittin up fae a gold-digger ay his ain n Chris's divorce hud just come through. Suffice tae say that the fair sex got a rough press on that fortnight! Did they no, though! A loat ay drug-takin n hooring went oan during that trip. Hud tae get Chris's stomach pumped twice. Happy days!

The thing is, while Lucinda soon realised the error ay her weys – i.e. that the fitba coach boy was a fuckin waster – auld Glen Urquhart here wis undergoing a wee renaissance. So fuck Lucinda, if you'll pardon ma French. Mind, no that many would say that now. Manners.

Aye, four simple words: *what dae ye say?*

They dinnae care what their bairns say now. And, fair dos, why should they bother aboot bedside manner when there's nothing for them? What's here? What really is the point ay this place and the people in it? Every cunt is depressed. Naebody has a life. And the poor young cunts, they're the worst ay them aw. Soon aw they twenty-year-aulds'll be fifty-year-aulds and nane ay them will have left the hoose. Aw they'll ken is the daft games they played online. And they dinnae seem tae bother.

Aye, so ah thought ah'd rent out my flat in Albert Street for the festival and move back doon here for a bit wi my sister Manda. She's no been well. They attempted hari-karis were a bit ay a jolt, ah kin tell ye. Terrible anxiety issues, eywis hud. Ah blame that Gary Templeton that knocked her up wi Jayden, n *mibbe* Jarred; dodgy as fuck. So the crux ay it aw is that Manda needs support. The plan was that ah would try and get my nephew Jayden on the straight and narrow, but that looks like a lost cause. Jarred, his wee brother, well mibbe that's another matter. That laddie might still be just aboot saveable. Might make a good plumbing apprentice oot ay him yet.

But there's other fish tae fry besides the stuff Manda boat oaf the van: poor auld Philly Matheson needs a send-off.

LITA (3)

The new centre had been rebuilt on a public park where kids once played games. This was part of a council deal with the developers of a private housing project. The edifice, replacing an old seventies pre-fabricated building, was in the same style as the new homes, a redbrick façade over its systems-built structure. It contained a bar and function room, designed for arts projects and events, but mainly used for birthdays, weddings and funerals.

It was the latter where Philip Matheson was being celebrated, having been laid to rest in a service at the old kirk on the main road. 'Philly' was a popular member of the community. It was he who had guided the youthful Glen Urquhart into local campaigns and socialist politics.

Philly had taken his own life. He left behind a pile of red gas and electric bills to augment a note that read: LEGACY CITIZEN: I HEREBY OFFICIALLY ANNOUNCE MY REDUNDANCY AS A MEMBER OF THE HUMAN RACE.

Lita and Jayden had arrived at the centre after hearing that there was free booze, paid for from a whip-round by several community groups. They needed a few drinks to take the edge off a crack-pipe blitz they'd undertaken to try to enhance sexual intercourse. This had proven semi-successful. When they got to the centre, the function room was packed with bodies as Glen, dark suit, red tie and sombre bearing, got up to make a tribute speech.

– Phillip Joseph 'Philly' Matheson was a man who loved life and loved the people of this community. Apprenticed at Parsons Peebles, Philly, an active shop steward, was on the tools till his redundancy. He fought tae make this place better for the working people of the area, and he did. The scattering ay National Front fascist interlopers in the late seventies; whae was involved? Philly Matheson. The campaign tae get recognition of the heroin and HIV crisis in community, whae wis *central tae that? Philly Matheson. The construction of the very building we are now in,* and Glen looked around the function room, – *central tae the campaign tae get this place built as a concession fae the developers, you guessed it: Philly Matheson...* Glen looked at Philly's widow, Hannah, sat in the corner, a wan smile fighting through her sobs as her children comforted her. The oldest daughter, Geraldine, he minded riding at camp in Skegness. It was so long ago that her breasts, vagina, arse, thighs could have belonged to any of dozens of women.

Jayden was uninspired by his uncle's speech. Growing bored and fidgety he left Lita sitting with a gin and tonic and headed to the toilet.

As Glen carried on, Lita too became antsy. It was the drugs but also the fact that Jayden had been gone for some time. He was probably outside having a smoke, and Lita decided that she should do the same.

When she went out the back there was nobody to be seen. Then she turned the corner to look down the alley at the side of the building, where they stored the big dump bins. It was here that Lita spotted Jayden in a compromising clinch with Andrea Raeburn.

Ah wis rattlin like fuck eftir last night n wi needed something tae sort us oot. Jayden sais aboot some auld boy's funeral at the centre whaire thir wis free peeve, so wi heads doon. This well-dressed felly is daein a tribute, good wi wurds, n Jayden sais it's ehs uncul. Then Jayden goes tae the lavvy tae smash a line. His ma, that Manda's thair, well pished, n ah'm waitin oan Jayden comin back wi that message. So ah goes tae hur, – Whaire's Jayden?

Well that cunt will usually no gie ye the steam oaffay her shite, so ah should've been suspicious whin she goes, – Saw um gaun ootside.

So ah goes oot tae see if ah kin find um. Nae sign, so ah looks doon that alley at the side. Couldnae fuckin believe muh eyes! Eh's fuckin well wi hur... eh's really fuckin well wi hur! – JAYDEN! WHAT YE FUCKIN DAEIN?

Eh turns roond aw yon wey, wi that ratfaced pus eh kin pit oan. – What ye fuckin talkin aboot?

– WEY HUR!

N ah hears her sortay snigger. Ah'm aboot tae tell um tae git the

fuck ben the centre, n hur tae git the fuck oot ay here, but he jist goes,
– Nowt. Stoap it. Jist causes arguments.

– AH FUCKIN WELL SAW YE WI MUH AIN FUCKIN EYES!
DINNAE DENY IT!

– Wi jist went outside fir a smoke, ay, eh goes.

– IT WISNAE JIST A FUCKIN SMOKE! AH SAW YIS SNOGGIN
EACH OTHER'S FACES OAF!

Eh jist shrugs ehs fuckin daft skinny shoodirs, but then she fuckin
well comes forward, dirty wee smile oan her face. – Jist a wee smoke,
fatso.

AH CANNAE FUCKIN WELL BELIEVE THIS. Ah'm jist lookin at
her, then lookin at Jayden. – YOU GAUNNY FUCKIN LIT HER
TALK TAE AYS LIKE THAT?

– Ah sais ah'm no wantin any argumints, eh steps forwirt.

Then she fuckin well goes, – Ehs cock wid need tae be ten fit long
tae git it up you!

Ah cannae believe this. N Jayden even fuckin laughs. Eh sais
sumthin like, – N it's only nine fit, then does that daft wee laugh ay his,
hi hi hi…

– WHAT! WHAT THE FUCK UR YOU SAYIN!!

– You heard. Ye deef as well as fat and stupit?

Ah runs forward in grabs hur by the hair! Fuckin bitch rakes her
nails doon ma face, but ah've goat her heid n ah'm bangin it oaf the
waw, n she's swipin at ays punchin ays n tellin ays ah'm deid but ah'm
screamin, – IT'S YOU THIT'S FUCKIN DEID, YA HOOR! N aw ah
hears is Jayden sayin, – LEAVE UR, n it's like a bad dream when
everything goes radge n they aw turn against ye n aw ah kin dae is
batter that Raeburn hoor's fuckin heid oaffay that waw…

JAYDEN (3)

In the distance, behind the wall of the litter-strewn alley, Jayden and Andrea, lips locked together, can hear the bawdy laughter that erupts from inside the centre. The faint trace of his Uncle Glen's voice fades to be replaced by cheers. Then ABC's 'All Of My Heart' strikes up, filtering briefly into their consciousness. The harsh shout of some foot-ballers from over in the park fails to jolt them. Or maybe it was a coach, from the sidelines.

It is warm and the little alleyway at back of the club in which they stored beer barrels has been put to romantic use. Jayden and Andrea, long on each other's radars, are both pleasantly surprised to find themselves locked in an embrace. For Jayden it was a marvel to be able to get his arms around a woman, to feel a slender body, her bones pushing against him, the grind of her hipbones on his, the ribcage under her small breasts. For Andrea it was great to feel those limbs around her, look into those flinty eyes and try to find him in them.

Ah'd went outside fir a fag n that Andrea wis thair. Hud a trackie jaikit n black leggings, hair slicked back. Fit as. – Ootside fir a sneaky yin, she sais.

– Aye, n ah'd gie you a sneaky yin n aw, ah goes, – tell ye that for nowt.

– What aboot fatty?

– What aboot the cunt, ah went, – gits oan muh fuckin nerves, n ah steps up n gits a hud ah hur.

– You're fill ay yirsel, she goes.

She starts talkin mare but ah starts snoggin her n feelin her erse n thir's a twinge in ma cock n want tae git it in her, but ah gits muh hand doon her leggings tae check if her fanny's wet, n it's dry at first at the slit bit but whin ah git it doon tae the hole, it's like a fuckin damn burstin! Hi hi hi!

Then ah hears that fat cunt shoutin…

We pills apart, n they start giein each other lip n then thir fightin. Lita's goat that Andrea by the hair n she's batterin her fuckin heid oaf the waw ay the pub.

Ah'm fuckin hard in muh pants, lookin at the radgeness in her eyes, then Andrea, aw defiant but it turnin intae fear as she screams 'you're deid' but it's mare desperate n she's feart n ah goes ower n sais, – She's hud enough. Stoap it!

Lita's pal Shiv comes oot n takes her inside n ah gits Andrea doon the road. She's greetin her eyes oot gaun oan about fat Lita n how she's deid. Ah'm thinkin ah'd have chucked the dozy fat hoor donks ago if it wisnae fir her mental brars. No thit they'd probably bother aboot a fat embarrassment like yon. But she nivir used tae be fat. See at fourteen, she wis a fuckin ride. Every cunt at school tried tae git up her. Ah goat oaf wi her at JB7's perty, n in the eftirnoons we'd take the day oaf school n ah'd gie her it aw weys, up the erse, like in the porn wi watched oan muh laptoap. That wis barry. But then she jist kept gittin bigger n bigger n pit oan mare n mare weight. Like her brar: that wide cunt Dessie. Ah dinnae ken if it wis the fat gene kickin in or aw the shite she eats. Ah mean ah like a Big Mac as much as any cunt – though ye cannae beat the fuckin chippy – but she takes the biscuit; cunt, she takes the fuckin packet ay biscuits! Hi hi hi.

So ah'm gaun doon the road wi wee greetin-faced Andrea n ah sais come back tae muh ma's n wi'll git that sare heid taken care ay, but ay. So wi does. –She's a fuckin cow, Andrea goes, – she's gittin it…

That Andrea but, she's gittin it. Joshy Boy Eight – the one ay the eleven Joshs fae oor mob at school n ooir group J-Firm thit ah hate the maist – that rode her last summer n wants tae fire back intae hur. Goat tae move quick, so ah detours past mine n gits her up tae ma room.

– Whaire we gaun?

– You need tae lie doon.

– Ah'm awright.

– Is yir heid sair, ah touches her soft hair. Thir's a wee bump on the side.

– It's no bad, she goes n she's brushin up against me. – Ah'll lie doon if you lie doon wi me.

So, ah goes, – Aye, cause ah'm hard, n ah'm thinkin aboot Adam Assbender, the American boy they caw 'The Brutalizer' cause eh's that barry at rough sex – mibbe even bettur thin Stonker – cause they say they cannae find lassies tae shoot skud wi um. N what eh sais tae git a bird intae bed, – You goat a fantastic boady... ah want tae tattoo it wi ma fists, baby...

She's goat muh cock oot muh troosers n ye kin pure tell she's watched a loat ay porn n aw, mibbe even strangleporn, cause she goes, – I love this dick... I wanna do all sorts ay things wi it and I want it tae dae all sorts of things tae me!

Barry. Start her oaf normal then work up tae clatterin her. – Ivir watch scud wi a felly?

– Aye. Love it.

– Ivir sook a felly's cock?

– Aye. It's ma speciality.

– Ivir git rode by a felly?

– Ah love a big, hard cock in my pussy.

– Ivir git rode fae behind by a felly?

– Ah love it so much.

– Ivir rode a felly wi you oan top?

– Ah love to do that, and play with myself and have a guy haul on my tits and ass when we fuck that way.

– Ivir been rode up the erse by a felly?

–Ah love anal... especially when a guy goes in hard...

This is fuckin great. Bet she likes tae git strangult tull she passes oot! – Ivir hud a felly cum in yir face n aw ower yir tits?

– Oh, I love the taste of spunk and I love to massage it into my boobs...

So: an experienced lassie in watchin porn! Aw the barry love talk. Cunt, nae wonder ah'm gittin fuckin hard but ah've nae blue boys n ah worry thit muh cock'll git too soft fir her erse, so ah tells hur we kin only dae it eftir ah git shot ay Lita, or her brars'll go fuckin radge. Ah tell hur we should leave it the now, n ah pits muh cock away n sais wi should jist play a game. She looks disappointit. – Whin we make love, ah tell hur, it'll be like the professionals in porn.

They boys kin jist git it up like that n they fuckin obviously watch porn aw the time, so it's daft tae say thit porn causes a reptile dysfunction. The reverse hus tae be true. Follay the science, as the cunts oan the telly say.

Wi plays a game ay *Dispersal, Deterrence And Damage: Exterminate Them!* n she's fuckin good fir a lassie: 54,734 furst score, even better thin that Lita! Then it's time fur me tae show hur how it's done. Ah'm gaun through the backs ay they hooses, like in New York (ah peyed good dough for that stuff), n ah'm takin oot aw they skanky wee villains, n ah'm deployin aw the weaponry, then smashin thum tae bits in singul-handit combat at close quarters! Dessie McCallum... take that, ya cunt! Ah'm in wi 66,321, which is brulyunt!

– You're awsum at this, she goes. – You could dae this oan YouTube n make some money.

– Ah try, but oan Twist ay, but they keep sendin ays aw things tae go tae, like the guvirnmint wi interviews n that, n it cuts intae muh screen time. Ah've no goat any work, but ah git enough fae sellin collies. But they guvirnmint cunts uv telt ays tae go up tae that supermarket the day.

– Ye gaunny go?

– If you chum ays, well. Whae wants tae work in a supermarket, but.

– It's a start, she sais.

– Right enough, ah goes.

So we go fir a walk up tae the centre. It's barry walkin up the road wi a bird thit's goat a proper boady n a right joab n aw. Hairdresser. Trainee. Fuckin sound. Nae cunt lookin at ye n sniggerin like they dae when yir wi a fat freak.

The supermarket wis meant tae be lookin fir mare cunts tae stack shelves cause ay that covid shite, but when ah sais tae the boy, – Ah hear youse ur lookin fir somebody tae stack shelves...

Eh jist looks at ays n sais, – What's your name?

Ah goes, – Jayden, but ah git kent as Jaygo.

Except fae that fat cunt. Hate the wey she sais Jayden.

– Right. What do you know about retail?

– Dunno, ah goes, – ah wis jist telt tae come here, but ay.

– I'm sorry, but I'm afraid we're looking for a wee bit more than that, Jason.

– Jayden.

– Sorry?

– It's Jayden, no Jason.

– Sorry, Jayden. Yes, I'm afraid we're looking for a wee bit mare in the initiative department.

Ah jist looks at the wide cunt. – Think ah want tae be ersed packin shelves wi fuckin mongols for a tenner an ooir when ah kin knock oot some ching n base fir ten times that? How much you gittin peyed an hour?

– Enough… the boy says but eh's blinkin n ehs Adam's aypil's bobbin up n doon like a bit ay shite ye cannae flush away.

So we goes, leavin um jist standin thair n Andrea sais, – You really telt him!

– Aye, ah goes, – ah did.

N she gies ays that look, a sneaky wee admirin look that ah used tae git fae Lita in second year, n aw ah kin think ay is how barry it wid be tae git hur back tae mine n giein hur it Stanley Stonker style! But muh ma n that wee cunt Jarred'll be back now, so nae peace. Jist means ah need tae plan oot the tannin she's gaunny git! Hi hi hi!

LITA (4)

Lita achieves a very decent score – her second best ever – on Xbox One at **Burnout Paradise Remastered.** *Even more satisfyingly, Andrea Raeburn checks in, sees her there and retreats! Along with the battering of Andrea, this second double victory leaves her feeling delightfully energised. After a brief snap of irritation when she can't find her phone, she locates it balanced on the edge of the bath. Calls her friend Shiv, urging her to come out.*

Shiv says she has to look after her infant daughter, Beyonce, who has a cold. Lita feels lost and at a loose end. It dawns on her just how few friends she has in real life; how much she has sacrificed for her relationship with Jayden. Now he was messing about with that whore Andrea and not returning her calls other to blandly text: **nothing happened.** *Fuck him. She needed a normal man, like one of the guys in the porn movies Jayden tried to model himself on. These boys had no problem in getting it up. If only he was the same. A hard cock, ejaculating decentish sperm into her pussy: was this too much to ask?*

Calls Jayden again. It goes to voicemail. Texts Jayden again. Nothing comes back. **That fuckin hoor Andrea!**

The house suddenly feels fusty and oppressive. Her absentee mum and dad are not missed, nor her drug-dealing brothers, but the presence of **someone else** *in the house would be welcome. She looks for Russell; checks his basket, then the cat flap. The food she'd scooped into his bowl untouched. It stinks. She throws it out. Another one who has gone. Opts to head outside and take in some air.*

Ah'm walkin doon the road thinkin ay how ah battirt that fuckin Andrea goodstyle n she's gittin it worsur if ah see her near ma fuckin Jayden again! Ah goes intae the Paki's n buys a Lotto ticket n some L&B's offay that Ranjeet. Whin ah gits oot that daft wee Jordan,

Jayden's mate fae the McDonald's, is comin up the path taewards ays.
– Whaire's Jaygo, eh goes.

– Dinnae ken, ah sais. *Problay wi that hoor. How could eh dae that tae us?*

Ah hate the wey ehs mates caw Jayden that. Even heard ehs ma say it the other day. Felt like sayin it's *Jaydun*, ya fuckin dopey bitch, you should ken that: it wis you thit fuckin well gied um the name in the furst place!

So me n Jordan's walkin doon the road the gither, headin fur Jayden's bit tae see if he's hame. Goat tae try n make it up wi um, now that Andrea's learnt hur fuckin lesson! Ah should fuckin leave um tae try n ride hur, see how that bitch likes soft tadger! Jayden's no right; that thing wi that Davina n giein her a bairn, sayin ey wis oaf his tits n meant tae stick it up her erse but pit it in her fanny by mistake. *Her pussy wis that tight ah thoat it wis her erse, that shows ye,* eh went, *that shows ye ah wisnae lyin!*

Aw a big fuckin joke, but that tells ays what eh's really like, deep doon inside. Muh brar Dessie wis right aboot um. Well, eh'd better keep the fuck away fae that Andrea cunt cause see if ah catch hur near um...

ANDREA (1)

Andrea Raeburn was daydreaming, placing Marko in the porn movie she had watched with Jayden. The hairdresser, Susan Logan, is cutting Alicia Bryant's hair. Marko walks past. In her mind's eye, she sees him reach out to lift his hands up under Susan's blue overalls. The arousing gasps coming from her colleague tells Andrea that the rummaging deft-fingered Serb has found Susan's clit and that her pussy is already wet. Alicia Bryant has turned round and, kneeling on the chair, starts kissing Susan on the mouth as Marko hikes up her overalls and skirt and pulls down her tight panties, entering her roughly from behind...

– Andrea! Marko shouts, breaking her train of thought, pointing to a middle-aged woman who is entering the shop. – A coffee for Missus Scrmygeour. Oat milk and one sugar, is it Maureen?

– Yes, you've got a great memory, Marko!

– Oh aye, ah always remember the oat mulk converts, Marko declares in Serbian-Scots tones.

Andrea catches Susan looking at Marko and Maureen Scrmygeour, her gaze wide, but a shiver of trepidation in her lips. Wonders if Marko has fucked her and if he can remember or even discern how her pussy is different from the other women he has had sexual inter-course with.

Then Andrea recalls an online interview with her idol, the adult entertainment actress Toni San Laurentis, who extolled the benefit of pelvic floor exercises in the tightening of the vagina. 'There's no excuse for a slack cunt other than laziness,' San Laurentis had declared in her confrontational American accent, 'and I run exercise classes specifically designed to get a pussy back in shape after childbirth. Having a tight vagina is not enough; the ambition must be to **fucking shred** even the smallest toothpick of a cock. I say to all women: weaponise your pussy! Gobble up that dick and spit the fucking remnants out!'

Gobble up that dick.

Then Susan's eyes meet hers, and Andrea flushes and heads to the back room to make a cafetière of coffee.

Ah'm pure nickin him oaffay her. That Jayden. Ah like the wey eh widnae ride ays right till eh'd goat shot ay her. Shows eh's goat something aboot um; no like maist laddies roond her. Even if it's wasted oan that fat bastard. N ah love the wey eh's goat ambition: dedicated tae ehs gamin career like ah am tae muh singin. Ah want tae use gamin tae highlight ma singin career. Ah've been writin songs aboot the characters in some ay the games, which ah'm gaunny sing oan webcam when ah play, once ah git good at thum. Jayden's right; it's aw aboot pittin in the ooirs n sometimes ah think this apprenticeship gits in the wey.

That Jayden.

Ah'm gaunny suck ehs cock like it's no been sucked before, like Toni San Laurentis in *Death Vixens 3: Prick Shredders*, that they aw say ah look like... the wey she licks it gently then sooks it hard, then gits it right doon her throat... oan her website n she sais it's aw aboot lookin up at the felly's eyes, that's whit gits thum gaun, never mind aw the technique...

Ah'm gaunny git up the duff wi Jayden. It'll be his bairn. That'll fuck her up! Wi Toni San Laurentis's pelvic exercises n that spiritual thing she does wi the pebbles up her snatch, ah'll git ma pussy back in shape in nae time. No like that fat cunt wi hur festerin pot ay rancid soup! Then ah'll be livin rent free in her heid, the fat hoor; every time she sees ays pushin that cart wi a wee Jayden in it! She'll git depressed, eat even mare n git even fatter! A slow fuckin death! *Think aboot me whin yir rottin away wi diabetes, ya fat hoor.*

Ah'll maistly leave the bairn at my mum's so ah kin concentrate on ma singin. Ah gits muh hairbrush n stands in front ay the mirrur, n thinkin aboot Jayden, ah starts singing 'Unchained Melody'. But then ah goes: naw, 'Unchained Melody'— isnae the best song for ays tae lead oaf wi, so ah pits oan that 'Just The Way You Are' but make it mare like a lassie singin tae a laddie.

Ah want Jayden tae lick ma pussy oot so ah gie it a guid shave. Ah'll show that fat bitch!

LITA (5)

Russell the cat had returned. He was sat on the battered garden shed, scratching authoritatively at the window, green eyes imploring. Lita could hear his mews through the glass, switching back and forward between psychotically belligerent outrage and plaintive begging. – Fuck off, Russell, ya wee radge cunt, she snaps, before being moved to apologise. – Sorry, pahhl, she throws open the back door as the cat weaves between her legs with quaking purrs, and she immediately scoops some Felix into the oft-deprived but always entitled beast's dish.

Then a text and file from a strange number pings into her phone. Lita looks at the message, opening the attachment in mounting excitement and anxiety. She cannot believe her eyes. Looks at it three times. Checks the ticket she bought from Ranjeet's.

At first ah thoat some cunt wis takin the pish, like whin ye git they fuckers pretendin tae be Vodafone n gittin the bank details oot ay ye, then cleanin oot yir account. Shiv goat ripped oaf that wey, or she wid've, but she wis it the end ay her overdraft lumit. Ah mind ah turned roond n said no tae gie cunts details oan the phone. She went, aye, but it looked that real. So ah goes: aye, but that's how they fuckin well git ye, Shiv!

So naebday kin say ah'm clueless aboot that sortay shite. Two big brars n a faither like mine, ye grow up double-wide. So they telt ays ah hud tae ring a number n then they pit ays through tae this guy tae check the numbers oan the slip. Eh sais they wir gaunny send sumday roon wi a cheque.

– How much is it, ah goes.

– Thirteen thousand, six hundred and eighty-two pounds on our local accumulator.

Fucker, ah could've knocked masel doon wi a feather. It wis real!

– Kin we bring a photographer?

Ah wis gaunny go aye, but then ah thoat: ah dinnae want every cunt roond here kennin ah've goat money; speshlay muh ma, dad n brars.

So ah drank aw the cider, rid bull n voddy that wis in the frudge. Then ah went up tae the Paki's n boat some wine n tons ay crusps n chocolate. Ah sais nowt tae Ranjeet.

– Celebration? eh goes.

– Life's one big celubrayshun, ah tells um, n gits hame.

Ah'm fuckin rich.

Ah'm right oan the internet n ah'm gaun private n gittin this fat sucked oot!

Ah text Shiv:

I don't believe it! I just got a winning Lotto ticket! IRL! Don't tell a soul!

Then shi phones ays, – That's barry, Lita, how much is it?

– Thirteen fuckin grand!

Shiv goes aw sortay quiet. Then, – Fabby, what ye gaunny dae wi it?

– Use it tae lose weight! Go private, git that liposuction done n muh stomach stapult!

– Right… she goes.

Dinnae like the wey shi's gaun aw quiet, – Mind, say nowt tae Jayden! What ye daein the night? Want tae come ower?

– Goat hur, but ay.

– The morn mibbe, we need tae celebrate!

– Mibbe. What ye daein, well?

– Goat a bit pished, ah look at the crusps, soon be the last ay thaim fir me. – Jist gonna play that *Battul Hardunt*.

– Awsum. *Dispersul, Deterrunce N Damitch*'s barry.

– Come chum ays roon the clunic Wednesday. Ah made an appointmunt oanline.

– Aye, okay. See ye then. Tro.

Then ah goes oan tae play *Dispersul, Deterrunce N Damitch* oan muh ain. Ah opts tae hide the score fae the group. Ah'm soon building up muh best result... 67,332... concentratin oan no gittin distracted by close cull, or rapin bitches n torturing prusnirs like ah loat ah laddies dae, just blastin ever fucker away...

... 71,643... but it's no stoapin! Ah cannae believe what's happenin here! Ah jist keep buildin n gittin bonus points as ah zap n blooter aw they cunts, thinkin ay that Andrea...

... in the back ay muh heid that T-Zone Rushmore, highest ivir score ay 126,739... naw, it's no possible... but ah've passed Joshy Boy Five, n ah'm *passin Jayden*... at 85,883!!...

... ah'm gaun aw dizzy n ah cannae believe it... huv tae keep focus, now ah'm jist shootin anything, but thir's a spinnin ay lights n bells n whistle n it's done n...

... MA FINUL SCORE IS 93,751!!! Bettur than Jayden ivir goat! *If only ah've been able tae git tae 100,000! Ah'd huv the best ivir lassie score!!*

Ah texts Shiv right away:

Guess who got 93,751! Don't tell Jayden!

My lips are sealed

Ah'm no tellin Jayden, no yit! Ah ken ah'm a bit drunk, but ah'm pure gaun roond tae see um! Ah git tae his bit n eh comes tae the door in ehs lime-green Fred Perry n lits ays in, but eh's aw that cocky wey. Ah'm ready tae gie um a piece ay muh mind aboot that Andrea when eh goes, – Come upstairs fir a line. Ur you pished?

– Jist a wee drink, ah goes. Ah'm no tellin um aboot the money, no yit. Nor the score oan *Dispersul, Deterrunce N Damitch*. No till ah'm sure that fuckin Andrea bitch is oot the picture. Ah ken wi aw dae daft things oan bevvy n ching.

– Want tae play *Call Ay Duty*?

– Aye, ah goes.

N wir right at it. He beats ays easy cause ah cannae concentrate. Then ah ask um aboot that Andrea, n eh goes, – Nowt happened.

– Honest?

– Jist a daft snog. Ah only goat hur doon the road tae save

arguments, eh shakes ays heid. – She's nowt tae me, you're ma burd, but ay.

Aye, right, well ah'm no convinced so ah'm still no tellin um aboot the money. Nor the score either!

JAYDEN (4)

The sun was out. Children finally emerged; mostly on the bikes their parents bought as an investment, as there were still jobs in food delivery. Adults worked the afternoon or evening shift, went home, had some dinner, watched television and went to bed. But in one house in the scheme, in a room with blinds drawn, lit only by the computer screen, two exhausted figures slugged it out.

Then the sun came up.

Fuckin well blootered Lita oan that *Call Ay Duty*! Hi hi hi! Played aw night till ah goat a splittin heid. We started at 18.22 and went ontae 6.22 exactly, in the mornin. Twelve fuckin ooirs! Aw she wanted wis ays tae ride her, but ah wis too tired tae waste a blue boy. If it hud been that Andrea it wid've been a different story. But Lita, ah'd huv jist fell asleep if ah'd goat it up her, like ah did the other week. Fuckin too many downers! Hi hi hi. Ah mind ah hur makin herself come by shooglin under ays, me bouncin oan toap.

Nae chance daein rough stuff oan her tae git the juices flowin: one mark oan the fat bitch n Dessie wid cull ays! Tried tae talk her intae gittin involved in a line up fir the boys, bit shi wisnae game, no like Lucy Lush in *Cum Bullets* oan Pornhub. The yin whaire ivray cunt oan that train rode her. That wis barry. Ah kin git ma hole dead easy, but ye huv tae think aboot yir mates. Perr Jordan's nivir even done it yit; want him tae pop the fuckin cherry, but ay. Goat tae look eftir the boys: tryin tae dae a good deed. Ah wis thinkin thit ye'd like tae keep quality fanny like Andrea tae yirsel, fir yir ain use, but Lita, git thum aw up hur. But she wisnae intae it, n went, – Ah jist want tae be wi you, Jayden.

Ah caught a sketch ay masel in the mirrur, – Ah kin understand that. But aye, ah wis too fucked eftir aw that gamin tae git it up hur. N ah'm no turned oan by fat, speshlay no now that Andrea's oan the scene! But tryin tae keep Lita oaf the scent, ah pushed a vibrator intae her fir a bit, n soon she wis squealin like a big whale gittin tanned in by a torpedo, n that bit wis mint, n ah goat hard enough for her tae gam ays n pill oot tae blaw in her coupon. So ivraything worked oot barry eftir aw! Hi hi hi!

But no as barry as whin she goes tae the lavvy n ah sees hur phone, n a text oan it fae Shiv:

> I don't believe it! I just got a winning
> Lotto ticket! Don't tell a soul!

> > > Leets that's amazin!

> Guess who got 93,751! Don't tell Jayden!

> > > My lips are sealed

What the cuntin fuck...

... loose lips count fir fuck aw if yuv goat loose fingurs! Ninety-three fuckin grand! She fuckin sais nowt! Well that's gaun in ma poakit cause if it disnae it'll jist git pilfered by Fat n Clint, n Lita's *ma* curlfren! Hi hi hi!

She comes back in, then we hears sumbday comin up the stair, n gaun intae the lavvy, but ah'm no giein a fuck.

– Ah'm starvin, she goes.

– Ah'm no wantin anything tae eat, ah tells hur. – Ah need tae keep gamin, but ay.

Ah hears thum outside, gaun back doon the stairs again. Disnae sound like ooir Jarred or Ma, whae'll kip fir ages anywey, but ay. They puhls.

– Ah've goat tae eat sumthun cause ah'm starving, Lita goes. – Blut shukur.

Ah need tae think things through. *Fat cow isnae gaunny tell ays aboot that dosh...* – Barry, you go doon n help yirsel, ah'm jist gittin oan back oan that *Call Ay Duty* while ah'm oan a roll. Need tae keep muh game time up!

That fuckin poppy's mine, n ah deserve it n aw. Tax for ridin a fat burd. Ah want that Andrea, n tae git shot ay Lita, but no git culled by Clint n Dessie oan the wey. Need tae try n figure this oot... mibbe uh should've rode hur... goat tae talk tae ooir Glen, he'll ken what tae dae!

UNCLE GLEN (2)

The house in Hemel Hempstead had afforded Glen Urquhart much pride. He'd done a lot of work on it himself. His sister Manda had come down a couple of times, but, although it was spacious enough, Glen had steadfastly put her off bringing the boys down. They were surly and their lack of manners was a terrible concern. It wouldn't have done to have them in the beer garden of the Harvesters, running around uncouth and feral when people tried to make friendly conversation. Glen Urquhart could see such potential interactions had disaster written all over them. Those savage urchins could turn a relaxing Sunday roast into the stuff of social nightmares.

On this, at least, he and his wife Lucinda and his daughter Roxanne, highly ambivalent to her young cousins, were totally in accord. It's not that Hemel Hempstead was even a particularly fussy place, Glen considered; Nige and Chris could eff and blind with the best of them. But the manners deficiency alienated people. A simple please, thank you and excuse me went such a long way.

So Glen Urquhart contemplates his diminishing circumstances: the lumpy settee in his sister's small new-build housing association dwelling, in a development that replaced the old maisonettes two streets away from where he grew up. Thank God for Cuthbert and the occasional respite of the Hotel Viva and covid lockdown, which had freed up the beds. But now that was over, and his sponsor was making grumbling noises.

Glen stretches out, massages some aches in his legs and heads upstairs to the bathroom to shower. As he mounts the steps the snores erupt from Manda's room, and the electronic pings and fizzes from Jayden and Jarred's domicile tell him one or both of his nephews has been up all night at the video gaming. After his shower Glen heads back downstairs. The gaming noises have stopped. It's Jayden's voice... plus a female one.

That Jayden is a fuckin lazy wee bastard. Sure enough, wee Jarred will learn his weys if eh's no careful. As a guest in the hoose, even on this poky sofabed, it's no for me tae say, but Manda should be pittin these useless cunts in the fuckin picture. Never peys tae lit them run amok. Mind you, she's in her kip n aw, snoring away on her tranquillisers.

Ah've work oan a contract ah landed wi a big letting agency in the New Toon, so a dusk-till-dawn job for me. Dinnae get me wrong, ah'm glad ay it; ah thought they'd have forgotten aboot Glen Urquhart up here. But my auld mate Billy Sim, well, who was the first guy eh called in when he broke his airm? Yours truly! Aye, plumbers never go hungry, but what they dinnae say is we work like fuck n aw.

The bathroom's a midden; two laddies, one ay them doped up tae the eyebaws, and a pill-popping depressive mother, so ye kin imagine! Obviously ah'm awready regretting this move. So ah'm showered n changed n ah'm back doon tae the kitchen. Ah'm opening the sliding cupboard doors, tryin tae decide what the breakfast options are (not a fuckin lot on this evidence, it has tae be said), whin ah hears a thumpin oan the stairs n a fat young lassie comes waddlin in. Ah seem tae remember her lurking in the backgroond wi Jayden at Philly's funeral bash. There wis some altercation ootside.

– Hiya, she goes.

– Hiya.

– Mand... Mussus Tempultun still sleepun?

– Aye... and I think Jarred's oan a sleepover at a pal's. And who might you be?

– Lita. Ah'm Jaydun's curlfren.

This lassie has a pretty face: fetching green gypsy-girl eyes, topped by Carrick Knowes a Gallagher brother would be proud ay and sweet, ruby-red lips. But, fuck me: she's cairyin some timber. Tae good effect on those threepenny bits, strainin away in a blue-and-yellay toap, and ah do like a big booty, seein the open palm ay this caressing right hand as a veritable space-exploration vehicle, traversing the lunar landscape ay that smooth terrain, but she's pushin the voluptuous-obese perceptual boundary tae the fuckin limit here! Oor Jayden is a bit young tae be a chubby chaser. Ah flash her a *cheeky wee smile*. – Lovely Lita, meet-uh maid... that wis the Beatles.

– Ah ken the Beatuls, n it wis Rita, she smiles, but wi a wee bit ay bashfulness, which might derail the inexperienced, but is read by the veteran cowper as *faux*.

– You're thinkin aboot the British Beatles. The Japanese Beatles sung ruvray Rita meet-uh maid.

She laughs a bit at that yin. – You're good wi wurds. Ah heard ye speak at that auld boy's funeral.

– Philly Matheson… a great man. Did you ken him?

– Nuht, we wir jist telt tae go thair fir the free drinks, but ay.

The lassie has obviously been corrupted by Jayden's malign influence. – So, Lita… Lita whae?

– Lita McCallum.

Now let ays confess that this is a sharp punch tae the gut. Yin that instantly cuts off the blood supply bound for cock, rerouting it back tae brain. The survival instinct suddenly comes tae the fore. Cause that's a name thit conjures up vivid associations. A rid flag, and no the sort ye want tae see flyin ower the Scottish Parliament or City Chambers. – Aw, right, nae relation tae Kenny McCallum? Or Clint n Dessie McCallum?

– Aye, muh dad n muh brars.

Well, if she's fae that shower ay wasters – *and now ah see dark, scapegrace een, n forget yon thighs tae get between* – oor Jayden hus royally shat the fuckin bed again. Big time. N tae think ah wis blaming him for scamming poor Philly's relatives for free drinks. Surprised she wis the only McCallum thair! – Right, n ah look at muh watch, thinkin aboot New Toon kitchens n shitehooses.

– Ye ken thum like?

– Aw aye, ah ken thum awright, n ah gies a knowin, evaluatin smile. Nods tae the kettle. – Ye wantin a cup ay tea?

– Aye, she goes. – Wis jist gaunny make masel some egg oan toast, but ay. Manda… Mussus Tempultin sais it's awright, the lassie goes, sly-eyed. – Ye want some scrambult egg oan toast?

– Aye, barry, ah goes.

So thair ah am, watching this chunky wee yin daein the cookin, usin aw the eggs in Manda's fridge, a twelve-pack n aw! N fuck me, it's some pile ay scrambled Nick Beggs! – Ah'll no need nowt else aw day, ah tells hur, as she pits the plate doon tae ays. – Just as well ah work hard tae burn it oaf. What's it you dae for a livin?

– Ah'm no working right now cause ah goat peyed oaf fae the bakery, but ay, but ah want tae open muh ain nail bar soon.

– Nail bar, ay? The entrepreneurial type!

– What?

– The service industry.

– Naw, ah wis telt at the school thit ah'd be guid at that.

– Nails... I'm sure you would, ah tell the lassie, whae's fairly demolishing that plate ay eggs. Funny thing is, ah nivir see her sae much as lift a fork tae her gob. They jist seem tae vanish by a kind ay osmosis. That egg n toast wi pepper n broon sauce oan it is soon sitting heavy in muh guts. – So, ye stey near here?

– Roon the corner. Yirsel?

– Stayin here for the duration ay the festival. No that thir's much oan during covid, but ah rented oot my flat in Albert Street. Ah'm jist back fae a long spell ay livin doon south. Hemel Hempstead.

– Whaire's that, Inklun?

– Aye. Near London.

– Ah'd like tae go tae Lundun. But ah'd go tae Ibiza first.

– Good choice. Ah've been a few times. First went thair in the nineties, a pure riot, and ah start tae think ay the good auld days. Nige, Chris and the boys. Great lads, nae drama wi thaim, no like some ay the bams up here. But ah suppose that's cause ah've nae history growing up wi everybody doon thair. There's nowt sae liberatin as a new start in a new toon, where yuv got nae past. Back up here ah kin feel it scannin ays fae behind every set ay twitchin curtains. – One ay ma best mates doon in Hemel Hempstead has got a big villa oot thair. Was daein some work on it for him, ah think ay Nige's barry spot. – Love it, n ah sweep ma gaze aroond the scabby kitchen wi its shitey worktoaps n presses fill ay non-matchin cracked crockery n contemplate muh reduced lot. – Better thin here, for sure. This place is gaun tae the dogs. It nivir used tae be like this.

– How?

– See, what this place used tae be aboot was solidarity. It was a community that stood the gither, fightin for real socialist values, ah say, thinkin aboot poor Philly Matheson and how his demise is indicative ay oor malaise.

– What? You're oaf yir heid, jist like yir nephew, she laughs.

– Naw, everything we've gained in life worth huvin is through working people standing thegithir. Have you ever voted?

– Aye, eywis voted, right fae the start. But when 5AM only goat thurd, ah sais that wis me done. Nivir bothered since.

What the fuck… – You've loast me a wee bit here…

– *X Factur*. Dinnae git ays wrong, ah liked Matt Terry, him thit won it, n ah'm gled ay beat that Finnish lassie… no thit ah agree wi a Finnish lassie bein in a show ower here… they must huv an *X Factur* in Finlund… but one ay the boys in that 5AM looked a bit like Jaydun… so that wis me done.

Aw that ah, Glen Urquhart, can dae is look at this dim lassie in abject despair. Aye, oor Jayden can fuckin well pick them. – Have tae rush, ah tell hur, – been an absolute pleasure, Lita, n ah dispense a saucy wee wink n point at her tits in yon blue-n-yellay boulder-holder. – That's an awfay sexy toap you've got on there, and ah watch her face ignite as ah head outside.

It's nippy ootside, fuckin deserted n aw. At least nae cunt's fucked aboot wi the van. Ah get inside and start it up, pulling oot the maze ay narray, double-parked streets ontae the main road.

Back at the lock-up, ah get the laptop oot n check my email. One fae Nige:

To: glenbraveheart@gmail.com
From: n.blakeley@hotmail.co.uk

Hello Glen,

Well, I hope the Jocko homeland is treating you well. The Double H news? After the big post-lockdown splurge, it's all gotten a little drab back here. I've chased the Council about with my building permit, but of course, Covid gets the blame for their incompetence.

Hot news: Lauren Brady stormed out the Horseshoes the other day, leaving poor Mick Carter standing around like a spare prick. I took him down the Harvesters and bought him a consoling lager. Fucking pandemonium! A mob of Watford scumbags had gotten off at the station. They were throwing their weight around on route into town. Thankfully they left after one. Bexey reckoned there was an HH firm of Tottenham taking an interest in their outing, but nothing kicked off. Apparently, some of the Watford crew went to Redz for a bop and to chance it with the local lassies, but left relatively quietly in a fleet of minicabs. Watford and Luton, they should move those bastard enclaves of shit back to the north or midlands, brick by brick, where they bloody well belong!

Dunno what your availability is like for doing some work in Espania, but Joe Watson was making noises about a potential big plumbing job in Torremolinos. Obviously, I threw your name into the hat.

Anyway, lets catch up soon, brother

Nige

Ah should be getting the fuck oot ay here, back south tae the land ay plenty! But blood is thicker than water, and ah need tae make sure that Manda's okay.

LITA (6)

Lita McCallum sits in her bedroom. It is decorated with posters of pop stars she once adored. It felt like centuries ago, yet tearing them down would seem a deep betrayal, not of the pouting, posturing, scowling subjects, but of the former self who had so appreciated them. As she stares into the wistful face of a doe-eyed young man who looks off poignantly into the middle distance, she can recall better times with her and Jayden.

The bedroom is a zone that nobody enters without her escort. Even her pugnacious, entitled brother Dessie was traumatised when he barged in to find his sister on top of his sweating, gasping underling Jayden Templeton. Dessie vowed never to set foot in there again.

Though distracted by her phenomenal score on Dispersal, Deterrence And Damage: Exterminate Them! – 93,751 was surely a freak accident – Lita has managed to browse holiday packages and several private weight-loss clinics. She signs up for a consultancy located in a new building off the St John's Road in the west of the city. It will take two buses for her to get there. But, like any procedure she opted to undertake, this would constitute money well spent.

Ah want tae tell *everybody* aboot the money, n Jayden aboot the score oan *Spersul*, but nuht, ah'm hudin aw that back! But ah made that appointment tae the private clunic, as soon as that money wis in muh account! Couldnae believe it when the hoaspital sais eh could take ays right away. So Shiv comes roond tae chum ays. We droap in some lentul soup ah made fir Manda n Jarrit, jist tae lit Jayden ken we're aw good again n tae make up fir they eggs. But naebody's in, cept yon Unkul Glen, whae tells us tae come ben the kitchun. – Fir Manda n Jarrit, bit you n Jaydun n aw, ah goes.

Glen opens the Tupperware boax n looks in. Eh gies ays a wee smile, then sticks it in the fridge. – Thanks. Who's this yin, then? eh goes, lookin at Shiv.

– Shiv, she goes.

– Pleased tae meet ye, darlin. Glen smiles that wey whaire ehs teeth look really big. Like pianny keys. It sortay looks mint, but.

Shiv looks aw nervous n goes tae me, – We should go tae your appointment, cause muh ma's goat Beyonce...

Then that Uncle Glen goes, – Ah would love youse ladies tae join ays in ma hostelry ay choice, the cocktail bar at the Hotel Viva, anytime that meets yir fancy.

– Whaire's that? ah goes.

– Ah... if only thir was an invention called the internet, whereby one could type in 'Hotel Viva' and find aw sorts ay information oan said establishment, including the location, Glen goes, n ehs brow goes up in the air. – Near the Waverley Station. Youse'll find it. So join ays. You lassies need some glam and sophistication in your lives.

– Mibbe, ah goes.

– Ah'd huv tae git a sitter for Beyonce, Shiv sais.

– See that you do just that, gorgeous, Glen grins. – You've never seen a cocktail bar till you've sampled the delights of the Hotel Viva, very Ibiza in its style. Bryan Ferry once drank in there.

– Whae's that? ah goes.

Glen looks a bit pit oot thit ah didnae ken this Bryan Fernie, but eh pills another ay they smiles. – You come by the Viva n ah'll play ye some ay his songs on the old Wurlitzer jukey.

– Right, done deal, ah goes. – Goat tae nash. See ye later, Glen.

– For sure, Lita, my angel. Don't you forget about me, no, no, no, no, at the Viva, n eh gies us a big wink.

We gits ootside, n ah'm thinkin, that song eh sung wis Sumple Minds. What's eh singin that for if eh's talkin aboot this Bryan Fernie? Then Shiv sais, – How wide is your Uncle Glen?

Ah gits a wee laugh at that yin. – Eh's no *ma* uncul, eh's *Jaydun's* uncul.

We heads tae that private clunic tae git ays *proper care*. Ah'm no knockin people fae roond here that yaze the NHS, cause they dinnae ken any bettur, but if yuv goat money, it's only right ye should be able tae jump the queue. It's two buses; at this big fancy place in they lush groonds which they sais wis Murrayfield, but tae me it's nearly Corstorphine.

– You're lucky, Lita, she goes. – Ah ken what ah'd dae if ah won money.

– Git a new wardrobe ay clathes? Ah'm waitin till ah lose the weight!

– Nuht, ah'd git Beyonce an operation oan her fit.

– Ah'd advise anybody tae buy a tickut, ah goes.

We gits oaf in they groonds, but: ah swear ah've loast ten kilos jist walkin tae the buldun! The receptionist asks ays muh name n ah tells hur. – We wir telt tae come here.

She looks up at ays. – Oh yes, you're in the right place.

So shi takes ays intae a white room, leavun Shiv waitin, whaire ah meets this doaktur guy. Hair aw swept back, a sortay beard… an aulder boy, but, well… ah'm no sayin ah wid, bit ah'm no sayin ah widnae! Then they dae aw sorts ay mentul stuff, weigh ye oan they big scales, take samples ay blood, pish, shite… ah thoat they wir gaunny take scrappins ay muh fanny fir a bit! Ask ays tae fill in this form aboot diet n exercise. Whin wir done ah talks tae the boy for a bit. Eh asks ays what aw muh goals ur. Ah tells um, then eh sais fir ays to go hame n thit ah'll git the results soon.

– What wis that like? Shiv asks whin ah git oot.

– It wis funny, ah goes. – Eh sais if ah wanted a bairn – wi Jayden, likes – it wid be bettur if ah wisnae sae big. But that doaktir boy, ah licks muh lips, – ah'm no sayin ah wid, bit ah'm no sayin ah widnae!

– Suppose so, Shiv goes as we git oan the first bus. The drivur tells us tae pit oor masks oan. Ah ey forget. Then, as we take oor seats, Shiv's eyes ur wide ower that mask. – That's what ah think aboot Jayden's uncul. That Glen.

– What?

– Ah'm no sayin ah wid, but ah'm no sayin ah widnae! We should pure go tae that cocktail bar!

– N ride that Unkul Glen?

– Nuht! she goes, then she looks at ays n laughs, – Well, mibbe, aye!

– Mind the time wi hate-fucked that grumpy auld Les Munro?

– Aye, him oan the buses.

– Whin ehs wife wis in hoaspital huvin thir bairn! Here, he's no drivin this bus, is eh? n ah points doonstairs…

Wir sittin at the toap ay that bus jist aboot endin oorsels! Then ah realises: ah'm fuckin well starvin here! Wir definitely gaun tae that McDonald's in toon before we go back oot tae the scheme, even if Shiv'll problay want tae go tae Nando's fur chickun, kennin hur!

JAYDEN (5)

The weather has changed again; it remained hot under the sun, when a tall building buffered you from the cruel Baltic winds that swirled down the Forth Estuary. However, such respite is only intermittent for the residents of the scheme. They find themselves being roasted, then frozen; this changing with almost every step taken.

Jayden James Templeton looks out his bedroom window, charged with excitement. Despite all this covid nonsense, his life seems to be opening up. The thought of Lita's ninety-three grand makes him giddy. He watches Joshy Boy Four struggle to retrieve a baseball cap the gale has torn from his head, sweeping it down the main road towards oncoming dock traffic. As first a car, then an articulated lorry, pound it into the tarmac, Jayden lets out an appreciative chuckle at the turn of events and JB4's gaping indignation.

Wiping sleep from his eyes, Jayden considers doing some drug rounds. He heads downstairs where he finds Manda standing at the back door of the kitchen. Smoking a cigarette, his mother stares off into the middle distance as the wind makes long, resonant whistles across the backcourts. **At least she's stayed thin, even if she blames this on her nerves.**

Jayden slyly checks the Lambert and Butlers on the coffee table: a near-full pack. His mother, her head fuddled with pills, will never miss a couple. He swiftly pockets two as he watches Manda exhale smoke, lost in thought by the door.

Ah worry aboot muh ma cause ay hur tryin tae dae away wi ehrsel. Ah worry n ah dinnae worry, if ye ken what ah mean. If she really wanted tae dae it she wid've done it. Ah mind some boy oanline sais thit eh worked oan the railways takin aw the deid boadies oaf the tracks. Peepul thit wir depressed durin lockdoon. Ah thoat, how does it take that long? Poor cunt's injured, git um tae the hoaspital right away. Eh's deid, git um slung away tae fuck soas the train kin git past. It's no gaunny make any difference tae him.

But this boy says naw, cause thuv goat tae git aw the bits; thir splattered aw ower the place whin the train hits thum that hard. Aw, ah says, it's like ye widnae even feel it, that's mibbe what they dae that fir, so that goat ays thinkin: if muh ma really wanted tae go, thir's a railway line no far fae here. But ah'll keep quiet aboot that: dinnae want tae go pittin ideas intae her heid! Hi hi hi!

But even muh ma sais it, aboot me n Lita, likes, n ye kin she's buildun up tae git at it again. She turns tae ays n shuts the back door, flickin the fag end oot, n goes, – Yir a gid lookin laddie, whit ye daein hingin aboot wi a fat cunt, n she's shakin her heid. – Nivir fuckin well broat ye up that wey!

– Fair enough, ah goes, cause muh ma nivir did. Use tae tell ays as a bairn if thir wis a fat cunt oan the bus, 'Dinnae stand up n gie that fuckin fat hoor a fuckin seat, ya fuckin dopey wee cunt. If these fat cunts want tae stuff thir fuckin faces it's nowt tae dae wi nae cunt else!' N she hates Lita. Whin the polis came tae the door for that Davina, Ma sais, 'If yir gaunny bring the polis tae oor door fir choking some lassie, at least make it that fat cunt, for fuck sake!'

Goat tae hand it tae her, cannae say fairer thin that, but ay. Cause it hurt muh ma, the polis comin roond, wi hur huvin the nerves. But she's no goat a guid wurd tae say aboot Lita. – Lita's no that bad… ah opens the fridge n points tae the Tupperware boax. – She left ye sum soup!

Ma said fae the start thit Lita wid run tae fat; funny how yir ma kens that kind ay thing. Her eyes ur ower n lookin at the egg boax. It's one ay they big yins thit huds twelve. – Soup… ah'm no wantin ur fuckin scabby soup… She opens the boax, n it's empty. – Ah dinnae believe it… that greedy… snidey fuckin…! Ye see it in the eyes! SHE STOLE MUH FUCKIN EGGS!

– Whae did?

– Your fuckin fat girlfriend! Broat some fuckin mingin soup ah nivir asked fur soas she could thieve muh expensive eggs! How many times huv ah fuckin telt ye aboot littin fat tramps in this hoose? She checks the bin, countin the broke eggshells.

– Might huv been Uncle Glen.

– Dinnae be fuckin stupit, she turns roond wi a right pus oan hur. – Thir's no a pick oan oor Glen. It'll be that fat hoor, she shakes hur heid n goes for the pack ay Lambert n Butler.

Ah'm shitein it in case she realises thir's a couple missin.

– Aye, a sly, skeekit cunt'll ey run tae fat. Cause they sneak eggs, she huds up the carton. – They sneak biscuits. They sneak cans ay Coke. They sneak bacon rolls. Watch the next time ye pass a Greggs. Go thair in the morning n lunchtime n it's aw office types n workies. Try gaun *ootside* that time, yi'll see a fat bastirt lookin aroond, eyes poppin oot thir heid, sneakin in, n comin oot wi pies n the likes, n then she goes, shakin the packet ay L&B, – THIEVIN MUH FUCKIN FAGS N AW!

N the thing is she's right. See, whin yir oot wi Lita n ye pass a McDonald's – funny, but Lita disnae like Greggs that much, which is barry – her eyes do pop oot ay hur heid. She ey says: *ur wi gittin a McDonald's?* Ah ey goes: *naw*, cause ah sumtimes want a chippy later. But she keeps oan: *when?* Ah goes: *five o'cloak.* She looks at hur phone n goes: *that's ages away!* Ah goes: *awright, but ah'm jist huvin a black coffee.* So wi'll go in n she'll git a Big Mac n chips n sometimes even a shake. Then wi'll git oot n ah'm starvin n git a chippy n she'll go: *ah'm wantin a fuckin chippy n aw Jayden.* So ah'll jist shrug.

Anywey, it's muh ma gittin oan muh nerves now, so even if it's cauld ah'm gaun oot, jist tae git away fae hur. No sayin nowt against Ma, but she kens how tae nip some cunt's heid. Ah cannae be ersed daein the roonds, sortin cunts oot for ching, way too early for that; ah'll wait till later oan whin ah ken thi'll be in. Maist cunts nivir phone or text back – until they want sorted oot. So ah decides tae git oot the scheme n take a walk acroas the main road n doon the hill tae the beach.

This wind is well fuckin nippy, but ah'm no that bothered cause ah've goat a gid jaikit n it blaws away aw the cobwebs n gies ye time tae think. Ah git doon the foreshore, n thir's gulls squawkin away, cunts better no shite oan ays, hi hi hi. The river's as oily as fuck, a durty grey stretch ay water, and Fife looks like fuck all, which it is. Huv tae be daft tae want tae live thair: thir's nowt till ye git tae Dundee. Dunfermline or Raith Rovers? They'll dae fuck all. Barry chippy near the

Raith groond, but: beyond yir wildest dreams. Or at least thir wis. Mibbe it's aw changed ower thair tae, wi aw this covid shite, which ah dinnae agree wi.

Whae's walkin up the grass verge, but the last person ah wants tae see... fuckin Dessie wi ehs two Staffies. One ay the dugs, ah think it's Rocky, is daein a shite n Dessie jist walks oan. An auld boy wi binoculars, whae's been lookin doon the rivur, turns n looks at um, sortay sayin wi ehs eyes: *ye no gaunny pick that up?*

Dessie catches um, goes, – Nose botherin ye, cunt?

The auld boy looks away. Ah hate Dessie, but it's barry watchin an auld cunt shite it!

– Dessie, ah goes.

– Aye... eh sortay sais, but it's mare ay a grunt.

Eh's a cunt, but ah need tae keep in wi um. – What's that radge sayin, auld pervert wi the bionculars? ah goes, lookin tae the auld boy whae's gittin intae a car, shakin ehs heid.

Cunt jist goes, – Nivir you fuckin mind! Heard ye wir messin aboot wi a wee scrubber!

Felt like sayin, *that's nae wey tae talk aboot yir ain sistur*, but ah goes, – Naw...

– If you fuckin touch another burd whin you're gaun oot wi ooir Lita, ah'll tear yir fuckin throat oot, ya wee fandan. Goat that?

Ah jist looks at um, wonderin if Lita telt um aboot the Lotto money. But naw, shi widnae be that daft. Then eh grabs muh froat wi that chubby hand... ah cannae git any air in...

– Ah sais: goat that?

– Ah... ah... ayeee... ah manages tae sortay git it oot... ah kin hear one ay they dugs growlin...

– Fuckin right, eh goes, n lits go, pushin ays away.

Ah'm strugglin tae git muh fuckin breath. Everything's spinnin roond... but it's barry, kind ay like trippin... ah starts tae laugh, even though ah cannae git breath in...

– Ur you fuckin laughin at me?

The dug, no Rocky, the lighter yin, eh's lookin it ays n aw tensed up, that low snidey growl again...

– Nuht... ah goes, hudin up muh hand, – ah wis jist laughin cause ah couldnae git breath.

– Laughin? Cause ye couldnae fuckin breathe? You're a fuckin wee mongol, pal, a fuckin spazzy wee weapon. Now git oot ay ma fuckin sight n dinnae lit ays see ye wi that stuck up wee hairdresser hoor or ah'll cut yir fuckin throat. Dinnae think yir wide cause ye goat that fuckin poseur ay an uncle steyin wi ye. He'll dae nowt. Cut his fuckin throat n aw. Ye hear ays?

– Aye, nae bother likes, Lita's muh curlfren.

– Ah telt hur ye wir a fuckin waster, but that's up tae hur. So, see if you mess her aboot...

– Naw, it's sound like. We sorted it oot.

– Phone, eh goes, hudin oot ays hand. – Open it.

If thir wis somethin aroond ah could pick up, but ah'm strugglin tae git muh breath. Ah jist opens it n hands it ower.

– Dinnae see nowt... what's this Freedom app? Heard some cunts on aboot it.

– You should git it, Dessie, ah goes. – Ah dae it fir aw the business. It's encryptit, n it deletes aw the chat. Bettur thin Telegram, Signul... ye kin even send things tae folk n they dinnae ken whae it's fae. Ah kin download it oantae your phone if ye want...

Eh slams the phone back intae muh palm. – No wantin you tae dae nowt, jist keep away fae other burds if yir gaun oot wi muh sistur. Right?

– Aye, Lita n me's sortit it aw oot.

– Fuckin better huv, the cunt goes, then turns away. – MOAN YOUSE, eh shouts at the dugs, whae follay him up the gress verge as eh spits oot a gob.

A bullyin fat cunt: bet Lita's gled they urnae in the hoose.

Ah gits hame, n muh ma's oot n soas that secretive wee cunt Jarred. But it's the best time: hoose tae yirsel. Hi hi hi. But then comes a text, fae the bane ay muh life, that fat munter Lita! Ah'm aw ready tae ignore it but ah mind whit Dessie sais, so ah git back tae hur. Nowt aboot muh ma's eggs: straight away she invites herself back roond! Well, lit's see if shi'll spill the beans aboot that fuckin money! Better no huv telt that Dessie cunt!

So much fir a healthy mornin stroll doon the beach! Ah gits a blast oan the crack pipe tae git a wee bit iced n swallay two ay that Viagra. Ah find Stranglelove.com oan xvideos.com n watch a bit ay *Gasman 3:*

Dark Love – the best in the *Gasman* series – whaire the big muscled cunt wi a cowl like Batman throttles this bird wi long black hair as eh rides hur. The wey the burd's eyes bulge oot makes ays want tae wank, but ah need tae deny it soas ah'm that desperate ah kin even see past Lita's fat tae fuck hur. *Ninety-three grand...*

She comes roond n wi huv a joint n git a bit stoned n she sais, – How is it that ye nivir lick ma pussy?

So ah'm thinkin *cause it's fuckin mingin*, see fuckin tryin tae find it in aw that flab, takes ye fuckin months bit ay, n it's like a fuckin swamp doon thair, what that boy oanline sais: Florida swamps, that's whit it wid be like, fuckin Florida swamps, but ay. Fuck knows when the time wis she could wash it. She cannae fit n a fuckin bath – the water wid jump oot if she jumped in – n ye'd huv tae send oot a search perty fir the fuckin shower attachment, ay! Too fuckin right, ya cunt! Hi hi hi! But, ah goes, tae keep the peace likes, n sais, – Ye ken how it is, doll, yuv goat tae try new things, but ay.

– Ah'm no littin ye choke ays, she goes.

– Ah nivir sais nowt aboot that, ah goes. Cause wi ma rep ah'd ride aw the burds in this scheme, easy! Oan that Teen Tinder ye kin git tons ay lassies: snobby burds n aw, but ay. Ah goat a differunt profile pic wi the new baseball cap n Stone Island jaikit. The posh burds dinnae fuckin like tae ride n ye git a bit para gaun up the toon wi the polis cunts n grasses aboot. Naw, ah'll stick tae bein doon here bit, ay. Sometimes wi mob up wi other gadges fae different schemes across the toon, thit ye meet oanline. Some ay thum huv joined oor gamin group, J-Firm. Tons ay rides doon here, like that Andrea. See if ah wisnae cockblocked by fat Lita n hur fuckin brars!

Think ay the ninety-three grand...

Whither yir in the scheme or up the toon, cunts fuckin look it ye like yir a fuckin mongul. Cause aw they see is an embarrassin fat cunt hingin oot wi ye. The likes ay that Andrea, fae doon the road, she's barry; it wid be fuckin mint ridin her up the erse, like Superdong Stanley Stonker or Gasman, that wid be awsum cause see if ah goat ma cock workin right ah'd fuckin split that pussy and that erse in two, fuckin right bit, ay. Bit no wi this fat cunt, that's a fuckin bloated liability. Waste ay a fuckin hard-on! Hi hi hi.

Think ay the ninety-three grand...

Well, she's gittin it, n wi starts snoggin, but ah'm saved by the bell cause muh ma comes back fae the shoaps. She shouts up, – JAYDEN!

– What?

– Whaire's Jarred!

– Ah dinnae ken...

– Whae's that up thair wi ye then?

– Naebody, ah shushes Lita. – Ah'm talkin oan muh phone!

That shuts Ma up. Ah hears the kitchen door shut. Then Lita goes, – What wis aw that aboot?

– She's jist nippy cause ye scranned aw her eggs.

– Charmin! Ah left her good soup! Did shi no git muh soup?

– Lit's jist sneak oot, cause ah'm no wantin argumints. McDonald's, ah goes, jist tae stoap hur fae sayin nowt.

Dinnae want seen ootside wi a fat cunt, specially no wi a big drug erection oan, but it goes doon whin ah gits intae the fresh air n oan the bus. The McDonald's is a treat, but see if they opened yin at the shoaps at ooir bit, it wid dae a great trade. Shouldnae huv tae go intae toon for a McDonald's. Cause see whin ye git in, apart fae the snobby students, it's aw cunts fae the schemes here. Ah dinnae like this yin cause thir's some south-side cunts hing oot here n JB6 chibbed yin aw thum. Coast seems clear, but. She hus a Big Mac, as usual. Ah jist hus chips, but ay. Ah watch aw the grease trickle doon the side ay her face. She's gaun oan aboot gittin an operation at some posh place in Murrayfield tae lose weight. Ah'm thinkin: mibbe ah could git you oan yir front oan the bed, git they two erse cheeks up n grease the pole n git it in yir erse, but like in the porn, aw that smooth wey, but ay. That's the fuckin problem wi no gittin a right hard-on or whatever the medical cunts call it, n even if ye do, it's nivir that smooth wey like they fuckin dae it in porn. N even if she wis up fir the strangleporn, ah'd nivir git muh hands roond that fuckin neck! Hi hi hi!

So wi gits talkin aboot love n relayshunships, n ah sais, – Ah'll ride ye up the erse, you oan yir front. Ah'm no gaun oan toap ay ye n daein kissin cause that's fuckin manky!

– Ah want it in ma fanny; ah'm needin us tae huv a fuckin bairn, she goes, n a wimmin wi two bairns looks roond.

Ah wish she'd keep hur voice doon. – Barry, ah sais, as no tae cause argumints, tryin tae think how big she wid be wi a fuckin bairn in thair.

Ah'm thinkin aboot ridin her up the erse, gittin the pole hard n right up thair while she's giein burth tae a bairn, the midwife gaun, push, push n me underneath that fat cunt cause ah widnae be able tae dae it fae the side wi a fuckin bairn's heid poking oot ay hur fanny, hittin the fuckin pipe n mibbe they bits fae the pipe – the embers, they caw thum – the fuckin embers burnin intae hur fat, like meltin intae it n hur screamin, n the midwife gaun: *it's comin, ya fat cunt, keep pushin*, n me no kennin what's happenin n, her back burnin, n the bairn comin oot ay her fanny, n then me fuckin blawin muh muck intae hur coal hole n wriggling oot fae under her, n they white sheets burnin, n her tryin tae buck n wriggle, n aw the fat flyin aw ower the place, n a bairn's heid comin oot – fuck knows if it's a laddie or a lassie, rather a laddie soas ah could take it tae the fitba, but no every game, jist the derbies – bit thuv goat a coffee bar here, n the barry thing is they huv that pan au chocolat which is fuckin mint scran, so ah'd be oaf!

Nae cunt wants tae watch a fat cunt huvin a fuckin bairn, how mingin is that? Ah droaps a wee hint, – What wid ye dae if ye won a million quid? n ah looks around. – Ah'd buy a hoose somewhere barry. Away fae here.

But ah git nowt back fae hur, she's jist starin ower at the counter. – Ken what, she goes, – that weed pure gied ays the munchies! Ah'm stull starving, n ah watches her waddle up tae buy another Big Mac.

She's sayin nowt aboot that money! Ah dinnae press it cause ah dinnae want her tae ken thit ah ken aboot it. Good thing is: if she's sayin nowt tae me she's sayin nowt tae any other cunt, like fat Dessie.

Goat tae git some ay that ninety-three fuckin grand before that fat cunt eats hur wey through it aw! Ah'm gaun hame – oan muh ain – tae think aboot how tae git that dosh, n tae watch *Gasman 2: The Choker Is Wild* again.

LITA (7)

It took a while for Lita to get ready. Having returned from McDonald's and leaving Jayden, she'd dyed her hair. Impressed by the bleached canary-yellow result, she is intrigued and excited at the prospect of a liaison with her boyfriend's Uncle Glen. Perhaps if she could befriend him, the antagonistic Manda might be better disposed towards her.

She puts on her best black leggings with a matching dress on top and walks through the scheme, heading for Shiv's, who is all ready. Her friend wears a pastel-yellow pleated skirt and an angora jumper. Her hair is tied up and pinned back, and Lita envies the visible cheekbones she once shared. Beyonce sits on the lap of Shiv's mother, Esther, permanently in her onesie and always apologising for this. – Here's me still in ma onesie, she announces in a drab tone between emancipation and defeat. The atmosphere is strained, and Shiv is anxious to leave. They quickly depart.

Shiv's awfay quiet oan oor way tae the bus stoap. Wi sees muh brar, Dessie, comin doon the street. – Say nowt tae him aboot muh money, ah whispurs tae hur. – It's jist you n me thit's tae ken aboot that.

Shiv goes, – Aye, but shi's goat a face oan hur.

But oor Dessie's here.

– Aye, ah goes tae um.

– Aye. Awright then, eh goes. – That Jaygo isnae muckin ye aboot?

– Naw.

– See eh doesnae, Dessie sais. – Heard fae Ma n Dad?

– Aye, still up at Gran's in Fort Wullium, but ay.

– Kin see thum steyin thair. Nice hoose she's goat.

– Aye, ah goes, watchin the maroon bus slowly comin up behind um. – Tro then.

108

– Tro.

Mibbe Dessie's right, mibbe Jayden is a waste ay space. N that cunt Manda: now ah'd buy the tight hoor aw the fuckin eggs she wants! No even thanks fur the soup!

Anywey, me n Shiv gits the bus tae toon, gits oaf near the station, tae hit this cocktail bar, the yin in that Hotel Viva. Thir's one ay they dash marks at the end ay the neon sign thit's fell oaf. Ah points at it.

– Exclamation mark, Shiv goes, but in a sortay snobby wey.

– Ah ken whit an exclumashun mark is!

Anywey, we gits inside, n thir's nae sign ay that Glen. Ah'm checkin us oot in the big murrur, wi muh sexy blonde hair, n ah'm thinkin, aye Jayden'll no be laughin if eh could see us now: me n Shiv, in a cool place up the toon!

Then Glen's standin up, waving at ays. Eh's sittin wi a smooth felly in a nice suit n a sunbed tan. – Pleasure tae see yis, girls, eh goes, leavun the smooth gadge still sat doon. Smooth Felly jist nods, n Glen takes us tae a corner table n then gits us two big gin and tonics, n then comes back ower n sits beside us. Eh looks at Shiv n sais, – Lookin gorgeous by the wey, doll, n ye huv tae admire the wey some fellys kin jist dae that. The likes ay Jayden, he couldnae walk intae a place like this n jist take ower – the gift ay the gab – no thit ah'm sayin Jayden's no goat it cause eh used tae huv it back it the school. Bit ah'm sayin Jayden couldnae dae it *here*. No up the toon. Eh'd go pure shy n shuffle aroond n look it ehs feet. Whereas this Uncle Glen is now touchin Shiv's hair n gaun, – Ah'd love tae make love tae you right now, by the way.

Which is mental cause ah've nivir heard any cunt say that before, n Shiv is gaun aw shy n pattin her hair doon! So ah goes, n it jist comes oot, –Ye reckon ye goat what it takes tae make love tae baith ay us, Glen?

– Shall we find oot? eh winks, downin ehs drink. We dae the same, and wi heads oot the bar. Glen nods tae a boy on reception, a big bald gadge, n the felly gies um a key. – Thanks Cuthbert. As wi goes upstairs, eh tells us, – They look eftir ays here. Plumbed this whole place, eh sweeps ehs hand roond. – Ken what ah'd like tae plumb now? eh asks as we step intae a room wi a big bed. – The depths ay depravity!

Shiv giggles n ah jist goes, —Aye right... that looks a barry drinks cabinet.

Glen takes the hint n makes us another two gin n tonics. Then eh goes tae the lavvy n comes oot in a bathrobe n tells us tae git intae one each. – Ah'm gaunny instruct you naughty ladies aboot real sex.

– Fuckin well suits me, ah goes...

– Ah've goat Beyonce, so we huv tae git oan wi it, Shiv sais.

So we gits the robes oan but nae real point cause thir oaf quick enough. Glen's goat ah good boady n aw: muscles, n eh kens it, sortay flexes thum, but eh's goat skinny legs. – Ah pump iron, eh goes.

– Ye pump lassies n aw, ah sais.

N eh sortay goes shy aboot that n sais, – What dae you think? Eh nods doonstairs, n fair play, eh's goat a big hard-on. Me n Shiv ur right doon n suckin oan it, takin turns each like in the fulums, n he's sayin, – Youse fulthy fuckin wee devils, ur as horny as fuck...

Aye ah fuckin am n Jayden kin git fucked cause it serves um right. N this boy, this Glen felly, eh gits ays oan the bed n pits it right in muh fanny, disnae moan aboot ays bein aw fat, n eh's giein ays a guid pumpin, but kissin Shiv, then eh's oot ay me n intae her, n eh goes, – Youse girls huv goat great boadies, different shapes... a man could lose ehsel in youse, ay, n ah'm thinkin: *aye, Jayden, this is whit you should be fuckin well sayin!* Cannae even git a ride oot ay the useless cunt, but this Uncul Glen's mental. – Ah'm gaunny be up youse two aw fuckin night... then eh stoaps n sais, – Here, youse are baith ower the legal age ay consent, aye?

– Aye, she's seventeen n ah'm sixteen, ah tells um.

– Goat ID, eh goes, pillin oot ay Shiv.

– Nuht... aye, ah goes. N shows um. Shiv's aw that twitchy wey, but she does n aw.

Well, he gits right back intae it! It turns oot tae be some fuckin night! Eftir whin we're gaun hame later, aw well rode, the burds singin n the light comin up, Shiv goes, – Muh ma'll go radge me steyin oot n leavin hur wi ur.

– Aye, ah goes. – N Jayden better no git tae ken aboot this, he'll go fuckin mental. It's ehs uncul!

– Aye, well if you keep yir fuckin mooth shut Jayden wullnae git tae fuckin well ken aboot it.

Serves um right fir gaun wi that Andrea hoor!

She turns roond n goes, – Well ah'm no a grass!

Ah'm thinkin *snitches git stiches* but ah sais nowt, ay. Ah jist goes, – Dinnae say a thing tae any cunt, mind.

JAYDEN (6)

*Jayden James Templeton had waited in his room hoping for a call from Andrea Raeburn. Nothing doing, he decided to masturbate to online pornography. Jarred was at football training, though his kid brother could come in any time. So Jayden smokes some meth and strips to his underpants. Fires up the new video from **Anal Vixens 3: Ass-fix-i-ation Nation**, featuring Tina Teen Trauma, a wide-eyed young woman with a wired rape-victim bearing, specialising in anal, rough sex and asphyxiation. He'd grown obsessed with her, and despite the blow of learning she was an ancient twenty-two instead of the young teen she looked, he is getting hard. The performer who plays Tina was rumoured to have taken out a lawsuit against Stanley Stonker (real name Daryl Johns) who had choked her half to death, but that may have just been to gather publicity for their forthcoming movie **Steam 3: The Final Breath**.*

Tugging violently on himself to the images, Jayden finally feels the blessed release on the terrible pressure that has built up in his testicles and brain, as he fountain-spurts in triumphant delight.

After a perfunctory clean up, Jayden heads downstairs. His Uncle Glen is not on the couch. Jayden goes into the kitchen, looks outside to see Manda in the back green taking down some washing. His mother comes in, two pegs in her mouth, which she spits into the light-blue plastic laundry basket she holds by its one functioning handle.

Ah wants Glen tae come soas ah kin ask um aboot Lita's money, n how wi git it oaffay hur. Ah sais tae muh ma, – Whaire's Glen? Thought he wis kippin oan our couch? Mind you, eh's goat ehs ain place in Albert Street n money fae that hoose bein selt doon in Welwyn Hempstead!

She pits the washin basket ontae the worktoap. – Aye, bit eh's stayin here the now. Watch…

She points tae the door, n ah kin hear a key in the loak. Then Unkul Glen comes through, wearin a trackie toap, Adidas, n hits the frudge. Takes oot a boatil ay wine. – A romantically drunken night up the Viva… bit early, but still… hair ay the dug… nods at ma n pours it intae two tumblers. They sit doon at the kitchun table, n Glen huds the boatil up tae me.

– How kin youse drink that shite, ah goes, shakin ma heid. – Ah jist like beer, but ay.

– Well, ah'll tell ye, pal, if ye drink beer yi'll jist end up a big fat radge, Glen goes. – Ah look at some ay the boys ma age… ah rest my case. In my twenties ah switched tae wine and spirits: white spirits like gin and vodka. Those that steyed oan the beer… the state ay they fat bastards, Jayden. Mark my words, you'll stay a skinny cunt till one summer, n eh pats ehs stomach, – mibbe this yin, mibbe the next, the pounds'll jist pile oan. You'll no be daein anything different; it'll jist catch up oan ye.

– Be a fuckin guid match fir you ken whae, Ma goes, lightin up.

– Fuck off; ah'll nivir git fat. It's aw tae dae wi how yir made. Ah take after you two's side ay the faimlay.

– It's no like yir faither's side anywey, muh ma laughs n tops up the wine. – Huv a wee drink wi yir mother n yir uncle, pal!

– Awright… but ah'll git a beer. Ah've a Tennent's in the frudge, ah goes. Tennent's is barry cauld, like ice cauld, soas ye cannae taste it.

– Good on you, Glen sais.

Course, soon as ah sits doon, she starts up, – So… ah'm tellin oor Glen aboot that Lita.

– Ah believe ah made her acquaintance, Glen goes. – She cooked us some eggs for breakfast.

The auld girl slams her fist oan the table. – Ah fuckin kent it! The fuckin thieving fat hoor! Thinks shi kin buy ays oaf wi fuckin soup! Ah ken how tae make muh ain lentul soup, thank you very much, n shi's up n pourin the soup doon the drain ootside.

– Well, she does huv a hearty appetite. Glen's smilin.

– Fuckin greedy fat cunt, Ma steps back in n washes oot the bowl n turns tae me. – What did ah tell ye?

– Stoap gaun oan aboot Lita.

– Comes fae a dodgy famelay, Glen sais. – Baith sides n aw, eh flips ays hand. –Well, it's a cause for concern, pal.

– So?

– You'll think it's bein nosey, Glen moves forward in the chair, gits right in yir face. Ah hate it whin eh does that. – But yir ma n ah care aboot ye, eh nods at muh ma. – Manda?

She jist scowls at ays n sits back doon.

– So… Glen goes, – this entire McCallum enterprise… we dinnae want ye tae git involved in something ye cannae git oot ay.

A bit fuckin well late fir that! – Ah'll deal wi Lita n her brars, ah goes. Fuck knows how he kens aboot what ah dae wi Dessie n Clint.

– But how, pal, Glen sweeps oot his hands, – how, pray tell, exactly will ye dae that? Eh gits up n walks tae the back door. Looks ootside, shakes ehs heid. – Look at us. My Roxy doon in Leicester; you, Jarred n yir ma here. Oor once great dynasty diminished tae this unpromisin rump.

– Charmin! Muh ma goes.

– But dae ye no see, Manda, Glen turns back tae her, – if we joined wi they McCallum lowlifes, how it wid constitute the ultimate defeat fir oor once noble house? That shower ay dirty, scruffy …

– Morbitly obese …

– … *morbidly obese*, thievin, chorin, plague-rat scum? God, we might no be much these days, certainly way short ay the rich bloodline that ran the docks, built the ships at Henry Robb, traversed the globe in the merchant fleet; but tae be reduced tae hooking up wi the McCallums? Tae crossbred with that mongol tribe ay savage, snidey, class-traitor scabs? Glen turns tae me. – Come oan tae fuck, Jayden son, ah'm no huvin it!

– Neither um ah! Ma shouts.

Ah dinnae believe this! N they dinnae ken what ah dae aboot Lita! – It's nowt tae dae wi youse!

– Is the wrong attitude! Glen's pointin at ays, sittin back in ehs chair. – You sais, in your ain words, that you dinnae want anything tae dae wi her, aye? Well, son, see us a resource in enabling you tae get rid ay said fat parasite.

Time tae shut this cunt up. – She won the Lothian n Fife Lotto. Ninety-three grand.

Aye! It suddenly goes aw fuckin quiet in the room. *Funny that, ay?*

Glen looks at muh ma, then me. – Well now... that's pit the cat amongst the pigeons, eh licks ehs lips. – The McCallums wi a bit ay seedcorn... well, what a waste. Literally: a *criminal* waste.

– Useless in thair poakits, muh ma shakes her heid. – Pished up the waw in nae time!

– Exactly, sis! We need tae box clever on this yin. Let's think it through.

Dinnae want this cunt thinkin he's in charge! – Thir's nowt tae think through, ah goes, – no fir youse at any rate!

– C'moan, Jayden, dinnae be like that, muh ma goes. – Ye awready sais some awfay hurtful things tae yir auld ma. Time flies, n ah'm no gaunny be here forever, son.

– Aye, well nane ay us will, n like you sais, youse'll live mare years thin us! Global warnin!

– That's no what ah mean, son. Ah brought you up best ah could, gied ye everything ah hud, she shakes hur heid. – You'll never understand a mother's love, pal...

– Point is, Manda, Glen cuts in, – we're faimlay, son. It's whae we ur. We need tae stick the gither. You want shot ay the fat lass, n we could aw dae wi a taste ay that poppy!

Fuckin too right. – Aye.

Glen's pacin up n doon, lookin that snide wey. Ye kin see the wheels in the cunt's heid gaun roond. – What if, ah, another felly wis tae seduce big Lita, take her off yir hands? Lassie's got a pretty face. Shed some coral n she'd be a knockout.

– She wis a ride back at school, right enough, ah goes. – Every cunt wanted tae git up hur. No now, though, nae cunt wid touch her wi a bargepole. So you're gaunny tell her radge brars no tae mess wi ays, aye?

– Let's no be too hasty here, Jayden, eh goes, – yir no thinkin strategically. Does it dae any good tae alienate the McCallums? Tae go tae war wi thum ower some wee fat hairy? One whae's sittin oan a healthy wad?

At furst ah took that tae mean thit eh wis shitin it oaffay her brars, but then ah gits tae thinkin thit eh might be right. Ah deal wi thum fir the collies, so besides a stompin or plungin, ma business wid be fucked!

– Naw, we need a mare sophisticated plan, Glen goes. – What if an aulder guy, a man wi proven expertise in the field ay seduction, wis tae woo her n take hur oaf yir hands?

– Aw aye, muh ma goes, giggling, – n whae might this be?

– Ah'm speaking hypothetically at this point, Manda, Uncle Glen grins, – but imagine if an aulder boy gied this wee fatty the message? Think ay the guilt she'd feel in betrayin ye. Eh half-shuts ehs eyes. Then eh opens thum n stares ay ays, – That's if you never rode that other lassie...

Ah gies um a *cheeky wee smile*. – Ah'm sayin nowt. But Lita disnae ken what ah did n didnae dae. Whae wis it you wir ridin last night?

– A gentleman nivir kisses n tells, Glen goes aw smooth, pattin doon that radge tache. – But if Lita betrayed you, that would put you in the position tae leverage a few bob, for sure.

– Mibbe... but what makes ye sure she'd want tae ride an auld cunt like you?

– Well... Uncul Glen tweaks his mowser again, – she rode a fuckin waster like you. That means any cunt's goat a shot!

– Christ, yir no fuckin wrong thair, Ma laughs, n they start cackling away the gither.

Awright, so eh's a dapper auld cunt: in decent nick for ays age. N eh's goat the gift ay the gab. N eh spent time in Camel Hampstead, n that's near Lundun. N a fat bird gittin attention hus goat tae be chuffed tae bits. N aye, if she felt she'd betrayed me, at the very least ah'd git a barry hoaliday oot ay it. N mibbe some money. Then ah'd tell her aboot me n Andrea. Seeken her fat pus! – So, what ye thinkin then, hi hi hi!

– Well, Glen goes, sittin back doon again, – what aboot this...?

LITA (8)

The Ibiza booking had been a spur-of-the-moment decision. Having secured some cheap flights, Lita was now searching for accommodation. Excitement ripped from her, tempered with a resentment that occasionally welled up into a bitter burn when she considered Jayden going with Andrea. This was now augmented with guilt at having slept with his uncle. So strange, she reflected, how those two things didn't cancel each other out, just added to your anxiety.

But she still has Jayden, and it is going to stay that way. And she has the money. She will get Jayden out of Andrea's way and reignite their relationship under a Mediterranean sun. Lose weight and get a better body than that skinny whore. Lita goes on Steam to look at new games and considers accessorising her existing ones. But if she pimped up the graphics, people in the groups and broader community would see she was spending money. Naw.

At her textual insistence, Shiv came round, leaving Beyonce at her mother's. Lita took her friend upstairs, and they sat at her console, playing **Dying Light**, watching Limmy blasting zombies on the webcam. After the game she once again emphasises the importance of Shiv saying nothing about their encounter with Glen. Then, on her urging, they watch **Love Island**. Lita invariably found this game show inspiring due to the life lessons it conferred. The contestants knew the ups and downs; there was always opposition. But the show's format ensured that someone would always prevail. Lita resolves that this will be her, with Jayden.

See whin ye love sumday as much as ah love ma Jayden, thir's nowt else thit matters. Whin ah wake up n eh's lyin beside ays, light shinin oan that smiling coupon, my hert jist flutters. Naebday can deny that magic. Ah ken ah've pit oan weight, but ah'm gaunny lose it for him.

Fir his love. That Andrea isnae gittin um cause eh's mine! Ah texts um:

Come round. Free house. Just me
+ Shiv. I have got a wee surprise

Eh's thair ten minutes later.
– We're gaunny git a Chinky, ah tells um, – ye wantin a Chinky?
– You gittin it, likes? eh goes.
– Aye, ah sais, – no thit you deserve it!
Eh's shakin ehs heid. – Ah nivir went wi that Andrea! It wis jist a drunken snog, like ah sais. Regretit it since!
Ah cannae believe how sincere eh looks, wi they big eyes. – What did ye go away wi hur fir then?
– Ah'm jist gaun doonstairs, tae phone, Shiv goes.
– Nuht, ah sais, – you're muh best mate. Ah want you tae hear this n aw. Your muh wicknuss, ah turns back tae Jayden. – What did ye go away wi hur fur?
– Ah telt ye! Ah hud tae try n talk hur intae no phonin the polis n gittin you charged! She wis gaun mental, n ah hud tae calm her doon, eh punches ehs chist. – Ah did it fur you!
– Gen up?
– Gen up.
Ah cannae resist um whin eh's aw serious n looks ays in the eye. – Lit's git that fuckin Chinky, well, ah'm starvin!
– Barry, Shiv goes, aw chuffed thit wuv made up.
Ah goes tae that Deliveroo app oan muh phone. Best thing aboot lockdoon wis discoverin Deliveroo! They even come oot here, tae the scheme! – Right…
– What youse gittin? Jayden goes.
– King prawn wi black bean sauce n fried rice, ah goes.
Shiv sais, – Lemin chickun.
– Nae surprise thair then!
– What's that meant tae mean?
Ah goes, – You eywis git lemun chickun.
– Naw ay dinnae, ah hud chow mein the other week.
Then Jayden goes, – Youse kin chow mein anytime yis like, n eh pats ehs baws.

Ah like it whin Jayden talks like that whin it's jist me n him, but no if it's him n me n Shiv. Ye kin tell she laps it up.

So wi orders n ah changes the subject. – The Chinky wisnae the surprise ah wis talkin aboot. Ken what else uv done? Booked us aw up fir Ibiza next week.

– Yir jokin, Jayden goes.

Ah shows um the tickets online! – See, ah watch ehs wee face light up.

– That's fuckin barry, ya cunt, n eh punches the air. – Ibiza!

– Need a fuckin brek, but ay. Aw that covid shite. Found cheap flights, us two n Shiv, ah goes tae Jayden, – Jordin n aw. Fir Shiv, ah sais.

Shiv pure gits a beamer. – Thir's nowt between him n me...

– Eh fancies ye, ah goes, – ay, Jayden? Your ehs mate!

– Aye, Jayden goes, aw half-herted.

– Dinnae worry, ah sais tae Shiv, – wu'll book seprit rooms! Ah looks at Jayden. – Eh does, but ay.

– Ah dinnae ken.

– Your ehs mate!

– Ah dinnae ken whit goes oan in ehs heid, but.

– So eh's no said nowt tae you?

– Nuht.

Shiv cuts in, – It disnae matter whae said what tae whae, ah cannae go. Ah've goat Beyonce.

– Leave hur wi yir ma for a couple ay weeks!

– Ah cannae... ah cannae keep daein that!

– But the sun'll dae ye good!

– Ah ken that.

– Aye, well moan tae fuck oan the hoaliday then...

– Ah'll go n ask muh ma, Shiv goes.

– Thair ye go! Yi'll soon be ridin plukey Jordan's cock in Ibiza!

– Shut up, Lita. Shiv's suckin oan her hair, lookin at Jayden. – You ey git pure manky.

– Naw ah dinnae, ah goes, but ah'm sayin nowt mare cos it'll jist make her gab, n ah dinnae want her tae mention Glen.

The boy comes wi the Chinky. No fae the one in oor scheme, but acroas the main road. It's barry, n thir's cans ay lager n aw. So wi sit n eat doonstairs, me n Shiv oan the couch, Jayden in the chair. Jayden wants tae watch porn, but ah goes, – You're disgustin, so we rewatch mare repeats ay *Love Island* n talk aboot whae the best rides oan it are.

Whin wir finished Shiv gits ready tae go hame. – Ah'd better git back tae the bairn.

– Mind speak tae yir ma. Ibiza.

– She's oan new puhls; ah'll wait till she's in a barry mood.

– Muh ma's oan new puhls n aw, ay, Jayden goes.

– Aye, Shiv goes, openin the door.

– Aye a bit ay sun, sand n sea, ay, Jayden goes.

– Mibbe, Shiv goes, n heads away hame.

So it's jist me n Jayden. – Now wi kin watch porn! Git us in the mood!

– Nah, yir awright.

That gits muh fuckin goat. – You nivir want tae fuckin dae it any mare!

– Yi'll git rode enough oan hoaliday, eh goes. – Ah jist like gittin gams.

Ah think aboot um gaun wi that skinny, cheeky hoor. – It's cause ye think ah'm too fat. Ye dinnae wank aboot me like ye dae they burds oanline.

– Different. That's jist a hobby.

– How's it fuckin different?

– How's it the same? They've goat different boadies.

– Like that Andrea's boady?

– Aw shut up aboot her, Jayden goes, aw stroppy. – You're obsessed wi hur! That wis a mistake, jist muckin aboot whin ah wis smashed. Meant nowt.

– Better no huv meant nowt, or ma Dessie'll batter your cunt in, Jayden! N if you've been seein hur again...

– Huv ah fuck!

– Huv ye fuck what?

– Been seein hur again.

– Been seein whae again?

– That Andrea.

– Ye'd better fuckin no be, Jayden! Ah'm no fuckin well jokun!

– Ah sais ah wisnae. Right? Eh goes, stickin oot ehs jaw that wey.

– Ah telt ye, ah fuckin stoaped hur grassin ye up tae the polis! C'moan! It's you n me gaun tae Ibiza!

So wi pits the porn fae the laptoap through the big telly screen. Jayden taught ays how tae dae that, eh is tech-savvy. Wi watches they two skinny burds takin it in turn tae gam a laddie wi a big cock. He's gapin at it, aw his attention oan the screen, no even touchin ays but, n no even sittin close. Ah thrusts oot muh tits. – Well, thir's plenty fellys thit like ma boady!

Jayden's heid whips roond. – Whit's that meant tae mean?

– Nowt, jist sayin.

– It means you gied yir hole tae some other cunt! Whae!

N ah gits aw cocky cause eh's jealous! – Nivir you mind, ah goes.

Eh turns away back tae the screen. Ah kin only see the side ay ehs face in the light fae it.

So wir sittin watchin this wee Chinky burd gittin rode up the erse by a big black felly. It looks well sare. Ah goes, sortay half jokin, – Ah think you want a threesome wi me n Shiv.

But eh jist laughs n goes, – That'll be the fuckin day!

JAYDEN (7)

Alone with Lita, Jayden is concerned that, as a reward for booking the Ibiza flights, she would expect sex with him. He is elated to get a text message from Andrea, who explains her phone had been mislaid but she'd been able to recover it. Did he fancy coming over?

Lita, scrutinising him, must have seen his face light up. She asked him who it was, and he manages to explain it is Joshy Boy Three, who was after some ching. It would be great to get money for Ibiza. He makes his excuses to Lita citing business opportunities and screen exhaustion from playing too many computer games, and departs.

Outside, he skips down the pavement full of joyful anticipation, towards Andrea's house.

Hud tae fuckin pish masel whin that fat cunt goes: *ah think you want a threesome wi me n Shiv.* Felt like tellin ur thair n then: it wis a threesome ah wanted, aye, *but wi Shiv n Andrea, no you, ya fat cunt!* But ninety-three grand, ay. Ah think mare aboot what Glen sais n if that mingin auld cunt wants hur eh kin fuckin well huv ur! Ah'll ride Andrea n mibbe Shiv n aw, if she didnae seem like a space cadet pushin that spazzy bairn aroond in yon go-cart.

But fuckin Ibiza! Cannae wait. Ah texts Unkul Glen:

Fancy Ibiza next week?
Big chance tae bang fatso.

Well ah thoat ah'll act the fuckin choirboy cause the fat cunt played right intae muh hands! Lit her pey fir the hoaliday, git hur tae pit some money intae muh account, then Glen rides hur so ah'm heartbroken n brek the news: *yir a fat hoor, n wir finished.* Tell hur ah've goat Andrea up the duff n then shag ivray burd ah kin git muh hands oan, foreign birds n aw! That'll seeken her pus! Hi! Hi! Hi! Git a Barcelona strip n pill the Spanish lassies. Or mibbe a Swedish blonde, they'll be barry rides, fuckin deffo!

Whin ah gits roond tae Andrea's she lits ays in, but this auld cunt, her dad, is standin there, airms folded. She tells um wir jist gaun up the stairs tae play music. Coupon oan this cunt, ye widnae believe it! Anywey, wi gits upstairs, but we cannae dae nowt cause she thoat they wir gaun oot, her ma n faither, but they changed thir minds.

Ah tell hur aboot Ibiza, n she's aw narky aboot it. – Thoat ye didnae want tae go wi a fat cunt!

– Ah dinnae, but she's the yin wi the poppy, but ay, n ah dinnae mention the Lotto dosh, no wantin another snout in the trough!

– Ah've goat money, ah'm comin n aw!

Well, ah'm thinkin, that would be barry! Ah kin really rub Lita's face in it then! Make dirty auld Glen's joab easier! Lita cannae stoap Andrea fae comin, no if she's peyin her ain wey! – Barry, ah goes.

– Bet she talks aboot me aw the time.

– Aye, ah goes, – she does, then Andrea n ah baith say at the same time, – Livin rent free in her heid!

That's the burd ah should be ridin! N once wi git tae Ibiza n Glen n me clean oot fatso, ah fuckin well will! Hi hi hi!

UNCLE GLEN (3)

Penny Holmes, rocking a glittering green dress, leans in a relaxed pose on the cocktail bar of the Hotel Viva. Glen Urquhart sidles up to her and, with a saucy wink, asks, – If ah said ye had a beautiful body would you hold it against me?

A measured stare greets him. – Who was it that sung that again?

– The Bellamy Brothers, Glen grins expansively. – So... what brings you tae this salubrious watering hole?

Her look sweeps over him in steady evaluation. Decides he's no good. Then resolves that no good is exactly what she needs right now, or she wouldn't be in this bar. – Well, I've been a wee bit down since I split up with my boyfriend. Thought I'd come out to cheer myself up.

– Well, your boyfriend is crazy, letting a woman like you slip through his fingers. That's a mistake he's absolutely guaranteed tae look back on wi a crippling sense ay regret.

Her smile, welcoming but with a harsh focus, tells Glen he is in. Moments later, when picking up the keys from Cuthbert Farquarson at reception, he reflects with satisfaction that he didn't even need to buy her a drink.

Wi the seduction ay the fair sex it's ey best tae stick tae the same tried-and-trusted methods, whether it's a wee fat dame fae the scheme or a mare sophisticated Hertfordshire filly. The traditional mix: decent shirt, no jeans, CK eftirshave. Ah love that stuff. Reminds they wee hairies ay thir faithers thit wir nivir thair. Cannae go wrong. Wi lassies that get past forty, thir aw confident ay thir place in the world and ken what they want. They've done the kids thing, or no done it, and are happy wi that or made peace wi it. Point is, it's no longer jist oestrogen driving them, they're charting their ain course. Like us wi testosterone. It goes doon tae a certain level whaire yir no tethered tae this drugged-up, serial-shagging bam any mare. Ye git tae make decisions oan behalf ay yir cock rather thin the other wey aroond.

This Penny lassie has a sleek, gym-hewn body, so bizarre tae think ay it compared tae wee Lita's, that teen rendered a shapeless, blobby mess by McDonald's. Lita might huv a decent mooth on her for one so young – plenty practice puttin things in it – but Penny's goat the goods. Course, it's pointless tae even talk aboot how much better in bed most lassies over forty are: it's another world. Ah'm sure it's the same for men, but ah'll take some other cunt's word for that!

Nae drama whatsoever in the morning, when, eftir a coffee n porridge brekie doonstairs (the Viva does barry Ipswich and Norwich), Penny departs. Numbers exchanged, nae fuss, leavin ays ruminating oan life. The couch at Manda's isnae that uncomfortable if ah kin get oaf intae the land ay nod reasonably early, and it's bearable if ah kin kip a couple ay nights a week here buckshee.

That wee fat yin hus the ninety grand plus in her purse. It willnae be thair for long wi the McCallums comin oot the woodwork ready tae pounce. Ah text Jayden tae try tae impress oan him how time-sensitive this project is. Love that kid, but eh's as dumb as a sack ay pebbles offay Silverknowes Beach. Lyin around in yir kip n playin video games aw day enriched nae cunt but the manufacturer ay that shite.

On Penny's departure ah switch oan the Nokia tae check muh texts. Then, fair play tae the daft nephew, Jayden's texted ays back wi the news ay an Ibiza jaunt. *At first ah shite it: if that clown Jayden goes oot thair wi her on his tod, he'll fuck it right up.* But the serendipitous fates are wi us: as it happens, when ah get intae my tablet ah've another email fae Nige Blakely in the Double H:

To: glenbraveheart@gmail.com
From: n.blakeley@hotmail.co.uk
Re: Double H Bulletin

Well Glen, the news that's fit to print from the Double H is pretty uninspiring. The Council are still – can you believe it – fannying about with my building permit. Old Misery Guts Stan George, you know, the copper that's retiring from the Met, complained about the roast on Sunday at the Harvesters. Poor Maureen in the kitchen wasn't exactly best pleased. But in the news that's unfit to print, you'll never guess who's been knocking her off? None other than our old mate Terry Jackson! They were spotted having lunch and canoodling at The Three Horseshoes, then on the towpath! I heard they met up at Finlays, had a bop and a bit of a snog and then went onto Redz and danced the evening away with the young guns! The only judgement you'll get from yours truly is that both parties very much needed to get their respective ends away! Hemel Hempstead is missing you in that department. And that brings me nicely to more potentially nefarious news, namely that Lauren Brady was asking after you. The bombshell is that she's split with Mick Carter, moved out into a flat and the house is on the market. Offers over nine hundred and fifty K. Bit naughty to try hauling in a cool mill from that shitheap, but location, location etc. When your name cropped up there was a certain longing in her voice and little spark in her eyes. Get yourself down here saaaahhhhhnnn!

Best

Nige

Lauren Brady... now there's lum ah would not mind giein a wee sweep. Bit of a Corbynista as well. Of course, we were not in the majority in the Harvesters, but all ah kin say is *2017 manifesto* and rest ma case! Ah'm thinkin about her seduction and how, wi this quality ay minge, ah'll need tae move in there sharpish, n wonderin how much ay the equity on that million-quid gaff is hers...

So ah'm right on the phone tae Nige, that stalwart ay the Harvesters pub-quiz team, and I'm tellin um that ah need the keys for his holiday villa in Ibiza next week. – No problem, mate, eh goes, – I was thinking we could all go, with Big Chris and some of lads from the Harvesters, but hey ho...

– Sorry, Nige, but ah'm scenting commercial opportunity here. Another time for a lads' trip.

– Alright mate, but when you do get to the villa, remember the bedroom that doesn't have the ensuite? We were discussing that it might be possible to knock out that cupboard and put a toilet and a small shower in there?

– Aye. Want ays tae have a look, take some measurements?

– Great. I'm going to text you the number of the box the keys are in.

So after giein muh hands a good moisturising, ah'm off the phone and oot the Viva, tippin Cuthbert oan reception a wee nod. Ah jumps in the van and heads doon tae the scheme. Just in the hoose when my sister comes in. Straight away she's swallayin some pills with a gless ay rid wine, Tesco's selection.

Ah text Jayden telling him ah've sorted oot accommodation in a big villa and get him tae tell Lita no tae book anything, as there's plenty room.

– What you up tae? Manda asks, slumping down in front of the telly.

– Ah'm off to Ibiza next week. Fat Lita's booked up; obviously usin some ay that money tae take Jayden and her pal Shiv and his mate. Best place tae make a move, away fae here n they McCallums. Fancy coming? Ah've goat decent accommodation through my mate down south.

– Ibeefa! No way! Git oan a plane, wi ma nerves? You tryin tae kill ays? Wi aw that covid? N hingin oot wi that fat hoor? Nae chance, ah'd nivir be able tae bite muh tongue. Besides, ma ravin days ur ower. Yours n aw!

– Ma ravin days'll nivur be ower! N ye kin relax thair withoot tearin it up, ah goes thinkin, well, *she kin.* – The sun'll dae ye good. Natchril vitamin C and D.

– Nuht, n it'll no dae Jayden any guid, hingin oot wi a fat mess, that's fur sure. Eh should be workin! Wi you!

– That's the mission, Manda, ah remind hur, – tae get those McCallum Lotto riches.

– Well, good luck wi that, muh sis declares, – but ah cannae be publicly associatit wi this. Ah'm no wantin the McCallums at this door, no wi ma nerves, n Manda's hands shake as she sparks up another snout. – N they cheap money-makin scams ur aw good n well, but ma Jayden needs a propur joab, git um away fae that crowd!

– Look, Manda, it would be the easiest thing in the world tae say ah'll gie muh nephew a start as an apprentice plumber...

Her cheeks buckle inwards as she inhales. – Dae it well!

– … but ah huv tae ask masel, as a businessman, is Jayden really apprentice material? It takes dedication, initiative, timekeeping and people skills, particularly in the realm ay manners. Has he goat them? Cause ah'm no seein them, Manda. Ah'm no seein them at aw.

– Ooir Jayden's goat skulls, ma sis declares, then struggling tae think ay any, snaps in muh pus, – What's manners goat tae dae wi anything?

– Jesus Christ, Manda! We go into people's hooses! In the New Toon! Dae ye think they're gaunny be impressed by an open-moothed, droolin, slack-jawed, drug-twitchin, mingin wee mess in a baseball cap and knock-off Stone Island gaun *whaaa… n ah wis telt tae come here* oot ay his goldfish gob when some posh auld fustoid asks him if he wants a cup ay tea n piece ay shortbried? It'll no play, Manda.

– So that's ma fault? Yir sayin ah nivir broat him up right?

– I'm saying *exactly that*, Manda, ah tell her, watchin her jaw hit the flair, – but it's no just your parentin deficiency…

– What?

– … check those desolate streets, ah points ootside. – Class inequalities, late capitalism and the changing technostructure have goat tae take their share ay the blame n aw. Trainin the laddie tae huv manners when there's nae employ might seem an exercise in futility, ah concede, before ah hammer in that home truth, – but aye, nae question at aw that the motherhood baw was decidedly droaped, Manda. Ah observed that at close quarters wi my ain eyes.

– It's no easy wi teenagers, you ken that!

– Meaning, Manda?

– Your Roxy! Spent aw yir time pillin laddies oaffay hur!

A fuckin low blow if ever their wis yin. – That's no fair, Manda! Aye, Roxanne exhibited behavioural issues when Lucinda and ah split up. For sure, the lassie took it badly n acted oot, ah'm no saying she didnae.

– That stuck-up hing-oot Lucinda!

– Whatever you think aboot her, and ah dinnae think a whole lot masel eftir her fucking cairy-oan wi that Raith Rovers bastard, she wis a good mother!

– N ah'm no?

– Like ah sais, ye sustained an early rid card in that key position, leavin team Templeton two short eftir the earlier dismissal ay hubby Gary. No exactly Alex Ferguson selection skills thair oan your part, Manda, ah expands, watchin her register this through her fog ay the meds, addin, – it hus tae be said.

Manda glimpses at the framed picture of Jayden on the sideboard. Her lip curls down and her eyes water. – Mibbe uv no been the best ma, but ah'm no a well wummin, she points tae they jack n jills oan the table, – ... so what kin ah dae?

Ah turns the picture tae the waw. Picks up the one ay Jarred, hands it tae her. – Forget Jayden, ah point at the back ay his frame. – The laddie's a no-hoper, a street-ruined drug-dealer. Only death or prison awaits him. It's now aw aboot Project Jarred, n ah taps the gless on the picture in her hands. – Still time tae get this boy intae shape. You work on the Ps n Qs n the bedside manner n ah'll get him involved in the industry; take him oot, show him the ropes.

A mercenary glint in muh wee sister's eye. – Will Jarred git peyed?

– Yes, *paid in experience*! He'll be learning the rudiments ay the trade! This will gie him a competitive advantage ower the likes ay Jayden n the rest ay them roond here, *if* eh seizes the opportunity and applies ehsel!

– Bit you're saying tae treat Jarred n Jayden different... ah thoat youse socialists believed that we wir aw the same!

– That's a fuckin Tory myth perpetuated constantly in their media tae undermine progress tae a just n fair society, Manda. We recognise the differences in people, but the fundamental truth is that we aw contribute and should aw share in the rewards.

– Aye, but no Jayden!

– Jayden n aw, but that's doon tae him and how much he chooses tae contribute. He's moving intae manhood, Manda, and it's gaunny be a rocky ride due tae aw the bad choices he's made. Jarred kin still make different choices.

Ah leave hur thinkin aboot that yin.

Ah ey tried wi my wee sis, for example, tae get her tae take an interest in Burns, but alas, no go. Dinnae embark oan doomed quests, play tae their strengths: Jayden is a hustler n we need tae get that McCallum blimp's money! The arbitrary crumbs-oaf-the-rich-cunts'-

table distribution mechanism ay late capitalism pit this in the hands ay the wrong representatives ay the proletariat, n it needs liberated fae they false-consciousness cretins. – As Burns sais, *Yet I, a coin-denied wight, by fortune quite discarded, ye see how I am, day and night, by lad and lass blackguarded.*

– What's that? Mare ay that daft Burns shite!

Doomed quests. Case rested. Nae point even responding.

N ah need tae text Lauren Brady doon in the Double H wi a wee note ay interest. Ah'm thinking ay they formidable breasts, especially in that tight lime-green toap she sported at the Harvesters Christmas bash, the one before lockdoon two. Decent handfays, firm enough looking tae suggest a plastic surgeon's attentions, which ah dinnae mind at aw. Women who make an effort are to be commended in this day and age. A Corbynista wi curves and killer pout… wasted on some Brexiteer fool wi an abundance ay lower-belly fat whae looks visibly intimidated whenever the convo moves beyond the realms ay Murdoch-manufactured soundbites. Waaay too much woman for Mick Carter, but perhaps just right for Glen Urquhart!

Ah leaves Manda n heads upstairs fir an Eartha Kitt, tae gie ehs peace in muh composition tae sexy Lauren. They exciting prospects ur stirrin ma inner workings aw weys as ah whip doon ma keks n sit oan the pan. Ah cook up n fire oaf a *cheeky wee* text:

Hey Lauren, so sorry to hear about you and Mick. Bad news travels fast. Obviously, I'm no stranger to heartbreak myself, so if you fancy a wee moan about the precarious state of modern romance, I'm your boy. I'm back down in the Double H soon, and it would nice to hook up for a coffee. Keep the red flag flying high! x

Ah'm sittin oan the crapper trying tae tease oot an unbroken one, when a text pops back in:

Hi Glen, yes, never easy. Brexit, Boris, Covid, lockdown and now this. It was being banged up together that made me realise we had absolutely nothing in common! Big YES to hooking up for that chat! Hope you're repairing nicely north of the border and avoiding all the usual HH dramas! Love, Lauren xxx

Bingo! Ah feel the weighty broon bairn drop in for its baptism, sploshing up some pish-water to help clean my hole, no that it even needs it wi that smooth birth! Game on wi LB fae the Double H!

Ah wipe ma erse n look at what ah've left in the pan. Beautful! Dinnae ken whether tae flush the bastard away or send him tae college!

LITA (9)

Lita had spent a sleepless night concerned about her new wealth and how to keep it concealed from predators; her brothers and her absentee parents mainly, but there was also the enemy within. Jayden was certainly chuffed with the prospect of the Ibiza jaunt, but he'd wanted to know where the money came from. She told him it was a settlement from the bakery, to drop her claim of unfair dismissal. It seemed to satisfy him for now. Then there was Shiv, who pointedly mentioned a medical procedure in Holland that would correct a birth defect in Beyonce's feet.

Lita rose, checked her online banking: 13,700.12 exactly, her existing 18.12 pounds supplemented by a deposit of 13,682. She could not stop staring at the screen. Resolving to treat herself to a full Scottish breakfast at one of the city's grandest hotels, far superior to Glen's shabby bordello, the Hotel Viva, she took a taxi into town.

The full Scottish is basically the same as the full English, omitting hash browns and substituting the worthier potato scone. It also features the subliminal square Lorne sausage and is generally replete with a healthy slice of black pudding and sometimes includes white pudding and/or haggis. In short, anything the full English offers in terms of heart disease, the full Scottish effortlessly trumps.

The hovering waiter, indulgently strained smile, stands by Lita as she studies the menu. – Ah ken that Lorne sausage comes fae Leith cause ay Lorne Street, but does link sausage n aw? Like named eftir the links?

– I do not think so, the waiter replies in what Lita registers as an Italian accent, – but I will ask.

Well ah jist asked that waitur boy, n eh goes back ben the kitchun n the fuckin chef only comes oot! Eh explains tae ays that naw, it's nowt tae dae wi Leith! It wis nice ay the waiter felly tae ask um, though. Barry scran, n they kept askin ays if ah wanted mare toast n coffee, the answer tae that bein aye! Ah gies thum baith a *cheeky wee smile* whin ah leaves, n gits yin back, n ah'm thinkin, ah'm coming back here wi Shiv fir a cocktail! Bet that waitur felly kens a few ay thaim! No sayin ah wid, but ah'm no sayin ah widnae!

Mibbe it's cause ah wis peyin for the hoaliday oat ay that Lotto win, but whin ah gits back tae mine Jayden comes roond, n eh's in a barry mood! N eh tells ays that Glen sais *he's* comin n aw, n thit *he'll* sort oot the accommodation! A swanky villa fae one ay his pals doon in Camel Humpstead or whatever the fuck they caw it! So Jayden bettur behave ehsel or it'll be ehs unkul thit ah'll be makin music wi in Ibiza! Eh'll pick up the chemustray between me n Glen, n that'll pit um oan ehs taes! N eh kin git fucked if eh thinks eh's gittin *ma* money. Ibiza's ehs loat! The rest is gaun oan me jist: gittin muh stomach stapled up n the skin stitched aw tight. Now ah've goat muh results n the doaktur felly said come tae thuh clunic n wu'll talk aboot it.

So ah meets Shiv, n wi gits one ay they trams back tae Murrayfield tae see the boy.

Like ah'd sais tae Shiv, that boy's a handsome felly, like a boy that used tae be a ride but goat auld, but managed tae stey *a bit ay a ride*.

Then the boy comes oot, n even if eh is a bit silver-fox auld, ah kin tell Shiv wid dae um n aw, n wi hus a wee giggle. – Ms Lita McCallum, eh goes, lookin at an iPad.

– Aye, ah goes. – Here tae git rid ay the fat, n ah grabs a handfay tae show um.

– Well, this is the certainly correct place for the procedure you require!

– Aye, ah goes. – So, when kin ah git this aw done? Ah'm booked oan hoaliday next week n want tae git intae a proper bikini.

Eh gies ays one ay they looks: yin whaire ehs brows ur gaun up. – The results... well, they were disappointing in some areas... but there is encouragement, too...

– What wis the best bits?

– Well frankly, Ms McCallum, the most hopeful aspect is that you are very young. Your skin is still tensile, you can lose weight and it should snap back. The downside is that you are morbidly obese, terribly so for your years, and are heading for type 2 diabetes and heart disease. Do you want to avoid these?

– Aye, course, bit muh main goal is tae git intae a bikini fur Ibiza next week, ah goes, thinkin ay Jayden n they yellay trunks ay wore at Portybelly beach last summur. Looked a ride.

– Well, eh goes, n gies ays a funny look n hands ower a sheet.

– What's this, bit?

– This is your diet sheet.

– Bit... ah goes, n ah kin feel muh mooth hingin open like a daftie, – ah thoat youse wir gaunny dae aw that. Ah wis telt tae come here, n ah looks at Shiv. – Ay, Shiv?

– Aye, Shiv goes, – we wir telt tae come here.

– I don't think you quite understand, eh goes. – You're morbidly obese. There is no quick fix. You really have to lose some weight. If you don't, you'll develop serious health problems. And shedding it will increase your chances of conceiving a child with your partner.

– It's him youse should be talkin tae! Eh kin barely git it up! Wankin off tae porn, fill ay Viagra n crack!

– Yes, well, excessive consumption of online pornography has been clinically proven to desensitise young men and make it more difficult for them to perform sexually with their partners.

– In this clunic, like?

– Sorry?

– Did ye dae tests oan thum in this clunic? Oan laddies?

– No, no, but it's commonly established that erectile dysfunction is enabled by excess watching of pornography.

– Tell ays aboot it! But ma Jayden'll no take a warnin. His idea ay a good night is takin puhls n jerkin ehsel oaf ower porn oanline!

He looks at ays like ah'm a dafty.

Ah'm fuckin ragin, but ah'm keepin it aw inside. Then ah goes, – Bit how? Ah mean... ah thoat... n ah grips muh stomach, hatin it, hatin this fuckin fat thit jist keeps gaun oan... – ah thoat youse wir meant tae take it aw away!

– I don't think you quite understand the process, eh goes. – I can see that you're very upset.

– Course ah'm upset! Ah wis telt youse could git rid ay muh fat!

– This is a dangerous procedure carried out under general anaesthetic. It stands a higher chance of success if you lose weight. You have to show willpower and motivation. You need to meet us part of the way and demonstrate you're a suitable candidate for this surgery.

– But ah've gaun private, ah'm peyin fir it! This isnae like oan the NHS; ah've goat the money, if that's aw yir bothered aboot! Ah turns tae Shiv. – Ay?

– She hus. She won the Lotto, Shiv tells the boy.

– Yes, but we need to consider the medical and psychological ramifications, not just the financial ones.

– Aw, ah goes. They ey try n trick ye wi wurds at they places!

N the boy tells ays tae come back in four weeks, n eh'll weigh ays again oan they scales.

Ibiza next week...

Ah'm in fuckin shock. Aw ah kin dae is git oot ay thair, clutchin this daft wee sheet eh went n gied ays. – N ah dinnae agree wi they scales, ah tells Shiv on the wey oot, – cause ah've goat better scales ben the hoose!

So wir walkin for a bit n comin tae Gorgie Road n passin that McDonald's, so ah goes tae Shiv, – Ah'm fuckin well starvin, hud nowt tae eat this morning cause ah kent ah wis gaun in n gittin weighed.

Ah didnae tell her aboot the fill Skoatish. Dinnae want her sayin nowt tae Jayden.

– Aye, but, Lita, Shiv goes, – that doaktir boy sais nae McDonald's n tae stick tae the sheet.

– Ah'm pure ragin aboot that, ah goes, hudin up yon sheet. – What sortay fuckin shite is this?

Shiv jist looks at ays through that fuckin annoyin flap ay hair.

– Ah kin start oan aw this stuff the morn, eftir ah dae a shop tae git the right stuff in. Right now, ah'm fuckin gaun tae McDonald's!

So eftir two Big Macs bit jist one chips fir me n one for Shiv (she's fuckin turnin anarexik), we gits back tae the scheme n ah goes up tae the Paki's n shows that Ranjeet the sheet. – Gies an avocado, ah goes.

– Nane, eh sais, – bit wuv goat cucumber n lettuce n tomatay.

Same auld rotten stuff, but ah buys it. – Goat any ay that rice?

– Wir a Paki's, Ranjeet goes, – course wuv goat fuckin rice, n eh hands ays a packet.

– Meant tae be broon, but.

– Broon rice? Seen broon skag roond here but nivir broon rice.

– Well that's what ah goat telt tae git oan this sheet, n ah shows um, but eh jist shrugs.

Ah cannae believe this, so ah walks oot the shoap! Jist as well ah've goat enough oan muh phone tae call the boy at the fat clunic oan the number eh gied ays. Eh comes oan n tells ays thit ah need tae go tae a differunt shoap that's nearly right back up the toon! A posh shop whaire they huv aw that stuff: Real Foods ay Broughton Street. So, ah jumps oan the bus n gits back up the toon. Well, no right up the toon, bit the bit ye git tae before ye git right up the toon.

It smells barry, but no like a real food shoap. Then ah sees aw this weird stuff n here. Ye couldnae eat thon! Nivir saw half ay it n muh life! Probably aw stuff that Pakis n Chinkies n posh cunts eat. The next thing is it's awfay dear. This laddie wi glesses n a beard, a sortay student-lookin laddie, asks ays if eh kin help ays. – Ah wis telt tae come here, ay, ah hands um the sheet.

– Oh… you're looking for all the stuff on this list?

– Aye, ah've goat tae start eatin duffrunt right away, that's what the doaktir felly sais anywey.

– Right… we'll have all this…

N tae be fair tae the felly, he shows us whaire it aw is. So, ah comes oot ay thair wi two bags fill ay it aw. Jist as well ah won that fuckin lottery: only wey ah could afford this shite! Ah'm tempted tae git a taxi, but thir's a bus comin so ah gits oan it.

Whin ah gits back ah goes oan *Dispersal, Deterrence And Damage*, ah gits 64,563, which is barry, but ah'll nivir beat ma highest score. Ah talks tae that Jillian Corbert oan Facebook n she goes, 'aye maist people will nivir beat that'. Nivir telt anybody aboot muh 93,751, but! Keepin that yin back!

Then ah'm nosin aboot n ah sees *hur* post:

AR 4 JT IRL

Fuckin dirty hoor! *Andrea Raeburn fur Jayden Tempultun In Real Life!* She kin git tae fuck! In hur fuckin dreams! Whin ah git Jayden oot thair in Ibiza next week, he'll be beggin fir it! That Unkul Glen n aw!

MANDA (1)

The hostelry lies in a former village just outside the scheme, close to an arterial road that connects the airport to the docks. Though long absorbed by the city, at certain times, like on this very hot day, it retains an almost rustic feel. Locals from the nearby old council developments enjoy the walk across the stone bridge to sample the delights of the pub beer garden.

Glen nods at two men, one with ginger hair. Doesn't know them, but they evidently know him. *Still a face in this toon,* he reflects, putting moisturising cream into his hands. He's taken Manda to lunch, and she tucks into prawn cocktail, followed by steak, mushrooms and chips and Black Forest gateau – one of the few places still offering this traditional dessert. They enjoy a long conversation about family, life, love and health. After three large gin and tonics they depart, Glen taking a taxi to the Hotel Viva, while Manda walks back into the scheme.

In contrast to the vibrant, almost festive atmosphere in the village, Manda finds the scheme completely dead. No children play in its streets, like she recalls from her youth, and she barely sees another soul on her journey. By the time she opens her front door, her head and heart are heavy, and something trembles up her spine like a scurrying rodent. Dismayed, she makes a cup of tea and sits down. Almost jumps out of her skin as her oldest son Jayden noisily enters.

Ah dinnae ken what tae dae wi that laddie. Wis only the other week when ah caught um breakin doon in tears. N that's no something ye want tae see, no in a young felly. Tried tae hide thit eh wis greetin. Too ashamed. Widnae talk aboot it.

Still goat a face oan um. – What's wrong wi you? ah goes.

Eh jist looks at ays n goes, – Is oor Jarred upstairs?

– Nuht.

– Is Uncle Glen no due back?

– Nuht, eh's away intae toon. That hotel bar eh knocks aboot. Jist left um.

– Ah need tae talk tae sumday, eh goes, slumpin doon oan the couch.

– What is it?

Then eh starts tae tell ays thit sometimes eh cannae git hard, like doonstairs, whin eh's wey a lassie! Fuckin sixteen-year-auld! Nivir happened tae laddies whin ah wis that age! Wish it hud happened tae ehs fuckin faither, tell yis that fir nowt! That wid huv solved a few problems! Aye, wid it no, but. Then ah thinks aboot that fuckin Lita eh's winchin. Maist lassies wurnae blimps in ma day: that must make a hoor ay a difference. – Well, Jayden, that fat Lita, what the fuck ur ye daein wi that mingin hing-oot… whit warm-bloodied young laddie could git a stiffer kennin eh's only gaunny be stickin it intae a tub ay lard?

Eh gies that daft wee pout, the yin eh's hud since eh wis a bairn, – Ah ken you dinnae like her…

It pits ays in mind ay his faither. But ah cannae even think aboot that cunt. Hud nae nerves till he gied ays thum: good riddance tae bad rubbish. – Jayden, it's no a question ay me no likin her, ah shake muh heid, – she's a dirty fat hoor n the whole fucken world kens that. That's no up for fucken grabs in the conversation …

– Bit you dinnae ken what shi's –

Ah waves muh hand, cutting um oaf. – Yir muthur's talkin! Ah ken we've hud oor ups n doons, but yir still muh laddie n ah dinnae want tae see ye squander the opportunities yuv goat in life!

– What opportunities? What huv ah goat in life? Whit opportunities ur thur here, fir the likes ay me?

Fair enough: thir's fuckin nowt. Husnae been fir years n willnae be ivir again. Bit ye cannae tell him that. Ye huv tae gie hope even whin ye ken thir's really nane, but ay. – Yir a fine-lookin young laddie, wi a guid heid oan yir shoodirs, no thit ye always yaze it –

– Bit –

– Bit that's no the point. Point is yi'll nivir git a chance tae yaze it wi that fat hoor draggin ye doon. Look at ye, yir getting a beer pot oan ye –

– Aw muh mates uv –

– N that's what she wants! Tae drag ye doon tae her fuckin levul! Ah've seen it happen! Dinnae lit ur dae it, Jayden, n ah points at um, – cause if ye dae yuv only goat yirsel tae fuckin well blame!

Eh says nowt aboot that, but ah kin tell it gits um thinkin. Eh gies ays a slow nod.

– This other yin lassie ye like, the Ibiza yin, she's no another fuckin fatty, is she?

– Nuht, she goat a barry boady. Like a modul's. Mind, she wis the yin fae the community centur?

Right, aye, eh did say. A step up; no thit that's sayin much. Rose West wid be a step up fae that fat cunt. – Bet ye nivir hud any problums wi her! Doonstairs, like.

– Nuht... but ah kin dae it wi Lita wi the puhls n crystal.

– Well, ah dinnae hud wi drug-takin. Ye ken ma views oan that. Anywey, ah goes as ah sees ehs eyes lookin tae muh puhl cupboard, – What's the big take-hame fae that? That's the sortay lassie ye should be pumpin, no a fuckin bouncy castle, Jayden, ah goes, n that grin oan his face thit minds ays ay muh ain faither; a guid man before the peeve rotted ehs brain. – Well make sure ye git the gither wi her in Ibiza, eftir ye clean that fat cunt oot furst! Yi'll feel mare ay a real man wi a proper lassie by yir side, instead ay a fuckin zeppelin!

– Right... eh's goat a text n eh's aw distracted again, n thair eh goes, oot the hoose withoot a wurd ay fuckin thanks!

Ma Jayden's slow sometimes, but eh's no fuckin daft. Dinnae care what Glen says, eh should be giein that laddie a trade. Flesh n blood. Hus tae count for sumthin. N it's no likesay he's goat a son tae hand the business ower tae. That snobby wee drawer-droapin hoor doon in Leicester – or whairever it is – she willnae gie a fuck aboot plumbin.

But oor Glen kin be stubborn; it's never gaunny happen. Nowt's gaunny happen wi him, but. Even wi Jarred. N eh's right aboot me bein a crap ma.

Ah sees muh puhls oan the kitchen table.

Grabs thum.

Heads upstairs.

Fuck this life.

JAYDEN (8)

Jayden James Templeton and Andrea Yvonne Raeburn had enjoyed a night of virtual passion, in their respective bedrooms. He had only needed two Viagra and a few grams of coke and a long watch of his idol Stanley Stonker going through his stock porn routine; blow job, frig off, pussy lick, on top, from behind, her on top, reverse cowgirl, anal, wank cum shot on face and over tits. He managed to spunk over the phone on Andrea's small, pert breasts as he went through the gay former wrestler Stonker's threatening vocabulary. It had been her responses – begging, pleading, squealing – that had got him off. He can't wait till they get together to do this in real life. And the two of them had decided that this would take place in Ibiza, where Andrea would coincidentally find herself on the same flight. Lita would be raging and would fall into the arms of Uncle Glen. Once that happened, Jayden would be in his rights to end the relationship, and he and Andrea would consummate their violent, asphyxiating love affair under the Mediterranean sun.

Then Andrea has to break off the call promptly, explaining that she is being shouted on by first her ma, then her dad, to come downstairs for her tea.

Now Jayden itches to test her, and his own erection. As the protagonist said in Gasman 4: Essential Maintenance …

… we gotta push onto new frontiers, bitch.

Ah cleans up muh phone n gits back oan the video. Ah could ride that Andrea withoot any drugs, ah'm bettin. It's that fat Lita that gied ays the reptile dysfunction, that's fir sure. Andrea'll sort ays right oot. Ah watches Gasman throttling this bird, then ah goes n FTs hur again. She's back in hur room. – What did ye git fir yir tea? ah goes.

– Fish fingers.

– Ah'll git thaim when ah see ye!

– Ah cannae wait. If that's what yir like oan the phone, ah cannae wait till we dae it in real life.

– It'll be barry. You'll git done Stonker style. N Gasman style n aw.

She sais nowt tae that, but she's no sayin naw. Then shi goes, – Ah pure want tae tell that fat cunt aboot us, Jaygo.

Ah shites it a bit then goes, – Naw, wait till next week in Ibiza, like we sais! Wuv goat tae watch cause her brars'll tan us baith tae fuck. She'll batter ye n then they'll rape ye tae fuck n batter ye, thuv done that tae lassies before.

– Honest?

Thuv no, but they wid. That's the type they ur. – Aye, besides we want tae see her face when you show up in Ibiza. N muh Uncle Glen sorted ye oot a room, so thir's nowt she kin dae. Be barry tae see that fat cunt's pus!

– But thi'll no batter n rape ays *eftir* Ibiza?

– Nuht, cause wuv goat it aw planned, ah goes. – Glen's gaunny ride her, fat Lita, n that gies me the excuse tae pack her in. Thir's nowt she kin say tae hur brars eftir ma auld unkul's banged hur! Hi hi hi!

– Ah like the wey you think, she goes, – you're no like other laddies!

– Aye, ah goes, – like Joshy Boy Eight? Josh Rattigan?

– We went oot fir a bit last summer, me n Josh.

– Right, ah goes. At least she's no denyin it. But ah dinnae like that cunt, n ah dinnae like the idea ay him bein up ur. Least favourite ay aw the Joshs. Ah'll fuckin well batter that cunt's heid in.

– Tell ye one thing, but, thir's nae other laddies like you.

Wonder what the fuck hur n JB8 did in bed? Ah'll dae mare tae hur! – Ah ken, ah'm mare like a porn star, ah goes.

– Cannae wait, she sais.

– No long now, sexy, ah goes. N wi end the call. N ah feel it, ah'm hard again awready! A skinny burd whae's game for a batterin or a choking ull dae that tae ye. Ivray time! Hi hi hi!

Then ah sees muh wee brar messaging ays:

Ma took loads of pills is in hospital
now don't know what to do

Fuck!

LITA (10)

Lita was trying to stick to her new diet, but the food was proving inedible. She found herself devouring sweet pastries at Greggs. Then the sugar rush was so intense she was compelled to visit McDonald's for a Big Mac to get the taste out of her mouth. On her way home she passed the household of the Raeburns and grew incensed.

From the pavement she looked beyond the grass verge to the balcony with its garden furniture. Then somebody briefly appeared in the window and pointedly pulled the curtains shut. Lita seethed in burning humiliation, unable to make out who it was. Probably not Andrea, who would be at the hairdressers, but her stuck-up mother.

Turning and marching down the road, Lita bristled with anger. She hoped to run into someone she disliked, giving them a piece of her mind; anything to vent the blinding rage.

But the streets remained abandoned.

Ken whit ah want tae dae wi that fuckin Andrea cow wi her snotty ma n faither? The ginger bastard whae sits in that lounge bar? Fuckin well fling a fuckin petrul bomb through thir snobby double-glazed windae wi the daft balcony! That cunt wi ehs gairdin furnichur oan that spazzy wee *veranda*, as they caw it! Aye, eh turned tae Shiv in the street one time. Pointed at it n went: 'that symbolises pride', in ehs durty, noncey wee voice. Then eh looks at the McWhirters' next door, wi thir washing hinging oot tae dry oan thair balcony: 'that symbolises nae pride', the cunt sais, same paedo sound comin oot ay his mooth, like forced oot ay his sinuses through ching.

Fuckin dick. If yuv goat a hoose wi a balcony course yir gaunny dry yir washing oan it. It's no like it's fuckin Spain whaire yir meant tae sit oan a balcony eatin wee bits ay food n drinking nice wine. In Scotland yir meant tae dry washin oan a balcony. How else wid they pit a fuckin balcony thair in the first place?

Ah gits back hame n goes oan Facebook. Furst thing ah fuckin well sees is that Andrea wi the scabby mooth oanline gaun oan aboot *in real life*. Well in real life she's gittin her fuckin cunt smashed in! IRL.

So then thir's a chap oan the door. Ah goes doonstairs, n it's Jarred, Jayden's wee brar.

Ah goes, – What is it?

– Ah wis telt tae come here.

– Whae sais fur ye tae come here, likes?

– Jayden.

– Whit fur?

– Muh ma's in the hoaspital.

– Manda!?

– Aye. She took too many puhls. Hur stomach goat pumped oot.

– Well ah cannae… ah mean… ah wis nivir telt nowt… whaire's Jayden?

– Eh went oot.

– Whaire tae?

– Eh didnae say whaire eh wis gaun, eh jist sais tae come here.

– Aye, well, come oan in then.

N the wey ah sees it, it's mibbe thit Jayden's tryin tae gie ays a test tae see if ah kin look eftir a bairn, no thit ah'd call Jarred a bairn exactly, but ye ken whit ah mean.

So this Jarred, this wee brar, comes in, n ah sits um doon oan the couch. Ah goes, – Ye wantin a cup ay tea?

– Nuht. Goat any Coke?

– Jist Diet Coke, ah goes.

– Aw.

– Ye no wantin it?

– Dinnae ken. Dis it taste like real Coke?

– Nuht, bit it's nae calories.

– So?

– So ye dinnae pit oan weight.

Eh looks at ays. – Pittin oan weight gies a lassie barry tits, but.

– Aw aye, ah laughs.

– Like you. You've goat barry tits.

The fuckin nerve ay that! – Ah beg your pardon, Jarrit Tempultin! Ah'm yir brother's curlfren! What dae ye think Jayden wid say if eh heard you talkin like that?

Eh shuts up.

– What's up wi yir ma?

– She took aw they puhls again. Did it before, but ay. Tried tae slash her wrists n aw.

Eywis thoat that bitch was mentul. – Right... ah've goat tae be somewhaire. Make yirself it hame.

So ah gits the bus intae toon, no quite intae toon but the bit before the toon centre which ah dinnae count as really toon. Ah walks doon the narray bendin street n sees the Hotel Viva, which is barry. Best thing is thit Glen phoned, aw durty talk, n sais for Shiv no tae come n aw, jist him n me!

Thir's a boy oan the reception, the yin thit's goat that shaved heid. – Can ah help you? eh goes.

– Ah wis telt tae come here, tae see Glen Urkirt.

– Glen's up in room three one two. Take the lift tae the third flair.

– Awright, ah goes n heads ower tae the lift n pushes the button. Thir's two lassies git oot the lift: skinny, dirty hooker types, n talkin aw foreign. It's a shite lift, awfay cramped. Ah gits up tae the third n finds the door n raps oan it.

Glen answers, wearin a bathrobe sortay made oot ay the same material as towel. Ehs pittin stuff oan ehs hands, like a lotion. Eh's goat a big smile as ah go in. – That looks cumfay, ah tells um. Ah sees ehs jaikit hinging oan a peg. Ah reckon the scabby wee auld phone eh hus'll be oan silunt.

As eh goes tae the bathroom ah checks, n aye, ah'm right. Then eh comes oot wi another robe, identikul, fae the back ay the door. Hands it tae ays. – So what's aw this aboot Ibiza?

– Ah jist want that Jayden tae ken thit eh's goat a rival!

– Aw aye, eh grins.

– Aw aye. If he disnae come up wi the goods thair, then at least ah'll git plenty romance.

– Ah hope eh disnae, Glen smiles, pushin ays doon oantae the bed.

Ah decide thit ah'm gaunny wait till he pumps ays before tellin um thit the doaktirs have pumped puhls oot ehs sustur. Jayden cannae ken aboot aw this; he'd be heartbroken. But Glen's barry at shaggin.

– By the wey, ah goes eftir, – you should check yir phone. Ye ken yir sustur goat taken tae hoaspital, right?

– What the fuck… Glen goes, mooth hingin open.

JAYDEN (9)

It took Jayden, once he'd walked to the Western General Hospital,
some time to locate the four-person ward where Manda was domiciled.
There seemed to be confusion as to where his mother was being
treated. When he was finally steered to the right place, he found Manda
laying in bed with her eyes shut and her mouth open. It was as if she
was caught in freeze frame in the middle of a belligerent argument.
Jayden tries to work out if this is a good or bad indicator of her health.
They hadn't told him much on the desk.

A female nurse enters and, completely ignoring him, bends over to
tend to his mother. Jayden gratefully scrutinises the line of the young
woman's panties through the uniform. Thinks about Andrea, then
Pornhub and the film **Orgasm Hospital**, *where Stanley Stonker is cast*
as an overworked surgeon who has to fuck comatose young women
back to life and then also let rip on some nurses. Feels a satisfying bulge
in his trousers. Then, as his thoughts stray to the possibility of a doctor
coming in and reviving Manda in this way, Jayden experiences both
disappointment and relief as the erection crumbles.

But the very fact that it had existed at all is cause for elation.

See! Ah dinnae need nae doaktir fir reptile dysfunction! Ah jist need
a burd thit isnae like a fuckin tub ay marjurine. The wey a loat ay
wideos come up, straight-faced but wi a wee smile pushin acroas the
lips, n go: *Ye still wi the same burd then, Jaygo? What's hur name*
again?

That sortay shite whaire they kid oan thir aw innocent, but ye ken
thir rippin the pish oot ay ye behind yir fuckin back! Soon tae be a
thing ay the past! Ibiza!

Cunt thit wis rumoured tae huv rode Andrea, that Chaymbo, he's
fuckin good at spreadin that sortay shite. But now ah ken he's ridin

naebody! Fae the hoarse's mooth n aw! Now every cunt's gaunny ken aboot that mind-treatin wanker! N JB8 n aw!

Mind you, that's what ah'm daein wi this nurse's erse, hi hi hi! *Bitch needs Gasman's noose roond hur neck.* The lassie finishes wi the auld girl, changing ur drips. As shi goes ah'm now thinkin aboot that barry porn fulum ah saw oanline whaire the lassie nurse n the lassie doaktir huv this boy aw encased in plaster except fir ehs eye holes n ehs cock that's stickin oot. So they start snoggin each other n lickin each other oot n pittin oan a show, n aw ye kin see is the boy's cock growin n gittin harder. Then they take it turns tae wank the boy off, then tae impale thursels oan ehs cock, while thir still playin wi each other's tits n kissin n that. Wish ah could mind ay the title! Fuckin barry! Giein ays ideas for Ibiza!

Bit sittin here lookin at muh ma in that bed, ah dinnae ken whither or no it's right tae go tae Ibiza n leave hur her like that. – Ma… ah goes, bit sortay soft.

Ah cannae believe it whin she no only opens her eyes but starts tae puhl hersel up in the bed. – Jayden… muh buiful laddie…

– Ah thoat you wir in one ay they commas!

– Nuht. Ah wis jist asleep.

– Aw. How ye feelin?

– Shite… sorry tae worry ye, pal. It's they puhls… thi'll huv tae change thum, n she's reachin ower tae the locker tae git water. – A wee drink fir yir ma, son…

Ah gits up n fills the cup fae the jug n gies it tae her: muh good deed fir the day. – Ah want tae ken if ah should still go tae Ibiza n leave you here, Ma.

– Go, she wheezes, – but take Jarred!

– Ah cannae take that wee cun –

– Ye huv tae take… n shi stoaps n looks ower muh shoodur.

Uncul Glen's come in. Eh's goat a blue corduroy jaikit wi a fur-trimmed collur. It looks dear enough, but it's auld cunt's shite. Eh's slicked ehs hair back, like mibbe it's jist been washed. – Goat here as soon as ah heard! What the fuck –

– It's awright, Ma croaks, – jist forgoat how many puhls ah'd taken… need tae git one ay they boaxes thit tells ye… wi the days oan thum.

Glen looks at ays like *he* disnae believe it either. Eh's goat some floors, aw different types like they huv in Tesco, which he pits oan muh ma's locker. – Nurse is gaunny bring a vase in a bit, eh says, n looks at muh ma aw sad. – Kid Sis... what's the Hampden roar?

Ma's voice is aw thin n raspy. – Uh telt Jayden tae go tae Ibiza... you still huv tae go n aw... but yis need tae take Jarrit...

– No takin that snidey wee cunt, ah goes.

– Yes, Manda, that Glen jumps in, lookin at ays aw stroppy, like. – We would never leave the wee man oan his ain. Besides, Nige, my mate in the Double H – you mind ay Nigel – he wants me to size up that job oan his luxury villa, and it might gie ays a chance tae scope oot whether the wee felly hus a plumber's eye.

N the cunt gies me that sortay look that sais: *you'll nivir make a fuckin plumber, pal.*

So ah gies him a look back thit goes: *stick yir fuckin plumbin shite up yir erse! Wir thair for fat Lita's poppy!*

– Aye... muh ma gasps, grabbing at the bedclathes like Lindy Lush in *Advanced Friggers* oan Pornhub, like when she wis gittin monstered by Stanley Stonker then they cut tae hur hand grabbin the sheet... it wis kind ay barry, but ye wanted thum tae linger oan her gittin choke-rode. – But what aboot you, Ma?

She pills ays close tae me, soas she thinks Glen cannae hear. – Jist fuck up that fat McCallum hoor. Git rid ay her once n fir aw! Promise ays!

But Glen's neb's in, – He will, Manda.

– Aye, ah wull, Ma.

– Promise!

– Ah promise!

– We keep our promises, son, the Urquharts, Glen goes.

– Ah'm no an Urquhart, muh name's Templeton, ah tells um.

– Aye, son, n whaire's the Templetons now? Eh? Whaire huv they ever been? Glen points at ehsel n muh ma. – But the Urquharts ur here fir ye, like thuv ey been! Notice that? Funny that, ay?

What's eh wantin ays tae say? – Aye...

– Aye what? Glen sais.

– AYE, AH PROMISE!

– Promise what?

N ah thinks aboot ridin Andrea aw weys, n specially chokin the horny wee bitch till ur eyes pop, n ah shout, – THIT AH'LL GIT RID AY THAT FAT HOOR!

A wimmin in the next bed tuts, n Glen looks at her makin ehs mooth go *sorry* bit no sayin it loud. – Keep yir voice doon, pal, it's a hoaspital!

Then ah hears the wispy voice comin fae the bed. – That's muh laddie... proud ay ye, son...

When wi gits oot the hoaspital, ah looks acroas at that Telford Arms pub n sais tae Glen, – Fancy a beer?

– Love tae, pal, but business, eh, n eh huds up ehs phone. – A plumber nivir stoaps. An idle plumber isnae worth a sook; thir's ey work needs done. Dinnae git too wrecked this weekend, mind this flight Monday mornin, eh goes, n eh takes a hud ay muh airm. – Listen... ah've goat yir pal Jordan sorted oot wi a ticket.

– Jordan n aw, n muh ma wants Jarred tae come, ah goes. – How come ye did that?

– Think aboot it. Siobhan's thair. If she feels left oot n gits nippy, the fat yin might take the strop n want tae hing oot wi hur. If Jordan gits oaf wi hur, it takes that oot the equation n gies us peace tae git oan wi oor work.

– Right... ah goes. Ye huv tae hand it tae Glen, eh kin be a wide auld cunt but eh kens whit eh's daein! But eh's no the only yin, cause ah tells um, – Thir's another thing, but. Andrea's comin.

Glen looks at ays wi a wee sneer oan ehs lips. Then ehs eyes go aw wide. – If Andrea's thair, Lita'll be pissed oaf wi you...

– Drive ur right intae your airms...

– ... ah work muh magic, which ah make sure the world finds oot aboot...

– ... then ah git intae Andrea, while you git Lita's account details n clean her oot.

Glen's eyes whip ower tae the boozer. Eh punches muh arm softly. – Mibbe a quick yin.

LITA (11)

The weekend dragged, but finally Monday arrived, and the tram took Lita, Jayden and Shiv as well as the late additions to the team – Jordan and Jarred – out to the airport. Glen had made an arrangement to meet them there. Jordan was immersed in the passing cityscape, confessing in awed tones that he had never been on an Edinburgh tram before. – These are barry.

– They'll be doon oor bit one day, Lita observes.

– Aye, mibbe, Jayden remarks.

– They wull, Jayden, thir fuckin comin right doon tae the bottom road! It sais it oan the plans!

Jayden looks at his girlfriend in rough appraisal, eyes narrow, lips light. – You seen the plans, like?

– Nuht, bit everybody kens it.

– What they say n what they dae ur different things.

Lita lets out a long sigh, addressing the assembled company. – Sumtimes ye jist huv tae believe thit things ur gaunny work oot for the best.

A conductor appears and asks to check their tickets. – You have to wear a mask, he tells them. Shiv, Jarred and Jordan are already so clad, Lita reaches under her chin and pulls hers up onto her face. Jayden hesitates for a second, looks at the unwavering gaze of the conductor, before producing a limp, sweaty effort from his pocket, fastening it in surly concession.

– It's nae real hassle. No really, Lita contends.

Jayden considers this and looks at Lita. A sabotaging surge of admiration for her insinuates within him as a smile ignites under his mouth covering. He can't stop it seeping into his eyes and moistening them as she briefly manifests as the erupting, full-bosomed siren of the playground. The glow coming from him briefly seems to fill up the tram. When she was prized back at school, it was Jayden James Templeton she had chosen to sleep with, from amongst a veritable rogues' gallery of adolescent sex pests. He recalls the magic of waking up with her that first time. That was two years ago, now so long it almost felt like another life in another world. Yet what he is presently experiencing is something similar. He keeps his gaze on her as she looks outside, pointing out a store to Siobhan. Wonders what she is feeling.

Can he betray her? Then his focus narrows in cold brutality at the flesh on her face covering those once lacerating cheekbones.

Yes, he can.

Because, ultimately, Jayden believes that Lita has betrayed herself by putting on that fat suit.

Lita turns and catches his stare, forcing him to look away. Not before she feels Jayden's love, but then also senses something else; perhaps it might be treachery. She shuts her eyes and closes her thighs, thinking of Glen in order to blot out the face of his nephew. The older lover had an easy style the younger man, even in his lustier days of last year, could never match. Glen's surprisingly deft fingertips, which sat so unlikely on the end of those rough-looking plumber's hands, probably due to his constant application of lotion, how they strung her orgasms together like pearls on a necklace.

By the time the tram goes through the dreary abomination of Edinburgh Park and arrives at the airport, Lita eagerly anticipates the appearance of her new lover. Her boyfriend's Uncle Glen is the fourth man she has slept with. The bus driver and an insurance salesman complete the list: both hate-fucks from previous occasions when Jayden was believed to have strayed.

So wi gits tae the airport wi Jaydun, Jarrit n Shiv. Spotty Jordan came as well, but eh's no a bad felly n ah think eh boat ehs ain fare, so thir's nowt naebday kin say.

Wir jist waitin oan Glen, whae's drivin oot, eftir gittin up at six in the mornin for a burst-pipe call, so wi goes n gits oor place in the queue. Ah'm jist thinkin, lit's go through n Glen kin catch us up once we git past aw that security shite. Jayden's heid's swivillin aboot like fuck, but ay. He's up tae sumthin. Eh's went n took ehs mask oaf. But fuck um. That wis some night the other night wi Glen. Eh kens how tae touch ye so ye jist come, n that's before he's even rode ye! Jayden cannae dae that!

Ah'm gled ay peyed fir Shiv tae come wi us. She keeps glancing at that Jordan like she fancies um eftir aw. If that happens it wid mean thit ah'd huv tae pick between Glen und Jayden, n see if Jayden nivir telt ays what really went oan wi that Andrea, ah'd pick Glen n leave him oan ehs ain! See how eh liked that! Ah whisper tae Shiv, – Once that Andrea sees they pictures oan muh Insta that'll fuckin well seeken her pus!

Shiv sais that she telt Catriona Polwarth n that crowd thit we wir gaun tae Ibiza. So tons ay awsum Insta pics fir everybody tae git well jel aboot! So, we goes up tae the check-in. Nice n early cause ay yon covid shite. Ah'm ready tae hand ower that new blue passport ah goat. Jayden, whae nivir even goat vaxinatit, is bein the big man, pushin forward, tryin tae take the lead.

– Hello, the lassie thair, big front teeth, at the desk says.

– We wir telt tae come here, Jayden goes.

– Where are youse flyin tae? the lassie goes.

– Ibiza, Jayden tells ur.

– Can I see your passports?

So, we aw hands them ower. Ah've nudged Jayden n pointed tae muh mask tae git him tae pit his back oan, bit eh jist shrugs.

– Whaire's yir covid test results? the lassie goes.

– Nane ay us huv goat it, ah sais, lookin at thum aw. – Ay-no?

– Nuht, naebday here's goat covit, Jayden says.

– Aye, the lassie goes, – but we still need tae see yir test results in order tae confirm this before we kin allow youse tae travel. N yis huv tae fill in a form for Spain, oanline.

Ah looks at Jayden. – Naebody sais nowt tae us, ah goes. We wir jist telt tae come here, n ah sees Glen walkin acroas the terminal taewards us, wearin this white T-shirt, shades pushed up oan ehs heid, n green-n-white-striped shorts, a blue bomber jaikit draped ower ehs shoodir. Eh stoaps n talks tae a boy in an airline uniform.

– You've no test results, the lassie goes, like she disnae believe us. She's got blonde hair aw tied back n a rash ay spoats either side ay her face. Which is shite fir hur cause she widnae be bad lookin if she didnae huv they spoats. It's a shame fir hur, like Jordan. Her Insta must be shite; jist aw pictures ay her mates! Ming-in!

– What test results, naebody telt us aboot any tests, or forums oanline, ah goes, thinkin ay yon clunic at Murrayfield.

– For the covid test, she says, stroppier. Then she looks ower tae an aulder wummin, short broon hair n a suit n goes, – N yis need tae pit yir masks oan.

– See, Jayden, ah turns roond tae him. – Should've goat vaccinatit n aw!

– What's that goat tae dae wi it?

–The guvirnmint spokesman sais it wis imperitif that ivray cunt's vaccinatit, Jayden!

–Thir's nae science behind mass vaccination. Maist cunts ur dying fae the vaxnation itself, and thir blamin it oan covit.

–Youse donuts really believe that a lying cunt like oor prime minister; a gormless, inbred puppet for big pharma and other exploit-ative commercial interests, Glen looks at ays, – or, eh turns tae Jayden, – some fucking anonymous conspiracy nonce citing other googling paedophiles, can be relied upon for guidance here?

Jayden sais nowt tae Glen, but n eh gits that mingin auld mask oot his poakit, n looks tae the lassie, – Happy now?

– Telt ye, ah goes n turns tae the lassie. – That covit's dangerous, ay?

– Aye, covid, the lassie goes.

– Takin away freedom, Jayden sais. – Makin it intae a polis state!

– Aye, but it cannae be helped cause ah'm afraid thit rules are rules, so thir's nowt ah kin dae, the lassie goes. N fair play tae hur, she ignores him n looks at me. – Test centre's through thair, n she points at they doors. – If you hurry you'll be able tae get a same day test n the resultsul be thair in two ooirs, so by the time ye git tae Ibiza ye should be awright. But mind, ah cannae tell ye this!

– Ye just did, Jayden goes.

– JAYDIN! Stoap gittin fuckin wide! Lassie's tryin tae dae us aw a favour!

– Why aw this commotion? Glen asks.

The lassie looks him ower n goes, – Your party havnae goat test results.

– Youse didnae get a PCR test? Glen looks at us like wir daft.

What's aw they daft cunts slaverin aboot? – Aye, we nivir goat that covid so it disnae affect us, bit, ay, ah goes tae Glen. Eh's aboot tae say sumthin, but Glen likes tae spraff n ye nivir git a wurd in, so ah tells the lassie, – Ah thoat ah'd goat it once cause ah woke up feelin shite, then ah turns tae Jayden, whae's noddin, – but it wis jist cause we aw goat fucked up the night before. That Mrs Syme up the road, she goat it n died, bit she wis auld n she wis gaunny die anyway.

– How auld wis she? Jayden goes.

– Auld. Fifty easy.

– She Antonia Syme's ma? Jayden goes.

– Aye... nuht... auntie.

– Ah rode it. That Antonia. No the ma or the auntie like, hi hi hi, Jayden goes. N ah used tae git a laugh at that sortay thing cause ah thoat eh'd changed whin eh goat wi me. No sure now, but.

As well ah rode Glen!

Glen's been listenin tae this like eh cannae believe it, while at the same time checkin stuff oan ehs phone. – This is daft. You'll no be able tae fly, eh goes.

– Ah've peyed fir they fuckin tickets! Ah goes. – N the lassie sais we could git yin here.

– Yes, the lassie's gittin aw worried, – as I said, there's a test centre here at the airport. It's outside in the lobby of the hotel. If you hurry up you'll be able tae git a same-day test thair, that's aw ah kin suggest. You really have to hurry, though. You should dae two tests, the latrul flow thit means *they might* lit ye oan wi if ye test negative, then the PCR test which yi'll huv the results fur by the time yis git thair.

So, we aw nashes roond tae this test centur. Some test centur! Just a wee tent in the hotel recepshun wi some chairs n a table. No very medical! Thir's two lassies, one quite fat n one thin, but thuv goat the same broon hair pinned up n the same blue overalls. Ah cannae believe it when they say it's gaunny cost a hundred n fifty quid each! Bit ah'm no wastin they tickuts, so ah jist gits thum. Then it takes ages tae fill oot the Spain forums oanline, mare ay that shite! Then fuckin Jayden goes, – Naebody's pittin one ay they things up ma fuckin neb!

– Jayden, git it up yir fuckin snotter hole, ah goes. – Yir ey pittin shite up yir nose! Wur no missin oor fuckin plane!

– Aye, fur fuck sake, Jayden, Glen goes, – workin men n wimmin died fightin fir your freedom tae act the cunt. Ye dinnae need tae yaze that power aw the time.

Ah'm sniggerin cause Glen's barry wi words, bit Jayden's goat a pus oan um. – What? Eh goes.

– Dae it, Glen snaps ehs fingers in ehs face.

– The lateral flow is self-administered, the thin nurse goes. – I do have to do the PCR, she tells us and explains that the airline'll probably accept the latrul flow tae git oan the plane, but tae git allowed intae Ibiza n no huv tae quarantine, wi need the PCR. But that'll no come in till wi git thair.

– See! Ah goes tae Jayden.

So wi does the latrul flow, but Jayden's no botherin, eh's jist touchin ehs nose, but it disnae matter cause wir aw negative!

Then the nurse tells us it's time fir wur PCR.

– You furst then, Jayden goes.

So, the nurse pits mine pit right tae the back ay muh throat. Ah'm pure gaggin n muh eyes ur waterin n ah'm makin choking noises...

Then Jayden goes, – She's usually guid at taken things tae the back ay her throat, hi hi hi!

Ah gits a beamer but ah hus a laugh aboot it, cause ye huv tae whin yir oan hoaliday. – Stoap embarrassin ays, you!

Then whin it's Jayden's turn, up ehs nose, eh moves ehs heid back soas it disnae even go up right. The nurse goes, pushin, – It needs tae go further up...

Ah gits muh ain back n goes, – Aye, eh's no that guid at gittin it up, ur ye Jayden!

That shut his mooth. Took the hump at that yin! Eh starts moanin aboot it bein sare whin she's done, but it's problay cause she hud tae fight through aw that gummy auld ching!

So wi aw gits done, n wi goes back tae the terminal. It's the same lassie, n she goes, – Yuv missed the flight.

Glen's no happy, nane ay us are, n eh's pointin ootside. – Ah bet the plane's still thair!

– But thuv shut the gate n yir still needin checked through, she sais. – Yis goat yir latrul flows?

– Aye... n Glen gies her aw they white chup things.

– Aw ah kin dae is book yis oan the lunchtime flight n hope thit the

155

PCR test results git back in time soas the Spanish'll lit ye through intae Ibiza.

– Well that isnae very satisfactory, Glen goes. – Ah'd like tae see youse treat Barnton people like that!

– It's aw ah kin dae, the lassie goes. – Ah'm really sorry.

– Bit that's no right, ah tells hur. – Youse ur aw jist here tae rip folk oaf n take thir money!

– It's no the lassie's fault, Lita, Glen goes, – dinnae blame hur for daein her joab!

Ah didnae like that one bit, cause ah wis jist tryin tae back Glen up, no huv him hit ays wi aw that. – Ah'm no blamin her, ah tells um, – ah'm jist sayin. Ah kin tell she agrees wi ays, but she cannae say nowt, ah goes, lookin at the lassie. She steys quiet but gits a beamer, which ah take tae mean she kens we're right.

– It's a dangerous epidemic, Lita, Glen goes, – n we cannae be silly or we'll aw end up back in lockdoon. Naeboady wants that!

– Ah'm no daein lockdoon again, Jayden goes, – n nae cunt's gaunny fuckin well make ays.

– You'll be daein it fae the fuckin jail if you're no careful, pal, Glen sais.

Then Jayden sais, – Lockdoon, lockdoon, suck muh fuckin cock doon! Hi! Hi! Hi!

Ah hus a laugh at that, cause that's Jayden's sense ay humour. No everybody gits it. Mister Henry fae the school, that awfay big nervous man whaes eyes blinked aw the time, the one that culled ehsel by jumpin oaf the Dean Brudge, he hated it whin Jayden, Johnny Joss, Jasco n Joshy Boys Three, Six n Seven (thir wis eleven Joshs in our regie kless at school) sterted rippin the pish oot ay um, jist daein aw thir pater. That wis whin ah fell fur Jayden. Ah still mind ay the poem eh wrote ays:

> That fuckin maths class
> It bored ays tae bits
> But ah went thair fir Lita
> N her barry tits.

Thir wis another verse:

Ah hate school dinners
They give me the shits
But I go cause ay Lita
And her barry tits.

Jayden nivur writes oot poeums like that now. Mantic poeums fir
me, like.

So, nowt mantic aboot this shite, n now they say wi need tae git
mare tests booked soas wi kin git back! Fair play tae Glen, but, he sorts
it aw oot oanline, n it hus tae be said thit Jayden – whae's awfay tech-
savvy – helps him oot loads, n wi gits booked oan that next flight.

It's still a loat ay time tae cull, so, of course, Jayden, whae's been
textin oan ehs phone, turns roond n sais, – We'll jist hit the bar. At least
it'll be better fir muh nerves cause wi kin git rid ay some ay this ching
um hudin.

– Ya fuckin idiot, Glen sais, n eh pills Jayden intae a corner ay the
big duty-free bit. – We could aw git huckled before we git tae Spain! Ah
telt ye ah've a fuckin connection thair whae kin sort us oot wi the best
n maist pure drugs! You n yir scheme ching! Be like gittin done fir tryin
tae smuggle Tennent's Lager intae the free bar in the VIP at Ascot!

Ah'm lookin aboot wonderin how easy it wid be tae slip ah boatil
ay voddy fae the shelf intae muh bag, as Jayden grins at Glen. – So
you'll no want any then? Ah've nivir cut this so it's awsum!

– It is, ah goes. See whin eh disnae cut muh brars' ching, it's really
fuckin mint.

– We have tae git rid ay it, Glen goes. – Honestly, though, son, you
need tae use the fuckin brains God gied ye!

– Ah'll git rid ay it, awright, Jayden sais, makin fir the toilets. – See
yis at the bar!

– Weapon, Glen sortay hisses as Jayden goes, n it makes um stoap
fir a second n ye think eh's gaunny cause a scene, but then eh carries
oan. Ah bet it's me thir fightin ower!

So thir's me, Shiv, Jordan n Jarred aw ready tae go tae the Wether-
spoons bar, but Glen makes us go tae this dearer yin. – Ah wouldnae
gie that Tory bastard the steam oaffay ma pish!

Wi gits a round ay drinks then another yin. Jayden's fuckin ages, n
eh forgets it's muh brars thit gied um that fuckin ching tae sell. Ah

keeps lookin at muh phone. Ah'm aboot tae text um. Then, whin eh comes back, ah cannae believe ma eyes... EH'S WI HUR!

THAT FUCKIN ANDREA!

– Look whae ah found! She wid've been gittin oan the same plane n aw, the early yin, but she's changed it tae ooirs!

That fuckin wee cunt's lit up tae fuck in aw, that big grin oan her coupon! – This is mental, she sais n gies Shiv n Jordan a fussy wee wave n smiles like a fuckin hoor at Glen. She's goat they big grey needlecord short skurt oan n a daft toap wi the name ay some band thit nae cunt's heard ay!

– What... what ur *you* daein here... you fuckin planned this... YOUSE PLANNED THIS! ah shouts tae Jayden, whae's laughin ehs heid oaf.

– Ah telt Jayden ah wis gaun tae Ibiza n aw... SHE FUCKIN SAIS WI THAT SOOKY WEE VOICE, – ... but ah didnae think it wis the same dates, nivir mind the same plane!

– AYE, YE EXPECT AYS TAE BELIEVE THAT YA FAHKIN HOOR...

– Free country. Believe what ye like, lead zeppelin!

– YA FAHHHKIN... ah charges at the fahkin hoor tae rip her heid oaf...

... Glen grabs ays by the shoodirs n pills ays doon in the seat beside um... – For God's sake, Lita, no here, you'll end up in the jail n no git tae fuckin Spain, n eh looks aroond...

Aw they peepul starin... nosey cunts... – Naw ah'll no! N wir gaun tae Ibiza, no fuckin Spain!

– Technically we're baith right, Glen sais, n eh's goat an airm roond ays, n ah hears that fuckin Andrea say something like *ah ey travel oan muh ain*... fuckin hoor couldnae cross the fuckin road oan her ain, but Glen's whusperin in muh ear, – Chill, babe. Look, Lita, ye cause a scene, she wins, n eh nods ower tae the bar, whaire a barman n barmaid ur lookin ower. – Never heard ay the phrase: revenge is a dish best served cauld?

– Nuht, ah goes, starin at her, n shi turns away aw snooty n shi's gaun up tae the bar wi Jayden, Jordan n Shiv.

– It means, stey cool n pick your moments for revenge, otherwise yir fuckin jailbait. Dae ye no think that's exactly what she fuckin wants?

Ah looks across at that grinnin coupon, she's aw ower Jayden like a cheap suit... – Lookit thum... they planned this...

Glen's whisperin in muh ear, – Ye really think thuv goat the brains for that?

– Bit she's oan hur ain!

– Fuck them baith. You're a real woman, Lita, no like that wee bag ay bones. We hud a wee tumble before, but that means nowt...

– Ye gaunny dae me in the plane lavvy, that mile-high club?

Glen has a cheeky wee glance at the lavvy, then sais, – Naah... when we git tae that villa, n we get the very best bedroom, ah'm gaunny make love tae you proper. You've nivir experienced real lovemakin before, hen, but fuck me ur you gaunny experience it now!

Eh's goat me like a wet sponge awready, n it's jist wi wurds. Jayden husnae goat wurds like that! Ah might huv tested negative oan the latrul flow, but ah've goat a latrul flow ay muh ain gaun oan doonstairs!

Fuck Jayden n that Andrea hoor! See how she likes dealin wi a daft wee laddie n ehs reptile dysfunction while ah'm gittin nailed by a fuckin man!

Him n Jayden huv made peace, cause Glen gits the wrap n goes tae the lavvy. Ah'm waitin oan um comin back, watchin that Andrea at the bar, tossin her heid back n laughin. Jarred's beside ays, gapin at ma chist. – What you lookin at? ah goes.

– Nowt, eh sais, turnin n lookin up tae the bar, at that Andrea. – She's no as big a ride as you.

Cheeky wee bastard's goat a wey wi the wurds! Ah'm aboot tae say somethin, but Glen's back wi the ching. So ah goes tae the toilet n smashes two lines, then wi drink up n go tae the gate. It's the same lassie fae earlier. – Right... here's yir test things, ah sais, giein her the latrul flow.

– Righto, that's acceptable, she sais. – Mind, if one ay youse has got a positive oan the PCR, they huv tae isolate in a bubble.

So, we gits oan the plane n we takes oor seats, me wi Glen. Ah'm no even lookin at Jayden n that fuckin hoor tae see whaire they ur! Ah sais tae Glen, – See what you sais earlier, aboot us gaun tae bed? Kin Shiv git involved n aw, like at the Viva? Ah dinnae like leavin ur oot, ah'm sayin as wi take oaf.

– If youse're baith very good girls.

– What if we urnae, ah looks at Shiv, whae's back behind us somewhair, probably near that hoor Andrea's seat… Jordan n Jarred ur gamin oan thir phones.

– Then I'll huv tae spank yis baith.

Ah'm practically fuckin breathless here… – Mibbe we will be a bit naughty then!

– Oh, youse'll be naughty awright, if yis ur hingin oot wi me, eh goes, then we hears laughin n it's Jordan, sittin wi Shiv. Glen droaps ehs voice n sais in muh ear, – Ye sais thir wis a wee bit ay chemistry wi the young Jordan felly n Shiv. Mibbe we need tae show him the ropes!

Then ah turns back tae see Jayden's fuckin sittin beside hur, that fuckin hoor Andrea, so ah starts snoggin wi Glen. Eh's goat ehs jaikit oaf, n eh pits it ower muh lap. Eh's wandrin hands creep under muh belly n eh's playin wi ays… the scent ay his efttur shave… – Sumday's awfay wet… yir soakin muh hand… eh whispurs.

Ah'm jist gaspin…

Then this voice shoutin, – WHAT THE FUCK! FUCKIN HUMILIATIN ME! SNOGGIN THAT AULD CUNT! Wi look up n see Jayden, ehs eyes burnin!

Glen pills ehs hand away, n ah'm pullin masel oan muh feet. – WELL YOU HUMILIATIT ME! SNOGGIN HUR! THEN YE BROAT HUR HERE EFTIR ME PEYIN FIR YE!!

Thir's cheers comin fae they drunk passengers, n a hostess is lookin oan, then headin doon the gangway!

Glen looks up at Jayden. – Sit the fuck doon! Then eh turns tae me. – It's no fuckin Jeremy Kyle, let's cool it!

– Please, sit down, the hostess says, n she's takin Jayden back tae his seat.

– Fuck him, ah goes.

– That's the spirit, Glen whispers. – Yir way too much woman for a daft wee laddie tae handle, n ah feel ehs hand gaun back tae muh wet snatch. – Goat tae keep you oan the boil…

Eh eywis waits till um aboot tae blaw, then eh eases oaf. – Dinnae fanny tease ays…

– Might as well tell the pope no tae pray…

Well, ah'm fuckin rampant whin we gits tae Ibiza! Wir jist waitin tae git oot through the passport bit n pick up oor luggage whin thir's a ping oan the phone n ah gits a negative. Wir aw comparing results, n it's only Jayden's thit gits positive!

SERVES UM RIGHT!!

– How's that? Jayden goes. – Latrul flow sais ah wis awright!

– This is mare accurate, though, Glen goes. – Like they sais, ye huv tae isolate.

– How is it thit ah huv tae?

– Cause ye do. Glen wags ehs finger, standin back fae Jayden n pillin ehs mask up. – Thir's two rooms oan the other side ay the pool! That's if they lit ye through, eh looks at the passport control people.

Then that Andrea goes n coughs, – Ah tested negative but feel shite, ah think ah've goat it fi Jayden oan the plane! Ah'm best steyin wi him n keepin away fae the rest ay yis.

Ah kin see what she's daein... – Ah'll stey wi Jayden! You tested negative, ah tells hur.

– You should keep away fae Jayden. You cannae afford tae git that covid!

– Aye, Jayden sais, – it kills fat people. Better safe thin sorry, but ay.

Ah looks away, fuckin ragin at they cunts. Then ah sees Jayden jist turn away behind this boy pushin aw they trolleys, n wi cannae believe it...

– What is fuckin...? Glen gasps under ehs breath...

... but Jayden jist slips right through, n eh's standin thair, oan the other side ay the customs barrier, no even goat ehs fuckin passport stamped! Eh's jist pointin tae us n laughin! Ah thoat eh'd git huckled, but nuht, eh jist walks oot then texts ays:

Pick up my bag off the belt.

– That fucking weapon will get us aw jailed, Glen goes.

– That's Jaygo, but, eh goes ehs ain way, that fuckin Andrea goes, n even sortay imitates ehs daft laugh.

– Fuckin straight tae jail, if eh's no careful! The idiot's fuckin illegal! Glen shakes ehs head.

Wi gits through n ootside tae the taxi queue, n it's that hoat ah kin hardly breathe... n ah'm watchin thaim laughin, Jayden n her, wi thir shades oan. *They fuckin set aw this shite up!*

Glen's went ower tae talk tae this boy in a taxi, bit eh disnae git in the cab. Ah sees um pit a packet intae ehs bag. Eh shakes the boy's hand n comes back.

Jayden's clocked this n aw. – What's that?

– Mind yir ain business, pillin aw that shite, Glen snaps. – Gaunny fuck ivraythin up!

– What, but? Jayden goes.

– Federico's sorted us oot. Proper shit. Now lit's git tae the digs, Glen goes, waving doon a big people carrier thit eh tells us eh booked earlier. – Right, everybody git thir masks oan. Jayden, you n Andrea git right tae the back! Wi goat tae try n observe that social distancin as much as we kin!

– Couldnae dae that oan the fuckin plane, so we'll no be able tae dae it in a motor, Jayden goes.

– The principle is thit we dae what wi kin, Glen snaps. – Lita, you're doon the front wi me, away fae they plaguers!

So wi thit we aw git in. Ah'm fuckin ragin, wantin tae tear hur – that Andrea's – face oaf. Glen asks ays what's up, n ah jist nods back at thaim, sittin behind us.

– Ah hate tae say it, but sadly ma knuckle-heided nephew, as dim as eh is, and ah cite enterin Spain illegally, is right *oan this particular occasion*, Lita. Studies've showed the morbidly obese tae be in the highest risk category. Wuv goat tae follay the science on this yin n isolate him ower the other side ay the pool, away fae us.

Ah sais nowt. Wir drivin oot ay the airport, then we go through a toon. – Whaire's this? Jarred's askin.

– San Antonio, Jayden sais, as the motor goes doon an awfay steep hull. – So ah'll need tae isolate at that back part ay the villa, n eh turns tae Shiv. – You comin wi me n Andrea?

– What aboot me? Jordan goes.

– Aye, you n aw, Jayden sais, bit ye kin tell eh's no bothered really.

Shiv looks tempted, bit ah turns roon n gies her a look, n goes, – Nae wey, cause see if you git it, you'll no be able tae see Beyonce whin ye git back!

This jist seems tae make hur even mare tempted. – But muh ma...

– Yir ma's gaunny look eftir Beyonce fir a month? Aye, right. What if she gits it?

This does the trick. – Nuht, she goes, lookin at Glen n Jordan.

– Cannae wait tae see this vulla, ah goes, giein that Glen a wee wink. His tadger's gittin sooked tae fuck: show that fuckin Jayden what eh's missin!

Wi turn oaf the road, doon a windin track tae this clearin, n thair it is! Thair's the hoose! Oor hoaliday luckchuray vulla!

JAYDEN (10)

The villa feels even more isolated than it is. It is situated in a forest, at the bottom of a trail path coiling to the edge of its garden from the main road above. A hazardous thirty-five-minute walk downhill, devoid of a pedestrian pathway and lined by bushy, overhanging trees, takes you into San Antonio.

A modern L-shaped construction, the villa is built around a large deep-and-shallow-ended pool. It has five bedrooms, three of which are proximate to a lounge/kitchen with floor-to-ceiling glass windows and sliding doors, opening onto a tiled patio and the piscina. The further two bedrooms are annexed on the other side of the pool.

It had been assumed that Lita would be with Jayden, or perhaps with Shiv if Jayden shared with Jordan, Jarred or Glen. Of course, such plans were scuppered, first by Andrea's surprise appearance then Jayden's positive covid test, which, although undetected (and undocumented) by the Spanish authorities, meant that he would require isolation from the rest of the party. It was agreed by everyone, other than Lita, that it was best Jayden and Andrea isolated together in the two smaller rooms across the other side of the pool.

Jayden Templeton looked around his bedroom, feeling fabulous about his own Machiavellian skills. Concedes to a grudging respect for those of his uncle. Of course, they had to pretend to be argumentative and antagonistic. It was agreed that their strategy would throw Lita off the scent.

Here's the norf Edumbruh news: Jayden Templeton is takin the fuckin pish oot ay aw they daft McCallums! Hi hi hi, best result ivir! Shimmy through the fuckin airport n they kin stick thir fuckin Brexit up their erses! We are Hubs, we go whaire wi want! J-furum! N hur snoggin auld Glen oan the plane in fill view ay us aw! Ah'll soon be proper shacked up wi Andrea, n ah bet ah'll be able tae talk Shiv intae coming ower n aw. It'll be fuckin mint. Shiv's decent oan *Call Ay Duty* tae, but Lita's mibbe a bit wide for this, so it'll be a challenge. Ah reckon, though, that Shiv, withoot clathes, might be a ride. She's no fat even though she eywis wears crap trackies. Jordan fancies hur, but a waste, the wey ah see it; ma ideal result would be fir him tae ride Lita eftir Glen did, n me tae ride baith Andrea n Shiv ower here. That wid be the best plan fir me, likes.

So ah'm gittin set up in muh room, Andrea next door, n then ah goes oot in muh dark-green shoarts tae stretch by the pool. It's hoat awright! Thir tests say uv goat that covit, but ah feel barry! It's only dangerous for auld cunts like Glen, so eh'd better no git cairied away wi aw this pretendin tae boss ays aroond! Then eh comes oot, ower the other side ay the pool, n ah'm wonderin what sortay gear eh's goat n if it's any guid. Then Jordan comes oot wearin a fuckin Hertz strip, n Glen goes, – Git that scabby retarded toap oaf, n git roond the pool. Vit C and D deficiency. That's how yuv goat bad spoats!

Jordan twitches like a shitein dug oan the Links.

– Seriously, sunshine will sort yir plukes right oot.

Then ah hears Shiv go, – Leave um, eh looks awright.

Ah'm aboot tae shout ower: *ye look like a fanny in that strip, n ah'm gled ah'm fuckin isolaytit cause ah'm no gaun anywhair wi you dressed like a mongol,* but then Lita comes ower, walkin roond the pool in they fat shoarts n vest, mask oan, keepin six feet fae us, layin doon the fuckin law. – Youse two better make sure yis stey at the endy the pool in they *two* rooms, she shouts at me n Andrea, whae's standin in the doorway ay her room, wearin a barry bikini thit's sortay turquoise.

– Ah'll jist be makin sure Jayden's awright, Andrea goes, actin aw that sweet wey, but like it's aw false. She's fuckin gittin it once Glen rides Lita n wi kin say it wis aw due tae jealousy. As Gasman sais: *we cross the ocean ay your tears, tae the promised land ay your pain, baby.* But *eftir* Glen rides Lita. Goat tae be able tae look her brars in the eye n say, she done me wrong. N see if they ask whae wi... well, Glen's no thoat aboot that, the fuckin great planner ay Camel Hampstead! Eh's no as fuckin wide as eh thinks! Cause whin it comes doon tae it, Jaygo here's the main man! Too quick for the Spanish customs n immigration cunts! Hi hi hi. – You jist stey wi Glen, ower thair, ah points.

Then ah gits ays this sad look, – This isnae us, Jayden.

Fuck sake... ah suddenly mind ay the good times, like that barry gam she gied ays oan Cramond Island, n ah nearly choke fir a bit. – Dinnae git too close, jist in case, ah goes. – Ah'll be fine... jist a bit ay stuff wi muh throat.

Lita nods n backs away a bit, then turns tae Andrea, – You mind whaes fuckin felly it is!

– Like you wir mindin whaes burd ye are... or wir? Messin wi his fuckin uncul oan the plane, Andrea goes.

Ah looks ay hur tae tell hur tae shut up. *We've got this. Me n Unkul Glen.*

– It wis jist muckin aboot, Lita sais, n eyes ays aw that beggin wey, but ah turns away, kiddin oan ah'm aw hurt whin ah'm laughin muh heid oaf inside! Hi hi hi!

So Lita turns n waddles oaf tae the other side ay the pool. Fuckin fat mess: wey they thighs wobble n that flesh hings ower they tight clothes...

– Gustin, Andrea goes, readin ma mind.

How could ah huv cowped yon?

Played right intae our fuckin hands, the daft blobby hoor! Nae muckin aboot, my erse, ah winks at Andrea n wi hus a wee giggle. She'll be gittin rode tae fuck n battirit tae a pulp as soon as Glen's up Lita, but eh'd better nash, cause ah'm no fuckin hingin aboot! Hi hi hi! Ah looks up tae the sun. One thing aboot it is thit it makes ye no sae bothered aboot video games, but ay. Hits muh room n racks oot a couple ay lines ay ching. Well. if Glen's no made any move tae share his gear!

UNCLE GLEN (4)

Glen Urquhart cringes as Ariana Grande's 'Dangerous Woman' blares out. Lita had got to the internet music system first. Gets on his Spotify. Briefly considers changing the track but declines, unready for a culture war, especially with Lita, whom he has to keep onside. Looks out through the patio doors to see her on a Lilo, scowling across the pool at Jayden and Andrea. His nephew seems oblivious; however, as they agreed, maintains a discreet distance from the thin girl. Glen concedes that Jayden played a blinder on that flight.

Going to his suitcase, Glen removes the urn containing the ashes of Philly Matheson. The deceased's ex wife, Hannah, had wanted no more ceremony. But Philly's daughter Geraldine had been of a mind to scatter them at Easter Road, Leith Docks or Silverknowes Beach. Glen had convinced her that, as an internationalist, the best tribute to Philly would see him whipping up in summer breezes all over the Mediterranean. The family had agreed, as this request obviously meant so much to Glen, who seemed more devastated than any of them by his old mentor's demise.

Placing Philly's remains on a fine wooden sideboard in the front room, Glen heads to the kitchen area, where he begins mixing cocktails. Back out through the patio doors, the others make themselves comfortable. The only person remaining indoors is Jarred, who lies on his bed reading The Adventures Of Huckleberry Finn.

The low frequency hoat air ay the lackeys n apologists ay kings and capitalists. In face ay thir folly, a catalogue ay potential disasters is only averted by baith chance and the reason that only good men n wimmin kin bring tae the fore. A text pops in fae one ay the best ay that ilk: the luscious Lauren Brady fae Hemel Hempstead. And ah dinnae need tae look outside tae experience the sun comin up!

> Is it a bit forward of me to say I've
> always held a candle for you?

Suddenly ah think ay Lauren pushing a candle intae ersel, me grasping her tits wi enthusiasm but a gentleman's decorum... the words ay the bard... *Her eyes are the lightenings of joy and delight, her slender neck, her handsome waist, her hair well buckl'd, her stays well lac'd, her taper white leg with an et, and a c, for her a, b, e, d, and her c, u, n, t, and Oh! For the joys of a long winter night!!!*... muh lungs feel aw starved ay air like they two bad days in June when that covid got a wee bit intense...

Course, ah shouldnae have worked through it, but follay the science was the fashionable phrase. So what if ah chose tae follay what Tam Carlyle called the *dismal science,* that ay economics, cause when yir self-employed ye cannae turn doon the poppy. Plenty plumbers waiting tae snatch your Dode Raft. Mind you, ah must have infected every cunt in that pub ah goat replumbed, poor bastards coughing and spluttering like a Freda Payne. It had to be done then cause muh boy big Lexo was getting it ready for reopening eftir lockdoon. Aw hands tae the pump. Ma hert's pumpin right now. And ah ken whae ah wish ah wis pumpin, n that's a certain Hertfordshire maiden! Ah shake the cocktail mixer like a daft cunt, then lower it tae the worktoap, n text back:

> Ah, how you make my day, bold
> Ms Brady! Let me inform you such
> feelings are highly reciprocal. If
> only you knew how much I've longed
> to hold you in my arms. xxx

Ma younger nephew, Jarred, ay silent wild-eyed stare and furrowed brow – a teen Jake Gyllenhaal oan crystal meth – is watching ma margarita construction wi unnerving intensity. That's good. Ah turn oan the tap at the sink. – Ah did that.

– What?

– Installed the entire plumbin system here.

– Aw.

So ah start explaining the rudiments ay said system tae him, n fuck me, if that slack jaw doesnae tighten as they bulging, vacant, screen-raped eyes gain somethin resemblin focus. Ah dinnae believe it, but Jarred seems tae be absorbin maist ay the information! Ah'm thinkin this boy might just have mare tae him than first meets the eye, when eh suddenly sais, – How much is a plumbin apprentice's wages?

– Depends oan how good that plumbin apprentice is, ah goes, spell broken, shakin that cocktail mixer again, glancing across at Philly on the sideboard. *Values aw tae fuck.* – Young Yousef ah hud doon in Hemel Hempstead was great. An immigrant, see: hungry, ah'm tellin Jarred, – no like the dispossessed mutant native underclass, aw initiative n manners robbed fae them by the evil screen, n ah pours the cocktail into a gless and hands it tae him. – Shouldnae be daein this, so dinnae tell yir ma, but one willnae hurt. Go on then. What dae ye say?

Jarred sips it. – No bad.

At that point ah huv tae look away in disgust. *Nae 'thank you'.*
Two simple fuckin words.

So ah casts ma beadies through the patio doors ower the bodies by the pool, principally that meatiest yin, n mind ay why wur really here…

… the McCallums are low-life, drug-dealin thieves whae prey oan thir ain class. Tae take fae they scabs is a virtuous n righteous act. N that daft, wee, fat hoor fell right intae the trap! Typical McCallum! Makes ays think that simpleton nephew ay mine – Jayden, ah mean – might just be coachable eftir aw. Of course, eh's playin the surly, daft laddie act tae perfection, precisely cause that's *exactly* what eh is. Therefore, it stands tae reason that his wee fat burd is a fuckin dipstick n aw. Ah'll chuck a few loads intae her n get that fucking account ay hers emptied in the process. A bit ay blimpishness in a young bird never deterred a seasoned campaigner!

Lookin ootside, muh eyes fair glintin in the Balearic sun filterin in fae behind the towerin trees, the big surprise is Siobhan. A fetching wee bit fat oan the lower abdomen, but otherwise a great boady in that bikini. Sittin oan the patio, yon sunlight's daeing her the world ay good. She's blooming like a flower in that skimpy wee two-piece; ah kin see Jayden's eyes fair poppin fae the other side ay the pool. Aye, less hunched at the shoodirs, much lighter ay heart, she's fair set the horn up in ays. But ye need tae focus oan the main prize. Ah gies the orange trunks a pat at the groin, leaves Jarred n steps outside.

As ah settle doon on the Lilo by Lita, ah hear they dulcet tones as Jayden shouts ower at ays, – Ah dinnae see how we huv tae isolate, it's no like this covit shite affects us!

Nae manners.

Nae sense ay community.

Nae nowt.

He's no jist playin the game for Lita's benefit; eh really is that fuckin daft. – Aye, but ye dinnae want tae kill the perr auld folks, ah shouts ower at um.

– How no? What huv they left us, n eh stands up n walks tae the edge ay the pool. – Global warnin, climate change, reptile dysfunction, aw the poison in food, in rivurs, n eh's shakin ehs heid, ehs hands oan the hips ay they dark-green trunks. – Lit thum fuckin die, the auld cunts!

The dopey wee Wyatt Earp's been hittin the peas n barley; of course, it's aw jist tae show oaf tae yon skinny wee Roger Moore eh's ridin. She's sittin thair aw snide-eyed, enjoyin ehs daft performance. Ah'm no huvin that. – But that's *rich* auld cunts, ah goes, – no the type ay ordinary auld people we come intae contact wi. Socialism, pal.

– So fuck! These cunts voted naw in the independence referendum cause they posh auld English public-school bastirts telt thum tae! Kept us doon n tied tae aw that shite! Then they voted tae go oot ay Europe n wir stuck wi they Mickey Mouse blue passports n treatit like fuckin lepers! Nae wonder ah took the pish!

Well, for sure it's a ching-fuelled rant, but ah've nivir heard Jayden talk like that, n ah admit tae seeing a wee bit ay potential in the laddie that previously escaped ays.

Ehs still nae tradesman, though, and the wide, wee cunt needs pit in his place. Covid or nae covid, ah'll be ower thair n tannin ehs fuckin jaw. Lit's see the bastards find a vaccine fir that!

LITA (12)

From her Lilo on the patio decking, Lita watches Glen Urquhart suddenly embark upon, and phlegmatically power through, a routine of push-ups. It seems obvious that this is a show of physical prowess designed to intimidate Jayden, increasingly lippy from the other side of the pool.

It seems to work, as Jayden goes back to rest on his lounger. Lita's rapacious eyes are on Andrea, lying in the shade close to him. The tirade from Jayden back at Glen has impressed Lita, in spite of herself. *It wis me. Thir fighting ower me!*

Jordan and Shiv sit at a table under the parasol and talk about their families.

All this is observed from the lounge, behind the patio doors. Young Jarred's eyes go from Lita's breasts, propped on top of her suitcase gut, straining against the bounding confines of the red two-piece swimsuit, to Shiv's yellow-and-black-striped affair and briefly to Andrea, wearing an aquamarine bikini with squiggly patterns. *No much tit or erse oan that.*

Behind the blinds Jarred touches himself through his leopard-spotted shorts. Wonders if those delicious tweaks on the head of his cock at the images from the other side of the glass officially constituted wanking. Or was that only the case when you yanked it to fuck? A brief look to see if anyone is behind him, but the only supervision comes from the sideboard and the ashes of Philly Matheson.

Then, as his head whips back, Lita rolls on her front, two large buttocks replacing the outsized breasts on display, and looks up at him. Jarred shrinks behind the blinds, mortified that she knows what he's doing.

With a satisfied smile, Lita raises herself up on her elbows, to get a sip of the latest cocktail proffered by Glen.

Jarrit... that wide, wee bastirt... another yin thit wants ays!!

... thing is, ah've found that Andrea's weak spot; a fuckin titless milkboatil that ey steys in the shade! Pure burns up, n thinks the sun's bad fir her skin. Vitamin C, ya mongul! Ah ken Jayden likes a lassie wi an awfay deep tan, like in the strangulporn fulums eh watches, so, of course, ah'm steyin oot here!

– You need some lotion oan that skin, hot boady, Glen's goat up fae ehs push-ups, – dinnae want you burnin up anywhaire but yon bedroom, n eh starts massagin that Tropic Heat intae muh back. Eh's goat good fingers, uses a loat ay *controlled* force. – Ah like tae go in deep, eh whispers in muh ear. – Dae ye like it when they go in deep?

Ah kin hear birds in the trees above makin noises. Thir's a wee stream at the boatum ay the gairdin gurglin like a bairn... beautiful fragrant smells like ye nivir git back hame...

Eh *does* go in deep, n it's awfay relaxin, well no jist relaxin, cause n ah'm gittin aw juicy doonstairs, tell yis that fir nowt! – Barry... ah whispers.

But then ah kin hear giggling, n ah kin feel aw muh back fat. Ah'm bettin it's comin fae the other side ay the pool whaire that Andrea n Jayden ur laughin at ays! Ah'm aboot tae tell Glen tae stoap, when eh undoes the clasp oan muh bikini! Then eh tries tae turn ays roond... – Nuht... ah goes... – fix the clasp...

– Ah dinnae think we need tae bother about that. We're awfay isolated here.

– Bit aw the rest ay thum...

– We'll aw huv our kits off soon, Lita. Ah think ay you as a leader, no a follower...

A *leader, no a follower*... so ah goes, fuck it, n thinkin ay that skinny Andrea – a barry meal wid kill her – ah turns roond n shows thum the loat!

Thir's aw shouts n whistles comin fae Jordan n Shiv. Then he whispers sumthun n she takes oaf her top n aw! Good fir Shiv! Only snobby cunt Andrea spoils the perty n turns away; jist cause she's goat nae fuckin tit tae speak ay! Then ah turns n sees that wee face in the windae, big eyes now aw Chinky. – JARRIT!!

Glen suddenly looks up, watches the blinds twitch. – Forgoat aboot the wee man. He shouldnae be witnessin this... n eh gits up, ready tae go through. But eh stoaps n looks at ays first, as ah manages tae clip the toap back oan, n spin it roond. – Good move on your part, Glen cracks that big smile wi they capped teeth. – If ah'd gotten a hud ay they beauties ah widnae huv been responsible for what ah might huv done, eh winks n heads inside.

Ah picks up muh bag n goes in eftir um. Eh's diggin in ehs wallet, n Jarred's standin thair by the fireplace, pretendin eh's seen nowt. – Mibbe time fir a wee stroll intae toon, pal, Glen goes. – It's gittin a bit adult oot thair.

– How? Jarred goes, open-moothed, but eh's grabbin the notes oot ay Glen's hand n stuffin thum in the poakit ay they jungle shoarts ay his.

– Ye dinnae want tae be hingin roond here wi us aw the time, pal. You'll meet some people yir ain age in toon.

– Whaes age ur you, but? eh goes tae Glen.

Glen disnae like that, n raises they slick black brows. – Ah'm the responsible adult that hus tae entertain everybody, n that's what ah'm tryin tae dae. Take yir Huckleberry Hound book, he points tae whaire eh's left the book, oan the couch, next tae muh bag.

– *Huckleberry Finn* –

– Aye, that's the yin, Glen snaps, then eh goes softer. – A relaxin wee stroll intae toon! Ah need a fill report as tae what's happenin doon thair! Muh man in San Antonio!

– Goan see the toon, pal, ah goes, jist wantin that Glen tae gie ays it bigtime. Ah gits intae muh bag n hands um another two twenty-euro notes.

– Ah jist gied um some money, Glen goes.

Ah jist want the wee perve tae go so ah kin git a length ay Glen's boaby up ays!

– How long's it gaunny take tae git thair? Jarred goes.

– Aboot forty minutes, Glen says, lookin at ehs laptoap.

– Ye might meet some nice lassies in toon, ah goes, n ehs wee eyes light up.

– Drink plenty water n watch yirsel oan that road, Glen's tellin um. – Make sure ye walk oan the side ay the oncoming traffic, no behind it. Eh opens the door. – N git a cab back if it gits dark.

– Right, Jarred says.

As soon as Jarred goes oot that door, ah sees eh's left ehs book. Ah goes tae shout oan um but Glen's ower n starts tae unfasten the clip oan muh swimsuit toap, so ah cannae be bothered, n a fling muh bag back oan the couch. – Naughty boy, Glen… ah'm rubbin that cock through ehs shoarts.

– The wee man's away, n you cannae afford tae let these beauties no git tanned aw ower, n eh's rubbin the cream n ehs hands n gittin muh tits n giein thum a good massage… ah've goat ehs cock oot …

– What ur youse up tae, Shiv shouts inside the doors, so wi stoap, n Glen scoops ehs cock back in n nods tae the door.

– We no gaun tae bed?

– Naw, ah want tae show them, including that wee wide cunt ay a nephew ay mine, how a real man handles a beautiful young woman, n Glen's goat ays ootside n back doon oan the Lilo. – Ah insist oan daein they legs, eh sais, n before ah kin say anything eh's squirted mare lotion ower muh thighs.

Eh's giein it laldy, kneadin muh thighs, n ah'm thinkin *he's no gaunny stoap, his hand's gaun right up muh fanny*, but eh ey pills back right at the last minute. Ah'm gaspin n wantin tae git at that hard-on in they orange trunks.

– You've goat a bananay in yir poakit, ah says in a whisper, but it comes oot aw cracked n hoarse. Must be the heat. Need tae drink mare.

– It's bein wi such a horny young bird that's gittin ma dander up. Ah'm gaunny git us mare drinks n cut oot some lines ay that *delicious* ching.

– But when ur we gaunny…

– Shh, baby, aw guid things come tae she whae waits…

N ah kin say one thing fir Glen, eh kin mix a margurita n a mojito, and we're drinkin loads ay thum by the pool, wi the music oan, aw that Ibiza house. Tons ay lines n aw, then the bumbles come oot, the stuff Glen picked up fae the boy at the airport. Ah takes yin, washed doon wi yin ay Glen's marguritas. Ah wis jist gaunny take half at first, but Glen says, – Go for it.

It hits ays like a ton ay fuckin bricks: ah feel muh mooth gaun dry n muh face gaun aw spazzy as ah cannae move muh legs or barely open muh eyes cause the blindin sunlight's everywhair… N wir aw comin up n laughin wir heids oaf, Shiv n Jordan ur gittin involved n aw, even

Jayden n that Andrea oan the other side ay the pool, n ah'm thinkin they kin dae what they like, we kin aw dae what wi like, n ah love Jayden, but Glen's barry n aw...

Wasted...

... aw us, except wee Jarred, away in toon... Glen even goes intae the pool wi a tray n brings drinks ower tae Jayden and cunty Andrea's side. They huv yin, but thir soon firin intae the beers. Ah'm gittin aw sad fur Jayden stuck thair oan ehs ain. – Kin we no let um come ower, ah asks Glen as eh climbs oot the pool.

– N infect us aw... no way, besides ah want the hoatest pussy for masel, n then eh's feelin ays up oan the Lilo. – Ye didnae think ye wir gittin away, did ye? Think ye wir gittin oot ay they lessons in love?

Ah looks inside, the blinds urnae drawn, n ah sees Jordan n Shiv snoggin oan the bed.

Glen wants tae mount ays, but the Lilo is nivir gaunny support us baith, so eh's pillin ays up n wi go intae whaire Shiv n Jordan ur oan the bed... kissin... n ye kin see thit Jordan's aw excited in ehs trunks n thit eh's a big laddie!

We're aw wasted... aw huggin n kissin, n it's like wir aw one so it disnae really matter whae pits thir cock in whaes fanny... ah'm in a trance... then Glen goes tae Jordan, – Siobhan's gaunny sook yir cock, n eh looks at Shiv, n she's giein a wee smile aw eckied n she's goat it oot his troosers. N then that durty Glen's gaun behind her oan the bed n pillin doon her swimsuit bottoms. Jordan gasps oot as Shiv sucks. Ah might no be gittin any action but ah'm still aw rampant... but they puhls are makin ays seek so ah makes fir the lavvy... ah see Glen's face... – You awright...? eh goes.

– Aye... ah sais, bit ah gits thair n think ah'm gaunny throw up... n ah do jist a wee bit in the sink, but then ah dae a shite n aw n it feels good...

... whin ah goes oot ah sees muh bag oan the couch, n ah'm hingin back by the door, n gits ma phone oot n uh starts fulumin the two ay thum roastin Shiv... Glen's fuckin her fae behind, n Jordan's goat ehs big knob doon her throat, n that daft bitch's eyes ur too dopey tae see me fulmin away!

Then Glen's suddenly pillin oot, so ah droaps the phone back intae muh bag, flings it oan the couch n comes right in, as eh shouts,

– Jordan! Ower here, before ye fuckin blaw yir muck, Glen points at Shiv's hole n eh sortay pulls Jordan roond tae git ehs cock in it...

– Ah'm missin oot, ah goes, fuckin rampant again.

– Ah dinnae ken, Jordan's aw spangled, – is this awright, Shiv...?

– Aye... aye... Shiv sais n then looks up at me n goes, – Youse huv tae leave us, but...

Ah dinnae ken what tae dae, but ah'm sortay laughin, n Glen turns tae me n goes, – Aye we've other business, jist wanted tae git the laddie started oaf...

– Barry...

– Too right... job done, Glen sais, wi that daft supervisin plumber face oan!

Jordan's pumpin Shiv fae behind. – Is it awright...? Ah really like ye...

– S'awright, it's barry. Shiv's hudin ontae the headboard n squeakin like a bairn's toy!

Glen's goat me by the hand, n eh's takin ays back tae ooir bedroom, but the blinds ur still open... then eh's goat muh swimsuit boatums doon n eh's right oan ays, starts eatin muh pussy oot... it's like a dream... acroas the pool, through the blindin light, that Andrea starts shoutin tae Jayden... n the bed's creakin as Glen's lickin ays, n ah kin see Jayden acroas the pool lookin in at ays, n ah hear um shoutin, – SO THAT'S HOW IT IS... n eh's goat a hud ay that Andrea... thir gaun inside his room... but Glen's still chowin oan ays n ma heid's wasted cause it's that hoat, the sun's burnin muh face through the open windae... then Jayden's back oot n shoutin at Glen, whae flicks um the Vs but then moves up n gits in ays n eh's pumpin ays... n ah feel that barry, but then ah feels this sickness deep in muh stomach n it's like ah'm gaunny pass oot...

ANDREA (2)

Andrea Raeburn and Jayden Templeton had watched in eager horror from across the pool as Jayden's uncle performed cunnilingus on his girlfriend Lita, thus symbolically ending the two-year relationship and freeing up their love. Andrea anticipated an overwhelming passion; a fusion of ecstatic, drug-fuelled holiday shagging, spiced up by the delicious operation of the scam. Now free of his weighty burden, courtesy of Uncle Glen, Jayden would surely perform with the porn-star technique of their online idols.

But Jayden was transfixed by the horror of the scene... Lita and his uncle... he looked at Andrea's snide, pinched face, felt the drugs in him and said to her, – Ye'd better make this worthwhile...

Andrea roared in approving scorn, – MOAN THEN, YA CUNT... and pulled him into the room, pulling the blinds shut behind them. They tumbled into bed, as Jayden took her through the standard porn-star sequence, before the darker tropes of Stonker, Gasman and The Brutalizer – Adam Assbender – only available from the dark web, filled his head...

... as a sudden hard, dizzying slap across Andrea's face was followed by a more violent tugging at her hair, then the declaration, – YA FUCKIN FULTHY WEE HOOR... DURTIEST HORNIEST RIDE UV HUD...

The sweet words rang in her ears as Andrea's brain wobbled in her skull under a flurry of blows. But she didn't properly pass out until his hands tightened round her neck, cutting off her air supply as her world darkened in a dead-eyed, juddering orgasm.

It's half an hour later when Andrea blinks into consciousness. Gets up, her traumatised body shaking. Goes to the window. Through her own bruising, visible in her reflection in the glass, she sees Lita lying alone and prone in her room across the pool.

Like a fuckin beached whale! Seems like it's sleepin. Jist like Jaygo. Ah gits back intae bed wi um. That wis a right session ay love. Ah'm battered, raw n sair, n muh jaw's throbbin whaire Jaygo really tanned it, like that Gasman boy eh likes did tae that Mirabelle Adams in that *Gasman 2: The Choker Is Wild.* At least eh nivir marked ays that bad, apart fae the bruises oan muh airms! Long sleeves when ah get back tae work! Ah sees the webcam eh positioned on the sideboard, recordin us.

But now eh's wakin up, n ah'm in Jayden's airms n that fat munter is ower the way, huvin been shagged by a daft auld felly! Ah call that a result! – You're barry in bed, Jayden sais, hudin ays tight.

Ah like aw the lovey-dovey bits best, eftir likes, but laddies expect ye tae let them batter ye a bit. Toni San Laurentis sais it's the ultimate feminism, showing yir strong enough tae take the punishment they kin dish oot. – That's right... ah want you tae dae anything tae me, anything ye want tae dae...

– Finally found a burd thit's game fir the type ay action ah like! No like fatso ower thair, humped by an auld cunt! Hi hi hi!

Ah lights us up two fags n looks at muh face swellin doon one side, – You're barry in bed, like ah porn star.

– That's cause ah ken what you lassies like, cause ah watch *tons n tons* ay porn. Ah'd say ah model masel mare oan Stanley Stonker, but Gasman's barry, n eh gits up n picks up the video camera, starts playin it back through the laptoap. – Need tae edit it, but we goat some barry stuff... phoah, ya beauty...

– Ah watch tons ay porn n aw. Ever seen *Paradise Bangs*?

– Aye. Seen it loads, eh pits the camera doon n jumps back intae bed.

– Dae ah no remind ye ay somebody oan that?

Eh looks at ays. – Aye! Right enough! What's her name?

– Toni San Laurentis! Ah sometimes ey git compared tae her.

– That bitch's boady is fuckin dope, but yours is better, eh goes, – tell ye that fir nowt, eh picks up the camera again n plays a bit back. It's the bit whaire eh's goat the belt roond muh neck n eh's ridin ays fae behind but ye cannae tell which hole eh's in...

– Aye? Ye think ah'm like Toni San Laurentis? Ye reckon ah could make money daein porn?

– Easy! You'd be minted! We should make a better tape, two cameras, n send it oaf, n eh waves the webcam. – Ah widnae like the idea ay other laddies ridin ye, bit... Coco Chambers... Chaymbo... he sais eh wis up ye.

– Wis eh nowt!

– Hi hi hi, thoat it wis bullshit!

Then eh looks at ays n goes, – What wis it like wi Joshy Boy Eight? Josh nivir battered ays as much as Jayden did then, that's fir sure. Ah'm gaunny huv tae try n git um tae calm doon a bit. – Wisnae as big or as barry in bed as you, but.

Jayden lies back n blaws smoke intae the air, a big smile oan ehs coupon.

Ah reaches for muh phone, but mind that ah left it ootside on the wee table by the pool. Ah tries tae move Jayden's airm.

– Whaire you gaun? eh asks.

– Ah wis jist gaunny bring ma bag n oor phones in.

Then eh's goat the *cheeky wee smile* oan again. – That kin wait, eh goes, n ehs stiff fingers ur pokin between ma legs. – Lit's git a close-up or two... fir the edit... n eh switches oan the camcorder.

Ah'm still sair n ah hope eh kisses ays for a bit so thit ah git wet before eh pits it back in. But nearly right away eh's wild at it again, pillin muh hair till the scalp burns n ah start tae feel hoat tears as eh sais mare barry things...

... then the pressure oan muh throat, n ah'm lookin intae ehs mad, burnin eyes, n ah cannae breathe, n ah'm thinkin this must be what it's like whin yir deid... slippin away tae the other side... ma whole boady aw shakin n that relaxed aw at the same time...

Eftir we wakes again, n ma necks's sare, n ah feel like ah've been stabbed aw ower wi a knife, ah sais tae um, – Ah could git that covid, you n me baith, n we'd be awright, but then wi could gie it tae that fulthy big fat hoor. That wid be her fucked!

Jaygo looks at ays like ah've said the wrong thing. Josh eywis sais that ah ey said the wrong thing. – No wantin any cunt deid! Jist want hur oot ay muh life n some ay that poppy that hur cunts ay brars'll jist git anywey.

– Course no, ah goes, – jist tae make sure she kens that she needs tae keep away fae us.

– Aye, Jaygo goes.

That's the thing about me n Jaygo: wi ey agree.

LITA (13)

Lita McCallum had a dream. A family holiday, and she could only remember two places they went to when she was a child: North Berwick, where they had a caravan, and Benidorm. The dream was dull but it set off a recall of the latter.

The hotel in the Spanish resort was luxurious to a ten-year-old Lita, boasting two bars and a large pool. But the break had ended in disgrace. After a boozy barbecue her father had glassed another holidaymaker, and the police had been called. No charges were pressed on condition that the family left the hotel and returned home the next day.

She recollects how two girls she had made friends with had subsequently avoided her, treating her like a leper. – We've been told not to play with you, one had said. – Your daddy pushed a glass into the face of that other man. There was blood everywhere!

Lita ran from the playroom and went down to the beach. She got back to be told off by her mum. Her father and two brothers were laughing as they threw stuff into bags, the incident already designated part of the holiday fun.

Now the holiday fun involves waking up next to your boyfriend's uncle.

Dinnae lit anybody tell ye thit thir's nae satisfaction at being smashed aw weys by an aulder felly; yin thit kens ehs wey aroond a lassie's boady. Ehs fulthy whispers in yir ear, specially oan they puhls. But it's no aw sweetness n light: thir's something mawkit aboot him lyin oan ehs back, snoring ehs heid oaf. N that sly coupon. Ah huv tae git up n open the sliding doors really quiet, n ah head acroas tae the other side ay the pool.

Ah sees Jayden through the gless, but eh's fast asleep... looks angelic wi that wee smile... but eh's wi that Andrea... ah'll fuckin batter that cow, covid or nae covid... but it breks muh hert, n ah cannae look! Ah'm aboot tae turn away, then ah see the marks on her, they bruises comin up oan her airms. Eh's hammered the cunt like in they rough-sex videos eh watches, n that dopey hoor's just lit um! If eh tried that tae me muh brars wid fuckin cull um!

Nuht.

Ah cannae look at thum.

Then oot oan the wee table by the Lilo, thir's two phones. One's Jayden's; it's green wi a Harp oan it n, 'Walkin the walk and talkin the talk since 1875'. N ah ken the code tae git intae it. It's 1875. So ah gits intae it. Muh heart pounds as a reads some ay the auld texts wi him n that Andrea:

> As soon as Glen has done fatso
> there ain't no stopping us!

N Jayden goes back:

You will get road every day
after that TRUE BY ME

The fuckin...

... ah sends Jayden the video ay Shiv gitting done by Glen n Jordan, through that encruptit Freedum, the yin Jayden uses for drug security. As soon as it goes intae his phone, ah send it fae thair oantae Andrea, usin WhatsApp. Ah kin see it pop in oan her screen notifications, even though ah cannae git intae it. Whin it does that, thir's nae sender ID n ye cannae tell whae it's fae unless they enable it. Ah ken Jayden's goat Freedum set tae delete everything eftir twinty minutes. So if they dinnae come oot n check thir phones before then it's mibbe gaunny work...

... then ah pit Shiv's roastin up oan YouTube, usin an account ah opened wi encruptit email address soas ah could git that x-treme porn n track Jayden. Then ah send hur it fae Jayden's Freedum account before deletin everything fae ma ain phone... ah look at thum, then pit the phones back...

... ah go back ower oantae the Lilo. It's barry tae relax in the evenin sun, but ah hears the telly oan, talkin in Spanish. Looks through the gless intae the lounge n sees Shiv n Jordan snoggin oan the couch. Whin they brek oaf eh hears um say, – N ah'd treat Beyonce like she wis muh ain.

– That's cause you're a jetulmin, Shiv goes.

So ah slides the door open. – Hi! Youse two stoap gittin aw lovey-dovey, ah tells thum. – Wis meant tae be a fuckin orgy!

They jist look up at ays n laugh. Then Jordan leans forward in the couch n sais, – Thing is, Shiv n me ur gaunny go oot the gither. Whin we git back.

– Good fir youse, ah goes, but ah'm no happy. No thit they care, cause thair okay, but they'll no be the now! Cause as soon as twinty minutes ur up, ah goes ootside by the pool n starts screamin...

UNCLE GLEN (5)

– JAYDIHHHNNN...

... the high-pitched scream bores into Glen Urquhart's consciousness. Sensing the mattress is again stable under his slim, muscular
body, he blinks awake. Concerned to find the bed empty – where is
Lita? – he throws his legs out. The tiled floor, despite the air con and
the falling sun, is still warm on the soles of his feet. The noise stops
as he stands up and looks out, but from his vantage nobody is visible
by the pool. Glen sees his orange trunks, discarded at the foot of the
bed. Pulls them on.

He looks in on Shiv and Jordan, wrapped up in each other, basking
in lovers' contentment. Otherwise the lounge is empty.

Where has Lita gone?

Then he hears sobbing coming from outside. Opens the patio door
to find Lita standing under the shading canopy, looking forlornly across
the pool. He's about to speak but she recommences her screaming over
at his nephew, who is emerging onto the patio blinking...

– JAYDEN! JAYDEN!

Christ, what's up wi that McCallum muck-bucket? Rode her aw
weys, and she still pines for that fuckin moron! – Lita, ah goes, but she
ignores ays, shoutin acroas the pool at Jayden.

– What? eh goes.

– What's aw the commotion aboot? ah shouts, – Come back tae kip,
Lita...

– HIM! EH GIED AYS IT! She points ower the pool. – CUNT GIED
AYS THE MILEY FUCKIN CYRUS! AH CANNAE GIT IT! MORBIT
BEESITY!! AH'M GAUNNY DIE!! CAUSE AY YOU!! Then she turns
back tae me, tears streamin. – Ah've goat ah the symptoms... dry
throat... poundin heidache... shiverin... cannae smell nowt.

– Easy… easy… ah fling an airm roond her n lead her inside, briefly glancin back tae scope Jayden's snidey wee pus. – Baby, it's just sunstroke. N a hangower. N ye cannae smell nowt cause yir beak's aw blocked up wi the gak!

That seems tae calm the dim wee oinker doon, as Jayden shouts fae across the pool, – AYE, THAT'S RIGHT! GO WI HIM, YA CHEATUN FAT SOW! WE ARE SO FUNISHED!

Well, it's gaun even better than ah thought! Ah'm aw puppy-dug eyes n reassuring whispers, as ah plonk fat Lita oan the couch. – Listen, baby, one thing ah ken for deffo. We're family now, we *look eftir each other*, whatever happens wi you n that boy, eh isnae takin care ay ye.

– Tell ays aboot it! Eh's wi that hoor! The chubby chowhound is irate. – How did that even happen? What's she even daein here!

– Calm doon, darlin, his loss.

Her eyes expand in hope. – But… dis this mean *we're* gaun oot the gither now? Like movin in wi you tae the flat in Albert Street? Or Camel Hampstead?

A grasping McCallum overreach; seen fae the moon. *No chance.* – Well, we're certainly bonded.

Her ruddy wee coupon is igniting the wey it did when ah banged hur. – But his ma, your sister, she hates ays!

– Well, that wis before ah came along n hud a wee wurd, ah wink, – pit her in the picture!

– Whit did ye say?

– Well, lit's jist say ah offered oor Manda a clear-eyed perspective, if ye like, as tae what's gaun oan wi you n Jayden, n ah rise n move tae the fridge n get oot two cans ay Stella. – Ah pride masel oan being able tae view social interactions wi a mare dispassionate gaze, ah say, as a text comes intae the Nokia fae muh sis:

> Have youse got that fat
> sow's poppy yet?

– The wey Jayden's treated ays… aw uv ivir done wis love um… she moans. – Wi you n me… ah dinnae ken… and starts greetin.

– Well, we aw love that laddie, ah points at masel, – ma sister's boy, ah tells her, n opens one Stella n gies it tae hur, then the other n takes a slurp, but ah need tae reinforce that he's no the wee angel, the blue-eyed boy some think, n ah hud up the can. – Nice cauld, ay?

Lita takes a sip, then a gulp, n nods. – Well, ah dinnae think Jayden's perfect, but we've been gaun oot fir ages n –

Ah raise muh hand n cut in, – ... But that's Jayden, Lita. There's the drug-dealing. The violence. The casual misogyny so rampantly endemic in scheme youth whae missed the healing tar ay the enlightened bourgeoisie's woke stick bein brushed against thir pallid skins...

– Ah like the wey ye yaze wurds, she goes.

– Ah like the wey your swing these puppies aboot, ah goes, lookin at her chest, n ah wouldnae huv believed a daughter ay Kenny 'Kaybo' McCallum's could go slightly bashful, but she certainly does that. – Stoap it, you, she sais, her sunburnt coupon further flushin tae they preorgasmic levels. – Ah'm gaun back oot tae git some sun...

– Me tae, ah goes, lookin acroas at Philly Matheson oan the sideboard. *Needs must, comrade...*

Then mare fuckin screamin n shoutin comin fae Shiv n Jordan's room. Me n Lita stall as spotty Jordan runs oot in ehs daft Hertz strip, – Some cunt posted us n Shiv oanline! It's up oan YouTube! Anonymous!

That wee cunt's cherry poppin, recorded for aw time!

Shiv runs through, looks right at Lita. – Youse wir the only cunts thair! Go intae yir phones!

The fightin McCallum comes oot in the wee chubster. – Everybody wis thair, it wis an orgy, n wi wis aw wasted! Ah wis in the lavvy, fuckin seek then shitein cause ay they puhls! Ye think ah'd dae that tae muh best mate?

– Ah dinnae ken...

– Dinnae fuckin well accuse ays ay daein sumthin ah didnae dae!

Thir squarin up tae each other, n ah signuls for Jordan tae git between thum n goes, – Girls, the best thing we can do right now is get this taken doon. If ma plumbing customers hear ay this... n suddenly ah'm worried aboot thaim, n Lauren in the Double H... ah steps outside oantae the patio, – JAYDEN! GET OWER HERE!

Acroas the pool Jayden pokes his glakit heid round the door, a tooil ower his shoodirs. – Ah cannae, but, cause ay that covit!

– GET THE FUCK OWER!

He looks at Andrea, n they come ower. Ah explain tae them, – Some cunt has filmed n posted Jordan n me roastin Shiv.

– Barry!

– Far fae it, ah snaps, – but first things first: did you dae it? You're the yin thit yazes that encryptit Freedom app!

– Did ah fuck! Ah'd'uv been in thair, no fuckin fulum it! Look, n eh opens n hands ower ehs phone.

Ah checks it. – WhatsApp… nowt… text… nowt… Signul… nowt… Telegram… nowt… Freedom… nowt. Fair enough, ah goes. – Now we need your tech-savvy skills tae get it doon! Ah hands um muh MacBook.

– Right… eh goes, n gits oantae it. – It should take nae time at aw. Whae pit it up?

– Hurry… Shiv begs.

– Inevitably the same cunt that filmed it, ah looks roond thum aw. – Which rules oot me, Jordan and Shiv, obviously, n ah focuses oan Lita. It would be a typical McCallum move: stupid and sleazy.

– Well yis ken ah nivur fulumt nay cunt, Jayden grins at Andrea.

– Dinnae look at me, Lita goes. N she's lookin at Jayden n Andrea, who ur standin outside the slidin patio doors. – N keep thaim oot!

– You wir here, Shiv sais.

– Ah telt ye, ah wis seek n went tae puke up… Lita sais, n she looks at Jayden n Andrea. – What wir they daein? They could huv come ower whin ah wis in the lavvy!

– We wir huvin fun. Eftir you n Glen wir, but, Jayden goes.

Ah wish that silly wee cunt would shut it. Lita looks at ays. – Ah wis in the lavvy, you ken that, Glen!

Ah ignore her. She did vanish fir a bit. Was she in the lavvy aw that time? – It was shot fae ower here. Ah looks at the images oan ma laptop (muh stomach does look flat for a man ay ma years, hus tae be said) n points through the bedroom door intae the lounge. – Could have been anybody, mibbe Andrea'll gie us her phone next…

– What? Andrea goes.

– It'll jist cause arguments, Jayden says, lookin up fae the laptoap. – C'moan, it's been a barry time, n ah've goat tae say, eh looks up at Shiv, – you seem like a barry ride. Ay, Uncle Glen?

– Top notch, ah sais, wonderin: *how can this wee cunt consider that right now?* He really is mentally retarded. But at least he's still workin away oan the deletion.

Shiv's a wreck, though, face trippin her. – Beyonce's gaunny grow up kenning whit a fuckin slag her ma is, she starts greetin. Ah nods at Jordan, in a *mind what ah telt ye* way.

So Jordan goes ower n pits ehs airm roond her. – It's awright… eh sais. Whispers something in her ear n starts stroking her hair. She settles intae his airms. That's muh boy, this is a kid whae responds tae coachin! Ye kin tell it annoys the fuck oot ay Jayden! N mibbe ehs new squeeze Andrea n aw. She goes tae the assembled company, – So youse ur sayin ah posted that?

– Wir jist hypothesising, no accusing, ah tells her. – But it could be Lita… or Jarred. Whaire is that wee bastard? He's been away for ooirs… ah looks up at the sky, now so black.

– Mibbe goat his hole, the pervy wee cunt, Jayden goes. – Problay him that fulumed n posted it! Ehs ey sneakin aboot daein that Peepin Tom act, n eh's the maist tech-savvy cunt here, mibbe even mare than me… eh goes, still oan the screen, mumblin, – … open *report this video… infrunches ma rights…* naw… bettur wi *infrunches ma copyright…* money shits thum up… entur timestamp… cut tae emerjuncy, illeekal post… then… eh huds up muh laptoap n sings in triumph, – Deletit!

– He's just a wee laddie… might be fuckin deid in a ditch… yir ma'll kill ays… ah thinks ay Manda's nerves n checks the phone, lookin for messages. Tries tae ring Jarred but it goes tae voicemail. So ah texts him. Ah'm jist aboot tae hit the panic button when we hear car wheels scrunchin on the gravel ootside. Then thir's a bang on the door n wir aw lookin at each other. – The fuck's that? ah goes, – … Jarred…

– Stall the now in case it's the bizzies, Jayden sais. – Git the fuckin drug stuff cleaned up. Spanish polis dinnae like that!

Ma nephew is fuckin thinkin at last…

LITA (14)

Both Lita's brothers, Clint and Dessie, had, like her father Kenny, served prison sentences. Her mother, Gerty McCallum, had only just escaped jail after nutting Margo Rooney and breaking her nose following a dispute over who had right-of-use in the communal drying area of the flats they then lived in. Gerty was spared a sentence as she was carrying Lita. The strategy of blaming the assault on hormonal imbalance proved effective, as the judge believed women were irrational creatures. There-fore, he recommended community service, where Gerty was compelled to stuff leaflets into envelopes at the arts centre for mail-outs.

This chastening and humiliating experience was one Lita's mother was disinclined to repeat. Since this, Gerty had reined in her inner crazy, attempting to provide a positive role model for her daughter. While not always successful, she was head and shoulders above Lita's father and brothers in this regard.

A turbulent domestic life had installed a scammer's worldview in the McCallum daughter. Though prone to flying off the handle, Lita could keep her nerve when the potential rewards were high.

Now Andrea Raeburn was facing her; face framed with toxic, shrew-like mien, indicating the scenting of blood.

This Lita McCallum perceived as a weakness.

The door knocks again. Jayden's in the lavvy, hidin the drugs, takin thum oot the stash boax. – Whae is it? ah goes.

– It's me.

– Whae's me? S'at you Jarrit? Back fae toon?

– Aye. Ah wis telt tae go n git a taxi tae come here. But the boy's ootside n ah've nae money tae pey um.

– Nae money!? How the fuck… ya chisellin wee cunt – Glen starts, then stoaps.

– S'awright, ah'll lit ye in, ah goes, shoutin ben tae them, – it's jist Jarrit! Sort yirsels oot! Ah opens the door n eh's standin thair. Thir's a taxi outside. – Much is it? ah goes.

– Fifty euro.

– Fifty fuckin euro fae San Antonio?

– That's what the boy telt ays.

Glen steps forwurt. – Bullshit. I'll send the cunt away wi a flea in ehs ear, n eh heads ootside.

Wi aw go oot n stand in the doorway. It's still hoat. Ah sees Glen talkin tae a big felly in a cab, whae's still wearin shades even though it's goat awfay dark. Glen's sortay moved ehs back tae block oor view, but ye kin tell thit eh hands something ower. – Bein, senor… lo siento, muchos gracias, eh goes.

The boy nods n the car pills away.

– Ye pey him? Jarred asks.

– Lit's jist say we came tae a mutually satisfactory arrangement.

– Did ye pey um the fill fifty euro? ah goes.

– Nivir youse mind, Glen sais, – it's sorted. We dinnae want tae draw attention tae oorsels, n eh sees Jarred listenin n droaps ehs voice, – wi the ching n eckies.

– Youse goat drugs here? Jarred asks.

– Nivir you mind that, Glen sais.

Wi go back inside n Jarred looks tae the telly in the front room. – Youse been watchin strangleporn oan that big screen?

– What dae you ken aboot that? ah goes.

– Dae it aw the time, but ay. Aw muh mates dae it.

– Strangleporn? At the skill? Glen asks. – Surely no.

– Aye. Well, no *at* school, but wi mates *fae* school.

– Jesus fuck, Glen goes.

Jayden's still hingin aboot by the patio door. Steps inside. – You shouldnae be watchin that, eh shouts at Jarred.

– How no? Jarred goes.

Jayden looks like eh cannae think ah a reason. – Cause… it's no… cause ah sais, right!

– It's no up tae you what ah watch. You're no muh dad.

– It's up tae me if ah punch ye in the mooth, aye?

– Aye, but –

– Well shut the fuck up then!

– C'moan lads, stoap aw this ruttin-stags nonsense, Glen waves them doon, n opens the fridge door. – Thir's cans ay Stella here. Wir oan hoaliday, fir fuck sakes!

– Right, Jayden sais.

– Goat that Coke Zero? Jarred goes. That makes ays feel guid cause it wis me what telt um it wis better thin Diet Coke.

– Ah dunno, Glen sais. – Huv a wee look n show some initiative, Jarred. Jayden, you git back ootside in the fresh air. Ye shouldnae be standin in here. Infect the loat ay us! Ah cannae afford any mare time of work cause ay this covid shite! Plumbin's a competitive game!

Jayden takes a can ay Stella. – It was you that sais tae stey here till wi found oot aboot whae shot n poastit the skud, ya bam.

– Aye, right enough, Glen goes. – Right, Jarred, lit's see your phone.

– How?

– Jist lit's see it. Yir tech-savvy enough tae huv done it!

– What? Jarred goes, but eh's ready tae hand it ower.

Jayden sneers, – Durty wee perve!

– What? Jarred goes.

– Open it, Glen sais.

So Jarred does, n hands it tae Glen.

Jayden goes, – Whaire wir you the day?

– That's ma business. You're no ma boss.

Jayden goes aw that quiet wey, like when eh offered Joshy Boy Eight a square go. – Dinnae fuckin push it.

Glen rolls ehs eyes, looks ower tae that creepy urn then Jarred. – We'll huv a quiet wee chat later, pal. But dinnae stey oot like that again! No whin it starts gittin dark! Hud us aw worried seek, n eh looks at the phone, the calls list then huds it up. – Muh wee nephew's in the clear, n eh turns tae Jarred. – Never doubted ye a minute, pal. No like some... but we hud tae check.

– What ur youse aw oan aboot? Jarred shrugs n takes the phone back n goes tae ehs room.

– Right... whae's next... Glen goes.

– Telt ye, Jayden goes, then looks at me, – That's you fucked! First ye ride muh unkul, then ye shoot a porno ay him wi your best mate n ma best mate!

– It wisnae me, right!

– Submit tae the process, Lita, Glen goes.

– Nuht, how should ah? ah goes. – It's ma phone!

That Andrea rolls her eyes. – Aye, right. If yuv done nowt wrong, yuv goat nowt tae hide, n she punches in her code n hands hur phone tae Glen.

Glen goes through the messages, then huds the phone up. Oan that Andrea's screen, Shiv gitting rifled by him, while gamin Jordan! But hur fuckin coupon... – Whaaa... naw... naw...

– She must huv thoat she'd deleted it, Glen snaps n turns tae hur, shakin ehs heid. – If you're gaunny be a snidey bastard, at least huv half a brain!

– You... YA FAHKEN... Shiv's gaun fir hur, n bein held back by Jordan.

– NAW! N Andrea points at ays. – IT'S HUR! SHE'S DONE SUMTHIN!!

– Well, ah've nowt tae hide, n ah goes intae ma phone n hands it tae Glen.

Glen goes through aw they applications, wi Jayden, lookin aw beady-eyed, helpin um, n turnin tae look at Andrea, whae's sortay pleadin wi um n mumblin, – Ah didnae send nowt... we wir sleepin, mind! WI WIR SLEEPIN!

Then Glen looks at Jayden, whae shakes ays heid. Glen goes, – Thir's nothing tae indicate it wis sent fae Lita. Sender and time unknown, sent fae that Freedom.

– But ah nivir fulumed anybody, Andrea goes. – Jayden, ah wis wi you aw the time! Tell thum!

– She wis, Jayden goes, then sais, – obviously wi wir crashed oot asleep sumtime...

– SO YE CANNAE SAY FIR SURE!! N IT'S OAN HER FUCKIN PHONE!! Shiv roars. She flies at Andrea and punches her, then rakes her nails doon her face. – EVERYBODY KENS WHAT AH DID NOW THANKS TAE YOU, YA CUNT!!

– Ah nivir... Andrea whimpers, backin away, n Jayden jumps in n pushes Shiv back.

Then Jordan springs forward. – Dinnae lay yir hands oan her, Jaygo!

Jayden cannae believe it. – *You? You're* gittin fuckin wide wi *me*?

– ENOUGH!! Glen screams oot n goes tae Jayden n Andrea. – Ah'd advise youse pair tae git back ower tae the other side ay the pool! Now!

– AWRIGHT, Jayden shouts. – WIR GAUN, DINNAE WORRY! FUCK YOUSE CUNTS! C'moan, eh sais tae that Andrea, n eh storms away, totally ragin, wi her troopin eftir him like a battirt dug!

Aw.

Ehs perr sad, beaten wee bitch!

Glen steps oot eftir Jayden, follayin um oot by the pool. – Need tae work on these manners, pal, you and yir wee floozy!

Jayden whips roond. – Aye, ye think so?

– Ah know so.

– How's that?

– Good manners are a set ay keys. They open doors, n Glen points tae us, through the patio door behind um. – Ask yirsel, will you be enjoyin sexual encounters wi lassies your age when yir ma age? Will ye even be here at forty?

– Fuck knows, whae kens aboot that? Jayden's ballin ehs fists, n that Andrea's tryin tae pill um away.

– Ye can guess. Stay a lean, fit man and learn manners. And keep away fae online pornography. It's obviously reinforcing yir appalling behaviour aroond the lassies n crushing yir libido, Glen sneers at um. – How tragic in one sae young!

– Fuck you, n eh points at Andrea. – Ah smashed hur aw weys while you wir ridin that fat mess, n Jayden looks at ays in spite n walks away.

Ah nivir kent eh could be such a horrible basturt. Ah feel the tears well up.

– Forgive my nephew, Lita, Glen kisses ays oan the cheek, – a young felly sadly lacking in those qualities that maketh a man.

Ah feel like sayin, *ah saw the fuckin texts: you wir in oan it,* but ah shut up.

Jayden gies us the finger n goes back tae his ain bit oan the other side ay the pool. At least wee snidey knickers isnae sae wide now! Hope she gits that covit oaf um n it fucks her right up! Oan toap ay it aw!

They walk roond the pool, bickerin at each other, her gaun aboot him littin that Jordan talk tae hur like that. – That Lita set ays up, Jaygo, ah ken it!

– SHUT UP! How could shi set ye up, ya daft cunt?!

She's nearly greetin, beggin um, – But she did, she did...

Fuckin barry music tae ma ears.

Then Jayden turns roond, cranin ehs neck ower the pool at Glen n me. – AH'M SEEK AY YOUSE CUNTS! YOUSE KEN NOWT ABOOT ME! COME OAN THEN, n eh starts walkin back roond the pool.

Glen steps oot n looks at him. – You talkin tae me, ya retarded wee fanny?

– YOU N ME! NOW!

– Dinnae fuckin make ays, cause if ah git covid ah'll make it muh worthwhile n dae whit yir ma should've done years ago; droon ye in that fuckin pool like a kitten!

– WU'LL SEE WHAE... wu'll see... wu'll... Jayden's gaspin fur air... then eh goes intae this coughin fit...

Andrea starts screamin, – HELP US! EH CANNAE BREATHE!

Glen's pit his mask oan n eh's acroas the pool n sais tae us, – Youse stey back, no wantin that covid! Some cunt phone an ambulance!

– Dinnae ken the number here, is it nine nine nine? ah goes. But Jayden's no breathin, so ah'm ower!

Ah grabs a cushion oaf one ay they chairs n pits it under his heid. Glen gits oan ma phone, n eh's goat me n that Andrea turnin Jayden oan ehs side. – Recovery position! PIT THAT OOT! Glen's lookin at the fag ah jist lit. Ah'm no happy, but ah droap it in the ashtray.

– Is eh gaunny die? Jarred goes.

– Nuht, ah sais, even though Jayden problay deserves it. For what eh's done. It wid stull be shite if eh did, but.

Eh's jist lyin thair, sortay fittin, until the ambulance comes n they gits Jayden oan a stretcher n loads um in. Ah starts climbin in, n that Andrea goes, – Ah'm gaun n aw!

– Naw, ah'll go, Glen sais, – eh's ma nephew.

– Eh's ma felly! N ah pushes that Andrea away n gits in the ambulance.

She jumps in behind ays. – Eh's no your felly, eh's ma fuckin felly!

– Ah'll git a taxi n see yis at the hoaspital, Glen shouts as the boy slams the back doors shut.

– YE WIR A FUCKEN REBOUND RIDE! Ah scream at her.

– AYE, THAT'S WHAT YOU THINK!

Ah turns n looks at perr Jayden, whae's a purpul colour, as the other medikul boy pits an oxygen mask ower um. – Eh's no well, that covit made um no ken what eh wis daein, ay Jayden?

Jayden's sayin nowt under the mask, but ehs eyes ur rollin as the ambulance goes up the hull tae the main road.

– Naw. It's no jist cause ay covid, Andrea's spiteful pus screws up aw hateful. – We've been at it aw the time! Tells ays you're no a real wummin, willnae lit um dae rough sex or nowt!

Cunt… ah fuckin looks at hur, then him, n ah goes, – Eh's ma felly, but AY JAYDEN!

Then wir baith lookin at Jayden, whae sais somethin under the mask thit we cannae make oot.

Ah try n take the mask oaf. – TELL UR, JAYDEN! AY YOU'RE MA FELLY! AY!

The wee ambulance boy is gaun radge, – No! Stop! Please!

– YOU SET ME UP! N the mental wee Andrea hoor fuckin grabs muh hair n pills it back. – EH'S NO FUCKIN WELL YOURS, YA FAT DOZY CUNT!

Ah lashes oot, batterin her right in the mooth, a proper hook like muh brar Clint taught ehs tae dae oan the heavy bag. Blood gushes oot, n ah feel her grip loosen oan muh hair. So ah've grabbed hers n ah'm twistin it back, n she lits go ay mine, greetin, n ah've goat her heid doon. Ah smack her in the face again, n ah'm thinkin thit the pagger's gaun right oot ay this bitch! But then she charges like a fuckin bull n batters ays against the side ay the ambulance. – YOU'RE FUCKIN DEID! She's screamin. Fuckin mental case!

Ah feel aw the wind squeezed oot ays, but ah'm punchin fuck oot ay hur. – WE'LL SEE WHAE'S FUCKIN DEID, YA HOOR!

– NO, NO, NO… the Spanish boy's tryin tae pill us apart, but she's goat muh hair again n ah've goat hurs, n nane ay us is letting go, but hur blood's spillin aw ower the place… then the back doors jist sortay fly open… like right at the toap ay the hull, and Jayden's trolley slides oot… muh hert's in muh mouth as ah thoat eh's gaunny topple right ower, but eh jist runs doon the slopin road, pickin up speed…

That Andrea n me lit go ay each other's hair, as the driver brakes the motor.

Ah screams at hur, – YOU DID THAT, YA FUCKIN DOPEY
HOOR!

– YOU DID IT!

Wi baith jumps oot n wir watchin Jayden rollin doon the road,
gittin faster aw the time. A car stoaps as eh passes right by it.

– JAYDUUHHHHN!!!! Ah'm nashin doon the hill eftir um, but
ah'm runnin oot ay breath masel in this heat. That Andrea bombs past
ays, n ah try tae keep up wi her, but she's nae tits so she's faster, n then
ah feel masel fawin ower… n that's aw ah remember. But ah ken ah'm
oan the ground, cause ay this wimmin n two wee bairns lookin at ehs
n askin things in Spanish.

Like ah'm meant tae ken any ay that shite…

Whin ah wakes up, ah'm in a hoaspital bed wi a mask oan masel,
jist like Jayden's… – JAY… DI-HI-HIN… whaire's Jayden… ah tries
tae speak, but ah'm coughin n hackin up muh lungs, n looks up tae see
the doaktir whae looks like that dago boy in fulums. Forget ays name,
but a ride…

– Take it easy, eh goes, in shite English, – you have bad shock. You
very dehydrate.

Ah'm thinkin, how kin ah be dehydratit whin aw ah've done is
fuckin well drink since ah goat here? Cocktails. Gin. Stella. Mibbe they
bumbles n that ching, but ay. Or mibbe it is that covit, eftir me kiddin
oan! That scares ays cause ah dinnae want tae be oan one ay they
ventilaturs!

But even if it's no that guid, the only cunt thit speaks English seems
tae be this doaktir. Suddenly ay reminds ays ay the boy fae Wiltshire
that ah fancied, the yin whae was oan *Love Ireland*. – You are very
obese.

– Aye, morbit beesity, ah tells um, – but ah cannae breathe…
Jayden's fault…

– Very obese to be pregnant… ees no good for baby!

– Pregnint? ah goes, n ah cannae believe what um hearin! – Barry!
Me n Jayden, n ah looks at the doaktir. Then ah laughs, cause that boy
disnae ken whaes bairn it is!

– You cannot be drinking and taking drugs, n eh asks ays aboot
what ah've hud.

Ah'm aboot tae tell um tae mind ays ain business, ah'm no

wantin grassed up tae nae Spanish polis, but ah'm thinkin the boy might no be like that n mibbe eh's jist daein ehs joab. Mibbe Shiv no follayin doaktirs orders is how Beyonce turned oot wi spazzy feet. She goat wasted at the Citrus Club one time whin she wis up the duff. Whae's tae say it wisnae the likes ay that thit did fir perr wee Beyonce's feet?

But here ah am in this hoaspital bed, so ah tells um. Ah'll keep quiet aboot the bairn tae the rest ay thum the now; ah'll pick ma fuckin time. But ah'll be pushin that stroller through the shoapin centre soon, n thi'll aw be sayin, *nice bairn.*

N it'll huv barry feet!

Thir's aw they peepul oan this ward, lookin fucked up oan drugs. Ah feel like shoutin oot: *ah'm nowt tae dae wi drugs, me!*

Jist as that doaktir boy leaves, Glen comes oantae the ward. Eh's goat a basebaw cap wi RAMS oan it, n eh's lookin roond. Eh gies ays a barry smile whin he sees ays. Ah'm thinkin, it might be his bairn, n see if it wis, wid it be the worst thing? The bairn wid huv personality! Ah mean, Jayden looks barry in that Fred Perry toap, but ah huv tae admit Glen's goat mare personality. N Glen eywis hus money in ehs poakit fae the plumbin trade, so the bairn wid want fir nowt. They daft cunts thoat *ah* hud money but it's no enough tae buy a hoose, n ah'd nivir even git a mortgage, even if ah'd held doon that joab at the bakery. If ah rent a nice place the money'll jist go. So might as well enjoy it, but ay.

– You okay?

– Aye.

– Ah've sent Andrea away fae the villa: a disruptive influence. Ah believe she's goat a place in toon. Couldnae huv her there wi Shiv gaunny kill her. Jayden's no wantin tae talk tae hur n –

– You n Jayden tried tae set ays up! Tae git that money oaffay ays!

– What money? Glen goes.

– Youse thoat ah won ninety-free grand oan the Lotto!

Glen's shakin ehs heid. – Jayden wis tryin tae string ye along, soas eh could ditch ye for Andrea. Eh kent ah wis intae you, so he wis tryin tae set us baith up, in mare weys thin one, so he could be wi Andrea. Ah wis nivir bothered aboot any money, n ah dinnae need it! Ah wis ey jist interested n gittin ma hands oan they titties…

– Nuht, beat it, wir ye fuck! N it wis only thirteen grand, ya daft cunts!

– Oh, I've nae doubt that Jayden hud nefarious plans for your cash as well as ditchin ye, but, as ah say, ah wis purely motivated by –

– Dinnae try n trick ays wi wurds, Glen!

Eh pits ays hands up like in surrender. – Ah'm no arguing aboot money, princess. The main thing is that baith you n ma nephew – though that wee toerag disnae deserve ma concern – are okay!

– Aye, right!

– Aye, it is right, Glen looks ays in the eye.

For a wee mind-treatin second or two ah nearly believe um.

JAYDEN (11)

Jayden James Templeton, his neck badly frazzled a scarlet-pink, is relieved to be inside the airport terminal building. He has endured a terrible week: a horrific forty-eight hours of struggling for breath in the sweltering heat had made him reluctant to leave the sanctuary of his air-conditioned room. Then several more days of utter boredom followed. He has lost both Andrea and Lita, but on the bright side achieved personal bests on both Fortnite and The Executioner: Quest For Eden, where he defeated Rudi Van Lauten, a rated Dutch gamer.

He still had to isolate on his return to the villa. This time he really was alone as there was no Andrea; she had checked into a cheap hotel in San Antonio, where, unbeknown to the others, Glen visited her regularly to prevent her getting too lonely. These outings were soon curtailed with the hospital release of first Jayden, then Lita.

The atmosphere at the villa could best be described as one of uneasy coexistence. Though both Jayden and Glen found Lita distantly polite, this suited them now that she no longer had the level of finance they'd believed. Glen resented Jayden fucking that one up and refused to talk to him. Both uncle and nephew could not share their joint worry that Lita was marshalling McCallum forces against them.

Lita mostly worked on her tan and slyly checked out baby sites online. Shiv and Jordan, enjoying their romance, were surprised when she declined drink and drugs. She refused to go clubbing, which was convenient for them. Like Glen, Jarred went his own secretive way.

For a while, things dragged; then, with the mysterious games time plays, it was suddenly over. They headed to the airport, their feelings of elation and trepidation that follow a holiday more manifest than ever.

Disembarking from the people carrier, they enjoy the blinding sun burning down on them for the last time. Shiv emits a yelp as she scorches her shoulder on the chassis of the vehicle. The blistered wound compels Jordan to visit the chemist in order to find some cream, while Jayden enjoys the terminal's welcome respite from the heat outside. He is concerned that they will see he has no stamp in his passport, having entered the country illegally, and is still infected by covid, which requires quarantine, but he is allowed to pass with only a cursory glance.

We are Hubs, we dae what we want... very least the Spanish cunts could dae... cause ah jist aboot fuckin well died thair, but ay. Whin ah slid oot the back ay that ambulance, then went intae the boy's car – jist as well eh braked – ah came oaf the trolley n rolled right ower the bonnet n hit the ground! No a fuckin scratch oan ehs! Bulletproof! Mare hassle fae yir ain country wi that passenger lokatur form shite! Wanted tae tell thum that ay dinnae download shite fawrums fae guv-irnmint websites, aw ah download is strangelporn, video games n fitba rows. But naw, ah bit muh tongue cause ay me bein illeekal. Thir's too much ay this fawrum shite. Ye buy somethin in a shoap, they send ye an email askin tae fill in a fuckin fawrum, like *how wis the service?* Git tae fuck wi that pish, ah jist boat a fuckin shirt oot ay Toap Shoap!

That covit wis shite, though. Fir a couple ay days ah couldnae fuckin breathe. Ah'd wait till they wur aw asleep when it goat less hoat, then go intae the frudge n try n smell that coffee. Nowt.

Andrea went n took the fuckin strop n moved oot, n she's sayin shi'll sit in her ain seat gaun back. Fuck her, tryin tae take the pish oot ay *me*. Ah mean, what the fuck, wi that fulmin shite? Then fuckin deny it tae sumday yir meant tae be gaun oot wi? Another bam.

Lassies ur duffrunt tae us.

N she must've sorted oot a diffrunt flight. Still, ah'll be able tae compare notes wi JB8 aboot who gied hur the best hammerin! Time the bros bonded again! Mibbe git him oan ma side whin it comes tae pickin the new moderatur fir the J-Firm group! Seeken Five's pus!

Aye, ah could've fuckin died, no thit the rest ay thum cared. Jordan wis gittin ehs hole oaffay Shiv fir the first time ivir, so *they* wir awright. Wey eh strutted aroond ye'd think the Jambo cunt wis fuckin Gasman. Lita said nowt whin she goat oot at the hozzy, but ah bet she grasses ays up tae they cunty brothers ay hurs. Jarred, muh fuckin wee brar, jist avoided ays, sneakin aboot, no sayin a word. N Glen... what a fuckin mingin auld cunt. Hingin aboot wi young peepul like us?

UNCLE GLEN (6)

For Glen Urquhart, trying to **scamduce** Lita and work with Jayden had felt like an unending and increasingly taxing babysitting shift. For a time, the health of both had been a concern. With potential McCallum reprisals outstanding, it was worse than just a massive waste of time and money.

Almost.

At least he'd got his hole off ten women, including the trio in the villa. The threesome with the two insurance brokers from Norwich after DC10 was probably the highlight. The day before this, he'd scattered the ashes of Philly Matheson on the beach, looking out at Formentera. Some of them had blown back into the camera shutters of a group of Japanese tourists. Their squabblings in their native tongue and broken English were just a background noise Glen barely registered as he watched the ashes float into the Med. – Farewell, socialism, he'd declared. He'd then went on a bender which culminated in the visit to Space and the threesome in a San Antonio hotel.

On arriving back in Edinburgh he's pleased to find Manda discharged from hospital. They meet at the beer garden of the village pub, where she is with a dapper Polish man named Woytek, several years her junior. His sister has a glow about her. Glen looks at the Pole; it's not just the new pills that have perked his sister up. Impressively wearing a new peacock-green dress that she tells Glen she'd picked up in a sale at the St James Quarter, as they had renamed St James Centre, she asks about Ibiza.

– Selt a dummy run, Glen says, advising her that the world is fucked up and not to travel. Woytek, who, post-Brexit, is having problems in getting back to see family in Katowice, solemnly agrees.

The festival is over, and it's time for Glen to return to Albert Street. Or perhaps even Hemel Hempstead. Chris has been on about a big plumbing contract in Enfield with a housing association. Lauren and *him are in continual text and FaceTime communication. He yearns to physicalise their relationship.*

It wasn't worth fighting over 13K. Lita is enough of a McCallum to earmark that money for herself. It was impossible to underestimate the greed of that clan, although Lita's cunning had taken him by surprise. The vanity and stupidity of his own nephew, less so.

After estimating a big replumb job on an old Georgian tenement in the New Town, Glen returns to his flat. He is reading an email when the buzzer goes.

Ah looks through the eye-spat tae see that Lita McCallum. She's a wee bit surprised when ah answer. – Hiya, gorgeous… tracked me doon, ay?

– What ur you daein here?

– Eh, this is ma hoose. Come in.

– Ah meant, ah thoat you'd be doon in that Camel Hampstead.

Jesus fuck almighty. Is there nae beginning tae these dopey wee cunts' education? Neoliberalism and the internet has made us aw intae dim, drooling serfs. In such circumstances, getting yir hole frequently, and fae multiple partners, is the only honourable stance for a true socialist.

She comes inside n sits doon. In the cauld light ay a driech Scottish day, fat blooters voluptuous right oot the windae. But then ah git an even bigger kick in the baws…

– Ah'm up the duff, n it's yours.

No the words a shagging man wants tae hear at any time ay life, let alone at mine. Ah dae some quick maths, ma age plus thirteen means dealing wi a mental teenager while in potential decrepitute: no happenin. Fuck me, ah was barely able tae cope with Roxanne, and that wis wi youth oan my side. – What makes ye think that?

– Aw, it's yours awright!

– Sorry, darlin, ah feel fir ye, ah really do, but ah huv tae be careful, it's ma livelihood, n ah'm no peyin for some other cunt's – pardon ma French – some other cunt's bairn. Besides ah've made nae secret ay muh desire tae return tae Hemel Hempstead now thit ma sister seems tae huv stabilised a bit. Thir's no a loat here fir me.

Lauren Brady... cannae wait tae rifle her...

– You'll dae right by me, or muh brars'll hunt ye doon!

A robust, if predictable, play by the fat wench: ah keep ma cool. – Dinnae threaten me, hen. Yir no dealin wi muh dippit wee nephew now. Ah ken villains baith up here and doon in London that owe me favours and whae make your brothers look like the two-bob shit panhandlers they are!

She gies ays that measuring stare, like she's weighing up if it's a bluff or no. Then she breks eye contact n looks deflated, starin at her shite trainers.

Time for bridge building, so ah brush the side of her cheek wi the back of muh hand. – But ah'm no fightin wi ye. Ah sais we wir famely, n ah mean that, n a lower ma mits oantae her shoodirs. – Now let's work the gither here, tae get what we want. Kin we dae that?

She lifts her eyes. – Dinnae try n trick ays wi words!

Ah droap muh hands. – Aw ah'm trying tae dae here, Lita, is tae work oot options, ah spread ma palms. – Are you sure the bairn's mine? Mibbe it's Jayden's?

– The dee em ay test'll prove it's yours. Jayden's no been up ays fir yonks cause ay the porn!

The auld quinoa and quorn will be the death ay alienated youth, fir sure. – Are you sure that you and ma nephew have never had full intercourse recently?

Her brow furrows, then her face opens as somethin starts tae dawn: that dredging up ay a no-so-special memory. – Aye... thir wis that one time whin eh wis oan the Viagra n crack...

– How the earth must have moved.

– Naw, bit eh goat it up, n shot a load inside ay ays, she sings triumphantly, – so it could be Jayden's!

For fuck sake, ma dim, drug-dealing nephew turns oot tae be ma git-oot-ay-jail caird! – Well, ah ken that doon in that scheme it's hard tae differentiate one gaming, violent, porn-watching, trudging-tae-the-Paki's-for-essential-supplies and shit-drugs-and-cheap-booze-ingesting day fae the next, ah tells hur, – but mibbe examine they dates?

– Ah wull!

– And... if you want a bairn: which you do, and also Jayden: which you do, right?

– Aye... she sais, lookin like she's still no quite sure.

– ... then mibbe be a *wee bitty flexible* aboot the actual date and time ay conception.

– What d'ye mean?

Ah sigh deeply. – It's a point ay detail as tae whether the bairn's mines or Jayden's. The main thing fir your objectives – i.e. getting Jayden – is that *he* thinks it's his.

A glint ay McCallumesque calculating greed smashes intae her eyes. – Jayden's goat nae money ootside ehs drug-dealin.

Fuck me, another play. – Perfect! You: with the single-parent allowance. Him: with a solid retail income in the black economy. Way tae hit back against the system and live oaffay the dregs ay a declinin welfare state!

– Aye, but it's no enough!

She's no that fucking daft. – Well, obviously, ah'd feel duty bound tae help oot my great niece or nephew in such a situation.

– Barry.

– So we have an agreement?

– Aye.

– Lita, Jayden is lucky tae have you as a life partner, and yi'll make a wonderful mother!

– Life partnur... ah like that, she says, and the fat lass leaves wi a spring in her step!

She's no the only one: could ah relocate again? Ah cannae stoap thinking ay Hemel Hempstead, a place designed for social mobility. Unlike the scheme: a veritable monument tae communal ossification. Aye, ah could fuckin relocate, awright. Right intae the fanny ay Lauren Brady!

Ah get upstairs n dae a crap, smooth and seamless. If wee fatso squeezes oot her bairn fae the front as easily, that wid be a result!

Ah text Lauren a verse ay ma favourite love poem:

> So fair art thou, my bonnie lass,
> So deep in luve am I;
> And I will luve thee still, my dear,
> Till a' the seas gang dry.

LITA (15)

*Lita goes home, surprised to find her parents back from Fort William. However, Gerty and Kenny assure her that their return is to be one of startling brevity. They seem detached, as Kenny sits watching football on the TV. Then he turns to his daughter and pontificates, – There's something aboot Scotland, the real Scotland, no this shit hole, which is just England really... the **Highlands** ay Scotland. Being at yir ma's ma's...*

– Youse are gaunny move thair, Lita burst out, in some distress. – Ah'm no movin up thair, she declared.

– Well, her father's grin expanded at the same time as a certain evaluating pity sparked in his eyes, – that was nivir gaunny be part ay the arrangement.

Through her rejection, Lita McCallum sniffed opportunity. This house could be hers. The baby, Jayden... she could have it all! Buoyed by this sudden revelation, she belted out, – Ah'm keepin this hoose then!

Her mother, reading a catalogue, lights a Lambert and Butler, casting her eyes around the spartan dwelling. – You are welcome tae it.

Lita decided to drop the bombshell. – Ah'm huvin a bairn, n it's Jayden Tempultuns!

But Gerty and Kenny barely reacted. There was not even any derogatory remark about the Templetons. – Ye made yir bed, ye kin lie in it, her father said, cracking open a can, as Young Boys, dominating against Manchester United, grabbed a deserved late winner. – Ferguson would never have stood for that shite, Kenny cracked with a satisfied grin.

– Worday advice, Gerty said, – if ye want sumbday tae git involved in bringing this Tempultun laddie tae heel, dinnae look at him, she pointed tae Kenny. – We're movin up their tae git away fae bams. Speak tae yir brars.

So that pits me in a right position. It's Jayden's bairn, ah ken it in muh hert, even if muh heid sais it's mare likely tae be Glen's... what the fuck ah'm ah gaunny dae? Ah'll huv tae git the test soas thit ah'm certain. But how should ah bother? If ah ken fir sure it's no his, Jayden might see it oan muh face. So fuck the test. Aw ye git is tests now anywey, n nane ay thum does any cunt any guid!

So ah'm wanderin roond the centre, thinkin aboot muh ma n dad gaun up north, thinkin aboot Glen gaun south. Then thir's Jayden. Still here. Ah've sortay forgeed um aboot Andrea cause she's right oot the picture. Ma Jayden nivir battered that wee bitch hard enough! We'll baith finish oaf the joab latur!

Ah pat muh stomach. Nae bairn ay mine is bein brought up like me or Jayden. That's fur sure. Then a text fae um comes in:

> Brought new jeans fae Cent
> James center. Eye feel barry
> now. Is just auld cunts need 2
> wurry n keep a look out

JAYDEN (12)

Those citizens of Edinburgh unfortunate enough to have to witness the terrible accident on Princes Street gawped in horror. A few battled through their shock to get on their phones. One man threw his light jerkin over the young man's damaged leg. – Don't look at it. It's okay, he told the confused Jayden James Templeton, who felt fear but no pain. Jayden couldn't move from his spreadeagled position, pinned by the crushing wheel of the huge bus. He could smell the fumes of diesel merge with the metallic scent of his own blood.

Just tantalisingly out of his reach, his smartphone, containing the record score of 89,769 on **Dispersal, Deterrence And Damage: Exterminate Them***, would time out soon, ending the game… – Muh phone, Jayden shouts, – GIES MUH PHONE!*

The bus driver has left the vehicle and is throwing up in the gutter, muttering between pukes, – Eh jist walked oot… oan ehs phone… nivir even looked…

– MUH FUCKIN PHONE! Jayden's screeches fill the air.

A horrified young woman, transfixed by the crushed leg, the white fibula bone shooting out through the ripped flesh, picks up the device and hands it to the stricken boy. Manfully, Jayden tries to finish the game. But his eyes are heavy, and the screen is a blur, and his deft fingers are clumsy on the keys. Then, aware of the black tarmac under him, with the maroon and white of the bus reverberating in his peripheral vision, he feels the world grow cold and dark as his head spins and his eyes close…

JAMBO CUNTS…

ANDREA (3)

Duncan Raeburn feels a vicious disdain for his daughter. Had he not worked hard to give her all the advantages? Everything had been about his family. He had even bought the two-bedroom balconied flat in the mistaken belief that the scheme would somehow come up, with all this private solar-panelled new-build stuff. But it was an illusion: the scheme remained the scheme. There was no sell-on value in the type of systems-built property he had purchased. Now he was stuck in the ghetto.

Andrea, though, she had a decent hairdressing apprenticeship. He wasn't about to let her blow it. She'd gone off to Ibiza with that...

... he hears a key in the lock. Turns down the TV by the handset. Watches his knuckles whiten as he grips the handles of the chair.

When ah git in, ah kin tell muh dad's determined tae gie ays a piece ay his mind. Eh's swivelled roond in ehs chair, n ehs eyes are blazing. – Sit doon, eh points tae the couch.

Ah does.

– Well? eh goes.

– Well what?

– You urnae a stupid lassie, even if ye ought to have done a lot better in your exams.

– Aye...

– It's they bloody games: you're oan that computer aw the time, n ehs eyes go narray n eh points ehs finger at me. – Keep away fae that bloody waster, that Templeton boy, him that was in the accident. Ah'll no have that rubbish in my hoose!

– Dinnae worry aboot that, ah goes, – so ower him, n ah gits up n makes tae leave.

– Whaire are ye gaun?

– Oot.

– Yir jist in! Where's oot?

– Ootside, ah goes n leaves um in that chair shakin ehs heid.

Ah takes the bus tae Leith Walk, gits oaf halfwey up n goes tae Albert Street. Ah gits tae a builder's yerd and ken that's the place when ah sees the van. Then he's gittin oot ay it n lockin it up. Ah follays um. Eh wis aw ower ays in Ibiza, whin ah wis oan muh ain. But eh's no phoned since. Fellys are scum. They either batter ye, like Jaygo, or ignore ye once they've hud thir way, like this bastard. But naebody made ays feel like he did in bed. Like a princess.

Eh gits in this stair, but ah cannae git thair in time tae keep the door open, n ah'm no sure which flat it is. Ah look up at the windaes.

Thing is, eh steps oot the stair door, fuck knows how eh seen ays! – What you wantin? eh goes. – Too busy for drama, pal.

– Jist tae talk.

Eh looks at ehs phone, then tae me. Pits it in ehs poakit. – Fancy a wee bit ay scran? Thir's a barry café roond the corner.

Ah jist shrug. – Aye.

We go thair n settle doon at a corner table. It's no bad. Glen is awright lookin for an auld felly, n she fancies um, that fat cow. Ah only rode Glen in Ibiza at first tae git at her. N Glen kin git it up withoot watchin strangleporn, n chokin n batterin ye, no like ehs fuckin psycho nephew. – Ye heard aboot Jaygo?

– Aye, awfay unfortunate. But gaming on your phone in traffic… ah mean, c'mon… n they reckon they'll save ehs leg.

– Thir sayin eh tried awfay hard tae finish his game, even through his pain, cause eh wis oan a big score. Yuv goat tae admire um for that.

Glen shakes ays heid. Aye, eh looks no bad, but ah'd never ride him back here, *waaay* too auld fir anything other thin a hoaliday fling! – Just nuts, eh goes. – Your ma and dad wouldnae like ye gaun oot wi him.

– No way. And eh's meant tae be hingin oot wi hur again! They say thir huvin a bairn!

– You are well rid, Andrea, Glen shakes ehs heid n twirls up some spaghetti. – Jayden lacks real enterprise, though he'll be quick enough tae claim compo n state n disability pensions tae look after him forever. That status ay worthless parasite would be demeaning tae maist men, but he'll hing aroond oan the margins ay life wi his dwindling sense ay self, no really carin too much.

– You sound like muh dad.

– He sounds like a wise man.

– Mibbe, ah goes. Then ah just blurts it right oot, – It isnae Jayden's kid; it's you that goat fat Lita in the faimlay wey.

– What? Whae telt ye that?

– You were wi her in Ibiza.

– Aye, but ye think a man in ma position doesnae take precautions? Wise up. It's oor Jayden's kid.

– Naw it isnae! Jaygo nivir rode that fat hoor fir ages!

– Aye, he did, this Glen goes, and the spaghetti Bolognese *is* good, n eh disnae look like eh's jokin. – He used ye, Andrea. Eh just wanted tae make Lita jealous so she would gie him the Lotto money. He even tried tae get me involved in this nonsense scam. Thought if ah rode Lita – his ain uncle – she would be indebted even further to him! That's his twisted logic.

– Naw...

– Ah've got the texts here. Ah wis gaunny show ye thum in Ibiza, but we were oan hoaliday n ah didnae want tae pit ye oan even mare ay a downer, n eh hands ays ehs scabby auld Nokia phone.

Be barry me riding Andrea while you're
shagging fat lita! I will do anything
to get her money

I will not be telling Andrea
about Litas money

– Naw... you rode Lita! It's your bairn!

– Ah'll tell ye something right now... ah couldnae go through wi it in Ibiza, Andrea. She's a fat mess. It's Jayden's bairn.

– Naw... ah'm tryin no tae greet, cause it wid mean eh took ays fir a mug fae the start... then ah minds, – But ah saw ye lickin her oot in Ibiza! Acroas the pool in that room!

– Naebody ever got up the stick through gittin licked oot, Andrea. That was as far as ah could go. Took ays ages tae find that pussy under they rolls ay fat, n a huv tae say, ah wis pretty turned oaf tae the point ay being disgusted. Did Jayden no tell you he rode her?

– Aye, ah goes, – but this wis jist up the erse!

– Eh's at it! Eh's been banging her for nearly three years, pal. Eh kens how to find that needle in the haystack. If eh kin get it up her erse, eh kin get it up her fud. Never mind that erectile dysfunction rubbish. They can take aw sorts ay drugs, including fuck drugs – crack, crystal meth, Viagra, amyl nitrate – you ken that!

Ah've goat a beamer cause Glen's voice cairies n two guys eatin look roond. But ah huv tae admit thit what eh sais makes sense. – Mibbe.

– He disrespected you, pal. Boasted tae me aboot how he only wanted to ride you up the arse, n knock ye aboot. Did eh make ye watch that strangleporn wi um? Lassies getting battered by wimmin-hatin freaks?

– Aye, but –

– Ah saw the marks oan ye in Ibiza. Didnae say nowt cause it wis your business. Consentin adults. But a boy shouldnae be tannin yir jaw n choking ye, n tryin tae pass it oaf as sex.

– Ah ken, ah wis stupit!

– Ye deserve better. His plan was eywis tae impregnate Lita, while only banging you up the erse n choking ye. That's why eh filmed it, soas him n Lita could watch you gittin knocked aboot. Her revenge. That's cheap n sleazy, Andrea. That's no the actions ay a real man. A gentle-man would never treat a lady like that.

Ah dinnae believe it… they've taken a len ay me… – Well Jaygo's far fae that, ah admit, tears comin oot muh eyes. – The thought ay him n that hoor laughin at ays gittin tanned… n it wis hur thit shot that video, ah ken it.

– Wi his help, nae doubts, Andrea. That lowlife scum were ey in it the gither. A Templeton. A McCallum. Case rested.

– Naw… ah cannae believe it, n ah starts tae feel they heavy sobs comin deep oot ay ma chist…

Glen reaches ower n squeezes muh hand. – Hey, angel eyes, come oan, ah'm no likin they tears, eh gies ays a spare napkin n ah dabs at it hopin muh liner hasnae run. – Your family, the Raeburns, ur good people. You shouldnae be mixed up wi the McCallums n the Temple-tons. The likes ay me shouldnae even be! Ah just came doon tae look after my sister, whae had stupidly married intae that twisted brood. Dinnae make the same mistake as her, Andrea. You've a trade apprenticeship! The likes ay a bloated, pie-munching cow n a drug-dealing feral shitbag will never understand that!

– Ah ken... muh dad's no speakin tae me, sais ah've been silly.

– You're just a very beautiful and talented young woman whae's lookin fir love. But yir daein it in aw the wrong places.

– Ah'm no beautiful! Ah'm no talented!

– The evidence of muh eyes, n Glen gies ays that *cheeky wee smile*, – n ears... cause ah listened tae yir tape... they tell a different story.

– What... you heard muh tape?

– Aye, n no the cheap scud yin ye made wi Jayden. Ah heard ye sing that 'Unchained Melody' on your YouTube site. Ah have tae confess, after you filmed Shiv wi me n Jordan, ma curiosity wis piqued.

– Ah nivir! Ah wis set up by hur, ah ken it!

Glen just waves ays doon. – That's no the point. The point is, it blew me away. That lassie should be on the stage, ah said tae masel.

– But... ah nivir... *ma* singin?

– Mare thin that, ah took the liberty ay sending it down tae muh mate Chris... in Hemel Hempstead, whae's in the music business. We should git you some studio time n dae a proper recording.

Ah cannae believe muh ears! – Ye really mean that?

– Aye. Ah've nivir been mare serious aboot anything in ma life.

Well, the wey ah see aw this is thit things happen for a reason. Wi sumbday like Glen guidin muh career ah'll finally be able tae brek through intae the industry. – Ah think we should go up tae yours n celebrate.

– Only oan one condition: wi pick up a boatil ay Moët-Chandon *en route*, or Moat-Shandon, as oor Jambo friends call it.

So wi goes up n takes the champagne tae bed. It's so good tae be wi a man that kens how tae touch a woman rather than a daft laddie that jist wants tae hurt one. What the fuck wis ah thinkin...

... we've just done it when a text comes intae Glen's phone. Eh sits up. – Fuck!

– What is it?

– It's oor Jayden. It's no good news.

LITA (16)

The surgeons at Edinburgh's Royal Infirmary were delighted to have the challenge of repairing the mangled leg of Jayden James Templeton. They felt deskilled: covid had made everything boring, taking all the beds and resources. Now, rather than conduct life-saving operations, they had to give priority to people who just got tediously sick and, with increasing rarity, died. The exceptions were gruesome road-traffic accidents where life-threatening injuries demanded immediate address. Matthew Gates, head surgeon in the unit, literally rubbed his hands in glee when he looked at the extent of the trauma the youth's leg had sustained.

Unfortunately, this elation quickly turned into despondency. After six hours' solid work under the theatre lights, the saving of Jayden's leg had proven far too big an ask. The only answer had been amputation just above the knee.

After the gruelling surgery, Gates had taken the team out for a meal in a Victoria Street restaurant he favoured. They'd gone to the wall for this surly youth, whose only visitor was an obese young woman who sat by his side while he recovered from the anaesthetic. Even the boy's mother had refused to come in, having described hospitals as 'awfay triggering' to one of the nursing staff over the phone. People were strange. The flesh, blood, organs and skeletal structures Gates could understand. The rest proved elusive.

Gates raised a glass, toasting the efforts of his team. – A young man lost a leg. But he didn't lose his life, and that's down to you guys. To you, and to young Jayden James Templeton! And everybody has someone, so to the loyal young woman who sat so adoringly by his side!

So, ah got up tae the unfurmury n they gied ays the whole story: Jayden's up the toon n oan ehs phone n eh's crossin Princes Street, so eh jumps oot in front ay this bus, but as eh gits past it another yin's coming up behind it, but quickur n eh cannae see it for the furst bus. Then eh sees it, but eh's no gaunny git past it so eh twists back, but the other bus has sped up, the corpie yin. The driver slams the brakes oan, n it hits Jayden, crushin ehs leg tae fuck. A boy wi a bike said it's good it missed maist ay um cause 'it wid huv crushed um like a Coke can' but, of course, Jayden, whae wis still tryin tae funish ehs game, shouts: 'fuck oaf, look it muh fuckin leg, it's hingin oaf!

Aye, they couldnae save it, so ah wis right up thair n ah wisnae leavin till Jayden came oot the anaesthetic. Took ays ages tae find the right ward cause they'd moved um twice. The furst place ah wis telt tae come tae sais eh wisnae thair, then the next place n aw, then whin ah goat tae the third ward n telt thum thit ah wis telt tae come thair, they finally kent what ah wis oan aboot. The surgeon felly wis quite young – no sayin ah wid, no sayin ah widnae – n eh sais ah wis brave stickin by ehs side.

Manda phoned ays whin ah goat thair. She widnae come tae the hoaspital: whatever ah've goat growin in me ah wid nivir treat it like she did Jayden. – Too triggurun, she goes, – me wi muh nerves.

Felt like sayin tae hur: it's no *your* nerves. It's you gits oan *ivrybody else's* nerves wi yir shan patter, but ah bit ma tongue.

Anywey, Jayden wakes up aw yon groggy wey. The nurse sais tae be gentul wi um as eh'll have that PMT post-trumatic thing peepul git whin ye cut oaf thir legs or airms. – They took it, eh goes.

Eh's goat this cage thing in the bed, so ah lufts up the sheet. Sure enough, nae leg. Ah ken it's no right, but the first thing ah thoat aboot wis ehs willie!

– That's right. Huv a good look at the cripple, Jayden goes, eyes aw moist.

– It's no that bad, ah sais, but it mibbe wisnae a guid thing tae say, cause it is.

Jayden disnae say nowt, bit ye ken by ehs eyes eh's upset.

– Peepul wi one leg lead normul lives, Jayden, ah goes. – Ye see they new legs, like oan telly, robot legs, better thin the real thing! The legs ay the future!

– Mibbe, eh goes, bit eh's awfay doon in the dumps. – Dae ays a favour?

– Anythin.

– Git muh stuff fae muh ma's n keep it at yours? It's jist games n clathes n that. She's gaunny fling ays oot. N ah dinnae want tae stey thair anywey.

– Right... ah goes. But ah'm no bein taken fir a fuckin dick again. – What aboot wee shitey knickers? That Andrea?

– Like ah sais, huvnae heard nowt fae her. She'll no want tae ken ays, no like this.

Aye, eh goat that yin right. – Bairn's yours by the way, ah tell um.

Ah think a wee light goes oan in ehs eyes. – Aye?

– N ah heard ye wir oan a guid score oan *Dispersul* n aw...

– Ah wis oan 85,613 wi three bonuses at levul 9!

– Ye'd huv beat ma 93,751 easy! N mibbe even T-Zone Rushmore fae California's 126,739!

– Naw, ah widnae, eh sais, n eh looks aw sad, like a wee laddie. Then another wee smile. – N the bairn's deffo mine?

– Aye, nae doubt aboot that, ah goes, n ah takes ehs hand n eh lits ays. Jayden's gaunny stey at mine: mibbe even perminint. – Ah'll look eftir ye, ah goes.

– You're the best, eh sais.

We hus a wee hug, n ah kin feel um gittin hard under the covers. – Jayden Tempultin, ah laughs, – they nivir took yir muddle leg!

Wi baith laughed at that yin!

Then ah gits hame n reads the email oan the computur:

To: sweetahLita@me.com
From: durtygurty@bt.co.uk
Re: Highlands

Dear Lita

As we told you we've decided to stay up in Fort William with your gran for a bit. She needs us and we love it up here. Your dad never gets a minute of peace in the scheme from bams bothering him. He's thriving up here in the Highlands. You're the most responsible of them all – not that that's saying much! But your brothers are wasters. Watch them. Keep them out of our house and your business. And do not let them leave things like packages and holdalls etc in the house! And that Jayden – keep away from him!

I ken you'll look after the place! Treat it as your 'ain wee hoose'.

Frankly: you're in no position to have a bairn. I'd consider other options. Your choice but.

Your loving mum,

Gertrude A Simpson-McCallum xxx

Hi sweetpea, dad hear no much wun for the riteing but like your ma says keep away from they Templetons an Urquharts RUBBISH ON BOTH SIDES TRUE love dad xxx

Ah'm keepin the bairn n ah'm no keepin away fae Jayden. Ah'm movin him in perminint now n thir's nowt they kin dae aboot it!

So later oan, ah'm roond at his hoose tae pack up his stuff like eh sais. Shiv comes n aw, helpin ays oot. That Manda just goes, – Wis bad enough a drug-dealer in the hoose, wi oor Jarret bein jist a bairn, but no a cripple... ah telt um, ah goes, sorry, son, but muh varicose veins ur bad enough fae aw that waitressin ah did tae pit food oan the table. Ah widnae be able tae look at a laddie wi one leg. That funny stump... nuht, she shakes hur heid like a dug comin oot the sea.

– Thir's mare tae it thin that, ah'm explainin tae Shiv, up in the bedroom. – Glen says that she met a felly at that oanline self-help group for people thit suffer fae suicide, no like suffer fae it, but try n dae it but dinnae succeed.

– So they help each other tae kill each other?

– Naw... it's like if they feel that wey like they might dae it, they try n stoap each other, like pit each other oaf.

– Like hide knives fae each other, boatils ay puhls n paracetamols n that?

– Aye... naw! They talk each other oot ay it!

– Aw.

So we take the stuff in bags doon tae ma hoose. Ah've jist goat Jayden's stuff packed, n wuv git it doon the road tae mine, n then Shiv's away whin thir's a knock oan the door.

Jarred's standin thair. – Hiya.

– Hiya. What is it?

– Ah wis telt tae come here.

– How?

– Hud a fight wi muh ma, so ah texted Jayden.

– Aw aye? Ye'd better come in then.

So ah'm thinkin, he might huv tae stey here fir a bit n aw: non-perminint, likes. Me n Jayden in muh ma's room n Jarred in mine.

Later oan, Jayden comes hame, no even in an ambulance but a taxi. So, it's the three ay us. The council huvnae transferred the tenancy oantae me fishully, but wir no sayin nowt aboot that! As far as ah'm concerint Jayden's here perminint!

UNCLE GLEN (7)

Laser-beam rays of light spilled in between the tatty blinds of the Hotel Viva. Glen Urquhart wasn't a consumer of online pornography; with regards to sexual activity, he was very much a participant rather than an observer. Yet he had to concede that there was something fetching about the generation of young women who had been schooled by its automated, brutalising routines. There really was little need for sex robots when we knocked out such a prolific supply of humanoid ones.

Glen's forte was romantic, devilish speech play, and when he turned this on Andrea Raeburn, it was uplifting to watch a nervy humanity insinuate into the girl, as, rendered moist-eyed and bashful, she sat giddily on the rickety pedestal his casually dispensed praise had constructed for her.

While enjoying the delights on offer, he found his thoughts straying to Lauren Brady, the full-bodied Corbynista of Hemel Hempstead. The post-coital chats with Andrea had quickly grown tedious. In the self-praise of her singing voice, she was almost unbearable. He yearns to scream in her face: **your vocals are fucking shit and you lack not only star charisma but any real personal charm.** *However, he restrains himself. Manners are important, and alienating a fit young ride is not an error a seasoned shagger is inclined to make.*

Wee Andrea, no a bad looker, and a fuckin decent enough cowp once reconditioned fae her porn education and the unsophisticated fuck-toy routines initiated by the likes ay muh nephew and his drug-woozy, ajar-gobbed robot mates.

But life gets mare complicated; wi every bit ay cheap praise ah can feel this lassie cling even mare tightly tae ays. Ah think of my ain daughter, whae's jist a few years aulder, and a cold sweat breks oot oan ays. It takes an age tae git her oot the bedroom doon tae the reception at the Viva! Cuthbert hands ays a big wrench ah'd left here ages ago, after replacing some rotted washers in old slow-leaking pipes. Dinnae want tae cart it aboot, but any tradesman will tell ye that tools walk if ye dinnae keep them secure or close. Ah stick it in my jaikit pocket, miffed that the weight ay it might fuck the Hugo Boss. Ah think aboot offerin Andrea a lift doon tae her bit, but mibbe best we're no seen the gither! She finally leaves, and Cuthbert tracks her oot the door, turnin tae me wi a slow nod. Approval? Envy? Contempt? Difficult tae ken wi that boy.

When ah get back tae the scheme ah opt tae keep the wrench oan ays. Dinnae like leaving tools in the van. One thing aboot aw the factories being shut doon here is that the air coming off the estuary is cleaner. The park is basically empty bar the staples: two wide young cunts wi shitin Staffies, a pregnant lassie pushin a pram and a few wee kids by the concrete adventure playground. Some mare new-build flats ur gaun up by the side ay the auld disused railway line.

Then muh hert sinks as ah see Dessie McCallum coming stridin towards ays. – YOU! URK-KURT! YA FUCKIN NONCIN CUNT! N eh's pointin at ays wi murder in ehs eyes. Starts tae run at ays. So ah dae tae: in the opposite direction, right across that fuckin park...

JAYDEN (13)

The physio and the occupational therapist had made separate appointments with Jayden Templeton, though the trauma counsellor's calls were left unreturned. Domiciled at Lita's, Jayden found his life had shrunk, and wheelchair navigation wasn't as easy as he'd assumed it would be.

Settling into a bed she'd made up downstairs, Jayden woke into a cold morning. Lita had gone out, and he missed her warmth. He got dressed, slipping into tracksuit bottoms, mortified by the absence of one limb and the perversity of doing up a single trainer. His new leg would be fitted soon, once the stump had healed, so the footwear wouldn't be wasted.

For want of something to do, he headed to the Community Arts Centre, hurling himself over the marshy park to give himself experience of navigating difficult terrain. The hardest thing was avoiding the Staffie excrement. Everybody in the scheme seemed to have one of those dogs, and he'd wanted one himself to take on his rounds. Had even procured a pup off Joshy Boy Four, but Manda had railed against it, claiming allergies in the presence of all domestic pets, and he'd been forced to return it.

He is just starting to work up a satisfying rhythm and feel the burn in his arms when a sudden pungent aroma assails him. He instinctively looks at his hand, which must have slipped from the propulsion ring onto the wheel. His fingers are stained a foul deep brown, and his stomach immediately heaves. – Fuck, Jayden snaps in rage.

Ahead, a discarded Metro newspaper flaps in the breeze.

A sense of powerlessness and frustration assails him. He attempts to propel towards the paper while avoiding touching the shitey wheel. Strains to pick up the paper, fearful that he'll tip the chair over. He grabs at it. Buoyed by this success, he tries to wipe the excrement from his hand and then the wheel. As he works, he battles to hold in the *contents of his guts. Fighting back tears, he thinks of what further humiliations lie ahead.*

Fuckin... ah'm tryin tae wash muh hands oan the gress withoot topplin oot ay this fuckin chair... this fuckin one leg... at furst ah didnae bother that much cause ah thoat ah'd probably spend mare time playin video games now ah've goat a wheelchair n thir giein ays money, but ay.

Ah'm nearly fuckin well greetin, ay, muh hands ur mingin, but ah keep at it n ah've got the wheel nearly cleaned. Ah git fitted fir a new leg, metal likes, next week. But things like this git ye doon. N nae cunt kin be bothered, or if they kin it's aw that pity. Fuck them aw: the new leg'll be barry, git ehs aboot n up they stairs, cause ah'm livin doonstairs right now. They sais they'd pit a chairlift oan the stairs fir ays, but ah dinnae mind it oan the couch-bed cause ah've goat muh computer n the telly n Unkul Glen made this auld broom cupboard intae a doonstairs lavvy. Eh's no bad really; ah think that money thit nivir wis turned aw oor heids.

It's good tae git intae the fresh air. So ah'm sittin by the bairns' swings whaire ah arranged tae meet Lita. She comes along n takes ower the pushin, so ah've goat that new game *Broken State: The Fight To Survive* oan muh phone, n ah'm rackin up a bramer score.

Funny how at night ah keep dreamin aboot ridin different burds, but the same burd, but yin thit *turns intae* different burds. Dinnae ken if that's me gaun mental or no, hi hi hi!

That Andrea nivir gits in touch, but Lita n me's gittin oan great at hurs. She's loast a wee bit ay weight. Seems tae be watchin her grub n no jist as it's gaun intae her mooth. Funny how she's huvin a bairn but losin weight! Ah pumped her last night, mare tae say sorry thin anything, but ah'm no bothered aboot ridin. Ye kin live easy withoot a ride, but ay. She disnae seem that bothered either. But ah dinnae mind steyin at hers. At least she kens how tae look eftir ays maist ay the time, no like muh ma. Ah look roond n the chair n we smile at each other.

Now Jarred's moved here n aw, but he's ey upstairs. Ah kin hear him n Lita muckin aboot, playin the video games. Whin ah ask um what eh's up tae, eh jist goes, – What's it goat tae dae wi you? Wee cunt's goat double-wide since ah hud the accident. But it's a barry result fir muh ma, she moved this Polish cunt Woytek in.

Then ah hears shoutin n turns tae Lita, whae's lookin acroas the field. Ah follays her sightline n sees her brar, that cunt Dessie, n Uncle Glen arguing by one ay the goalposts. It's like Dessie's been chasin Glen, whae's oot ay breath, ehs hands oan ehs knees. Then Glen points behind them and as Dessie turns n then turns back Uncle Glen pills this huge monkey wrench fae ehs jaikit n tans um a beauty! Dessie goes doon, n Glen's right oan um, pummellin that big heid wi ehs fists.

– DINNAE GLEN, Lita screams. – Eh's fuckin batterin oor Dessie!

– Dinnae git involved, ah goes, but she's leaving ays n gaun ower. Ah'm tuggin oan the wheels, tryin tae git them acroas the muddy gress.

Ah gits closur, muh phone oot, n Uncle Glen's standin up, bootin fuck ooy ay Dessie, whae's oan the deck spangled. Lita's screamin fir um tae stoap, but Glen's talking tae Dessie, as eh stomps um. – Ah fucking hate violence, n look what you've made me dae, n eh kicks um in face, snappin ehs heid back, – you've debased ays. Happy now? Yuv won, eh goes, tannin um in the coupon another beauty. – Taste that fuckin victory; savour it!

– Stoap it, Glen! Lita's right up tae um.

Ah stoaps fulmin oan muh phone. Pits in in ma poakit. – IT ISNAE GLEN'S BAIRN, ah shouts at Dessie, – it's mine!

– SEE? YA FUCKIN IGNORINT, LOWLIFE, TWO-BOB CUNT, Glen twists away fae Dessie, points tae ays in the wheelchair. – IT'S HIS!

Dessie is tryin tae sit up, hudin his mooth tae stem the blood. Eh looks at ays, n ye kin see his eye comin oot, swellin up n shuttin. – Is that right? eh sortay gasps.

– Aye, ah goes. Eh looks barry, like some cunt hus hud rough sex wi um! Gasman Glen! Ken whit ah'll be watchin the night, n ah taps muh phone in they trackie boatums. Hi hi hi!

– See, Glen wags his finger at the daft cunt, then turns tae me n Lita, lookin ower the park. – This is fucked! Solar-panelled hooses! Doon here? Eh turns back tae Dessie, then sticks oot his hand. Dessie looks at it fir a bit then takes it, n Glen pills him tae his feet. – We aw square?

– You noaked ma fuckin teesh oot, Dessie shouts, but backin away. – How ur we aw square!?

Ah nivir kent Uncle Glen wis that wide. Heard it said, back in the day, but ah jist thought eh wis a weird, noncey plumber whae went oan about socialists aw the time. It makes ays gled ah nivir hud that square go wi um now! – You nivir did yir hamework, eh points at Dessie. – Ye called ays a paedo, accused ays ay daein something ay didnae, threatened ays withoot hearin ma side ay the story or takin intae account thair side. Ye fuckin chased ays. So, aye, ah wis feelin a wee bit threatened. So, aye, ah responded. Sorry aboot the teeth n that, but violence isnae an exact science!

Dessie spits oot some mare blood. That eye is really shut, reminds ays ay a baby burd thit fell oot a nest. Great seein the bullyin cunt like that, n ah cannae help but smile. Eh sais tae Glen, – Ye shink yir shome big fuckin gangshter doon in London?

– Well, a lot of villains have properties in Spain, Glen goes, hands oan ehs hips. – Ah go out there and dae the plumbing for some ay them. Ah dae good work, ah never take the pish wi the billing, always finish oan time n oan budget. Maist ay them get mates rates as ah'm happy to be oot in the sun. And aye, they show gratitude, and a few would be maist fucking upset if any two-bob cunt was daft enough tae incapacitate *thair* boy. And they have contacts here whae they exchange favours for. Ah think you ken who ah mean.

– Aye well, ah've goat mates n aw –

– Aye, exactly, and ye want tae start a fuckin war over some daft wee bairn gittin another yin up the duff? Glen thumbs ower taewards us. – Grow the fuck up.

– You grow the fuck up, Dessie sais, but eh seems tae realise eh's made a cunt ay it!

Ah looks up at hur. – Kin we go now?

We head oaf n ah git her tae droap ays at the community centre. Ah kin git back oan muh ain fae thair. They say tae dae as much as ye kin tae build up the strength in yir airms, n ah dinnae like being beholden tae nae cunt. N oan that note, what she disnae ken is that cause ay the accident ah've goat two huntrit n twenty-eight subscriburs now!

– Soon yi'll huv that new leg, the one like that Terminatur's goat, n Lita rubs her gut.

Kin tell she's starvin, n the coffee bar here does bowfin rolls. – S'at you oaf then?

– Aye, this diet's gittin me doon. Ah'll make you fush fingkurs n chups oan a roll fir yir tea, but ah'll jist be oan salit again.

– Right.

– See ye later, bunnyhunch, dinnae you be late, n she kisses ays oan the cheek n front ay aw they cunts at the centre! Ah'm gittin fuckin treated like a bairn! Sooner the real bairn comes n ah git that new leg the bettur!

– Aye, ah goes, – see ye in a wee bit, n she gits oaf.

At the centre it's barry cause thuv goat the *Evenin News* n ah'm in it:

NO SHAMER FOR LEGLESS GAMER

Jayden Templeton (17), the dedicated gamer who made the headlines by trying to finish his phone video game, the controversial *Dispersal, Deterrence And Damage*, after a horrific accident in Edinburgh's Princes Street left his leg literally hanging off, is now suing Lothian Buses. The shocked driver of the vehicle, Chris Arbuckle (52), said: 'I couldn't believe it. He just stepped off the curb, not even looking up, far less where he was going. It was horrible to witness. I've been in counselling since. I'll never unsee that smashed leg.'

Templeton himself said: 'I might have lost a leg, but it's Lothian Buses who don't have a leg to stand on when it comes down to this claim. I could have made the top three, or even number one, of global players on *Dispersal, Deterrence And Damage*. I'm claiming loss of earnings and sponsorship.'

But the self-described 'professional gamer' has attracted some scorn in gamer circles. Golly D, the London-based gamer who grossed over four million pounds last year, and has close on two million subscribers said: 'Nobody has heard of this guy. Good luck to him, but I'd like to see his earnings statement. Money talks and bulls**t walks.' While a neighbour of Templeton's, who wished to remain anonymous, said: 'If "professional gamer" means "drug-dealer" or "thug", then this guy is certainly one.'

Dispersal, Deterrence And Damage has long attracted controversy. After being quasi-illegal and available only on the 'dark web' it was finally approved by the Games Rating Authority (GRA) division of the Video Standards Council. The content is highly violent, involving the wiping out of civilians, including women and children, and with close-range functions. Conservative MP Nick Wallingham-Hendry, a former chairman of the game's parent company Ethical Games, and now a chairman of the Commons video licensing advisory committee, said: 'The gaming industry gets a bad rap for the evils of society. It employs many creative people and it should be less regulated than it is.'

But Dr Rachael Smedhurst, of the University of Edinburgh School of Psychiatric Medicine, said: 'The World Health Organization recently designated "gaming disorder" as a mental-health condition. The case of this unfortunate young man shows what can happen when this behaviour develops into fully fledged addiction. Gamers are literally playing with fire.'

Fuckin cunt... some cunt grassin ays up... notice thir too feart tae gie thir name, n that gamer cunt in Lundin... ah checks muh subscriburs... up tae 317 now! N it's a bramer picture tae; black Stone Island jaikit, New York Yankees basebaw cap, hair cut short like a young Eminem, as Lita ey sais. That should reel in the fanny! Hi hi hi!

Whin Jordan came roond the other night, wi Joshy Boys Three, Six n Twelve, wi played the accidunt back oan YouTube; me scramblin for muh phone wi muh leg hinging oaf... it wis a barry laugh... hi hi hi... aw they cunts fae the telly n papers wantin tae talk tae ays!

The guid thing wis it wis only the second-best video wi watched; the best wis oan muh phone, watchin Uncle Glen batter the fuck oot ay Dessie, but! If ah kent eh wis that much ay a fuckin pussy ah'd huv done it masel! Wish that wis oan YouTube. JB6 hud went, – We should batter him again, and ehs fuckin daft brar. Thir no that hard. Your Unkul Glen proved that, Jaygo. We should run the gear roond here, no they cunts.

Ah said something like, – Wait till uh git muh new leg furst, but it's sumthin tae think aboot. Fuckin too right.

LITA (17)

Lita McCallum was happy to leave Jayden Templeton at the community centre where he liked to sit and play video games. It was a nice outing, and Jayden got peace there. Now Lita had decided she would tell Manda Templeton of the pregnancy, while offering duty-free purchases picked up in Ibiza. There were Lambert and Butler cigarettes and Beefeater gin, which she believed were Manda's favourites. She had made similar purchases for her mother, father and brothers Dessie and Clint. Wondered if Dessie, his jaw wired, would thank her now.

Peepul say ah huv tae be mad tae take in Jayden eftir what eh did, n the wey eh treatit ays. Ah jist say, naw, cause eh's the faither ay ma bairn, n that hus tae count fir sumthin. Now ah've goat tae try n make peace wi Manda, n tell ur the news. Jayden, fair play tae um, wanted tae come wi ays, but ah sais, naw, no eftir hur flingin you oot ay yir ain hoose.

The scheme's empty, like a nuclear bomb's hit it. Ah dinnae see one singul person aw the wey tae Manda's. Jist as ah gits tae the door, a big Polish felly comes oot, younger thin Jayden's ma. No sayin ah wid, but ah'm no sayin ah widnae! – Is Manda in? ah goes.

– Aye, eh goes, but in a Polish voice.

So she comes tae the door behind um n goes, – What you wantin?

– Jist tae talk, ah goes. – Brought ye they fags, fae the duty free in Ibiza. Didnae ken what tae git ye, but ah thoat: ye cannae go wrong wi fags.

– What ur you gittin ays anything fir?

– Ah've goat some good news. Kin ah come in?

– Suppose, she goes, takin the bag wi the fags n booze n headin in. Ah follays her, shuttin the door behind ays. – Tryin tae drive ays tae an early grave… she goes, pittin thum oan the worktoap.

– Aw, ah goes, pickin up a fags carton n hudin it up, – so yuv stoaped then?

– Ah didnae say that, she goes, aw panicky, grabbin thum back.

– N yir favourite chun n aw.

– Whae says that's muh favourite gin?

– Jayden...

– Like he'd ken.

– N you did, mind yon time at the centre?

– Ah meant Gordon's... then she looks at ays, – ... but this'll dae, even if ah shouldnae wi muh puhls.

– A little ay what ye fancy...

– Aye well, wi'll see, she goes, pourin two glesses wi ice n lemon n flat Schweppes tonic water fae an auld boatil in the frudge. She hands ays yin n pits yin oan the tabul in the kitchen. – So what ye wantin?

– Ah'm in the faimlay wey. You're gaunny be a grandmother!

Hur mooth hings open n hur eyes bulge oot. – A fuckin what...?

UNCLE GLEN (8)

Glen Urquhart is heartened by the impending visit of Hemel Hemp-
stead's sexy socialist Lauren Brady. This aside, the only things keeping
him in Edinburgh are several outstanding plumbing jobs and a com-
pensation claim he is advancing on behalf of his nephew, Jayden, with
a New Town lawyer he had done work for.

Manda has fallen for Woytek Lebowski, the Polish carpenter she
met at the suicide-support group. Woytek was in the habit of sending
all his money back tae his family, but Manda has put a stop to that. –
Yuv goat tae live, Woytek!

Manda, more buoyant than in many years, had even come round on
the baby, deciding to invite the family to dinner at her place.

Well ah was shaken up, no doubt about it, by that confrontation wi
Desmond McCallum. Technically ah came out top, but nae real
winners: eh forced me intae his game ay pittin negative energy oot there
intae the world. But the straw's better oaf in his mooth than mine: ah
like ma solids. Dessie was ey just wind, though: his brar Clint'll be a
mare formidable prospect. So ah'm treading warily in the scheme as ah
head back fir this family dinner: an Uber straight in and right back oot!

It's good ay Manda tae have us round for a Chinese takeaway. Of
course, yours truly has footed the bill. Fair play tae Woytek, the boy
offered tae chip in, but ah insisted it wis ma treat. Ah only made two
stipulations: one was that Shiv and Jordan would be invited. Ah'd
found out fae Geraldine that the boy was hers and none other than
Philly's grandson! It wis the Hertz strip that threw me off scent: a man
like Philly Matheson would never have entertained maroon progeny.
Gerry shamefully admitted it was the boy's faither that carried the
Roseberry stain: a Wheatfield regular. The other condition was that we
would all sit doon at Manda's kitchen table, which, as far as ah kent,

never had they extension leaves pulled out ay it. She had tae borrow mare chairs fae next door and git Jayden's wheelchair in at the end. Manda really pulled oot the stops, *real* plates (except fir two which were paper) n plastic knives and forks, *and fully functioning* salt and pepper cellars.

So ah helped her load up the food on the various plates. Ah have tae say it wis generous ay ma sister extendin the olive branch tae Lita, even though she's no sure aboot the impending grandmother status. (Or mibbe auntie, if ye want tae split baw hairs.)

– Well, this is a happy occasion, ah goes.

– Aye it is, says Jayden, – only thing is, he looks at Jordan n Shiv, – what ur they daein here?

– Aye, Lita goes, – n ah'm no bein wide, barry tae see ye n that, but this is meant tae be jist faimlay.

Ah gies that *cheeky wee smile*. – Ah wanted Jordan here soas ah could ask um if eh's prepared to train as a plumber wi me.

– Aye, barry, the boy goes, aw excited. Jayden, Manda and Lita's chins fair hit the table!

– How's that, Jayden goes, jist as a notes a text fae the lovely Lauren hus popped intae muh phone. *English rose ay Hemel Hempstead, soon tae be bound tae ma bedstead!*

Ah watches Shiv cuddlin Jordan. Thir delighted! – Of course, it'll mean relocation to Hemel Hempstead, ah tell them.

Ah see fear ignite in Shiv's eyes. – Ah cannae go thair n leave muh ma.

Jordan looks shattered, but eh glances at Shiv, then me. – Nuht. Sorry, Glen, it's awfay guid ay ye, but wi huv tae stey here. Thanks, but gie it tae Jayden.

– Aye, gie it tae me! Jayden goes.

– Aye! Yir ain fuckin nephew!

– Sorry Manda, but if *you* cannae have a raspberry ripple in the *hoose*, then how dae ye expect me tae huv one *oan site*? Plumbers ur up n doon stairs aw day n it's no the kind ay trade for a laddie… sae… disabled.

Well that fair sets thum oaf! As they squabble away ah checks Lauren's text:

I can't wait for you to show me the
delights of Edinburgh! To be honest
I think I might be ready for a fresh
start! Too much baggage in Hemel
Hempstead. Thoughts? xxx

Aw aye… ah starts typin…

The Athens of the north is a beautiful
place, but could only be enhanced by a
(red) English rose! My motto is always
'suck it and see'. (Make of that what
you will!!) G xx

Ah look up at thum, and they faw silent. In Jordan, ah see a young
me, even as ah hear ma ain voice assume the gravelly wisdom ay Philly
Matheson himself, – Have you ever heard ay the phrase: huvin yir cake
n eatin it?

LITA (18)

At the dinner table Glen's good humour had jarred on Lita. She had taken on Manda's obsession that he should apprentice Jayden in the plumbing trade. But the outrage of this unlikely alliance fell on deaf ears. Glen would not be moved, and Jordan and Shiv were euphoric.

Now Lita gloomily considers her lot, pushing Jayden home in the wheelchair. Jarred walks alongside her, and she suddenly feels his hand rest on her buttock. She stops, as Jayden looks up from the chair. Jarred withdraws his hand as his brother asks, – What?

– Nowt, Lita says, pushing again, as Jarred's hand returns to her arse, groping at its giving heft. When scowling at him, she is met with a wink.

She walks on and pushes on.

That Jarrit's turnin a right cheeky wee bugger! When we git hame, ah go upstairs tae muh room, leavin Jayden doon thair in front ay telly. So Jarred comes up n only starts gaun oan aboot muh tits bein barry! – Thing aboot you, bit, yir erse is mint n aw. It wis great feelin it up ootside!

So ah suppose ah started aw that daft flurtin, cause ah'm gittin nowt oaffay Jayden as per usual, n as fir that Glen, well he's deffo ridin somebody else. – Ye want a wee feel ay thum, then?

– Aye. Ah pure want tae sook yir nipples. Ah bet ah kin make thum stand oot!

– Aw, ye think so?

– Aye.

– Aye, well wi'll start ye oaf wi a wee feel n see how we go. Honestly, see youse laddies, yis uv goat one-track minds!

– Ah've hud muh hole, ah ken whit it's aw aboot! What dae ye think ah wis daein in Ibiza!

– Jarrit Tempultuhn! ah goes, but aw sortay schoolmarm like.

Then eh looks at ays wi they twinkly wee eyes. Fill ay mischief. – Jayden's no intae ye. Everybody kens that. Eh's problay still ridin that Andrea.

– Naw eh's no!

– Well, see if eh wis, eh shrugs, – ah'd think eh wis mad. She's too skinny. Ah like a real lassie wi a barry body like yours.

– You're an awfay charmer!

– Aye, so when ye gaunny gie ays muh hole? Like proper?

– Yir too young for that! How auld ur ye, twelve?

– Thirteen!

– Makes nae difference, n besides ah've goat a bairn in here, ah pats muh stomach. – Yir brar's bairn!

– Disnae affect it.

– What dae you ken? Listen, Jarred, ah'm no giein ye a ride n that's that! Yir Jaydun's brar!

– Eh disnae treat ye right, cause, see, if eh did, then ye'd nivir huv lit oor Uncle Glen up ye. Jayden's goat one leg n nae prospects. Ah'm gaunny be a plumber wi Uncle Glen one day, eh goes, – once Jordan's aw trained up.

– Aye?

– Aye, eh sais, then they wee eyes go aw insistent again. – Jist gies yir pussy, it'll be barry.

Ah huv tae hand it tae Jarred fir sheer persistence. Reminds ays an awfay loat ay Jayden whin wi wir first gaun oot. – Aye, that'll be the day! Ah dinnae jist gie anybody a ride, son! Ah telt ye, n a thrusts muh tits oot, – ye kin git a wee feel ay thaim.

N eh starts feelin thum. Ah tell um tae go soft furst, then squeeze thum a bit harder. Eh does. – Ye want a wee gam, but then, ah sais, aw croaky.

– Goan, gies a ride, but.

– Nuht, ah telt ye!

– A dry ride then. Keep yir tights oan.

So ah takes oaf muh leggings quick, cause ah'm worried thit Jayden'll come up the stair n they crutches, n Jarrit's goat ehs jeans doon n eh's oan toap ay us, humpin away, gropin muh tits. Then eh stoaps n goes aw spazzy, makin aw they noises as eh comes, n eh's sayin

things, bit it's no aw stuff fae the porno oanline, it's something like, –
Ah wis telt tae come here…

Didnae take um long!

… n eh's lying back wi ehs eyes shut n in a strange wey, n again it
reminds ays ah Jayden whin wi wir first gaun oot, n ah ken ah should
feel bad aboot this, but mibbe fuckin peg-leg Jayden went oot and
fucked that hoor Andrea again, n anywey they tried tae git muh money,
so ah dinnae.

His daft wee cock spunks aw ower ma belly, n it takes ays ages tae
git it oot they folds. Jist as well ah've loast a wee bit weight. Still,
under the knife next month, n it's aw a thing ay the past. – Dinnae
you tell yir brar aboot our wee daft games, Jarrit, ah goes, – or yir
uncle!

– Think ah'm daft? eh sais. Then eh smiles at ays. – Ken what wid
definitely make ays stey quiet? You giein ays a real ride. Me gittin it
right up ye.

Ah looks doon at ehs cock, n it's gittin aw hard again, n eh's jist
blawn!

– Goan. Gies a ride. Lit ays git it up ye…

– Beat it, you!

– Goan…

Ehs daft wee face! – Bit Jayden might come up!

Jarred gits oaf the bed n opens the door. Jayden's crutches are in the
hallway, against the waw. – Took thaim upstairs wi us, but ay. Cunt's
gaun naewhair!

The next thing is Jayden's shoutin up the stairs, – What's gaun oan
up thair? Whaire's muh crutches?

– Git thum in a second, Jarred goes, – jist finishin this game… n eh's
pillin muh tights doon, wi the egg-white spunk still glistenun in the
material… then eh's goat ays oan the bed n eh's oan ays, then ah feels
ays cock pushin inside ay muh wet fanny… this isnae right, but ah've
goat ehs thin wee erse in muh hands n ah'm pillin um further in… –
This is barry, eh's gaun… kent you'd be a barry pump, but ay…
euughhh…

… n eh blaws again, this time inside ays.

– LITA! JARRIT! Jayden shouts fae doonstairs. – What ur youse
daein?

– Gamin, we both shouts doon at once! Then wi laugh, n ah goes, – *Call Ay Duty: Modern Warfare*!

Ah hear Jayden's voice. – Ah want tae play!

Ah turns tae Jarrit n whispers in his ear, – Yir brar's playin days ur ower... but yours huv only jist begun!

GRAND
UNION

JOHN KING

Autumn, 2021

RAY DIDN'T APPRECIATE Stan's use of the Nutter tag, but took the comment in his stride, knew the younger man was just excited hearing *40 Years Untamed* for the first time. And who could blame him given the line-up? Ray was the one who'd told him to hurry up and listen to the album in the first place so could live with the 'Nutter class' rating. It was meant as a compliment, and his irritation turned to a warm respect for Stan and his love of Oi. No words were required. Quiet or otherwise. Whispered into his shell-like or barked with a glare. Ray was a different person these days, and while there had been one or two wobbles along the way, the distant echo of fist and boot, the skinhead was solidly on the straight and narrow. He was loved up and living with Priscilla. Running the firm. Had never felt happier.

With Terry and Angie in Jamaica, these last two weeks had been his big test. After years as a driver, he'd served his apprenticeship on the management side as well now, and while he knew Estuary Cars inside out, this was the first time he'd been left in sole charge. Nervous in the build-up to their departure, he'd driven home after dropping them off at Heathrow sure he was going to muck up, but things had gone better than even he'd hoped, and no way was he going to pull up one of the boys over a stray comment. Good leadership was built on mutual respect. He was at peace with the world. And so Friday afternoon rolled into early evening at a leisurely pace in the Union Jack Club, Ray enjoying a light ale with some of the chaps, and by a light ale he meant a *Light Ale*, the bottles ordered direct from Young's by barman Buster.

– Have you seen this? Stan asked, turning his phone towards Ray.

Taking the Samsung, he recognised Merlin from the England games. Born and bred in Birmingham. A lorry driver by trade. Supported Aston Villa. He was wearing his blue Levi's jacket with the Led Zeppelin, Black Sabbath and Slade patches. Never wore anything else. He was football mad. Watched the Villa youth as well as the first team. When he wasn't away working. Ray remembered him raving about a youngster called Jack Grealish. How England had to stop Ireland getting hold of him as they risked losing a special talent the same as they'd lost Ryan Giggs to Wales. Jack was playing for the full England side now, thank God. About time as well. Gareth Southgate didn't seem to fancy him as much as the supporters, who were desperate for an injection of flair.

It was the same with Declan Rice. Another near miss. Chelsea had already fucked that one up letting him go to West Ham as a kid, even though it was only a matter of time before he came home. It was going to cost the club a fortune, but Ray wished Roman would get his finger out before Pep or Klopp stepped in. With Rice and Mason Mount bossing the midfield, Chelsea were going to win the lot. They should try Conor Gallagher in there as well. But then what did you do about Kanté, Kovačić and Jorginho? Mount, Rice and Gallagher were the future. That's what Ray reckoned. He wouldn't want to lose Kanté, though. Kovačić wasn't bad either. He didn't mind if Jorginho left. Not after Italy had beaten England in the final of the Euros.

– It's Merlin, Stan said.

Grealish might have looked like something out of *Peaky Blinders*, but the Brummie headbanger had been right. Jack was a rare, maverick talent. Transported from the 1970s. An Alan Hudson for the 2020s. From back when football was still the people's game. And men were men. He couldn't imagine Peter Osgood wearing rainbow laces in his boots as Chelsea welcomed West Ham to the Bridge. Or Chopper Harris taking the knee at White Hart Lane. Or Charlie Cooke diving and trying to con the referee into giving a penalty. Not against Man United with George Best and Bobby Charlton on the pitch. No chance. Ray hadn't seen these players in person, but knew all about them from his Uncle Terry. The same standards applied to those who'd followed in their footsteps and entertained Ray. Kerry Dixon, Joey Jones, Pat Nevin.

– I know. Who else could it be?

The Villa man was another maverick. Always on the road. Haulage or football. He had probably eaten in every caff and diner in Britain, slept in every lay-by and drunk in most of the pubs. He had crisscrossed Europe as well, been to cities as far apart as Helsinki, Lisbon and Istanbul, but whether it was one of the more glamorous locations or a grim industrial town or a remote trading estate, Merlin always had an adventure. He had a knack for finding the best local restaurants and bars when abroad, and despite his scruffy appearance seemed to attract the ladies. It wasn't all eating, drinking and romancing, though, as he made sure he saw the more traditional sights. He particularly enjoyed visiting the homes of writers and painters, locations that featured in their novels and pictures, museums and buildings dedicated to their work.

Franz Kafka, Hans Fallada and Albert Camus were three of the writers he had told Ray about after an England away in Warsaw, late at night in the hotel bar when the police had reclaimed control of the nearby streets. Ray was an Orwell man and had mentioned *Nineteen Eighty-Four* for some reason, started Merlin talking about the European writers he admired. And artists like Picasso and Matisse. He had dropped a load off outside Nice. Slept in his cab for two nights. Spent a day in Antibes and two hours in Château Grimaldi. Another in Vence with an hour at the Matisse Chapel. He had shown Ray the photos on his phone. Added a few words of French.

– What's he up to? Ray asked.

Merlin had also been to every ground in the top four English divisions, keeping his membership of the 92 Club up to date as fast as he could after a new side arrived. But he wasn't at a match or in his lorry in this particular shot. He was sitting at the front of a barge.

– Have a look at the next ones, Stan urged.

Ray flicked through several more photos of Merlin and the barge, wasn't sure why he was looking at so many that were more or less the same, but then he did a double-take as the man became a goat. He brought the phone closer to his face to make sure. It was definitely a goat. He looked at Stan, who had been waiting for his reaction.

– Keep going.

Ray moved to the next picture. Merlin and the goat were standing by the side of a canal. Somewhere industrial. Dirty, depressing, dramatic. Northern. Thousands of bricks rose up behind them. A factory wall. Another photo showed Merlin crouching down so their heads were level. There was an iron bridge in the background. Black. Bolted together. With the height advantage removed, the goat seemed bigger and stronger, and the idea that it was smarter made Ray grin. Maybe it was in charge. The captain. There was a picture taken next to a lock. The flash had gone off and lit up the animal's eyes. Ray felt a childish chill run across his skin. But only for a split second. He handed the phone back.

– What's Merlin doing with a goat?

– Don't know. Likes him, I suppose.

– Is that his barge?

– It's a narrowboat. He insists on calling it that. Got to get the names right. The kitchen is a galley. He's been travelling around England since the first lockdown. Just the two of them.

– It's a good-looking animal, Ray admitted. Intelligent.

He passed the phone to Buster.

– He's a clever one all right, the barman agreed.

Stan wasn't sure what they meant. It was a goat.

– They'll be in Uxbridge tomorrow, he said. Merlin's getting some work done on the hull and there's a yard there everyone uses. A few of us are meeting up.

– What sort of time? Ray asked.

– Twelve onwards. You should come over. I'll get there a bit earlier, though. His name's Gary.

– I only know him as Merlin. It's the same with a lot of the people you meet at football. Only ever know them by their face or a nickname. Doesn't matter where they come from, there's always the same mix of characters. More or less. There's not many like Merlin around, though.

– The goat, I mean. He's called Gary.

– Gary Goat? Better than Gareth Ramsbottom. Next manager of England. Must be hard him living on a barge. Where does he sleep? The goat…

– It can't be inside, can it? On the roof?

– I've never been on a barge.

– Me neither. And it's a narrowboat. Honest, he won't let that go. There's quite a few people turning up. I phoned around. Everyone's keen to meet Gary. It's an excuse for a session.

Ray emptied his bottle and nodded to Buster, who opened another light ale and passed it over. Stan was only having the one as he had to go home, eat and change, pick up his brother, collect Darren, drop his brother off, then drive back to the house to dump the car and call a cab so they could get over to The George and meet Matt. Ray had his own plans. Light ale was an easy early drink.

– What's Merlin's real name? Ray asked. Do you know?

– Ramsbottom sounds about right. Arnold? He's northern, so it has to be something like that. Arnold Arkwright?

– Is Birmingham in the North? Is the Midlands? I mean we say it is, but I don't know. Mercia and Wessex were Saxon kingdoms. There again, so was Northumbria.

– Must be, Stan said, checking the time. It's all northern monkeys soon as you get past Watford. Right, I've got to get going.

– Can you send me a couple of those pictures? Ray asked. I want to show someone.

Stan did this quickly and was on his way. It was quiet this time of day, but the Union Jack didn't depend on the money that came across the bar. It was used by a lot of the drivers, but separate to Estuary and not Ray's responsibility, Buster and Hawkins in charge while his uncle was on holiday.

While the beaches and sunshine would be nice, Terry had chosen Jamaica because of the music he'd been listening to since he was young, keen to soak up the atmosphere and maybe see some of the places where ska had originated. For Terry, it was about the recording studios where the likes of Laurel Aitken and Prince Buster had started off, and he'd already booked up a visit to Orange Street. It wasn't as if he could stroll through Trench Town late at night, eating jerk chicken with Coxsone Dodd and smoking ganja with Jimmy Cliff. As he'd told Ray, he wouldn't be doing an Ivan, standing there watching Toots And The Maytals record for Leslie Kong. But if he could find a local who knew his stuff he'd pay him well for a tour.

Ray had been invited round to watch *The Harder They Come* two nights before they left, along with Terry and Lol demolishing a king-size Chapatti Express delivery with the help of some ice-cold Caribs. His uncle felt odd jetting off to a four-star hotel, an all-inclusive deal with an excursion thrown in he didn't fancy and would leave to Angie, but that was just his humble nature. He deserved the trip and would love it, sitting by the illuminated pool in the evening, drinking rum cocktails as a steel band played. Angie had sent Ray a nice clip. Typical Tel wearing a blue Fred Perry, sunglasses perched on his freshly-cropped head, giving the camera a big thumbs-up.

Walking over to the jukebox, Ray chose 'Skinhead Girl' in memory of April and in honour of Angie, watched the 45 being lifted up and dropped into position, the needle lowering as the machine worked its magic. Terry's second wife had made a massive difference to his life after the years of grieving, and it was good seeing him with someone special again. The music boomed. His uncle was a young tearaway done well. Self-made. Someone who had never forgotten his family and friends. Yes, Terry would be loving every second of his holiday in Jamaica.

Nobody was perfect, though. Not even Tel. And while he was a giver not a taker, when it came to his Rock-Ola he refused to share, the records that made it onto the jukebox strictly controlled. It was a running joke between uncle and nephew, these two strands of the English family and the wider skinhead world, while even Terry's son Lol was denied access. Not that he minded. Ray's early attempts had soon been brought to an end as the Estuary and Rock-Ola supremo had a lock specially fitted. But with Terry away, he had tracked down the key, been sure it was somewhere in the Union Jack, and searching the empty premises early last Sunday he was about to give up when he'd found it on a hook under the bar.

Terry must have forgotten to take it with him, or maybe he'd left it there for Buster and Hawkins in case of an emergency. It was a long time since any new singles had been added. Much too long. Ray was picking Terry and Angie up from the airport tomorrow and would come here first, add his selections and continue to Heathrow. He couldn't wait to see the look on his uncle's face. As he watched 'Skinhead Girl' spin he wondered which single to replace it with, whether it should be Cock Sparrer or The Last Resort or one of the newer bands. Returning to the bar, he chatted with Buster, finished his drink and checked the time, should really get going himself as he'd arranged to pick Priscilla up from Uxbridge station.

It was an easy drive over listening to Knock Off, Tear Up, LOAD, Crown Court, Boilermaker, B-Squadron and Hard Wax. He turned the music off when Priscilla called. She was at Rayner's Lane. Her train had been delayed after an incident at Wembley Park and she said she'd meet him in the Queen's Head. Their special place. Ray wasn't going to drink as he was driving, had already had three light ales and told her he would wait in the station, but she said not to worry about that, she only wanted a half, was hungry and fancied a curry. She could drive. What did he think?

– It would be rude not to, he responded, referring to the offer of a drink, ruby and lift home, musing on the rule of three and how everything was going his way.

Turning up Windsor Street, and when he reached the top looping back down from the Underground, Ray parked outside George's and headed for the pub. He ordered two pints of Guinness and downed the first of these in three goes, took the second and sat at an empty table by the window. Feeling poetic, he considered Priscilla and how she was like the head on his stout. The perfect topping to his perfect world.

He saw three men Stan's age passing outside and thought again about the younger driver's love of Oi, the emerging bands who would remain outside the mainstream, the same as always. Life repeating itself. Stan's best mates Darren and Matt made up another trio, and Ray returned to this idea of the same sort of characters mixing and balancing each other out. He wondered if a study had ever been done. Probably not. Stan was the solid one, Matt more flamboyant, Darren the loose cannon. A reliable man, a ladies' man, a hard man. Ray smiled as he dissected their little firm. Frowned as he tried to work out where he fitted in. If he was Stan, Matt or Darren. It would depend on the stage of his life. There were other depths, of course, things going on below the surface. Reasons and rhymes.

He wouldn't last five minutes these days. Not behaving like he used to do. Not with the cameras and everyone filming on their mobiles. He wouldn't be able to release the anger he'd felt in the past, and fuck knows where that could have led. But that was all gone now. He was older and wiser. Happy watching *Breaking Bad* and *Better Call Saul* and *House Of Cards* on Netflix with the love of his life.

Ray's phone vibrated. Priscilla was on the train. Asking if they could go straight to George's when she arrived. He was disappointed as he had the taste now, but didn't let it show. Agreed. A change of plans. Made calculations. He had time for another pint. A quick one. At least.

Maybe he shouldn't. It would be an act of solidarity to resist. But an empty gesture. He drained his glass and went to the bar. Returned to his seat. Looked at the pictures of Merlin and Gary again. He fancied going along tomorrow. Merlin was a good bloke, and it had been years since he'd seen him.

The England boys were turning out, and he wondered who Stan had invited. Should have asked. It would be a proper session. He had other things to consider, though. Had a thought. Forwarded a picture of the goat to Priscilla. There was something different about these creatures, even if he wasn't sure what. They were part deer, part sheep, part unicorn. Gary was a rarity. At least to Ray. Same as a barge. Narrowboat. And he studied Merlin's new home. Wouldn't mind seeing that either. There was a romance about the canals as well. A timeless mystery. Whether he went along or not really depended on Terry and Angie. He couldn't pick them up and rush off. Priscilla was going to have some food ready for when they got back to the house. And there was the jukebox to think about. He had to be there when Terry put on a Clancy Eccles or Laurel Aitken record and heard the voice of Micky Fitz or Roi Pearce instead. What if he wanted to go over there tomorrow afternoon?

His phone vibrated again, and Ray finished his pint and walked up to the station. Stood near the barrier. The Bakerloo service pulled in and the platform filled. He spotted Priscilla right away. Shimmying when he waved. She came through the machines and put a finger to her lips so he didn't speak, leant her head on his chest and hugged him. He drew in the smell of her perfume and felt her body, and as they turned she slipped her hand through his arm, leaving the station and heading down into Windsor Street.

– I hope someone didn't jump at Wembley, she said. Or fall. They didn't say.

It was still early, and The Raj was half full, their favourite table empty, and once they'd removed their coats and these had been hung up they settled in and were soon into the poppadoms and a generous relish tray, a pint of draught lager and a bottle of cider backed up by a jug of tap water. Ray knew what he was having, but still liked to examine the menu and consider the alternatives, which while it often led to some late uncertainty rarely influenced his final decision. Priscilla had arrived with a more open mind and was thinking about a vindaloo instead of the Madras she'd had last time, although she was also tempted by the jalfrezi. They would probably share an aloo chat and onion bhaji, as those had become their regular starters.

George wasn't in tonight, but Young George was his usual friendly self, and Ray had often thought he must feel the pressure at times, being the son of such a legendary local character, but if so he never showed any nerves. With their orders taken, they were able to relax, Priscilla removing her mobile from her handbag and finding the photos Ray had sent.

– He's spooky looking, don't you think?

– Merlin's fine. He's got a heart of gold. Supports Aston Villa.

– The goat, I mean.

– Gary?

– Gary Goat? Is that his name?

– That's what Stan at work told me. You've met him. A big, cheerful lump. Stan…

– Look at the eyes.

Ray knew what she meant, but didn't admit he'd felt that split-second chill. It was only the flash on the camera playing tricks.

– That's a nicer picture there. He looks more normal.

– Why is he living on a barge?

– It's a narrowboat. I don't know.

– What's the difference?

– Suppose it's in the name. A narrowboat's narrower. Smaller than a barge.

– It sounds like a children's story, doesn't it? You know, living on the canal with a goat. You can rent barges, can't you. Maybe we should do that. Travel up and down England for a couple of weeks.

Ray didn't reply as their starters were being delivered with a flourish, but while he saw the romance involved, he wasn't sure he wanted to spend his holiday on a canal. The novelty would soon wear off. He could be wrong, of course, and once their food had been arranged he raised his lager and Priscilla did the same with the cider. Her phone was on the table and Gary's eyes watched them as they drank, until she noticed and put him away inside her handbag. Yes, Ray had to admit that life was very sweet indeed. A cooling beverage and a scorching ruby then off home to Shepherd's Cross to watch *The Irishman* for the fourth time.

There were moments when he missed his nuttier self, but these were brief and he knew how to avoid putting himself in situations where he could make a mistake and ruin his new life. He had a lot to lose. While drink had played its part in his mistakes, and love and work were the positives that kept him stable today, it was as much about his age. Getting older had brought him benefits he'd never have imagined when he was young. *The Irishman* clocked in at three and a half hours, ran across the decades of a man's life, except there was no remorse and no mellowing. De Niro and his friends were killers, gangsters who murdered other human beings for money. Ray wasn't like that. And yet he loved the movie for its friendships, the same as he did Scorsese's *Mean Streets*, *Goodfellas*, *Casino*, *The Departed*.

Ray was a good-time boy who enjoyed a social drink. The same as Stan, Matt and Darren. At their core. Which one of them he resembled most, he did not know. He'd never been a heavy. More like an overgrown kid. As Mum used to say. They all were. It might have been a long old film, but each time he watched *The Irishman* with this gorgeous lady, who was sitting next to him delicately devouring her aloo chat, it felt shorter than before. They always had a break to get some ice cream from the freezer. Ray chose vanilla. Priscilla chocolate. Maybe tonight they'd have a bottle of beer each. That would be nice. He had some light ales at home. Thanks to Buster. And in the morning he would wake up with a clear head and a clear conscience. In control. Happy. Living his best life.

At first it was hard travelling on the canals together, but after a month or so Merlin and Gary had calmed down and settled into a routine. The goat had the most to lose. He was clearly oblivious to the dangers facing him if they failed to get on, and because Merlin took his guardianship role seriously he made the same allowances as he would for a small child. Even so, Gary had to play his part. There had been some unpleasant incidents early on, as well as the inevitable headbutting and petty vandalism, even a flash of temper, but Merlin understood that the lack of a shared language was always going make a tough situation tougher. He only wished he could explain the reasons behind what were some big changes for both man and beast. Covid had altered their lives forever, and, as they settled down for the night outside Rickmansworth, he knew that it had altered them for the better.

As more time passed they had come to respect each other's customs, and eighteen months after setting off Merlin believed they had developed a genuine friendship. The headbutts continued, but were playful rather than the more aggressive attempts at establishing command, while the breakouts and damage caused were normal for such a curious and nimble creature. Gary was intelligent, yet still a creature of instinct who knew nothing of football, music, literature, art, politics or religion, unaware even of the pandemic and the harm it had done to so many bodies and minds. Merlin accepted these limitations, but while it was irrational it did irritate him that his friend had no knowledge of economics, didn't appreciate the effort that had gone into the buying and maintaining of their new home, the cost of provisions and fuel, the hassle of obtaining these during the lockdowns.

Relaxing on his bed while Gary slept soundly in the wheelhouse, the story of a man who woke up one morning to find that he had changed into a giant insect filled Merlin's head, and when he turned a page of this Kafka tale and felt its rough edge, found half a nibbled paragraph, he was taken back a few months, remembered how these cultural divides had been emphasised and had to laugh. They'd been relaxing on the roof of *Wizard's Journey* in the brilliant Lincolnshire sunshine, the only sound the rustle of grass when a breeze skimmed the surrounding fields, Gary dozing, dreaming his goaty dreams, Merlin resisting the urge to nod off and join him in that parallel world, excited by a pick-up it had taken him weeks to organise.

He was holding brand-new copies of Albert Camus' *The Plague,* Hans Fallada's *Alone In Berlin* and Franz Kafka's *The Trial,* along with Kafka's *Metamorphosis* collection, fiction that fitted the times in which they were living. The paper was mint and clean and smelled fantastic, and while it was years since he had read these books, the effect they'd had on him as a young man remained. With time to reflect, he'd found himself thinking about Linda and how she'd introduced him to authors he would never otherwise have known about. She had got him reading, at least for a while, and now he wasn't working he had decided to go back and read them again.

He'd tracked Linda down online, glad to see she was married with four children and lots of grandchildren, choosing a different path to the one he'd ended up on. She had known what she wanted early, been decisive, whereas he'd drifted, although he supposed he had done okay in the end, sitting here in the heat, sniffing black ink and drawing in the summer air, deciding the smell had to be unique to Lincolnshire, very different to Cumbria or Norfolk or Somerset. The cities, too, of course. These mixtures changed by the second and would be impossible to measure and analyse, but didn't the best perfumers rely on their noses?

His own sense of smell was the sharpest he could remember. It was the same with his hearing. Best of all was his vision. He was seeing the world more clearly than ever before. It was as if he was being retuned, and he guessed his increasing awareness was logical with so many of the old distractions removed. There was more to it than that, though. Life on the canals was quiet, but he was experiencing an intensity of being that made him feel as if he was coming out of a deep sleep. This hadn't happened right away, and he'd been through spells of loneliness and doubt, but he was linking with his surroundings and evolving, taking on another sort of form. It was hard to explain, but exciting. A revelation.

As a buck, Gary gave off a strong odour, yet Merlin had quickly got used to this and within a week barely noticed. A couple of friends he'd met up with reckoned the smell was transferring, but he didn't care. If he was domesticating Gary, then it was only right that he was being rewilded. His friends laughed at this, reminded him that dogs were meant to be man's best friend, that their owners took on their looks, and perhaps it was the same here as his face had become more goatish. Merlin was pleased. He loved his talkative mutt who was part ante-lope, deer and sheep. He liked the idea that he was going through a physical and mental shift.

Gary'd had no choice when it came to living on the canals, been press-ganged into joining a crew of two, although he didn't exactly pull his weight, was more of a passenger. To be fair, while the goat's curiosity meant he liked to roam, and he'd broken out on numerous occasions, he had never tried to run away. Anyway, coming to live on the *Wizard* had saved his life. Merlin had learned a lot about goats since, on the internet but mainly through experience, and he couldn't help smiling as he remembered the first time Gary had pissed on his own front legs and face, spraying his urine about in order to attract the ladies, even though there were no nannies for miles. That smell really was horrible.

Merlin had known one or two men who'd done similar over the years, drunks who splashed the front of their trousers in the Gents and wondered why their chat-up lines never worked. His cousin Colin had gone further on a Great Yarmouth weekender, drinking so much he'd pissed himself in the pub while they were sitting in a booth with a couple of women from Harlow. The memory remained vivid after all these years, Colin cunning enough to shift the blame when the Harlow girls started twitching, blaming these old boys who were sitting at a nearby table, his wet jeans hidden by the table. Merlin had aided and abetted his cousin, finishing his drink fast so the women went to the bar to get another round in, joining them while Colin snuck out and returned to the chalet, showered and changed, made up some story about why he'd vanished, the details forgotten. At least there was a reason for Gary splashing it all over, which made him a lot smarter than Colin, who'd struggled to explain why his jeans had turned into slacks.

It would have been easy for Merlin to make life easier for himself, but no way was he having his friend castrated. Gary, not Colin... The farmer who owned the field where the goat had been living kept on about this, bringing it up every time the rent was paid. Castrate the beast and he would become more docile. Less smelly. The farmer was one more Giles, a bully with a knowing smirk Merlin had found creepy at the time, and in these more relaxing and enlightened days perverted. He'd always hated violence, and once the first lockdown started and he made the decision to head off on his narrowboat, it was clear he had to take Gary as well. If he left him behind it would mean castration or slaughter – probably both. He'd saved the goat when he was a kid, found him somewhere to live, wasn't about to abandon Gary now.

Merlin returned to that day in the Lincolnshire sun, when the smell, taste and effects of the cider he'd been drinking added to the aroma. It was homemade and strong, bought off Madeline, who used her dad's old press and sold it by the towpath outside Leeds. He was savouring his books, flicking pages and absorbing a recycled paper mix that was meant to be cutting down on deforestation. When he needed a wee he'd gone below instead of into the nearest field, didn't want to disturb Gary, knew he'd try to follow if he left the *Wizard*. Stopping to make himself a sandwich, he returned five minutes later to find the cardboard packaging chewed and the books nibbled, Gary standing there smiling as he bleated a cheerful welcome back. Merlin rarely got angry, and definitely not when he was looking at this picture of innocence, the goat only doing what goats did. The love he felt for this gentle soul had soared despite the damage, an empathy that spiralled to include the farmed and labouring animals of the world, the tethered and beaten and ignored, in those brief seconds seeing Gary as a figurehead for their suffering. It had been another epiphany, one of the many lessons he was learning, a series of realisations.

They had stayed with a lady living five miles from the Sheffield & South Yorkshire Navigation. A florist from Doncaster who'd inherited a house in the countryside, one with a big overgrown garden, which had allowed Merlin to bring his four-legged friend along. She'd picked them up in her van, and it had felt as if they were going on holiday even though they were on the move and exploring England, the goat quickly making a start on tidying up her garden. Diane liked his appetite if little else about him, and especially not the smell, insisting Merlin put his clothes in the washing machine as soon as he entered her house, running a bath and telling him to take his time.

This he had done, spent ages soaking in and topping up the hot water, a luxury he'd missed. Diane knocked on the door after half an hour asking if he had drowned and should she call an ambulance, and when he finally came out in the dressing gown she'd lent him, this woman he'd met years earlier while working and staying in a pub overnight was waiting on the bed he was meant to be sleeping in, naked and playing with herself. A couple of days had turned into a week, which had become two, and while he started to feel restricted living with another human being, the house was warm and spacious, and Diane was good company. Despite this, he missed the *Wizard* and began worrying it would be stolen or broken into, which was silly as he'd never felt threatened on the canals, not even when a drugged-up scally had climbed aboard in Manchester. Gary started screaming a friendly hello, and the kid freaked out and ran for his life.

The skunk Diane grew was powerful stuff and it would have been rude to decline her offers, especially as she was making him these fantastic meals, the sort of food he hadn't tasted for many months. He wasn't a smoker at the best of times, and it wasn't long before he was feeling lethargic, his clarity of thought muddling, which only made him realise how healthy he had become. It was a hard one, knowing whether he should stay or go, but the decision was made for him when he started crying in front of his hostess. It was thundering outside, really pouring with rain, and he'd gone over to her bedroom window and looked out, searching for Gary in the darkness, couldn't find him, not until the lightning flashed.

The goat was sheltering under a tree. He was soaked. It looked as if his fur had been shaved off. Skin stripped from his body. The head seemed oversized, thanks to his horns. Merlin couldn't see from this distance, but was sure he was shivering, from fear as much as the cold. A wave of sadness engulfed him. This creature was frail and alone and defenceless. His kind were farmed and brutalised, sacrificed to gods, cast out as scapegoats, castrated and milked, slaughtered and even raped by the lowest sorts of humans. He'd mentioned these things one night, in the morning wishing he hadn't, relieved Gary didn't understand. Merlin would have felt terrible if he had, but not as bad as he did now. The goat had been left to fend for himself by the one person in the world that he trusted.

This well-travelled lorry driver who had hauled heavy loads and dealt with every sort of problem, a fearless road warrior who liked a drink and was no weakling and knew little fear, began to cry. He had no idea where this had come from at the time, and neither did Diane. The look of disgust on her face had made him feel very ashamed. She'd taken them back to the narrowboat the following day, and once she was gone the two friends had been overcome with relief, happy to be home and moving on, their freedom restored.

Despite Gary's simple animal nature, Merlin had been talking to him at length and in greater and greater depth. The goat may have been noisy at times, but he was also a good listener. While clueless when it came to the specifics of what was being said, he did pay attention and after a while seemed to be reacting. At first Merlin thought this was due to his changes in tone and speed of delivery, shifts that reflected emotions, but after a while he had started to wonder if something else was going on. Generally speaking, his voice had a soothing effect, but when he became excited Gary reacted, bleating more than usual. It was as if he was trying to separate words, his attention increasingly focused as though he was linking sentences and learning the language. This was ridiculous, and maybe the first sign of madness, but, whatever the truth, these one-sided chats were appreciated, as without companionship an animal was bound to become as lonely as a human.

Merlin loved to wax lyrical about his favourite football team and the magic of Jack Grealish. Villa were one of the sleeping giants of English football. Newcastle were another such club. Local rivals Wolverhampton Wanderers, West Bromwich Albion and Birmingham City were big, but nowhere near the size of Villa. They were not giants of the game. He stressed that he didn't mean this literally, wasn't talking about huge mythical men shaking the earth with their footsteps and terrorising the locals, but the history and culture of a footballing institution, the support that had gathered on the terraces since long before he was a boy, back in the days when people weren't forced to sit down and pay through their noses for the privilege. He told Gary about the Ron Saunders side that had won the First Division, Tony Barton and the European Cup, how the club was on the rise once again.

It was a shame the goat had no concept of history, whether it was football or the canals they were travelling along, the latter a subject Merlin had started investigating as soon as he bought the narrowboat. It was an incredible network that ran from north to south, east to west, and he had long appreciated the thought and labour that went into creating infrastructure, the way roads and canals and railways connected people and elevated their lives. He had loved most of his time as a long-distance lorry driver, seeing the UK and Ireland and travelling further afield and exploring Europe. The cab was his hotel on wheels, even if it was more like a cheap B&B minus the breakfast, but he had freedom and stimulation, the many friends he'd made among the other drivers, the people met along the way, the sights he had seen.

There were too many pubs and bars to remember, women charmed and occasionally paid for, although he always felt guilty afterwards, adding extra to make up for what he considered a wrong. His work was an extension of his football trips, following Villa and England away, but he'd become irritated and then angry at his pay and conditions, the lack of respect shown by the authorities and wider society. The facilities provided were a disgrace. Another insult. Without drivers like him working all the hours they did the country would grind to a halt. He was a self-employed man doing a hard job, believed in the dignity of labour, but those in control saw him as little more than a modern-day workhorse.

There was an aura about the canals, the place where a decaying industrialism met the constant renewing of the land, a silent claiming of past and future, but along with the planning and construction of the network, there was a dark, satanic side. Life had been tough for the humans working the canals, but a lot worse for the horses providing the muscle, beautiful creatures moved from the forced labour of ploughing to slave on the towpaths. Taken from their rural homes they were beaten and driven forward until their hearts and bodies failed and they were sent exhausted to the knacker's yard to be slaughtered and turned into glue and dog food.

He'd been thinking ahead when he bought the narrowboat, the idea to one day travel around the country and see it from the shadows, move silently through the back channels for another vision of England. It had been offered to him at a price that was too good to ignore, a friend connecting him with a friend. It was an investment for when his body failed him or the work dried up, but really it was an escape from a life that had started to tilt in the wrong direction. He had talked excitedly about the narrowboat but doubted he could stand this life for long, as he was used to speed and power, moving long distances fast, hearing different languages and seeing all sorts of odd places, discovering the unusual. He needed company, liked to be around people, lived alone but didn't want to *be* alone.

Covid had made a vague plan real. Maybe he would never have used *Wizard's Journey* for more than a week or two at a time without the pandemic, but when the first lockdown was under way and the work he'd lined up was cancelled, he couldn't face looking for more, even though it was obvious lorry drivers were going to be needed. He admired the doctors and nurses and all the other essential workers, but he'd left the rollercoaster and couldn't see himself getting back on.

He had lasted three weeks stuck in the house before he had to either get out or go mad. Giving his landlord notice, he left the flat the next day and dropped the stuff he wanted to keep at his brother's, gone to collect Gary and after ten minutes managed to put him in the car and drive to the canal, the next morning setting off. He had been nervous at first, but the best way to learn anything was on the job. It was the mental change that had been hardest, and he knew he had to look after his head, balancing the long periods of isolation with company, meeting up with people he hadn't seen for years, tapping into his football connections. As his friendship with Gary grew he'd felt less alone, happy to accept that this was another stage of his life. Going to football again had been a relief, and he could do that from the canal, but he wasn't attending as many matches as before, could see that fading away one day. He would always want to see his mates, though. That was never going to change.

He was looking forward to tomorrow and meeting up with some of his England pals. They would have a good drink and maybe a curry in that restaurant he'd heard about. On Monday he was putting *Wizard's Journey* in to have the hull sorted out, staying at a friend's place in Colnbrook while it was being done, before continuing his journey into London. Smithy was a driver whose old man ran a small firm locally, and there was an empty caravan in the yard, some land next to it where they kept a couple of horses and a donkey. He would be there for two nights, and once *Wizard's Journey* was back in the water would head for Brentford and a couple of days there, before coming back and joining the Regent's Canal, crossing the city from there, his destination Limehouse and a drink with his West Ham friends.

He hoped Gary would be all right away from the *Wizard*, knew Colnbrook wasn't the ideal location for an animal with strong senses of smell and hearing, being so close to Heathrow, that the atmosphere was going to be a lot different to what they'd become used to, and yet there was petrol and oil floating in the air as he laid on his bed. He would keep a close eye on the goat. They had moored in cities before, and while none came close to matching the size of the capital, he knew from other bargees that there were plenty of nice spots to be found.

Folding the page he'd been reading and closing the Kafka collection, he turned off the light and rolled onto his side, didn't mind feeling this tired so early, because that was another amazing thing about life on the canals, the depth of his sleep and the clarity of his dreams, the way he woke up so refreshed and excited every morning. There were nights when it was as if he moved beyond the human, and maybe that was why he had cried in front of Diane, embarrassing the woman so much she'd wanted him gone, his sleep disrupted by the sex and drugs and fine food, the new order of things turned upside down.

As he began to doze off he heard the clicking of hooves, but wasn't scared, knew the horses were in a better place, that there were no ghosts and no killers on the towpath. Gary hadn't got out either, as he could hear him dreaming. The goat was an innocent who'd never had a wicked thought in his life, saw the world in a much purer way, and Merlin's best nights were spent inside his head. There were more clicks, this time on the wood above his head, and he was reassured, knew that the moon was sinking and the sun was being prepared, and certain to rise.

Stan wished he hadn't shown his brother the pictures of Gary, that he hadn't told him there was a goat coming to Uxbridge with a man called Merlin. He'd just thought it would be nice if Stephen came along to meet him, the idea that there was going to be some mental religious angle to it never entering his head. It was meant to be a friendly get-together in a pub on the canal. A session with a star attraction. A football drink to coincide with the arrival of their Brummie mate from the England games. Everything innocent and above board. At least until Stephen started talking about the Devil and his wizard and the plague that was destroying the country and how the Evil Ones had to be stopped and by that he meant killed and their bodies burned.

– It's only a goat, Stan had said. You'll love him.

– Have you met the beast?

– Not yet, but he's harmless. Lived in a field and now he lives on a narrowboat.

– I thought it was a barge.

– They call it a narrowboat.

– Real goats don't live on the water. Have you ever seen a goat out sailing before?

– I don't go looking, do I? I cross the canal sometimes, but that's it. There could be millions of goats travelling up and down for all I know.

– Don't be so stupid. Have a look at those pictures again. Can't you see the likeness? Satan, Lucifer, Pan, Baphomet, Beelzebub. Call him what you want, but the Devil is coming, and he plans to enter London through the Uxbridge portal so he can spread his pestilence.

– You're joking, aren't you?

– Of course I'm not joking. Think about it. Why is he travelling with a sorcerer?

Stan went to say something, but was too slow.

– Because he's carrying the final variant of the virus, that's why. The strain that is going to wipe out every single person on the planet. Merlin is his servant, the one who makes the poison.

– Merlin's not his real name.

– What is it then?

– I don't know.

– Why not? That's mental.

– He's called Merlin because he's got long hair like one of those Druid priests. He isn't a sorcerer. Mind you, he can magic a pint away fast enough. Make it vanish in front of your eyes.

– You see, black magic.

Stan wasn't sure if Stephen was being serious or not. He always had to be on full alert, though. Consider everything he said. Just in case. He worried about his little brother. More so recently. That was never going to change.

– Merlin's master will draw the witches down from the hill and into the valley. They can smell the goat from hundreds of miles away. The stink of his rancid breath and arse. Leaking cock and balls the size of footballs. You know that, don't you?

– What are you on about? There aren't any witches, and what's all this stuff about leaking cocks and football-sized bollocks?

– Trust me, the witches are on their way. Some will already be in the woods on the road to Slough. I wonder if they'll arrive together? Probably not.

– Leave it out, for fuck's sake.

– Others will be travelling in from the West Country at this very second. That's where the crones like to rave. Inside the stone circles. Who do you think makes the crop circles? Have you ever thought about that? These corn dollies can enchant anyone. Especially men like Matt, who'll shag anything that moves.

– That's not very nice.

– Ladies made from wheat, oats, rye, barley. I'm no expert, but they will do whatever is required to mate with the Devil, and if not Lucifer, then his familiar Merlin.

– Come on, Stephen.

– He's the great deceiver. You think the human is in charge of the animal, but it is Gary who controls Merlin.

– You're doing my head in.

– Did you know Thor rides a chariot drawn by goats? And that every night he kills and eats them? And in the morning the goats have come back to life?

– Merlin's a lorry driver. He owns a narrowboat, not a chariot, and if he's ever eaten goat meat it would've been curried. I don't think Thor likes Caribbean food.

– Don't make fun of me, Stephen said in a stern voice.

– I wasn't. But you'll like Merlin. And Gary's an ordinary goat. You can pat his head and feed him a carrot.

– Sounds more like a rabbit.

– I don't know what goats eat.

– You've seen *The Lord Of The Rings* too many times, that's your problem. You've got to face up to reality. This isn't Gandalf we're talking about. Anyway, there are no good wizards, and no such thing as white magic. Gary and Merlin have to be erased from the face of the Earth. I'm going to shoot them and set fire to their remains, and there is nothing you can do to stop me.

This exchange had taken place three hours ago in Stan's car, sitting outside the family home where Stephen lived with their parents. Darren hadn't helped, smirking in the back as he listened to the brothers. He hadn't tried to calm things down as he normally did, instead doing the exact opposite, going into his pocket and taking out that fucking troll cross, a four-pound curved iron loop bought off eBay.

It had been funny the first couple of times Darren flashed it in the pub, two fingers slotted through the middle so it fitted nice and snug, more like a knuckleduster than the charm he claimed it to be, but the novelty had soon worn off. To be fair, it had acted as a miracle worker on one occasion, that night he'd showed it to a couple of lovelies they'd been chatting up, explaining how it protected him from danger and meant he was invincible. While one of these ladies decided he was making fun of her, the other had a sense of humour and played along. Darren had pulled, which was unusual, as women usually kept their distance.

This was a couple of years ago, when the boys were pissed and care-free in a public house, not sober and serious and stuck in the motor like earlier. It was strange he still carried the cross around with him, but maybe he'd brought it along specially, which was even worse. Darren knew Stephen was fragile. He fucking well knew. The last thing he should be doing was encouraging his madness.

– You can borrow this if you want, Darren had said, stretching an arm between the driver and passenger seats, the cross in the middle of his open palm.

Stephen turned and took his glasses off, leaning in close to see more clearly.

– What is it?

– A troll cross. It will protect you from harm. It's Norse.

– Pagan?

– Maybe originally, but not any more. Everyone converted. We're all Christians now. At least in this car.

– The Devil really is coming, Stephen said, raising his head and staring at Darren. Don't say he isn't. Lucifer and his drug-addicted magician and cock-sucking whores.

– Sex-mad witches? Darren replied. I wouldn't mind some of that. But the virus is getting weaker. Satan's fucked. I don't know much when it comes to black magic, but this cross will save you from the wicked ones.

– And how will it do that, good sir?

– You carry it in your pocket. It's especially powerful when you're crossing a bridge, because that's where a lot of trolls live. Under bridges and in ditches. I don't mean just trolls, but anything nasty.

Stephen took the cross.

– What about monsters who travel on water?

– It will definitely protect you against the sneaky fuckers who use the canals to move around unseen.

Stan couldn't believe Darren. Why would he talk about trolls and put more ideas into his brother's head? He tried to snatch the cross and Stephen screamed, closing his hand and forming a fist.

– Leave it alone! Let Darren speak.

Stan wished he hadn't tried to grab the cross. It was making things worse.

– You can borrow my amulet, Darren continued. Keep it for as long as you want. Forever if you like.

Stan fumed.

– I'm not a fool, Stephen insisted. There aren't any trolls in England, only on the internet, and they could be living anywhere. If we were in Scandinavia it would be different. If I was a Norwegian or a Swede or a Finn, but I don't think Finland is part of Scandinavia. Trolls? You're taking the piss, you piss-taking piss-taker.

Darren laughed, and after a few seconds so did Stephen.

– When you meet the Devil, hold it up and see if his face catches fire.

– That won't work. There are better ways to burn the Devil. I know what I'm doing, Mr Piss-Taking Piss-Taker.

Stephen slipped the cross into his jacket's inside pocket and glared at Stan before jumping out of the car and hurrying towards the house, too fast for his older brother who fumbled with his seatbelt as he tried to follow, the front door opening and closing before he could catch up. Stan had stood in the street trying to decide whether to follow Stephen inside or not, knew that by doing so he could do more damage, make Gary and Merlin and the cross seem more important than they were, had to hope this would be quickly forgotten. That often happened, but Stan had a bad feeling, his attention turning to the wanker sitting in the back of his car.

It hadn't been the right time or place to have a go at Darren, not with Stephen watching from the living-room window, and now that they were in the pub and he had a couple of pints inside him it felt as if he had overreacted and taken all that nonsense talk too seriously. Matt had joined them, and the mood was immediately lifted by his carefree attitude, the three of them bouncing off each other like they did, focusing on the more important things in life.

– What the fuck have you done to your hair? Matt was asking, running his hand over Darren's head.

– I cut it myself, he said, lowering his face and presenting his skull for further inspection.

– Looks like it as well. Did you do it blindfolded?

Darren grinned and moved back, happy to be out with his mates, holding a pint in his hand. It was true for all three of them, and around the pub and across the country groups of men felt exactly the same way.

– I bought some clippers after the first lockdown, Darren explained. It was horrible having long hair, and I wanted to be ready if there was another one, just kept cutting it once I got going. I must be doing a good job if this is the first time you've noticed.

– Same here, Stan said. I had a haircut as soon as I could. Angie at the cab firm does the drivers.

– Terry's wife?

– Ray The Nutter's second auntie?

– Oi The Nutter... I put my foot in it earlier.

– You called him Nutter? What happened?

– It slipped out, but I didn't exactly call *him* Nutter, it was more a comment about an album he recommended, this brilliant compilation *40 Years Untamed*.

Matt and Darren knew their Oi through Stan, but weren't as dedicated.

– What did he do? Darren asked, bringing the conversation back to Ray before Stan started listing the tracks, like a lot of these music-lovers did, sharing genes with the trainspotters and matchbox collectors and birdwatchers.

Darren admired Oi The Nutter. The bloke was old school, and he had seen him in action a few times, even shared the back of a police van and a court appearance, part of a tradition that went back through Nutty Ray's own family to Terry English and the original Shed boys. He thought about the FLA marches, the lads who'd turned out from across the country, everyone united against their common enemies, the terrorists and traitor scum who made excuses for suicide bombers and paedophiles, the dregs of polite society that allowed the abuse of white children by racist, fundamentalist filth.

They had been good days out, with Ray and Terry among the many Chelsea who had attended, and while at first Darren had hoped things would get lively, there'd been no real opposition, and anyway, it had always been meant as a peaceful show of strength. The mutual respect was clear, with all the rivalries and stereotypes put to the side, part of the spectacle that made their terrace culture special. A good number of those present were older and wiser, and it was the chance to show their shared roots never mind any political affiliations. Not that the MSM would ever report it that way, but they were part of the problem and nothing positive was expected.

– Ray was fine, Stan said. For a moment I thought he was going to say something, but he's mellowed. I told him about Merlin and how we're meeting up.

– Is he coming?

– Don't know, but he asked me to send him some photos, so maybe. The narrowboat and the goat. He thinks Gary looks intelligent.

– That fucking goat, Darren laughed. Yes, mate, he's the brain of Britain. I don't see why people are so interested in him. Same goes for the barge.

– It's a narrowboat. And how many people own or get to meet a goat?

– I heard Matt's got one at home. Reckons he's servicing his clients, but I don't know.

– You think what you want, Matt laughed. That's all in the past, anyway. Remember, I was charging CAT. Top rate as well.

– Fucking rent boy.

– I'm not complaining. Interesting, well-paid work. Keeps me fit.

Darren scanned the pub, leaving Matt's bullshit behind, absorbing the movement and noise.

– How many are coming? he asked Stan.

– Should be a good turnout. Locals, obviously. Chelsea and the West London clubs. Some Arsenal and West Ham are travelling over. Millwall, too, I think. A carload of Merlin's Villa mates. Newcastle are in London. Reading and Wolves. I even heard someone is flying over from Norway. A Chelsea supporter.

– I think I've met him, Darren said. Björn?

– The bloke out of ABBA? Matt asked.

– Your favourite band.

– You need a bit more punk and Oi in your life, Stan said. Some Infa-Riot.

– I don't mind ABBA, Matt admitted, deciding to take things further for Darren. I like a good tune. It's music for the ladies. Songs for smooching and getting them warmed up and in the mood for love.

– Matt the gigolo.

– There's Björn and Benny, he continued. Best of all Anni-Frid and Agnetha.

– Did you hear about the ABBA concerts they're planning? Stan asked. It's going to be the band from 1977 performing.

– What are you talking about?

– They're using avatars or something. It's a virtual show. Digital performers. Mad, isn't it? Sounds good, though.

A flashgun went off in Matt's head. Faces from the recent past. Surreal horrors. Real and imagined. Fear replaced with the relief of escaping a world he had seen and did not like. He was in a photographic studio. It was high end and professional, traditional rather than trendy in its decor, the technology state of the art. He was standing at the back behind some serious kit, the main camera positioned on a tripod, flanked by bulbs, the lens directed towards a white canvas background. He could see the legs of an antique chair, but not who was sitting on it, his view obscured by a make-up artist. Somehow he knew it could only be one of two people on the chair, unless they were posing together, and he felt that earlier fear returning, realised what he was doing, couldn't be thinking of both these characters as human.

The make-up artist was applying some sort of powder, raising a brush in the air, small clouds puffing and floating into the canvas. She had a blonde beehive and was wearing a short red skirt, white top and black boots, a timeless modernist style that was classy and upbeat. The photographer was watching this scene through his viewfinder, zooming in and out, adjusting the focus. He was older and also smartly turned out, from the same era if another generation. Matt couldn't see either of their faces as they were facing what he realised was a small stage. There was another man present. He hadn't noticed him before.

Shocked, Matt didn't know how he could have missed Terry White. He was wearing a black Crombie. White was the snappiest person present. Sensing that he was being watched, Terry White turned a wooden head and focused his glass eyes on Matt.

He wanted to run, but knew that would be a mistake, and anyway, he hadn't done anything wrong. Terry scared Matt. More now he was getting taller and the strings were clear, this marionette a lot stranger than those avatars and dancing queens. Matt blinked and Terry was gone, the make-up artist leaving the stage and coming into the shadows to stand next to him. She was an illustration that turned into Natasja. The photographer was advising Little Terry, who was the one sitting on the chair. This was the real marionette, not Big Terry. Another blink of those shutter eyes and the two Tels were united. Terry sat on Terry's knee. Their features followed the grain of the wood and the slash of a blade. Powdered and dangerous, the flash faded and Matt returned to the pub.

– You haven't invited any Tottenham along? Darren was asking.

– Of course not.

– But you've got West Ham and Millwall? Locals and outsiders.

– It'll be fine. England united.

– Wasn't so friendly after the Germany game, was it? Who are the West Ham?

– Potts and Lenny. They're getting the Metropolitan Line from Aldgate.

– So there could be a few of them?

– I don't know, but Merlin's going over to East London and they can see him there.

Darren was shaking his head.

– Potts and Ray? It's not a good idea putting those two in the same pub. Not after the Germany game in the summer.

– They had an argument, that's all, Matt said.

Stan had heard of a disturbance in the Chandos after England beat Germany 2-0 in the semi-finals of the Euros, but he'd been out of the area by then. He was glad Matt had said that. He was less of a wind-up merchant than Darren, didn't push things to the edge in the same way. At least Darren knew when to stop. More or less. Unlike Stephen.

– I could be wrong, Matt continued. Thinking about it...

Deep down he knew he had been careless.

– So how's the new job going? Matt asked Darren.

– It's brilliant. Best I've ever had.

– Doughnut Darren.

– That's me. Honest, I love it. Shouldn't tempt fate I suppose. Only been there six weeks, but the days flash by. It's the smell. The happy faces.

It had to be one of the best jobs in the world. That's what Darren had thought when he saw the post advertised, surprised to be called in for an interview once he had sent in his application, shocked when he received a call two days later offering him the position. Doughnut Delights had only been going a couple of years and was already expanding, with a second shop recently opened. The work had saved his life. Rachel was in charge of this new place, and while she could be bad tempered and rude, she had taken a shine to him and was friendly and some even said flirtatious. He didn't see that, was just pleased to have a full-time job with lots of overtime.

– You can call me Doughnut Darren or Doughnut Boy or maybe plain Doughnut. Seeing as it's you, Matt.

– Plain doughnut? No filling?

– Traditional, me. Covered in granulated sugar. Powered is nice and glazed is okay, but nothing beats granulated. Raspberry or strawberry jam, but not vanilla custard. That doesn't belong inside a doughnut. Each to their own, though. Whatever the filling, there has to be enough of it, and Double D is more than generous. Part of what sets us apart.

– Double D? Sounds like a bra company.

– Doughnut Delights. We do a much bigger range than just the traditional doughnuts. I never knew there were so many types until I started there. I get a nice staff discount and have tried them all.

– He's delivering as well, Stan said. Brought a box to the Union Jack for one of the drivers' birthdays. Nutty Ray knows the company, where it started and that.

– I get some healthy tips as well. Personalised service. Lots of parties.

It was Darren's birthday tomorrow, but he never mentioned it so nobody knew or remembered. He found it interesting how different people handled these and other anniversaries. As far as he was concerned, his birthday was another number on the calendar. His parents had died when he was a young and he had no brothers or sisters, so nobody had ever made a fuss. The aunt who had raised him had marked it, but that was a long time ago and best forgotten. There were lots of men out there with big families who kept quiet, while others told everyone and loved the attention, really did see it as a celebration. He had never understood this as it meant another year closer to death. He didn't know if there was a right or wrong approach. Christmas was the same, and although the others invited him for dinner, he preferred to spend the actual day alone. He always made sure he had a session the night before and slept in late. He still cooked himself a proper meal, but was glad when Christmas Day was over.

– You wouldn't think many people had doughnuts delivered, but you'd be amazed, he continued. Huge boxes of them, and some are even gift wrapped. I took fifty to a children's do last week. This wasn't a rich family either.

– Must have brought fifty or thereabouts to Estuary.

– You should have seen how excited the kids got. Twenty beaming faces. Everyone likes a doughnut, don't they? It was the same with your lot at the Union Jack. Boys in men's bodies, hurrying to the box to see what was inside.

– That's true, Stan agreed.

– The thing about the job, as well as the smell of the doughnuts, is that everyone you meet is smiling. Sounds odd, I know, but maybe it's like being a clown. Well, not a clown exactly. I mean, a lot of people are scared of them these days. The greasepaint and that. Huge red mouths. You can do a lot...

Matt returned to Terry White's wooden face dusted in white powder. It smelled like talcum rather than anything more expensive and specialist, and there was nothing sugary or doughy about it either. Again he was replaced by his marionette self, Little Terry. This was one nasty fucker, and he was off the chair and charging towards Matt with a chisel in his right hand. ABBA were more fun. Terry was back on Terry's knee as the flashgun popped.

– Jesus, Matt said.

– You're scared of clowns? Darren asked.

– No, I was thinking about someone else. *Something* else.

– You know, one day nothing is going to be real, Darren said. Everything will be done by avatars. Not only bands, but the crowd as well. Look at football during lockdown. The crowd wasn't needed once they added sound effects.

– I was thinking about that, Stan said. If we could have got in there and taken over the soundtrack for those games it would have livened things up. Playing classics from the old days. *Hello, hello, Chelsea aggro, Chelsea aggro, hello…*

– That would have upset a few people, Darren said. You can't say this, you can't say that. Fucking wankers.

– *You're going to get your fucking heads kicked in…*

– *With hatchets and hammers, carving knives and spanners…*

The three friends were imagining the outrage, thousands of New Fans and Numpty Beloveds spluttering into their eight-pound Italian lagers as they headed straight to Twitter and Facebook to express their disgust.

Stan, Matt and Darren were back to normal, drinking fast, ordering again and again, kept on going, lifted up and happy. Until Darren returned to the next day's meet and who was coming and how he should have held onto his troll cross and not given it to that nut-nut Stephen because he was going to need some protection when it kicked off and the pub was demolished hadn't Stan thought about that what a fucking plum he would end up banned for life. Darren was pissed and only mucking about. Everyone knew he loved Stephen. Tomorrow wasn't down to Stan or anyone else. They were all adults. Grown men. But it must have come out wrong.

While Stan knew some people saw humour in madness, he wasn't laughing. He was suddenly sick of Darren. The realisation hit him hard. They'd known each other since they were kids and it was too long. Matt was easier going, and while it was true that Darren had been good with Stephen over the years, maybe it was because they were similar. There was something not right about Darren, and the good times were no longer worth the bad. The lockdowns had broken a lot of bonds and that could be part of the reason he was feeling like this, but it didn't matter as the anger bubbled over and Stan put his glass down and before Matt could stop him threw a punch that connected with a thud, following it up with a second and third before Darren recovered from the shock and began fighting back.

Gary stood on the roof of *Wizard's Journey* and felt the love flow through his body as Nanny Goat Great brought England back to life. She was coaxing the sun awake with wisps of her sacred breath, stirring the simmering embers to spark and flare, a gentle puff causing the fire to roar and blaze. Gary drew deep on the cool canal air. It was refreshing his lungs and heart, while the first burst of light warmed his mind and channelled his focus. This magical voyage was revealing a world he could never have imagined, and he was no longer scared when he woke up in the morning, only felt excited about what would happen on the next leg of their adventure. Later today they would enter the wonderland known as Uxbridge, where they were going to meet some of Captain Longhair's cheerful, football-loving friends.

The goat's old world had been the corner of a field, his company the sheep who came and went on the other side of six lengths of stretched wire, a crow that perched on a pole and spread rumours. She swore the metal sheds he could see in the distance were full of cows whose children had been taken and murdered so humans could drink their milk, while the concrete blocks beyond housed pigs who had never been outside and didn't know the sun existed. The lorries that thundered and made him shake as they passed took these pigs to a factory where they were bled to death and their bodies dismembered, so the same sort of people could cook and eat their flesh.

The crow was mixing horror with fantasy and insisting it was the truth. Did he never wonder what happened to the sheep? What about the smell in the air? Why was he living in the corner of a dirty field? Little Billy Boy Silly needed to look more closely at the humans he saw. Gary did as she asked, and while he could accept the men were unfriendly and appeared unhappy, he didn't for a moment believe her stories about cows and their babies, the pigs and factories, sheep vanishing into dark holes. It was too terrible to be true. Such things were impossible. He felt sorry for the crow, but couldn't deny that he was unsettled.

Longhair was a different sort of character, a kind soul who brought gifts of apples or bananas when he came to visit, on the day he took Gary away arriving with both. The car ride was scary, and it had taken ages to clamber into the back seat, which was due to his own uncertainty, but once on the move it was also fascinating. A series of novel scenes changed and repeated, accompanied by the soft rhythms of an engine that had linked with what he would later know as the sound of Led Zeppelin. Boarding *Wizard* had felt dangerous and he'd panicked, climbing onto this same roof with the idea to run somewhere more solid, but faced with an expanse of water he'd been forced to stop. His saviour had left him to settle his nerves before offering food and drink and later luxurious quarters where he could rest for the night.

It had taken a while to adjust to what were some big changes for them both, but after a month they had settled into a routine and over time become firm friends. He owed his new life to the noble captain, the only time he'd doubted him when he learned that Longhair had driven a lorry in the past, but his loads were quickly detailed, and no calves, pigs, sheep or other creatures had been involved. The relief he felt showed how fiction sold as fact sowed doubt, while it also reinforced the belief that Nanny Goat Great was watching over him. Each day spent on this journey saw Gary's old anxieties ease. He would instinctively remain vigilant, but while his first exposure to humans may have been negative, he was an optimist who only wanted to see the best in his fellows.

He trusted the captain, and as the months and seasons passed the idea that he was more than just a friend and protector developed. Perhaps he was a guardian angel sent by Nanny Herself? This may have been fanciful thinking, but Gary was noticing something of the goat about Longhair, and as he began to understand the language and appreciate the mysteries of human religion and especially the churches of Aston Villa and England, the holy canal system on which they travelled and eventually the terrible virus that had paradoxically led to his salvation, perhaps something of the human was transferring in the opposite direction. His reactions to Longhair's monologues were certainly unusual. Their minds seemed to be synchronising, which wasn't so strange, seeing as they were both animals with heads, hearts, brains and limbs, although the captain hadn't been blessed with horns or a visible tail, forced to walk on two legs not four.

The canals were a pathway, even a body of sorts, more treelike than animal, but a manmade structure with its own arteries and blood, a spine that sprouted into small arms of hollowed-out bone, a marvel of engineering that had demanded mental brilliance as well as both human and non-human labour, the tasks involved in this massive undertaking divided according to class and species. Horses were the slaves, apparently beaten and abused by masters, sent to their deaths when they weakened with age. Gary had listened to Longhair talk about this, his friend's sadness bouncing around inside both their skulls, yet the feeling faded and they carried on, enjoying the magnificent variations of landscape, the mixing of dead industry and huge swathes of living land, the green fields where Gary liked to browse and feast and be merry.

Nanny Goat Great's love filled every cell of his body, washing through his veins like the purest water, and he thought of those fields through which they had passed, stopping at the tree he had climbed with Nanny's guidance one morning last spring. He didn't know its name, but had seen a crow perched among the buds, recognised its voice but wasn't sure if it was male or female, if its name was Colin or Colette. It was eating a berry and wobbling on the branch as if intoxicated by its juice, and when Colin *and* Colette saw the goat below it apologised for urinating, the flow hitting a nearby molehill, adding that it must leave now and change its feathers in a chalet, which seemed odd as didn't birds live in nests? He had never seen a crow wearing human clothes before either. It was perplexing, to say the least.

Colin and Colette had flown away, his or her wings huge like an eagle's and tiny like a sparrow's, Gary curious to share its view from the tree. He had wondered if there was a map of the canal network spread out over the surrounding land, and if he would be able to see it from the crow's favourite branch, the highlights marked with bright-yellow felt pen on a giant version of the map Captain Longhair had pinned to a wall inside the *Wizard*. This he brought out to show Gary when the weather permitted, spreading it on the roof of their ship, and while it was a temptation, this was paper the goat would never chew. He'd had no qualms about the Camus, Fallada and Kafka tomes he had vandalised more recently, as this was heavy literature for a mind that needed lightening.

Gary had meditated in this place of elevation, but climbing down from the tree had been more difficult. When Longhair arrived, he had talked about cats and ladders and firemen for a while, eventually leading his friend to safety and a good night's rest before they negotiated the next lock. These were what most amazed the goat. He never tired of these miraculous inventions, loved the gates and sluices and chambers and the way the water rose and fell, the control established with shaped woods and metals. His friend had been to the temple of every professional football club in the country, and now his sights were set on the seven wonders of the waterways. His ambition was infectious, and Gary listened closely as his hero waxed lyrical. This delving into the future with planning and plotting was a mesmerising mental ride that could be unsettling, but he was more goat than man and had coped.

The first of these wonders experienced had been at Tardebigge on the Worcester & Birmingham Canal, a stretch of thirty locks it had taken them six hours to negotiate, an endurance test for a rookie captain and crew, true, but an incredible achievement that lifted their confidence to great heights. Gary had offered encouragement as he watched from the water and the shore, taking turns between the two. It was said that the greatest wonder was to be found at Caen Hill on the Kennet & Avon, with twenty-nine locks set out over two miles, the sixteen squeezed in at the top the ultimate. He was looking forward to seeing these locks, maybe more so even than Longhair, as he had none of the captain's responsibilities.

There were one thousand, five-hundred and sixty-nine locks in England and Wales, and they were determined to use them all, as well as travelling through and across the fifty-three tunnels and three hundred and seventy aqueducts. There were canals of varying widths and branches connected by rivers to experience, with reservoirs and official moorings and an adjacent path that seemed endless. Gary was surprised and pleased by the attention he received when they paused near a busy lock or other junction, and he accompanied Longhair ashore. People flocked to them, many leaning and crouching down to stroke Gary's head, some bringing food, most referencing his good looks. The goat was modest and knew no vanity, but was conscious that he had a certain handsomeness. Comments were also made with regards to his intelligence, as if this was surprising, but Gary took it in the generous spirit in which it was intended and bleated his thanks with great love and respect.

These admirers asked Longhair questions, and after a while Gary noticed how extra friendly some of the women became, openly flirting and in some cases sending phone numbers. The presence of a goat told them that this was a kind and gentle man, one who had refused to leave an innocent to fend for himself when he set out to explore England. While it made Longhair more attractive to these feminine souls, there was also the trust it engendered. The ladies who dallied with Longhair Love on the canal banks were very different to Madam Diane, the temptress who had waylaid the good captain with hot baths and tasty meals and strong skunk, talking filth about his leaking cock and heavy balls while Gary was left outside to endure the wind and rain. He would never judge this lady, who clearly disliked him, but was aware of the confused thoughts on the matter lodged in the Longhair brain. Life had returned to normal, no doubt partly thanks to the mighty influencer Nanny Goat Great, who was much more in tune with the human opposites of good and evil.

Longhair had spoken at length about the coronavirus, where it had started and what it was doing to the human population and the societies it had created. He discussed the arguments for and against restrictions, the vaccines that had been developed, while Gary believed that more important were the pandemics that had gone before, detailed by his companion but never dwelled upon. There was the influenza that had killed fifty million people a century earlier, outbreaks of which returned each year, and through this he became aware of the First World War, stunned that the brilliance that had gone into designing the canals and locks and viaducts and barges that floated on its water and the machines that ran on engines and could apparently fly in the sky was so flawed, that the same humans had deliberately designed death tools such as guns, tanks and bombs. These were in a constant state of development, the human race accepting of slaughter between its tribes, but brought down by a virus, a form of life too small to even see.

There was an infection that had spread through men who loved men, its origins in the continent of Africa, the home of the beautiful yet frightening lion. Its origins were said to lay in the human killing and consumption of monkeys. This was particularly horrid, given the similarities between the two species, and the goat decided this was an analogy he had missed. There was another pandemic which had also lasted to the present day and transmitted through mating, Gary shocked to hear that syphilis may have been spread by men raping sheep. Perhaps even goats.

He would stare at his captain as he spoke of such things and remember the crow Colin and Colette who sat on the pole in the wire fence where he had lived a long time ago, maybe even in another life, and who he had found in a tree in a field, the memories faint and fleeting, firm and fixed, fading and returning. Longhair was an honest man, but the horrors he detailed couldn't be correct, and were perhaps due to a malady in the invisible entity that lived inside his silver screened machine. For a while Longhair had fixated on the virus's origins, and while Gary wasn't able to help with words, he provided the gentle headbutts and nuzzles that showed his friend that he wasn't alone. If what Longhair said *was* true, then surely the lesson had to be that humans should stop abusing the rest of the animal kingdom. Wasn't that obvious? But these stories were ridiculous, the cause of far too much angst and depression.

His friend had been through periods of gloom himself, the sort of despondency Gary had never known, whether through loneliness or excessive laptop use, but that was in the past. They kept moving, stopped when the whim took them, and while Gary preferred the countryside, he had become accustomed to towns and even cities where they drifted unnoticed through areas that were derelict or regenerated, forgotten or rediscovered, and he had come to see the different designs and conditions as works of art, expressions of that restless creativity that drove the dominant species. All of these places felt safe, and even the incident in Manchester hadn't been a concern.

When a young male moptop boarded uninvited one night, Gary had simultaneously welcomed him aboard and alerted the captain, the intoxicated state of the perp and the element of surprise no doubt helping as the lad cried out before stumbling away along the towpath and into the darkness. Longhair had asked Gary if he was all right, hugging him and saying something about bravery, that he was as good as a guard dog. This and other memories were proving longer lasting than they would have done in the past, which was one of the effects of living with a human, and as the time passed Gary was taking on more and more of Longhair's quirks, could feel these increasing as the dawn took hold.

Sunlight was spreading across the water, and when a pair of ducks appeared he turned his head to watch them paddle past before looking to the other side of the canal to where a swan was nesting. This was a big, confident bird who had chosen a concrete ledge on which to settle, a narrow strip protected at the front and side by water and at the back by a concrete wall. Swans were impressive creatures, and he wondered how they saw the universe, having grown up free. Queen Elizabeth owned these swans, and they'd always have felt at ease with that sort of protector, but while his own guardian wasn't as rich or powerful as Her Majesty, he was an angelic man of the world who knew how to move through society. He had his trademark kind heart, yet thanks to his football interests was able to mix with every sort of character.

Gary had been careful not to wake Longhair when he left the wheel-house, treading as lightly as he could once he had climbed onto the roof. He had his private space, with bedding and a favourite blanket, extra hay during the cold months, a hot water bottle arriving before shuteye. The captain would rise when he was ready, and a mutual respect was assured, although the click of hooves would have already registered as their thoughts kept transmitting, Longhair receptive to the wisdom of Nanny Goat Great and the Goat Laws established by the Goat Sages of yore. The flow was two-way, in waking and dreaming, and Gary's optimism had clearly helped the captain.

Gary was a good listener and Longhair liked to talk, his mono-logues interesting for one keen to learn, and yesterday he had returned to his love of football, or at least the men who spectated rather than played the beautiful game. They revelled in an alcoholic sacrament, communal singing and a devotion that could sometimes overflow into wild passion. These were secular Christians who believed in teamwork and loving thy neighbour, while the tale of Baby Jesus was one that had captivated Gary early doors, as it did so many millions of human and non-human creatures. The Son of God had been described as a lamb, which was close enough, and Gary decided that he too belonged with Christ. Saint Longhair must have thought similar, creating a small stable below the sacred wheel that guided their vessel. There was always room for the goat. No casting out into the desert. No scapegoating with the invention of mutants. Babies and children saw clearly, and Gary had experienced this at locks and along the towpath, and weren't human children often referred to as kids?

Yes, they loved to hear stories about Billy Goat Gruff, and he was fascinated by these mini-folk. The Goat With No Name, who he had met but couldn't remember where or when, or if he had been pure vision or a physical messenger from Nanny, had told him about these beings, having spent time in a petting zoo, describing miniature persons pushed in wheeled contraptions, unable to stand or survive alone for long post-birth. Most surprisingly, they wore wrappings that caught their urinations and droppings, and sat in these gurgling until an adult could clean up the mess. Again, Gary did not comment, accepting difference, however peculiar, and closing his eyes as the sun shone into them he heard quacking and thought of ducks and the Donald, heavy-metal thunder, the taste of cardboard, paper, ink, denim.

Since his visits to the farm, Gary had been fascinated by Longhair's jacket, a garment of jean fabric with inherited patches dedicated to the choirs Led Zeppelin, Black Sabbath and Slade. Local to both man and goat, they were symbols of a pre-birth era when the invisible net did not exist. He had developed a fondness for the music in small doses and at moderate volumes, the headbanger at the controls adjusting the beats in response to his bleats. Led Zeppelin were Gary's preferred choice, with 'Rock And Roll' and 'Kashmir' favourite tales, while Slade came a close second.

In the early days of their voyage, Longhair's mind had been restless and needed filling with information in order to stop his inner turmoil rioting. Reading about Black Sabbath he'd discovered a picture of vocalist Osbourne holding a dead chicken. He was laughing as he posed with the corpse, which had a cigarette inserted in its mouth. Osborne was reported to have worked in a killing factory, and Gary felt Longhair's reaction, his protector turning the screen so that he, too, could see. Most humans dismissed this sort of thing as playful jinks, but for Gary it was worrying proof of the crow's warnings. The mockery involved exaggerated the obscenity, and Sabbath no longer shook the *Wizard*.

Another voice that boomed from Longhair's machine belonged to President Donald Duck. A big man with a glowing orange face, he was either loved or hated, although Gary wasn't certain of the reasons. Donald enjoyed grabbing pussycats and running up huge debts, while putting America first and supporting the industrials denounced by his defeated foe Hillary. She was the mate of former leader Bill, famed for a peculiar liaison in a government building, namely the placing of his winkle in a young lady's mouth. This was an odd custom and far from hygienic. All of this was happening in a far-off land called USA, where the planet's two-legged herds had migrated in search of freedom. It was said they had decimated the native tribes and killed tens of millions of buffalo in order to establish democracy, which was ridiculous. The students of London had paid tribute to President Duck when he came to visit Queen Elizabeth three years earlier by building a Baby Donald doll, which they then raised into the sky. Gary was confused by this, guessing it represented some sort of nappy cult.

Longhair's early upset at events both far and near had lessened as his laptop usage fell, although the frictions stirred remained as metaphorical ghosts. These and current concerns threatened to damage his dreams, which would in turn ruin his days. This couldn't be allowed. While he admired the captain's many fine attributes, Gary's honed goat senses saw and heard far more than his friend. There were no spirits on the towpath or anywhere else, the souls of every living being, whether animal or plant, moving into the sun when their physical forms faded, and it was here that Nanny maintained the bliss he was currently enjoying. It was the present that mattered.

The goal of every human religion was to escape the chaos of what might have been and what could one day be, and as Merlin stirred these were some of the thoughts that must follow him into his early waking state. If he lived a healthy life according to goat principles and kept growing that budding goatee on his chin, then Nanny Goat Great would guide him as she did her other favourite son.

Merlin opened his eyes and brushed the hair from his eyes, squinting as the light flowed through his window, bringing with it waves of sheer joy, the knowledge that today was going to be extra special. He heard shuffling and imagined a horned god blowing on the embers of a fire, causing it to spark and roar and become the sun. Gary was awake and moving about above and inside his head, would have climbed onto the roof as he liked to do, drawn by the dawn, his excitement shared by Merlin.

Rolling out of bed, the captain heard his hooves click on the wooden floor, looked down and saw only toes, relieved and disappointed, the notion he was half-man and half-goat returning, Gary half-goat and half-man, two cheerful fauns learning from and becoming each other. He really did love the clarity and intensity of his dreams, at the same time pleased when they faded and he was fully back inside his own mind. Walking into the galley, he put the kettle on and banged on the ceiling to let Gary know he was up, that breakfast would be on its way as soon as his coffee was made.

Darren cupped the soap in his hands and rubbed his palms together under the cold tap singing 'Happy Birthday' as Johnny had advised softly lullaby-style washing slowly to make sure the job was done properly but the water was too cold so he turned on the hot and listened for the click of the pilot light in the kitchen the pop and whoosh as the spark lit the gas and fire boomed pipes gasping air popping in pockets the warmer water meaning the soap frothed as he reached the end of the song and started again rubbing a little harder as he'd forgotten to disinfect himself last night coming home drunk with a large portion of chips that needed dealing with before they got cold and a crusty bloomer to cut and butter plus two pickled onions to spoon from the jar in the fridge and a new bottle of Asda ketchup one of those upside-down plastic jobs with a seal hidden under the cap that had to be peeled back this was fiddly any time let alone when he was pissed Johnny's wise words forgotten the short memories of humans easily distracted and while Darren was groggy he knew that it really was his birthday receiving punches as presents in a public house putting the plug in the sink he tried to remember the details mixing hot with cold and turning both taps off he stopped singing leaning forward cleaning his face humming the tune inside his head instead and the soap was stinging cut skin there would be no cards no presents no cake no candles and no reason anyone should know he would be with his mates later and that was enough he was the sort of man who didn't like a fuss made and once he had dried his face with the towel he emptied and rinsed the sink and finally stood straight staring into the mirror inspecting his split lip and a black eye that was more like purple but not too bad – considering.

He couldn't work out why Stan had been so angry. It was out of character and out of order. Darren had known Stephen since they were children and never treated him any different to his other friends, which meant having a laugh and on occasion taking the piss. It wasn't as if Stephen didn't do the same back, and he could be pretty brutal with his humour as well, but Darren wouldn't let anyone bully or make fun of him in a serious way, more annoyed at Stan for thinking that's what he'd been doing than the punches. As for encouraging Stephen's madness, well, a lot of what he'd said over the years made sense.

There had been a couple of times when he'd come out with stuff that was properly mental and sent electric shocks racing through Darren, but more usual were his observations about people and events that made little sense at first yet seemed obvious once the words sunk in. This could take a few hours, or a day, or even a week, and there was the risk that some half-heard pearls would fester and cause chaos, but Darren had decided that if he concentrated and didn't switch off he could probably stop this happening.

Most of Stephen's difference was in how he responded to everyday life, the paths he went off down, harmless fascinations and levels of obsession, and Darren liked the way he drifted away from a subject before coming back in to destroy the mainstream version. It was like a fighter pilot appearing out of the sun and shooting down a bomber. There was a flamboyance about Stephen at these times. He became a showman. Not always, but when he was at his best. Darren was different again. He prided himself on meeting life head on. Talking straight. He didn't want anyone's advice or help. Opinions led to indecision, and that made a man weak. In times of crisis he had to be strong and decisive. Neither did he want sympathy. This was lucky, as it was in short supply when it came to his kind. For better or worse, he was ordered and self-reliant.

He did love a good tear-up at the football, though. That couldn't be denied. Outside the ground in the surrounding streets, near a train station, a town centre, somewhere nice and crowded. Or in a pub. Nothing was better than getting into a drinker on enemy territory with a good firm, powdering the nose and wetting the whistle and finding the opposition and have a fucking good row. Every generation knew this feeling. It didn't have to be football, but it had been for generations of young men since the Sixties, before that the racecourses taking things back to two world wars. Men enjoyed mobbing up. Not wankers, but the boys. It was normal, natural, healthy.

The old chaps in their seventies and eighties might have lost their physical strength and mellowed, but he was sure the urge remained. It was an escape from the boring everyday and made Darren feel alive. He'd struggled during the lockdowns, but that was due to the isolation and boredom, a set of extraordinary circumstances, and his troubles were private so there was no lasting damage or cause for concern. Being out with the lads again had revived him, and there was a lot of lost time to make up. He was keen to pick up where they'd left off, although he feared not everyone felt the same way. Things would even out and normal service would be resumed. He fucking hoped so, anyway.

As well as his brother, Stan needed to believe in his friend. Hadn't Darren helped him out at school, going right back to when Stephen first started? Darren had been with the brothers all the way through, dealing with the usual playground politics in his direct manner, even at six ready to take on bigger boys and superior numbers. He could well remember the thrill he'd felt that first time, steaming in single-handed and having Stan and Matt following him, and to this day he liked it when the odds were stacked against him, although perhaps it was a memory he'd built up, as he'd been small and couldn't have done much damage, the next level coming that time outside the shops when they were twelve or thirteen. That had been a lot different. Fucking mental when he thought about it now.

The boys concerned were from another school and Darren had never known their names, the faces little more than smears. There'd been this one lump who'd wrapped his arms around Stephen so he couldn't move, while two of his friends pretended they were crying, mimicking their victim, a fourth boy setting fire to his coat. Darren could see the skinny cunt now, holding the material up as he flicked his lighter, the way the flames had started to grow. The human straitjacket kept holding Stephen so he couldn't run away or put the fire out, and it was spreading as Stan ran towards them, overweight and much too slow, Darren getting there first and digging his teeth into the fingers holding Stephen, the kid shocked and letting go, staggering and falling to the ground when he was pushed.

Darren was on top of him digging his teeth into hands that had been raised to protect a blubbery face and he remembered how free he'd felt as if the straps of his own straitjacket had been released and not just loosened but cut with a razor so they could never be tied and tightened again he hardly noticed the kicks to his body and head before Stan and Matt arrived and they stopped but there were other older voices the sound of grown men it must have looked as if this nutter was trying to rip the other boy's face off but he wasn't even though there was blood in his mouth no he wasn't a fucking vampire didn't care about that he was more interested in the bones under the skin because he could feel these and might be breaking some of them dogs loved gnawing on bones from the butcher's didn't they there were hands coming down and pulling Darren off one man holding him firmly a sweaty middle-aged baldie saying the police were on their way and what the fuck was wrong with him his mate shaking his head the kid is a fucking lunatic and thinking about this now Darren felt a little bit embarrassed but more than that he was pleased.

He'd done this nut-nut routine while the responsible adult was holding him, but only for a minute or so, had started growling as if he really was a dog, sensed the confusion this was causing and barked, knew he was upsetting the men who had broken up the fight, two good citizens doing the right thing the same as Darren would now if he saw a couple of boys fighting like that, and the thought made him realise how bad he must have looked, and eventually he'd howled, could see the indecision in the men's faces, they didn't know if he was winding them up or truly demented, and that's how he felt about Stephen sometimes, knew Stan thought the same, and Darren had turned into a wolf or more like a werewolf, although looking back he wasn't sure if he'd done this for effect or to celebrate or for the sheer joy of being free or maybe all of those reasons put together. He'd had a lot of grief off the police. And his aunt. Which wasn't unusual.

Less dramatic, but probably worse, was that time when they were older and really he'd only just escaped going to prison, battering that wanker in the Bricklayer's, the one with the black-rimmed glasses who thought he was a villain, the sort of two-bob cunt who watched too many gangster films made by posh boys, thought he was a cinematic Kray twin, a naff British gangster hugging everyone as if he was in the Mafia. He had a lot of friends, though, and liked to embarrass loners and oddballs, make them feel small. Darren had seen him holding court in the past and thought he was a dickhead, but never said anything. He wasn't a regular in this pub and if he went around clumping everyone who got on his nerves he'd have spent most of his life in jail. He couldn't remember why he'd arranged to meet Stan in there, but he was standing at the bar drinking when the brothers walked in. The wanker made a comment and those around him laughed.

Darren was older and didn't go all werewolf this time, but when Stan stopped he was up and over and spraying the man concerned with CS gas, cracking him in the face with a chair and breaking his nose. He hadn't stopped there, as when one of the bully's mates tried to brain him he'd clouted him with the remains of the chair, not realising there was a nail sticking out of the leg, which became embedded in the bloke's head. Playing the scene back, it was comical but frightening, as it could have ended up with the man dying or being brain damaged, neither of which Darren wanted to happen. The CS gas filled the pub and innocent bystanders had become scared, some running outside, and he regretted that, could hear a woman screaming, thought about Stan last night, understood his concerns about today, as going on the names mentioned there was going to be a proper turnout. A volatile mix. Darren had ended up in the cells, been lucky nobody grassed, not even the landlord who he compensated for the damage caused.

Yes, Darren had done the business for Stephen and expected better from Stan. Some respect wouldn't have hurt. That's all anyone really wanted. And where was the loyalty? That worked both ways. His feelings were hurt, and the more he thought about it the more obvious it was that Stan was going soft in the head. He knew what Stephen was like. Well, he didn't, not in the way Darren did, but he had to be used to his ways by now. Surely? He'd had enough time. No, Stan was listening to the propaganda and it was rotting his brain. He should be standing with his family and friends, not criticising them, and definitely not attacking a lifelong mate.

There was too much soppy talk and not enough action, and it was affecting morale. England was on the receiving end of every lame cunt going. Chinless wonders and spineless wankers. The rich were still in control, but there were plenty of well-paid numpties refusing to challenge the official views. Mind you, they never did on the way up either. Wouldn't have got anywhere if they had. It didn't matter if it was mad stuff like men being able to have babies, arguments that made language meaningless, they just agreed and did whatever they were told, enjoying easy lives they'd never earned, part of an Artificial Intelligentsia running society from inside their iClouds.

Few normal people made it through, so it was all relative. You had the rich boys Boris and Rishi in the top two jobs ordering arse-lickers like Hancock what to do while Starmer sat in front of the mirror blow drying his hair. Darren had enjoyed seeing Boris bossed by Chris Whitty, Patrick Vallance and the guv'nor Jonathan Van-Tam. Those TV covid briefings were easily at their best when JVT was involved. Nobody fucked with Johnny V. He could see the bloke on a school football pitch as a boy, charging around and getting stuck in, clobbering the showboaters, fair but hard as nails, only deliberately fouling an opponent who had kicked him first.

JVT was the bulldog engine of his side and took no prisoners. He would play in either of the full-back positions if required, but lacked pace and could be exposed by a speedy winger, mistiming tackles and causing some serious injuries. Johnny had an attention to detail which reminded Darren of Martin O'Neill. A refusal to let anything go. JVT didn't care who he was talking to when he had a point to make, would have stood up to an unfair referee even as a nine-year-old, putting the man with the whistle firmly in his place. Not that he was ever rude. Johnny was polite and respectful, but adamant when he knew he was right. He also listened, concentrated on what he was hearing and replied in a direct manner. JVT was the footballer's footballer.

Darren was seeing his PE teacher at school. Mr Rodgers, better known as Perfect, as in Perfect Cunt. He was as well. Dictator material.

Tall and thin, he looked like the Syrian leader Assad, the one who massacred his own people and used chemical weapons on children. Perfect dressed more like a prefect than one of the staff, had probably been a lanky cunt when he was still a pupil. Darren wished he'd battered someone who, thinking back, was a bully like the fire-starter and pub gangster. Worse in some ways, because he was hiding behind his position of power. If only JVT had been in Darren's school. He wouldn't have let anything go, knew how to handle the likes of Perfect, at the same time calming Darren down and easing him in a safer direction, and wasn't that what he did with Stephen? Darren listened, agreed, coaxed, defused. This was possible because he understood him. And Stan didn't.

Darren also liked Chris Whitty, although not as much as JVT. Chris had a different style, but was also someone who cared. He laid awake at night worrying about those he was trying to save. To be fair, they all did. It was easy slagging people off from a distance, and yet Darren didn't believe in lockdowns or vaccinations. The pubs being forced to shut was the final straw as far as he was concerned. Lose its public houses and England was finished. The rich had been at it for years, taxing and cranking up the price of beer, turning old London drinkers into gastro bars before moving to these craft-beer set-ups. When the lockdowns were eased there was that madness about having to give your details to be let inside, and once there asked to sit at a table and wait to be served, charged extra and told to put a mask on when you went for a piss. What the fuck was that about? Luckily he knew a couple of places he could walk to where they didn't bother with that sort of nonsense, but it showed how fast things could change, how society could be shut down within days.

Covid had been a disaster for Darren. He had lost his job and spent a year out of work, but there was nothing new about his bad luck, as he was always the one who got shat on. Not that he was moaning or feeling sorry for himself. It was just the way life went for some people. He kept this to himself and racked up the debt, at the same time wishing he had a gun and could shoot Hancock and do the bumbling lefty ponce Boris at the same time. The only one of that smarmy bunch of front-bench wankers he liked was Pretty, and he had thought about her a lot during the first lockdown.

It was fair to say he'd had a crush on the woman, and missed seeing her and his other favourite lady MPs in a packed Commons on the Parliament Channel, forced to relive memorable moments on YouTube. Pretty had a saucy smirk that was barely hidden behind the stern faces she pulled, a knowing that convinced Darren she was a handful behind closed doors. She was his SARS Lockdown Babe and gave him a hard-on to this day. He liked Nadine Dorries as well, but government by Zoom left him cold.

There was nothing right about any of them, but despite this he'd taken a shine to Angela Rayner. He couldn't work it out. She was gobby, ginger and northern, but had touched his heart. He had no sexual feelings for her, saw the attraction as more a marrying of minds, soulmates who, if given the chance, could change the world. He was sure that if she'd had the power and known about his predicament Angela would have helped him out. Pretty and Nadine were highly charged and tough, and would turn their backs on him if he started whining.

Angela belonged in that special band of female politicians he didn't necessarily agree with but still admired. These included his favourite, the former prime minister Theresa May, but also the patriot Arlene Foster, nationalist Nicola Sturgeon and green queen Caroline Lucas. Outside of Parliament, and more within his own age range, he had soft spots for Stacey Dooley and Alex Scott. With these ladies he was always the perfect gentleman. Darren wasn't some sort of pervert living a dodgy parallel life, not like his rent-boy mate Matt. And any violent thoughts were only ever directed at male MPs or sneaky fuckers like Dominic Cummings and Alastair Campbell. He wondered if those two had come out of the same laboratory, as they shared a slimy feel, clearly despising each other because they came from the same egg. Sibling rivals. He could see the Wuhan scientists brewing those two up easy enough.

He'd thought about trying to talk to some of these politicians in person. If he waited outside Parliament on the green where the media did their interviews and said he worked for BBC or Sky, depending on who he wanted to attract, perhaps they'd stop and talk. He would have to be convincing, need to dress and speak nicely, be polite and respectful, even with the MPs he thought were scum, but he definitely wouldn't be letting that looney with the loudhailer interrupt him, the Mad Hatter who stood there shouting the same sentences again and again.

These things would obviously never happen, whereas Stephen could talk about them for a day or two before making himself some sandwiches and packing his backpack and heading for Westminster. That was the dividing line. Darren was a realist. Who was going to believe he was a reporter? A professional journalist? Was Pretty going to fancy him when she had her pick of the posh boys? It would be better to hang around in one of those pubs on Whitehall, although the area would be under surveillance and he didn't fancy being shot by a protection officer before he'd got a chance to discuss the important issues of the day. This had been impossible when the pubs were closed, and he'd thought about this more seriously, wondered why more people didn't just go to Whitehall and drink themselves silly. Take a chance. See what happened.

Where was the fairness? The accountability? It was Darren who had gone over and sat in the garden with Stephen, talking for hours while Stan was on furlough doing up his house at the tax-payer's expense. How had that happened? And while he was sawing and nailing and drilling and filling holes and painting and decorating, Matt had been doing the same to his customers. That had upset Darren for some reason. It worried him to this day. More than the vaccinations. Those fucking jabs.

He wasn't having the government inject him with something that had been rushed through in a panic. No chance. Stan had had a go at him about that as well, but only verbally, pointing out he'd put plenty of drink and drugs into his body over the years yet was worried about an injection that could save his life. You had to trust someone, and if you couldn't trust the NHS who could you trust? There was a lot of truth in that, and Darren believed in JVT, but he would do things his own way. Stand firm.

The drink-and-drugs comment did make him laugh, though, particularly when it came to his beer consumption. Like a lot of the football lads he knew he had gone too far with the coke on occasion, but didn't soldiers going into battle like a tipple first? He saw himself causing mischief in Leicester, Newcastle, Liverpool. Further afield.

Overseas. Good times. Chelsea and England. But those vaccinations were different, and the French tart Macron had been right to slag off AstraZeneca, even if it was for the wrong reasons, sulking like the moody cunt he was, despite the fit ex-teacher he was servicing.

Stan had never understood Stephen and was pussyfooting around him more than ever. He had been infected with an overload of dodgy information meant to frighten people into silence. The joy and humour was being sucked out of him so he only saw his brother as this weakling who could never be joked with in case he took it the wrong way, like one of these soulless cunts you saw on the TV. Stan seemed to think Stephen needed to be shielded and sedated with blandness. It was normal he was worried and more cautious than Darren, who wasn't family, but he'd changed and was taking it to an extreme that wasn't right. There were excuses, but none that made up for the way he had behaved last night.

Darren knew he should respond, hunt Stan down and hurt him, but he just didn't want to, and anyway, his reputation wasn't at stake, as far as he could remember Matt the only one who'd seen what happened. If Stan wanted to take things further he would defend himself, but Darren refused to turn against him. He didn't care about the damage done to his face. He'd had far worse. It would be terrible if their friendship ended this way, when they both wanted the best for Stephen. His heart wasn't in a fight. He needed Stan and Matt. They were the closest he had to family. But he couldn't look weak and had to decide how best to handle things later on. His phone vibrated. It was the mischief-maker himself sending selfies.

The first of these two pictures showed Stephen standing to the side of what looked like a tunnel. He was holding Darren's troll cross in the air. This was hard to make out at first as he was in the shade, but the outline became clearer and it made sense. The second photo saw Stephen in the same pose, but this time he had something bigger and more solid in his hand. It took Darren several seconds to identify this, and longer to believe. But the silhouette was clear. Stephen had been talking about his friend from the psychiatric hospital. The armed bank robber. They'd gone to a Greek restaurant that served the best vine leaves either of them had ever tasted. This man had moved up the pecking order since his release. He was a professional criminal.

Darren realised he had got this badly wrong. Stephen had lost the plot. He was tooled up and dangerous and on the loose. Darren tried to call him, but went to voicemail. Leaving his damaged face in the bathroom mirror, he took the brick from the floor and placed it on the toilet seat, made sure it was centred and everything was secure before hurrying into the bedroom where he put on his shoes and jacket, grabbed his keys and phone and wallet, accepting that Stan had been right. He did this easily because they were friends. He wasn't going to pretend otherwise. Darren was honest. Loyal. He stopped before leaving the flat and studied the pictures again. Stephen was by the canal. It was easy enough to guess where the tunnel led and what he was about to do. He had said as much. And only Stan had properly listened.

Stephen prayed for his mother – for the soul of the woman who had given him his life – conceiving and nourishing and shielding him from evil – radiant as she carried this miracle of creation inside her body – Mum in her younger glory – glowing skin and a golden halo – she would have sensed there was something different about this baby – terrified the goblins would find out and try to flush him away – and even though Stephen was inside God's House he could hear the Devil's hooves click-clacking on the cobbled streets of her unconscious – the muttered orders and giggling obedience of the Diabolical's lackeys – he saw the outline of a horned head at the stained-glass window lining her dreams – because the old truths may have faded but they never really died – these were impressions that would have kept her vigilant as Stephen developed – until he was ready to enter the outside world – strong enough to survive and prosper with the help of this lady whose love was unconditional and without limit – he was the issue of a sacred union – a holy conception that wasn't immaculate but near enough – he was no test-tube foetus produced in a laboratory – he was flesh and blood and thought and emotion and wished he could remember the months before he was born – how it had felt as his organs expanded – further back as the spawn separated and a tadpole freed itself and sprouted limbs to become the frog that moulded into his human form – an amphibian baby with a big bubbly head on tiny smooth shoulders

– there was no webbing on his fingers and toes and Stephen had told the girl behind the counter in Greggs as it was important she understood he repeated it twelve times and once more for luck to make up a baker's dozen so the information stuck in her mind and wouldn't become lost in the orders for sausage rolls – he wasn't built of pastry or wicker or corn or gingerbread – Stephen was no mud-caked golem – no zombie – but he was sidetracking and returned to his prayers – apologised – asked God for forgiveness – and that He protect Mum as she had protected him – that she be allowed to live a long life free from physical and mental sickness – she was kind and generous and deserved to be happy – had done her best for all of her children and the idea that she could be sad and fearful made him tremble inside – if only he had been less of a burden – his spirits crashing as the evil fleas nipped – they had to be fought – he was her son and Mum loved him and said so every single day – when the end came and her soul left her body he was confident she would be rewarded – there had to be some sort of fairness – the Devil knew this – it was why he tempted people off the path and away from the light – the reason he infected minds and bodies and collected souls and drove serial killers and paedophiles and loved to bully and torture and maim and murder.

Stephen prayed for his father – for the soul of the man who had supplied the seed that had fertilised the egg that led to the birth of the individual God desired – the idea that Satan had somehow interfered flaring but only briefly – Stephen was good not bad – special not strange – Mum said and Dad said and Stan said and Sarah said – if he didn't have a father on Earth he wouldn't be sitting in the front pew of this church talking to his father in heaven – leaning forward with his hands gently clasped – head bowed in a respectful manner – Dad had fought the demonic threats of hunger and homelessness – protecting his young family and providing solid foundations – his life could have been easier though – Stephen praying that the physical labour eased before it wore out his mind and body – perhaps one day he would never have to worry about money again – how this would happen Stephen didn't know – and he resisted the urge to ask for the favour of a Lottery win – it would be a crass request – but surely God knew what he was thinking – if he heard his prayers – yet there had to be some sort of privacy – secrets were essential – white lies equalled good lies – nothing had ever been said but he knew he'd been another weight for his father to bear – this beast of burden with the cross of a donkey tattooed across his back – and when they were together just the two of them Stephen relaxed in a way he never did with anyone else – even now as an adult – Dad protected him in a different way to Mum – that first boss after he left school – the one who'd made him run home crying – said he was stupid and Special Needs because he'd forgotten to put detergent in the pail and had mopped the toilet floors with cold water and hadn't he fucking noticed – sorry God – he relived the shame he'd felt and reminded himself that it was the Devil and not this boss responsible – he wasn't wicked – maybe the detergent would have stopped Lucifer's infection – head in a bucket – mouth washed out with soap – it was important to hate the sin and love the sinner – Dad had no interest in religion – came into the factory the next day and punched his boss and made him apologise in front of the others – they'd ended up in the police station and a sergeant said he would have done the same if it was his boy there couldn't be a repeat – Dad and Stephen had stopped for a pizza on their way home – he saw them sitting by the window eating deep pans – it was a sweet memory although Stephen reminded himself that it was better to turn the other cheek – even if he felt good recalling the shocked look on his boss's face – which was wrong – and he apologised again.

Stephen prayed for his big brother Stan – asked God to watch over him in the years to come – especially in these dangerous days of bachelorhood when he was drinking in public places and attending football matches with Matt and Darren and other ruffians – that he would one day fall in love and settle down and marry and have three or four or even five children – Stephen was looking forward to meeting these nephews and nieces – they would call him Uncle and he could spoil them with presents – and while he himself would always remain single he didn't mind in the slightest – stressed that he didn't care at all – he'd been made for other purposes than procreation – in the shorter term he prayed that Stan would stop fretting over truths revealed – he was a simple soul with a good heart but struggled to process Stephen's wisdom – that sounded unkind and even a little arrogant but wasn't intended as such – it was normal and God understood – Stan had never been embarrassed by his younger brother – not even when they were mixing with other children in the playground or playing football in the park – yet while their bond was eternal Stephen had to put some distance between them this morning – Stan couldn't be involved in what was about to occur – Stephen was a bold Christian soldier and would soon be marching as to war – Darren's troll cross the cross of Jesus going on before – he was doing the Lord's work and this required the focus of a righteous assassin – the blessed precision that came with a sober spirit – the battle between good and evil ebbed and flowed and the best a conscious man could do was offer to surrender his life when the balance tilted too far – the Devil had come out into the open – Gary was strutting and issuing orders – Merlin giggled and leered – the Diabolical was flaunting his wickedness.

Stephen prayed for his sister Sarah – that her nightmares would end and she'd be able to sleep properly – that her rosacea would clear up and he'd never see her crying again – not just crying but sobbing – like a child in their mother's arms – this had shocked Stephen – he wasn't stupid – knew the care home where she worked had been hit hard by covid and that a lot of people had died but it was still upsetting to see her in such a state – Sarah didn't suffer fools – everyone said it – she was tough – he used to think hard – as far as he could see she had never hidden or wanted to quit even though she was frustrated and then angry at the shortage of PPE – his sister must have been terrified she would fall sick yet said nothing – they'd drifted apart when they were teenagers – she didn't want her mad brother hanging around when she was with her friends – he couldn't blame her – he was older and had to admit he'd enjoyed embarrassing her at times – thinking it was funny to use his difference – sorry now but nobody was perfect – he had a streak of naughtiness and asked God for forgiveness – absolution was immediately granted and he felt better – Sarah was still bold and brash – more like Granny Claire than Mum – but he saw her clearly now and was very proud of his baby sister – she had set an example he hoped he could match – if he was successful in his mission the nightmares would end and her sleep would be sound and full of the sweetest dreams and her rosacea would vanish and there'd be no more tears no more crying no more sobbing – God would grant these wishes he was sure – Sarah had been doing His work after all – Stephen helping the best he could – not just clapping his hands in the street but calling her every other day when he knew she'd finished work and been home for a couple of hours – at first he'd worried he was intruding though not enough to abandon her to the flat and that wanker of a boyfriend – sorry God – he'd kept things brief but there were times when they'd ended up talking for ages – and his guilt drew him back to their teenage years even though God had forgiven him – how he'd come out with things her friends thought were odd and strange and mad – they were – he guessed a lot of siblings became closer as they grew older – it was hard to imagine what it must be like to be an only child – the Chinese had had a programme of one baby per couple which meant eventually nobody would have a brother or sister or cousin or nephew or niece which is probably what the Party intended – he didn't know if that was still the law in that godless land where the Devil did whatever he pleased – would have to find out.

Stephen prayed for Granny Claire – mother to his mother – as boisterous as Mum was reserved – she drank a lot of vodka and pinched his cheek when he went round to see her and Grandad – made him these huge doorstep sandwiches – cheese and pickle or cheese and salad cream – cooked shepherd's pie and bangers and mash – if she needed ingredients she'd send him to the shops and while Stephen didn't have much money he made sure he either paid or pretended he preferred one of the many tins of soup she'd stockpiled – it had been tough not being able to visit her and Grandad when everyone was locked up – they were old and he didn't know how much longer they had – this was a terrible way to think but the truth – he couldn't bear seeing his grandparents imprisoned – Stephen would go for long walks and end up outside their house standing by the window watching Granny Claire on the other side of the glass shaking her head at Grand-dad when he moved to come outside or invite Stephen in – he would place a hand on the window and his grandparents took turns doing the same – it was brilliant being able to see them properly again even if Granddad was dipping in and out of this world – he remembered Stephen's name but Mum had warned him that would change – they'd spent a lot of time in the garden this summer – Granny Claire treating herself to a generous double once four o'clock arrived – it had been a blissful time in their miniature Eden – one he would never forget – Stephen prayed every night that Granddad would get better but understood God was looking after him and Jesus would be waiting and that it was the Devil responsible for his illness – Stephen had never really known Dad's parents – Grandad Stan who he'd met when he was small – Granny Mo who'd died before he was born – only ever seeing pictures of her and mainly the one in the living room at home – he didn't know what they were like as people – Dad said they were nice and changed the subject – a bland description – Stephen's memories of Grandad Stan were vague and he reminded himself to find out more about them – moving on and praying for his aunts and uncles and cousins and now his friends – the choices and connections he had made.

Stephen prayed for Heavy G – despite only seeing him last week picturing his friend as he'd looked nine years earlier – short rather than shoulder-length hair – clean shaven not bearded – wearing a bowling shirt like Tony Soprano – back when they first met in what had to be the safest safe house in the land – a haven of rest and rebirth where the voices tormenting Stephen had been banished – he wasn't mad as some people maybe thought – it was just that the words had speeded up and become distorted and nastier until he was overwhelmed and according to the doctors a danger to himself – it was Heavy who'd welcomed him to the sanctuary with a smile and a handshake and a short tour that ended with two mugs of hot drinking chocolate – the building had been built with special bricks and glass that protected those inside from the insanity outside – Heavy sharing this vital information within ten minutes of meeting Stephen – delivering his message of hope with impressive respect and awe – and it didn't take them long to realise they had a lot in common – despite the robbery and firearms offences Heavy G was a sensitive fellow – tough when it came to business and even violent if crossed but otherwise caring and considerate – he was the only criminal Stephen had ever met and they'd stayed in touch after he left – continued their friendship once Heavy followed a year later – they'd spent many good hours in the relaxation room while sectioned – playing dominoes mainly – an easy game that allowed them to chat and put the world to rights – they spoke freely and listened closely and nothing had changed with last week's chinwag taking place in a Greek restaurant recommended by Heavy – they'd been served a feast that included the best vine leaves either of them had ever tasted – and after finishing their meals they'd broken out the dominoes and had three coffees each over the next hour and a half – the only ones left as the afternoon moved towards evening – Heavy knew the owners and they were happy for the two friends to stay – it was when the one waiter remaining went into the back that Heavy produced the gun he'd promised – placing it on the table and explaining its capabilities – nonchalant as only a professional villain could be – Stephen was very nervous – scared they would be seen – but he couldn't be rude and interrupt – if a passerby spotted the gun the police would be called and he didn't want them to be arrested – especially as it would mean a long prison sentence for Heavy – so Stephen had begged God to pass the weapon over – which He did – and now he asked Him to forgive his friend those trespasses and to keep an eye on Heavy if he wouldn't mind – he'd made mistakes but that was the Devil infiltrating and not his fault – some people were responsible – others were not – the man was an innocent – Stephen felt he was a good judge of character and Heavy G was one of his two best friends in the world – three if he counted Darren.

Stephen prayed for Liam – wondered where he was and what he was doing – hoped he had a place to sleep that was safe and warm – somewhere with a roof and a bathroom – the weather was changing and before too long it would be winter again – he shouldn't be living outside when the temperature dropped – shouldn't be sleeping rough whatever the season – nobody should – Stephen had this fear that when he was older and less able to defend himself Liam would be held by one man as another set him on fire and two more stood and mimicked his screams – Stephen and Liam were burning alive – victims of the beasts who worshipped Satan – witches danced around their charring bodies – responsibility had to be taken for this crime – and countering the urge to judge and condemn with humility and respect he asked the Lord to urge Liam to get in touch – to please whisper it in his ear – it was nearly a month since he'd seen him and Stephen had searched in the places he'd frequented before the emergency – the government had done the right thing and brought him indoors but the Devil kept stirring – exploiting temptations of housing and rent – encouraging the greed that meant homes were seen as little more than investment and profit – it was nothing new as Mary and Joseph and Baby Jesus knew – Liam back on the streets – returning to his routines – the alcohol and drugs – his visions and Bible study.

Stephen prayed for Darren – his brother's friend – his friend – *their* friend – they'd known each other since he could remember and maybe he'd taken his kindness for granted – if so he apologised to God who was Darren's father and would let him know in His special way – the handing over of the cross was another thoughtful act – it would stop Stephen being dragged off the path and into the darkness – the trolls would remain under their bridges – the seed planted in his mind exploded – there was a humpback bridge on the canal – the perfect place to wait for Gary and Merlin – he would have a clear view of their approach – Darren was the loyalest of friends – accepted Stephen – *understood* – and while his discipline broke down when it came to a street fight there were reasons – Darren's aunt had always scared Stephen – they hated the sin and not the sinner – there were plenty of people out there who suffered and had no support – were always alone – and Stephen thanked God for looking after him and putting him with a family that would never turn its back – and for giving him friends like Darren and Liam and Heavy.

Stephen prayed for everyone he knew and had known and those he had yet to meet and would never meet – the unborn and the babies who arrived physically or mentally damaged and sometimes both – the children they became – their youths and middle age and final years – he beseeched God to better the Devil and ease their suffering – to calm the longing to fit in and release them from those terrible feelings of rejection – the isolation and loneliness – a pain that only deepened with age and awareness – teenagers struggled at school – wanted to work when they left but were rejected and even ostracised – he prayed for those who would never fit into the mass and were going to spend their lives on the outside – and for those who were admitted and buried alive – Stephen prayed for the children abused by adults – the boys and girls sexually molested with nobody to save them – orphans whatever their age but especially when they were small – the sex slaves transported – he prayed for the poor and everyone who was hungry and couldn't afford food or clothes – refugees fleeing their homes – the men brutalised by war – the women raped and butchered – for the souls the Devil had targeted and enjoyed tormenting – and despite his best intentions Stephen damned the sinners as that tougher side of God emerged – the part fed up with excuses – it was becoming too much and no time for restraint.

Stephen prayed for the courage to stand firm and not turn and run for his life when he walked out to meet the Devil on the watery path running through the fields beyond Uxbridge – he could already smell the dank blend of grass and dung – see the fear in the eyes of the horses who lived there – hear the hum of demons – the beating wings of Beelzebub's shit-sniffing fly army and its bluebottle officers who were much better fed and oozing protein – bigger than ravens spewing aerosol – goblins left their grottoes as frog boys climbed out of ditches and witches emerged from the woods naked their slits shaved lubricated ready to mate with Dirty Gary – and while this was going on the citizens of London carried on regardless stuck in their modern state of denial even though the new variant had been identified and warnings broadcast – but the scientists responsible were godless materialists who denied the existence of the psychopath responsible and this encouraged Gary and the cocksucker Merlin – a pair of tricksters experienced in conning the gullible – there was even going to be a welcome arranged by Stephen's own brother – Stan thought he knew best because he was Big Brother – throwing open the gates to the city – and once London was contaminated the virus would spread out from Heathrow and ride the winds first class and second and cargo and exterminate every last person on the planet – Stephen couldn't let that happen – he wouldn't take the easy option and pretend this wasn't happening – worse was to beam a numbskull smile and buy the sorcerer a pint and present the Devil with a slice of juicy watermelon or maybe a burger off the barbecue – this goat wasn't going to be sticking to grass – no chance – no – Stephen refused to hide he would fight the good fight with God on his side what did it matter if covid was brewed in a Wuhan laboratory or a Wuhan wet market or anywhere else these were the cracks the Diabolical exploited as he kiddie-fiddled in the shadows until it was safe to emerge into the light using his deceit and theatricals to con Western civilisation into dismissing him as nothing more than a backward superstition – surely this was a rejection of hope itself – a gutless surrender in the eternal war of opposites – God didn't want this – He was with Stephen every step of the way and the soldier's body shook as he was filled with the electric ecstasy of the Holy Spirit – fearing no evil as he heard distant hooves – Stephen had his own army and there were no rancid flies and no bluebottles in its ranks – his friends were willing him on – Darren had given him his defence and Heavy G the means of attack and Liam a vision of the world – the Devil was out in the open – overconfident – which made him vulnerable the cocky cunt – sorry – and unclasping his hands and raising his head and standing up Stephen walked back up the aisle towards the church door – stopped at the font to stare into its special water – he was calm – fully focused – removed Heavy's revolver from inside his coat and made sure it was loaded before hiding it in his backpack – and once he was outside in the daylight he moved through the graveyard – climbed over the furthest wall – heading for the Grand Union Canal where he would kill Gary and Merlin.

Matt had been lucky. At least that's how he saw things now, looking back to the start of the pandemic. There had been some big downs, obviously, but lots of smaller ups, a couple of strange shagging episodes and some proper eye-openers along the way, and with money in the bank and Nat living with him these last three months he was feeling positive about the future. It was important to make up for lost time, and he didn't understand Stan attacking Darren like that last night. They should be happy, not fighting among themselves. It made no sense. Not that he was over-bothered, as he knew they'd be laughing about it later.

Like everyone, Matt had missed seeing his family and friends when the restrictions were in place, but he'd kept working, fortune smiling on him from the off. Builders were meant to be key workers, and while he'd never been sure if this was official policy or not, he'd carried on and been left alone. Driving to work during that first lockdown he'd felt like a king, as if the streets had been cleared specially, enjoying the novelty of a white-van man being shown some respect for a change, one tiny part of a workforce suddenly noticed and valued. The casing had cracked and the cogs driving the machine that kept society functioning were out in the open, Matt thankful he didn't have to drive a bus full of virus or sit on a supermarket till or, worst of all, care for the sick and dying in hospital.

Because he wasn't going to the pub or football he'd worked a lot more hours than usual, doing six and even seven days a week, which meant he'd been earning and saving some serious wedge. This had started him thinking about the realities of supply and demand, interest rates and investments, how the rich used their capital to become richer while the masses sweated and were forever struggling to make ends meet. Covid had made this divide crystal clear as the wealthy stayed at home and the plebs brought them their food and drink and whatever else they fancied.

For a while he'd felt sure there was a change coming. Once life started getting back to normal, those who did the hardest jobs and were the core on which everyone else depended would no longer be looked down on and exploited, but as the time passed it became clear this wasn't going to happen. Matt had little interest in politics, but he could see an opportunity passing and thought it was a shame, deciding that when the big killer virus arrived one day he wanted to be indoors waiting for his doughnut delivery to arrive, not out there grafting and dying. He couldn't help smiling as he imagined a familiar face on the scooter pulling up outside, an ageing Darren coming to the door dressed in his polka-dot uniform, a company cap perched on his thinning head.

Doughnut Delights had done well out of their deliveries, a move driven by the need to survive rather than any long-term plan, providing what the average person saw as a luxury item, the decadence of granulated sugar and a Double D dose of raspberry or strawberry jam. It showed that someone with imagination could come up through the ranks, and Matt wanted to be one of these success stories, but knew that while hard work and ambition were important, luck was essential. It was about being in the right place at the right time, drifting into position like a thirty-a-season goalscorer, a skill that couldn't be taught.

The first lockdown had been announced two days after he went to look at a job for a couple he'd done work for in the past, a horrible pair who'd fucked him about when it came time to pay. At first he hadn't bothered answering their messages, but they wanted a new conservatory and his work ethic meant he couldn't ignore them forever. Arriving at the house he'd felt ashamed of himself, after five minutes remembering it was the husband he hated most, a smug cunt he wanted to lamp, a know-all who thought his work and wealth protected him. It did, which made Matt feel even worse, and as he drove away he swore he'd to turn the job down, even if it seemed immoral and a bit petty.

Covid arrived and he had his excuse, but the wife messaged him five times in six hours and he finally spoke to her, would have felt bad blanking someone who seemed frantic. She said they were determined, refused to let the virus interfere with their plans, that he shouldn't be scared of catching it from them as they would keep their distance and rarely if ever see each other. Matt had agreed to send a quote. He needed another reason to turn the job down now, decided to ask for silly money, adding an extra fifteen percent CAT on top of that, plus VAT. He was taking the Michael and not expecting a reply, to his amazement asked how soon could he start?

After thinking about this for a while he decided they probably thought they could get away with not paying him at all this time, seeing as the world had shut down. Either that or they'd invent a problem and demand a big discount. This was his third chance to justify not doing the job. He told Mrs Edwards he would need fifty percent plus the cost of the materials upfront, the rest when he had completed half the job. This had been agreed within minutes. These people had to have what they wanted, no matter what else was going on. It was as if the cost didn't matter when it came to the crunch. It was a hard thing to get his head around.

Mrs Edwards had one condition. While he would be left alone to get on with the job, which meant there was zero risk of transmitting the virus, she would like to see how the work was progressing occasionally. They could keep their distance easily enough, but she asked they both wore masks at this time. Was that agreed? It was fine with Matt. It suddenly felt as if he'd hit the jackpot. As well as the threat to health, the pandemic was as much about work and the means of survival, which on top of the isolation had to be causing a lot of stress to a lot of people.

Matt was learning lessons and going to target a high-end clientele from now on, raise his prices and offer the full virus-free service, look to advertise in new ways. He had to reach those people, couldn't rely on personal recommendations as he'd done in the past. He kept returning to the fact he had asked Mrs Edwards for what he thought was a ridiculous sum, yet to her sort it was peanuts, and it was his failure to see this that had been holding him back. He wouldn't be thinking like this if he was out on the piss with Stan and Darren, but might as well do himself some good, make the time work to his benefit. There were other things he could do, like dressing in a suit when he went to cost a job, maybe take some elocution lessons. Or maybe not.

A month after he'd started, Mrs Edwards turned up with a mug of tea and a sandwich. This was a surprise, as she normally arranged her visits a day in advance, and while they had spoken a few times, these were formal conversations about the progress being made. She was cold and superior, and he felt as if he was being interrogated, but really didn't care. Now she was suddenly warm and friendly, came close enough to put the mug and plate on his workbench, quickly moving away but staying to talk.

She was wearing a pair of yellow washing-up gloves as well as her mask, taking no chances with the virus, and it was a more casual chat, which worried Matt. The woman was up to something, turning the charm on and off as it suited her, probably thought he was too thick to notice, a manipulative madam used to getting her way. He wasn't going to change his price or not insist on the second payment which was about due, if that's what she was thinking. There was more to this, though. It was as if she'd had a personality transplant, and he guessed she was bored being stuck inside, fed up of the repetitive misery being pumped out by the media. The house and garden were big enough, and she was better off than most, but even so, he couldn't help feeling sorry for her, would have preferred the colder version.

Perhaps it was a twin or doppelgänger, a marionette ordered by Terry White, and there was something about her face… He pushed the thought away. Mrs Edwards came to see him three days running, and he realised she disliked her husband a lot more than he did. Mr Edwards had gone to stay at their cottage in the country, and she seemed to be flirting at one point. He dismissed this as imagination, just wasn't attracted to this snobby lady who'd been looking down her nose at him from the start.

On her fourth visit she brought a fresh mask with his tea and sandwich, asked him to put in on in place of the one he had been wearing, to humour her please, and once he had she marched over and started unzipping his jeans. Matt's principles vanished inside a second as she told him it would be best if he took her from behind as an extra security measure, as she didn't want to catch anything. Mrs Edwards didn't ask him to wear a condom, just the fresh mask, reminding him several times to make sure it covered his nose as well as his mouth. She emphasised there could be no kissing as the exchanging of saliva was very dangerous and could prove fatal. It was mental, but Matt wasn't complaining, more than happy to oblige.

After a few days of this, she said she was worried about the masks they were using, feared they might break and leak, had read they weren't as good as she'd thought, that being forced to wear them on buses and trains was an infringement of liberty for little gain, and while she didn't agree about the freedom angle, she did take onboard their lack of effectiveness. To that end she had ordered two masks that were far better, and she would like them both to wear these when they were fucking. She had used that exact word, and Matt was shocked.

He was more than shocked when she produced these masks. They covered the head and were made from some sort of black rubber, with a snout and huge glass eyes and an oversized filter. They looked like they had been built to wear during a nuclear attack. Or after the release of a deadly nerve gas. Or by a perv into S&M and gimps and fuck knows what else. Deviant sex. That wasn't his thing, and he was sure it wasn't Mrs Edwards's either, but he was in for another jolt after he'd been invited upstairs, following Her Ladyship into one of the guest bedrooms where they removed their clothes for the first time. Everything but the masks. And when he saw himself in the dressing-table mirror he had become one of the two human dolls with ant heads banging away. The image had distorted since, seemed less and less real, part of a porn film, before returning with a thud. It had happened. There was no doubt about that.

When the conservatory was finished she changed back her stuck-up self, and he was dismissed with the comment that she was pleased with his building work and the service he had provided. Driving away he felt used, which was odd as he'd been paid so well, and been lucky enough to have some fun on the side. It was her tone that grated, the sheer arrogance of the woman, and he again felt ashamed that he had sold his soul like so many men before him. It had taken him a while to laugh this off, swearing it would never happen again, six months later something similar developing with a client living in the riverside developments in Battersea.

Matt was installing a luxury bathroom for a glamorous character who owned and ran an Italian restaurant, someone who'd worked her way up from waitressing to the kitchen, management and finally ownership. Elaine was a good twenty years older, petite and tough, irritable when she returned to the flat in the late afternoon, shouting at him if he was too noisy when she was resting before going back to work in the evening, but she did it with humour, and was kind, brought these fantastic meals home, insisted he help himself to anything he wanted from the fridge while she was away. He liked her, and this time it was Matt who'd tried it on with a handful of subtle compliments that were ignored. He wondered what he'd been thinking, forgot about it and finished the bathroom, had tidied up and was ready to leave when she said she wanted to test the shower and make sure it worked. Would he mind waiting?

He had stood by the main window of her apartment and watched the river down below, its miniature boats and barges drifting along the Thames in slow motion, toy cars chugging across the bridge and through the streets, ants dotting the pavements, model houses running into the distance on the opposite shore, over towards Stamford Bridge where he had spent so much time over the years. It was a fantastic view he'd marvelled at every single day he was here, sitting in an armchair next to the glass when he had a break, or was enjoying one of Elaine's meals, the thrill never wearing thin. The clouds were constantly changing the scene, and he would never have known how important they were to the colour and mood of a place without this job.

He was going to miss this luxury pad in the heavens, had enjoyed his time here, the work and company and relaxed atmosphere, ten minutes later Elaine appearing in a too-small towel and strolling towards him. Once again Matt was thanking his good luck, knew his winning streak was going to continue for a while yet. There had been another request, one that was repeated on his numerous returns, that they had sex in front of the window.

This sheet of glass was huge, reaching from the floor to the ceiling, the apartment one of the best in the block apart from the penthouses, and because it was so high in the sky and for the most part facing the river it wasn't as if they had lots of neighbours who were going to watch and film them in action. Even so, he had felt awkward that first time as she turned and leaned forward and raised her bum in the air, placing her hands on the glass saying she wanted the sun to finish drying off her back, and it had been a hot day and he had sweated buckets, servicing this noisy lady who demanded fast, deep penetration.

These sessions had continued for the next three months as he was asked to carry out a series of small improvements and odd jobs. She had mentioned an ex who lived on the other side of the river before any of this started, and one evening when he'd been working late and Elaine had the night off she insisted on placing a standing lamp next to them, and as he was shagging her Matt wondered what the bloke would think if he had some high-powered binoculars or a telescope, an odd thought that popped into his head and was quickly forgotten. A week later Elaine told him she was getting back with her former husband. He missed her and was jealous and had walked into her restaurant and proposed for a second time. She kissed Matt formally on each cheek and handed him his coat. A couple of days later he found an envelope in his pocket with two-hundred-pounds'-worth of twenties inside.

It had been an interesting time inside a sad time, more than anything a bizarre time, and while he had enjoyed the money and the sex and the fact he had come through the pandemic better than most, it seemed surreal and unreal and for a while had left him confused. He was either stupid or naive, because eventually he twigged Elaine had used him as much as Mrs Edwards had, and maybe more so, that he was little more than a human dildo, the vibrating builder asked to wear a rubber mask and perform on a stage, that he was more gigolo than fuck-buddy. This had annoyed him for a while, and he was glad to be working for normal people again, even though it meant a drop in income, his big mistake telling Darren after a drink too many.

His agitation cleared when he heard from Natasja, a message out of the blue saying she was coming to London. He hadn't expected to ever see her again, the mention of a parcel and Terry White filling him with dread. He had met up with her and they'd clicked and a month later she was moving in, and here she was sitting on the sofa in their living room. So far it had been good. They got on well. Nat had her iPad propped on a cushion she'd arranged on her lap, Frank sprawled out next to her with his front paws crossed, the rich smell of Asda's own Italian blend filling the air.

Matt kissed her on the forehead when she raised her face, a shot of happiness racing through him like the caffeine he craved and would be drinking in a minute. Natasja was on the mend and it was a relief, their worry fading with the easing of her post-covid complications, the foggy-headedness and tiredness that had made concentration so difficult, a frustration for someone who needed her focus. They were looking at the positives, though, Matt seeing her quick recovery as another example of his good luck. She'd got off lightly compared to a lot of people, among them Darren's auntie and their Chelsea mate Ian Stills.

Darren had never said what he thought about his aunt's death, which didn't really surprise Matt, as they rarely spoke about their feelings. At least he'd told him and Stan she'd died, but maybe only because he was late meeting them and it had just happened, moving on and leaving them wondering about someone who had always been a mystery. A strange lady. It was terrible, people banned from being with their loved ones when they were dying. He didn't understand that. Darren was strong. Nothing seemed to bother him too much. And yet...

Ian had died after being moved into intensive care and put on a ventilator, a young man who'd had a tough start in life the same as Darren, and Matt saw those runs of luck that escalated, the bad as well as the good, and maybe some people really were cursed from birth, which would explain why things played out as they did. It was unfair and he didn't see the logic, couldn't believe in God, in heaven and hell, rewards and punishments in an afterlife. From what he could make out the reason Stan had gone for Darren in the pub was to do with Stephen and Merlin's goat, some old-school religious nuttiness, the madness of superstition. He wasn't sure, though, had only picked up bits and pieces. Wasn't going to dwell on it, whatever the truth.

More interesting was what Natasja was doing on her iPad. She had added the cogs of the machine to a goat. Not just cogs, but pipes and springs and bolts, welding brass and iron to a silver body. She had also drawn steampunk elephants, rhinos, rabbits, krakens and horses, even a dog that looked like Frank, but this was her first goat. Matt had told her about Gary and there he was, a mechanical being with tubes for horns and screws for hooves. Nat had created human figures as well, Victorian mavericks in waistcoats and top hats and goggles, navigators and aviators, a dwarf sporting some serious Diddy Man headgear, ladies with spiked hair wearing corsets and petticoats, and Matt suggested a barge, one with a clock on the front, drawn into this cheerful steampunk universe she had come to love.

They had watched a series of old films together, *The Time Machine* from 1960 and *20,000 Leagues Under The Sea* from 1954 two of the best, Matt's favourite the more recent *Hugo*, but he was happy just sitting on the sofa with Nat and Frank, tapping into her ideas and following where she led. He liked everything she did apart from the insect man with the big black head, a body that looked more like a toolbox, seeing himself in a grand house and a luxury apartment, places he didn't belong, spotlights shining on a human workhorse, flashguns popping. When the real killer virus arrived in five or six years' time he would still be out there grafting. Or if the work dried up maybe delivering doughnuts for Darren and boxes for Amazon. There would be no more CAT and no more shagging his employers either.

Nat asked if the barge should be parked at the side of a canal or pulled by one of her horses, although weren't there tractors that came later? He didn't know, but he did think these animal designs worked better than the humans, reckoned the goat was nearly as good as his favourite, the steampunk elephant. Despite her new drawing, Nat wouldn't be coming to the pub to meet Gary and Merlin in person, as she still needed her rest. This suited Matt. It meant he could have a proper drink with the boys. Different rules applied. Especially when it came to a football piss-up.

If Natasja was with him, he would have to behave in a certain way, turn into another version of himself, although maybe it was the other way round. When it came down to it, he supposed everyone was two or three people. More even. Life was easy when he was with Stan and Darren. They never took things too seriously. Not usually. Well, Darren did at times, but he had his reasons. Apart from Stan thumping him, his luck was changing, and that's what Matt wanted. Everyone happy. Laughing. Normal service resumed.

Stan ordered his first pint at eleven. He hadn't spoken to Darren since last night and didn't want to either, more interested in finishing what he'd started, knew he couldn't be doing that today, though, not with some of the faces turning up. This was meant to be a friendly meeting of the likeminded, but one punch could lead to a lot more when the drink was flowing. Add some ching abuse and the violence it stirred in already excitable characters, and things would get very messy very quickly. His anger at Darren, concern for Stephen and the realisation that he'd probably been careless with the invites had blended with last night's beer and shots, his mind speeding so fast he'd hardly slept. He was feeling twitchy and trying not to panic, hoped the Doom Bar was going to settle his nerves.

There would be women in the pub, pensioners and regulars, locals from the barges moored nearby who were used to chilled-out lives, so he needed to forget about Darren and focus on keeping the peace, try and talk to Stephen and calm him down. This was proving difficult, his brother leaving the house before Mum and Dad were awake and not answering his phone. It was true that when the weather was nice he would get up early and set off on an extra-long walk, bury his mobile in his backpack and lose track of the time, which, along with a flat battery, could explain why he wasn't picking up. But it had been raining earlier and the sky was overcast, plus Stephen was a Wikipedia nut and meticulous about keeping his phone charged.

It was possible he'd forgotten about the goat. Stan remembered Julian Assange, how after a week spent reading the leaks that had got Assange into trouble Stephen packed a bag and spent two freezing nights outside the Ecuadorian embassy, turning his phone off for the duration and scaring the family, who'd had no idea where he was and reported him missing. According to Stephen, he'd left the grid for security reasons, in order to protect his loved ones from possible reprisals, as supporting Julian was considered a terrorist act. There might well be a long, pre-execution interrogation, with family members transported to a foreign country where torture was tolerated and US agents flew in specially to enjoy their fetish for waterboarding.

He had met other Assange followers and returned home raving, going up to strangers in the precinct at one point to list various state-sponsored crimes and conspiracies, swearing a CIA hitman was prowling the market, that the shoppers needed to hide their faces from the cameras to ensure they were safe once they left. This had badly upset Granny Claire, part of a generation raised to believe a person should keep their politics, religion and how much they earned to themselves. Roaming the shops ranting about the CIA and assassinations and God knows what else would get the boy shot. Stan had reassured her nothing like that was going to happen, but it had taken a while, and he'd been disturbed by her reaction. And then Julian Assange was forgotten. Or at least never mentioned again. None of the family had dared to ask why in case it set Stephen off.

Yesterday's anger was different. Stan had never seen his brother like that before. Maybe it had transmitted and was making him feel like he did. Stan was hoping for the best, but fearing the worst. Knew something was badly wrong.

– I'll have one of those please, Matt said, arriving as the Doom Bar was being placed on the counter.

The barman went to get another glass.

– Look at your mouth, Matt continued. I wonder what state Darren's in. You surprised him. Surprised me. What the fuck were you thinking?

Stan shrugged and didn't answer.

– You're lucky he didn't batter you. He could have done, you know. Darren let me stop him. I couldn't have held him back if he'd really wanted to do you.

Stan stared at Matt, but still didn't speak.

– Have you two kissed and made up yet?

– No, and we won't be either. He's a fucking idiot.

– What's the matter with you? Come on, life's too short.

– He does my head in. Doughnut by name, doughnut by nature.

– Cheer up, for fuck's sake. Think about the strawberry filling. The raspberry...

– I'm not in the mood, Stan said, his voice hardening.

Matt wanted to talk about granulated sugar and traditional values, but held back. This wasn't the Stan he knew. He'd been sure he would be regretting what he'd done by now, and the more Matt's head cleared the worse that seemed. Really, what the fuck had Stephen done to stir things up this bad? He was still only curious, not desperate, and would find out later, when the time was right, hoped Darren would be in a better mood, that they weren't going to be miserable and moany all day.

– Thanks, Stan said, paying the barman when the second pint was delivered.

They stayed at the counter and drank. Thinking about it, Matt hadn't considered Darren's reaction properly. He had landed a couple of good punches but was only defending himself, and there was a good chance he wasn't going to be feeling so generous today. Why hadn't he sorted Stan out last night? He was loyal, true. Everyone knew he was loyal. But even so...

Matt was happy to be in the pub and wanted to enjoy the day, look to the future, went back to Nat's steampunk drawings to keep himself cheerful, trying to image how she would design his two best mates. Stan would make a fine hippo. Like the big boy in *Madagascar* with the piggy nose. A cogged version. Hubcap nostrils. Matt smirked, wiping it off his face before his chunky hippopotamus pal noticed. Darren would be more straightforward. A tin soldier with a giant key in his back to turn him on and off. Except nobody ordered this trooper about. He marched in time, took precise steps and never backed down, but chose his own enemies. He would definitely have to ask Nat to draw his friends. Cheer them up as well. A hippo and a tin soldier.

– I'm thinking of adjusting my rates, Matt said, keen to break the silence and lighten the mood.

Stan didn't seem to hear. Maybe he was thinking about Darren as well, realised that he could come charging through that door at any second and nobody was going to be able to stop him putting Stan in hospital. Matt saw Darren running into that pub up North. In and out like a human whirlwind. Old Bill couldn't believe what they were seeing. He was on a different level when he got going. Yet there was that touch of class about him that meant he was unlikely to maim a lifelong friend. Matt just hoped he was right.

– What rates?

– CAT, he said. Maybe I'll increase it by another two or three percent. I'm not getting the select customers now things are back to normal. I'm not charging enough.

– How are people going to know until you price a job, though? Stan asked, irritated. He had more important things on his mind than this rubbish, noticed Dobbin inspecting the pumps behind Matt. He hadn't seen him arrive.

– Not talking about your sex tax again are you? Dobbin asked.

Matt turned, imagined himself blushing. Why the fuck had he told Darren? And why had Darren opened his mouth? Like Stan, it was out of character. Could have been jealousy, he supposed. Or Dobbin ear-wigging. Covid had reordered the world. Affected every single person. Darren had to make do with his fantasy MPs, while Matt was doing the business for real. He concentrated on the new arrival.

– What do you think? Two, three, four percent extra?

– I'd go for five.

Dobbin turned to Stan.

– Is that right Potts is coming over?

While Stan's head moved up and down, Dobbin's shook side to side, but both these motions were slow as if the speed had been adjusted, ready for the slapheads Alan Shearer and Danny Murphy to pass judgement, or Ian Wright wearing one of those oversized caps the baldies liked. Versions of working-men's caps. Partisan headgear. It was as if Stan and Dobbin were mucking about. Reflections in cracked glass.

– Ray's not going to be too pleased, Dobbin added.

Matt saw they were serious. But why the glum faces? Who cared? So what if a nutty skinhead nutted a Happy Hammer? So what if he'd been servicing Mrs Edwards and Elaine? He was a single man at the time and why shouldn't he be pumping his good fortune into these lucky ladies? The masks and stage were his private business, and he returned to those images, watching himself from the outside, a giant doll with the head of an ant, a marionette performing in front of a window. His bosses pulling the strings. Again… Terry White. So fucking what? And he laughed out loud, which caused the others to stare and soak him in their gloom.

Taking a big mouthful of Doom Bar, Matt spotted Two-Ton and a couple of others sitting outside at a picnic table, the West Drayton man eating a pizza from its box, said he was going outside to say hello, get some fresh air and clear his head. And there Matt stayed, apart from returning to the bar get a round in as more of the lads started to arrive, by one o'clock the pub and its garden packed.

As far as Matt was concerned, the atmosphere was relaxed and friendly, as he'd expected, but Stan saw things differently and remained tense. There had been an unfortunate exchange at the far end of the bar between some locals and three Welshmen who were working and living in Hayes. Two were regulars at England games, like many of those descended from South Wales miners their earlier roots in Somerset and Wiltshire. Sheep- and then goat-shagging had been mentioned, the Welsh lads unimpressed that the predictable comment had been delivered by strangers. Threats were made, and it was only Ray stepping in and smoothing things over that had stopped an early bundle.

Stan was relieved, but it wasn't a good sign, while Matt felt it was another example of his own good-luck story, Oi The Nutter having just arrived, saving Matt from having to try and help Stan break up a fight. Ray knew both groups of men, which along with his reputation and some well-chosen humour was enough to restore the peace.

Looking at Ray, Stan was worrying more and more about Potts and the West Ham lot, who'd be on their way by now. They were meeting in an Aldgate pub before catching the Underground straight through to Uxbridge. There were other possible flashpoints apart from Ray and Potts, and he tried to work out why he was so wound up when everyone got on at the England aways or when they were in London for a home game. It was more than him just feeling responsible. There was a heaviness in the air, or at least filling his head, and he wondered if it was no more than Stephen putting his ideas in there, stirring him up with that mental talk about the Devil. The sense of dread was real, though. Maybe it was a premonition. But Stan didn't believe in that sort of thing. How could he?

– It's a flexible regime, he heard Matt saying ten minutes later. CAT only applies to those who can afford it, and more than that, it is reserved for people who deserve to be taxed. The snobs. Arrogant cunts.

– Anyone who sneers, Ray suggested.

– Progressive taxation is the ideal, Dobbin reflected. I'd raise it a lot further. Tax the rich to the hilt. You must be earning decent money, Matt?

Stan was standing by the back door of the pub. Matt was enjoying himself, refused to take the fight last night seriously, wasn't bothered about the pub getting smashed up, didn't know or care about Stephen's troubles. Yet it was Darren he had the hump with. And where the fuck was his brother? Stan tried calling again. No answer. The beer garden was heaving, the arrival of the barbecue clearing a path as it was wheeled into position.

Two-Ton was doing the honours and had brought along an apron and a chef's hat, took these out of a plastic bag and put them on. For a laugh. At least Stan thought it was. There would be no gourmet dining here. No gastro-pub shit. Burgers and sausages were the only items on the menu. With buns, ketchup and brown sauce. Stan watched Two-Ton as he tried to light the coals, used too much lighter fluid so the flames shot up and he jumped back, bowing to hide his relief as everyone cheered.

While Stan fretted and Matt had fun explaining the details of his CAT system and Two-Ton Tony (From West Drayton) struggled to get the barbecue going, Darren was approaching the tunnel where the Grand Union passed under the Uxbridge Circus end of the Western Avenue. He slowed as he went inside, the light dimming, struck by the stale pong of hidden water, a pinched claustrophobia that increased with each hesitant step. If anyone had been about he'd never have given the smallest hint he was afraid of the dark, would have walked tall and straight and probably exaggerated his movements.

He had only ever told one person about this fear, an error he'd never repeated. Even though he was a child at the time, he should have known better, quickly learning to keep his feelings buried as he built the inner will that meant he was strong enough to destroy weakness at its source. Yet the darkness still scared him. His confession had led to the closing of his bedroom door at night, a blanket pushed against its base on the outside to stop any stray light entering. The curtains had already been tightened and were soon replaced by a much thicker material. Fear turned to terror, and he struggled to sleep. The problem was easier to handle now. As an adult he could leave his bedside lamp on, in control of the situation, but as he moved deeper into the tunnel the old terror was returning.

He heard his aunt cooing in that pigeon voice she'd used when she was making fun of him, talking about the grotesques who loved to pull the heads off boys his age and suck out their lungs, how they were drawn by lights left on at night, the wasting of electricity and spending of money she didn't have, and did Darren know that his brain wasn't going to die right away, which meant he would have to watch those dirty little beasts chewing on his insides in the seven minutes he had left. The grotesques came into a house through its toilet, and that's why he had to make sure the seat was down before he left the bathroom and not to leave a mess as they liked the smell of pee-pee almost as much as those night lights. He must also add bleach before he lowered the seat. She was here to protect him, and who else wanted to do that? Nobody else cared what happened to silly little Darren.

Moving away from the wall to the edge of the towpath, he resisted the urge to speed up as the light dipped, couldn't risk falling into the canal. Fuck knows what was down there waiting for him to make a mistake. The grotesques would roll him over and wedge his body in a crevice and cover him in mucus and slime as his head was clamped in a huge jaw and removed. Normally, it didn't matter what the odds were, as he was fearless and enjoyed the challenge, but he had never seen anything noble in those dirty little beasts, the dregs of the fairy-tale world. He thought of his aunt and would never speak badly of the woman, would always keep their private stuff private. He owed her a great deal.

Darren's loyalty was a quality he cherished. It made him proud and it made him strong, and as he moved through the tunnel he was seeing himself standing in the corner of a bathroom facing the wall, a boy told not to fidget, frozen for an hour listening to a sad soul speaking in her precise way, his mind running away as she told him about parents he didn't know, listing her sister's faults in particular, from the petty to the serious. He'd often match the sound of his aunt's voice to the noises made by different animals, stirred by the pigeon comparison, a bird he liked to this day.

His aunt would put a length of string on the floor behind his heels, sit down on the toilet seat and talk, swearing that if he moved and touched the string with his heels she would pull his trousers down and smack his bare bum with the ruler she had kept from her schooldays. Teachers used to do that sort of thing. There was nothing wrong with corporal punishment. Darren didn't like the idea of being exposed like that, but when he drifted off one day and touched the string she carried out her promise, and yet he had only felt sorry for his aunt. He was an obligation. A nuisance. But he couldn't resist stepping back again and again, to upset her he supposed, but maybe so she'd feel better. He didn't know. Couldn't remember. What did it matter anyway? Covid had taken her away. He'd watched her die through a window at the home.

He came back out into the open and was revived, continued along the deserted canal path, scanning the fields for Stephen, saw horses over by the trees, but that was it, and he kept walking, heading towards Harefield. He'd gone out with a girl who lived over that way when he was sixteen, and the name matched the area, her brothers into their lurchers and hunting rabbits. She was a gypsy who held a grudge, and he'd been lucky to get away in one piece. He'd never had a serious relationship, and maybe she was the nearest he'd come, but she'd turned nasty, taking him for someone he wasn't, and he imagined running into her brothers out here on his own. If he wasn't trying to find Stephen he wouldn't have minded. He had done two of them when she set him up, could batter them again if he had to, plus anyone else they brought along. They were two or three years older, cocky and lazy, hadn't expected him to go all nutty on them. She was proper horrible at the end, and had only escaped the same punishment as her brothers because she was a woman and Darren had standards.

There was a white smudge up ahead, and as he got closer he saw that it was a small humpback bridge, a minute or so later making out a figure standing in the middle at the top of the arch, knew this had to be Stephen. He was facing the other way and couldn't see Darren, focused on something further along the canal. When the stretch of water there became clearer, Darren could see a narrowboat approaching, guessed it was Merlin and Gary, moving towards their deaths. It was the perfect place for an ambush. There would be no escape once they reached the bridge.

Darren shouted and started to run, his eyes moving from the bridge to the canal, from Stephen to the barge, and he could see Gary more clearly, standing at the front, a harmless goat who didn't deserve this, and neither did Merlin, of course, who was vaguer, at the back steering, the details becoming sharper, Darren distracted and stumbling and nearly falling to the ground or into the canal, keeping his balance, the tunnel terror gone, pretend monsters who popped heads off and sucked at lungs and pulled boys and men into the depths. This was grotesque right here, the killing of Merlin and Gary Goat, a brutal act that wasn't going to be dramatic or romantic or funny, nothing but a vicious double murder that made Stephen into something Darren hadn't thought him to be, a reversal of that gypsy girl's opinion, carrying a gun and using it another world away from a football fight or a kid pretending he was a dog or a young man teargassing a bully or a lonely old woman with a piece of string and a ruler. Stephen would end up in prison or a mental hospital. Either way he would be locked away and confined with no more long walks or fascinations, pumped full of drugs and forced to avoid miles and miles of white string. He would go truly mad. Totally insane.

Darren reached the bridge at the same time as the barge, but he was too late. Stephen had raised the gun and was steadying it with both hands. The Christian soldier heard nothing. All his attention was on the Devil leering up at him. God was on his side and standing next to him on the humpback bridge. It was a fantastic feeling. Good would always defeat evil. But it needed the brave to step forward. Stephen pulled the trigger and fired straight into the face of the goat.

Ray was on another high. Life just got better and better. He'd picked Terry and Angie up from Heathrow, on full alert in case his uncle wanted to nip into the Union Jack on the way home. Which he didn't. There had been no mention of the club, and Ray had planned to hang around for the duration, in case Terry decided he was going to head over there later. He had to be present when his uncle realised the jukebox had been breached. That some proper Oi Oi skinhead 45s had made it onto the Rock-Ola. But Terry and Angie were tired and eager to get back to the house, and once they'd tucked into the buffet Priscilla had made while he was doing the honours at the airport, there was no way they were going out again today. Terry had suggested a pint tomorrow lunchtime at the Union Jack, in the English tradition.

They'd had a brilliant time in Jamaica and looked fantastic. Tanned. Relaxed. And Ray had felt good telling them how smoothly Estuary had been running. Like clockwork. He'd loved being in charge. Embraced the responsibility. The strength of his emotions had come as a surprise. Gratitude, relief and pride colliding. He'd proved himself. Ray was a skinhead, and as such believed in hard work and the dignity of labour. Nothing could upset him today. Certainly not those two no-marks at the bar. Especially the cokehead who'd aimed a sneer at the back of one of the bar staff. Ray didn't know them from Adam. Hated people who sneered. But he put it out of his head. Wasn't about to follow them into the khazi. It wasn't his style. Not these days. He was on the path of the righteous. The straight and narrow. No words were required. Definitely no old-school aggravation. No fist and boot.

Ray was enjoying a quiet drink with friends. Celebrating his good fortune. Priscilla dropping him off and saying to call her when he was ready. She would pick him up. He didn't want her having to drive back over, though. It was easy enough to order a cab. He was one of the Estuary bosses. Remember? She'd kissed him and run a hand up the inside of his leg. Left him with a hard-on. She wasn't bothered about meeting the goat. Gary scared her, even though she knew it was daft. Ray guessed she wasn't keen on spending the day in a pub full of football hooligans either. Men on the lash. Doing what they did. Saying what they said. Anyway, Ray would have more fun on his own. That's what she'd told him. Priscilla really was perfect. Gorgeous. Inside and out.

The narrowboat appeared from under the humpback bridge, but this one was red not white, the width of two lanes of traffic rather than a single path for farm labourers and animals moving between fields. With the clouds having thinned out, the sun caught the water along the watery V of the approaching *Wizard*, and for a few seconds the voices on the bank dipped, a brief hush as the majesty of England's canal system hit home. The drinkers in the beer garden cheered as Merlin put the narrowboat into reverse, slowing it down and shunting towards the towpath on its starboard side, the raised voices and its chugging engine bringing more men outside.

Gary stood at the front. He was certainly a fine-looking goat. Calm and reflective. Some thought he appeared intelligent. Others wise. The excitement grew. There was a man sitting next to Gary with his legs dangling over the bow, but this wasn't the helmsman Merlin, who remained at the back steering. The figure at the front raised a hand and waved, Stan surprised to see that it was his brother. A weight lifted.

Stephen's other arm was draped around the shoulders of the goat, who looked unconcerned and maybe even pleased. Another man appeared. Darren climbing onto the roof and walking to the front to join Stephen and Gary, and as he stood there it was obvious to Stan that his friend had put himself out once again, tracking his brother down while he'd waited in the pub. Stan felt guilty on several counts. Darren loved Stephen like a brother, and what had he got in return? A right-hander. Darren had always been loyal. Stan's guilt turned to shame. The bloke hadn't deserved to be punched. There was no excuse.

Once the narrowboat touched concrete and was secured, Stan greeted his brother and friend, shaking their hands but avoiding eye contact, looking now at Gary, who was watching and didn't seem phased by the number of people present. The goat stared into Stan and his mouth moved, as if he was speaking, which was impossible. It would be a simple bleat. A couple of beats. The engine had cut out and Merlin was on the roof, saying his hellos but keen to get to Gary, make sure he was okay. It was a touching display of friendship, best appreciated by those who were closest. Merlin set about checking the rope attached to Gary's collar, before leading him ashore.

Later, Darren would explain how Stephen had fired his gun and hit Gary full in the face, the fact that the holy ammo inside the water pistol hadn't blown his head off or set the animal alight proof that God loved the goat and wanted him to live. As Stephen had told Darren on the bridge, and later Stan and Matt, and then those he was meeting and greeting inside and outside the pub, the Devil was playing a bigger game. Decoys and distractions were being employed, but this attempt to breach London had been real enough, and while it was important to hate the sin, it was more important to love the sinner. Gary had been infected by the Evil One, but the variant was on the wane now and wouldn't destroy humankind. No, he didn't consider himself a hero, and when he focused on the stranger who had asked this in a half-mocking tone, there was a goatish glint in Stephen's eyes.

With Gary saved, Merlin was in the clear. The pistol had done its job. None of the boys had met this Heavy G character, but heard how the armed robbery that had seen him committed to the same hospital as Stephen nine years earlier had involved the use of a similar such gun. The exact model in fact. It had nearly got him killed by police marksmen, but Heavy still loved his firearms.

It was turning into the best of days. Everyone was united, the goodwill that came with the goat infectious, while Potts and his pals had gone on a bender in the East End and never reached the station. Someone said they had started fighting among themselves, but that could have been a rumour started by Millwall. Ray appeared at the bar where the young firm were standing and bought Stan, Darren and Matt a pint before going over to say hello to Merlin. When things eventually quietened down they would sit and talk about Orwell and Kafka, the Orwellian and Kafkaesque trends of the present day.

Stephen told Stan that he thought it would be a good idea if the family bought a goat. They were friendly animals and if they were all like Gary very clever. Darren said that was a great idea and Stan wished he hadn't, but kept his mouth shut.

– I'm sorry about last night.

– Don't worry about it, Darren replied.

– No, seriously, I was out of order.

– It's fine.

– Go on, Matt said, in a mushy, encouraging tone. Have a cuddle.

– Fuck off, they replied together.

– Fucking rent boy, Darren added.

– Can you please not swear, Stephen said. You'll upset Gary. And rent boy is a homophobic term. There might be some faggots in this pub who will hear and be offended.

The others studied Stephen's angelic face. They were never quite sure...

– Gary can't hear us, Stan said. Anyway, he doesn't understand English.

– He knows human, don't worry about that. And he has ultra-sensitive hearing.

Stephen turned to Darren and produced a birthday card and started singing 'Happy Birthday'. Everyone joined in, the sound rising up and moving Darren who hid his emotions well, lowering his head and nodding as if there was no need for a fuss, although secretly he was chuffed. It was the first time he'd had anyone except his aunt sing this to him, and that was a long time ago, in her mocking chirp.

– Speech! Matt shouted.

Others followed, but Darren didn't know what to say. He raised his glass. Kept it simple.

– To the footballer's footballer. Johnny Van Tam.

– JOHNNY VAN TAM.

Gary remained in the beer garden. A huge bald man knelt down in front of him and patted his head, a short youth waiting nearby with treats okayed by Merlin, who was keeping an eye on his fellow traveller. He had tied Gary's rope to a picnic table, as he didn't want him wandering off and getting knocked down on the nearby road. The trucker-turned-bargee was discussing the current Villa squad with some friends who had driven down specially, moaning about the Cockney pint in his hand, the price and taste and lack of a head, even if this was out of habit and in jest. The goat revelled in the attention he was receiving, watching and learning, taking everything in with a sparkle in his eyes and a smile on his face, noticed Darren glancing over at Stephen, who was talking to three strangers, one of them swaying from the effects of the drink or drugs or maybe both.

Stephen kept raising and lowering his water pistol, squeezing the trigger and squirting the man, who laughed but not as hard as the others. Darren was trying to see if they were doing this with Stephen or at him. His fists tightened, decided they were enjoying their friend's embarrassment, loosened them again as Ray came and stood next to him, his eyes directed to the same place, the nutter calm like he'd never seen him before. Darren felt good with Ray by his side. He opened his

316

card and read the printed message rising through the bubbles of a pint glass, moved to the words inside. Raised his head.

Stephen was looking straight at him and winked, turned and continued with the story he was telling, a long description of Beelzebub and his filthy fly army, the nature of evil and the Black Death, how the Devil took over goats and other animals and even men and made their cocks leak and balls swell, the smell drawing witches out of the woods and across the heathland, down into the valley, the sort of mental, drawn-out tale that was going try the patience of a saint, and with the occasional squirt of water maybe even lead to a disturbance on the banks of the Grand Union Canal. Out on the edge of West London. In the place known as Uxbridge.

LONDON BOOKS

FLYING THE FLAG FOR
FREE-THINKING LITERATURE

www.london-books.co.uk

PLEASE VISIT OUR WEBSITE FOR

- Current and forthcoming books
- Author and title profiles
- Events and news
- Secure on-line bookshop
- An alternative view of London literature

London Classics

The Angel And The Cuckoo *Gerald Kersh*
Doctor Of The Lost *Simon Blumenfeld*
The Gilt Kid *James Curtis*
It Always Rains On Sunday *Arthur La Bern*
Jew Boy *Simon Blumenfeld*
May Day *John Sommerfield*
Night And The City *Gerald Kersh*
Phineas Kahn *Simon Blumenfeld*
Prelude To A Certain Midnight *Gerald Kersh*
A Start In Life *Alan Sillitoe*
There Ain't No Justice *James Curtis*
They Drive By Night *James Curtis*
Wide Boys Never Work *Robert Westerby*

NEW FICTION

THE SEAL CLUB

WARNER WELSH KING

The Seal Club is a three-novella collection by the authors Alan Warner, Irvine Welsh and John King, three stories that capture their ongoing interests and concerns, stories that reflect bodies of work that started with *Morvern Callar*, *Trainspotting* and *The Football Factory* – all best-sellers, all turned into high-profile films.

In Warner's *Those Darker Sayings*, a gang of Glaswegian nerds ride the mainline trains of northern England on a mission to feed the habit of their leader Slorach. Welcome to the world of the quiz-machine casual.

In Welsh's *The Providers*, the Begbie family gathers in Edinburgh for a terminally ill mother's last Christmas, but everyone needs to be on their best behaviour, and that includes her son Frank. The ultimate nightmare family Christmas looms, where secrets and lies explode like fireworks.

In King's *The Beasts Of Brussels*, thousands of Englishmen assemble in the city ahead of a football match against Belgium, their behaviour monitored by two media professionals who spout different politics but share the same interests. As order breaks down we are left to identify the real beasts of the story.

London Books
£10.99 paperback
ISBN 978-0-9957217-6-0